IN
COLT
BLOOD

By Jody Jaffe

Horse of a Different Killer
Chestnut Mare, Beware
In Colt Blood

IN
COLT
BLOOD

Jody Jaffe

FAWCETT COLUMBINE
THE BALLANTINE PUBLISHING GROUP • NEW YORK

A Fawcett Columbine Book
Published by The Ballantine Publishing Group

Copyright © 1998 by Jody Jaffe

http://www.randomhouse.com

Library of Congress Cataloging-in-Publication Data
Jaffe, Jody
In colt blood / Jody Jaffe.—1st ed.
p.   cm.
ISBN 0-449-00084-2 (alk. paper)
I. Title.
PS3560.A3125I5   1998
813'.54—dc21   97-43681
                                   CIP

Manufactured in the United States of America

First Edition: May 1998

10 9 8 7 6 5 4 3 2

If you're lucky you get one great horse in a lifetime.
In memory of
Brenda Starr
4/21/75 – 4/28/97

I decided early in graduate school that I needed to do something about my moods. It quickly came down to a choice between seeing a psychiatrist or buying a horse . . . I naturally bought the horse.

Kay Redfield Jamison, *An Unquiet Mind*

PROLOGUE

When Fuzzy McMahon started becoming fertilizer, she finally became useful. Too bad it took a smashed-in skull to give her life some purpose.

And she'd have completely realized her biggest accomplishment—making the grass greener—if a fat, gray pony named Blue By You hadn't made such a commotion.

"Lord have mercy, what's wrong with Blue this morning?" said Ebert Darnell, a tall spindle of a man who did the morning feeding and cleaned stalls at Anyday Farms. "Look at him, will you? What's he in such a fuss about? Tearing around that field like his tail's on fire."

The woman standing next to Darnell shook her head. "As slick as that grass is, and as bad as my luck's been running, that pony's gonna kill himself for sure or worse, bow his damned tendon like that colt in the barn did. That's all I need this morning. Leave it to them to get a pony that won't stop bucking unless he's turned out twenty-nine hours a day. Quick, go catch him before you-know-who drags her sorry butt down here."

Darnell might have argued that you-know-who doesn't move her sorry butt from bed until the morning thunderstorms in her head die down, and the only thing that chases that storm away is more Johnnie Walker Red. But Ebert Darnell wasn't one to argue or even think unkindly of the less fortunate.

"Want me to hose him down?"

1

Cathy Sullivan shook her head. "Better not, this March weather can be crazy. It already feels colder than it did an hour ago. Just make sure you walk him out good and cool him down. Don't forget to brush the sweat marks off him. We wouldn't want the little princess to find a dirty pony."

It was a wonder to Darnell that Cathy Sullivan had stayed as long as she had, talking about them the way she did. Not that every word of it wasn't true, and then some. In the fourteen years he'd been cleaning stalls, feeding horses, and fixing fences at Anyday Farms, most of the barn managers never lasted from one hay shipment to the next. This one even the hay men knew by name.

"Hey, Cathy," they'd call as the bright green rectangles of sweet alfalfa made their way along the conveyor belt, clickety-clacking up to the hayloft. "Can't believe you haven't told them to shove it yet. That must be antifreeze you've got inside you, girl."

No question about it, it took a special kind of person to put up with the owners of Anyday Farms. It wasn't only that the missus was a drunk. Some drunks dry out pretty good between the wet times, maybe even feel a little bad for how they've behaved. Not this one. She was meaner sober than she was drunk.

She'd come down to the barn, tilting this way and that, screaming as if she'd been violated if she saw a lead rope hanging the wrong way on a stall door. Or hay in the aisle or horse manure in the stalls.

"What the hell am I paying you for?" she'd start each rampage.

Hard as it was to believe, Darnell felt sorry for the woman. He surely felt forgiveness for her, and that's why he'd lasted so long in her employ. But he figured forgiveness was his job as a Christian. He truly felt sorry for what her life had become. No matter how much prayer he put into the subject, she just kept getting worse.

When he'd started there, she'd been just a normal spoiled rich lady. She wanted things her way, but what rich person didn't? If she was demanding, she could at least find the kind words to frame her wants. Over the years, it seemed she'd lost that part of her vocabulary, as if Johnnie Walker himself marched right up into her brain and snatched away all her pleases and thank-yous and would-you-minds.

She looked different too. Not the regular kind of aging with lines here and there. It was more drastic than that, like her face had fallen in on itself, as if her internal footers had crumbled to dust. She'd never been what you'd have called a car-stopping beauty; her face was a little too round and her eyes a little too small. But back when Darnell started working there, she'd still had a softness to her looks, the kind peonies get just as they blossom.

Her flower wilted fast, between the alcohol eating at her insides and the meanness eating at her soul. What started out as a pleasant-enough-looking face ended up looking like a shriveled Halloween mask of Porky Pig's sister. Darnell couldn't help but wonder if that was God's plan; He'd give you this clean, shiny face full of life and promise to start with, then let you do what you wanted with it, from the inside out.

Darnell didn't know when the meanness took over. Not when he first started working at Anyday. He'd seen many flashes of kindness to her then, especially with the young girls who boarded their ponies at the barn. The mothers would swing open the heavy doors from their Mercedes, Volvos, and BMWs and out would come one ponytailed girl after the next waving good-bye as the cars went back down the narrow gravel lane to Route 16. That's when she'd step in, playing proxy mother to all the little horse-crazy girls; tying up the long, straggly laces of their paddock boots, reaching high to bridle the ponies who knew just how much bigger they were than the girls. And when the girls tumbled to the ground, she'd pick them up, dust them off, give them a few "there, theres" and leg them back up at the count of three.

That wasn't to say she didn't have her snits. But back then she knew a way out from the dark moods. She'd saddle up one of her horses and take him deep into the woods and come back without a holler in her.

If Darnell thought about it hard, he'd probably pinpoint the changes to right before the baby came. She'd hated being pregnant, at least hated how it made her look and made her husband look at other women. Though Darnell could've told her it wasn't her swollen belly that made her husband's eyes slide to places they shouldn't be. He'd had slippery eyes since the day Darnell had met him, and surely way before that. Darnell didn't like to think unkind thoughts, but it was as clear as a cold day that a handsome man like that, with his big, curly brown hair and I-know-what-you-want smile could've had any woman, no matter how gorgeous, he'd wanted.

Darnell was sure that during the lonely nights she'd been up there in the big house, she'd been wishing she'd had as much looks as she did money, which is something she had plenty of. He'd never been to the art museum over in the rich section of Charlotte, the one they made from the old mint building, but he'd heard there was a two-story wing with her daddy's last name plastered all over in fancy, gold letters. She drove the biggest Mercedes he'd ever seen, and the barn at Anyday Farms had been in one of those shiny-paged magazines that ran pictures of Cher's house. Still, with all her money, big cars, and fancy buildings, Darnell knew she was alone at night with only the company of Johnnie Walker. Her wealth might have gotten her a husband, but it sure as anything didn't keep him.

It wasn't only his eyes that roamed. The husband was never around anymore, except to drive his truck through the back fields checking his cows. He might come to the barn to shoe a horse, if the owner was pretty and slim, or to see what the latest barn manager looked like. But the missus got smart to that after a while and started hiring fat girls with big noses.

So it was just her and the baby, a girl blessed with her father's looks and cursed with her mother's disposition. It would have been hard to figure who was worse, mother or daughter. Except the daughter had two excuses: she was still just a child, thirteen years old with a set of hormones churning and swirling away at her like she was nothing more than a twig going down the meanest parts of the Chattooga. And secondly, look what she had for a mother, a woman who could blame her rottenness on nothing but too much money and too little to do.

Darnell shook his head and asked Jesus to watch over them, the only thing he could do when he got thinking about that whole sorry family. He started walking to the pasture to catch the pony, who was still racing around like he had bobcats chewing at his hooves.

"Ebert," Cathy Sullivan called, "take a can of feed with you in case he's hard to catch."

He went back to the barn and into the feed room, where he scooped a few handfuls of small green pellets into an old Maxwell House coffee can. When he got back to the field, the pony still hadn't settled down. He'd gallop up the fence line and then go back down even faster, slamming to a stop at the lowest end of the pasture, near the manure pile, where he'd rear up and strike down at the ground, again and again.

As much as Darnell tried, the pony wouldn't be caught.

"Wait a second, I'll come help you," Cathy Sullivan said. She joined Darnell in the field, carrying a coffee can in her hand.

"That's your problem right there, Ebert," she said, looking into his coffee can. "You've got pellets. Don't you remember this pony said he hates pellets? Let's see if I've got it straight, he said he's only going to eat the sweet feed from now on, because the pellets get stuck in his teeth and then all the other horses make fun of him."

Cathy Sullivan let out a big, snorty laugh. And Ebert Darnell joined her.

5

"That was sure something," Darnell said. "How much they pay that woman, anyhow? Saying she could talk to the horses. What'd she call herself again, a horse what?"

"A horse communicator. She claims she can talk directly to a horse, like you and I are doing right now with each other. Charges a hundred bucks a chat. Of course, she throws in a massage afterward, 'cause she says the horses need the relaxation. Got to hand it to her, though, she's done all the barns in Weddington, Matthews, and Waxhaw, and the owners swear by her. I thought some of the boarders here would get a kick out of her. I should've just minded my own business. I wished I'd have been a little psychic myself, I'd have never brought her here. And to add to my already awful day, she's coming back this morning for some of the other boarders. I just hope you-know-who doesn't come in during her little séance. Man, I can't take two of her volcanic eruptions in one week. Besides, how was I supposed to know?"

"No way you could have," Darnell said. "Don't worry about it. It'll pass. I've seen her blow bigger and say even more hateful things than she did the other day, then come down to the barn a few days later and act like nothing happened. That's her way. She just needs a couple, few days to cool off, that's all."

"I wouldn't mind her staying away for a couple, few years."

As the two talked they walked to the bottom part of the field where the pony was rearing and screaming and still striking at the ground.

"We sure as hell could use that horse communicator now," Sullivan said. "What's he yelling about? I've never seen him like this before."

Blue By You paid no attention to either coffee can of feed, and it wouldn't have taken a psychic to see that this pony had other things on his mind besides food-clogged teeth. His ropy veins pumped hard against his coat, now sweat-slicked dark to a deep, steel-gray. His nostrils flared wide and he snorted short, violent bursts of air. But it was his eyes, popped wide and darting around, that made Darnell know something was wrong.

He smelled it first. Stronger than he'd smelled it at the barn this morning when he'd assumed it was just an old woodchuck rotting in the woods or a run-down opossum oozing on the road. The closer he got to the stream, the surer he was that the smell wasn't coming from a small animal.

"Must be a dead deer that's got that pony in such a fuss," Darnell said, saying a prayer that he was right but knowing for sure he was wrong. No four-legged animal gives a smell like that.

"Whew, that's thick," Sullivan said. "Let's catch him and get out of here. I'm going to lose my breakfast any second."

And that's exactly what Cathy Sullivan did.

"Oh my God," she said between retches. "That's no deer."

Ebert Darnell walked toward the manure pile. A bloody arm dangled down. With shaking fingers he dug through the dirty pine shavings, rotted manure, and matted hay and got to hair, yellow hair swirled black by dark clumps of dried blood, looking so much like the marble cake his wife had served for dessert last night that Darnell found himself choking back his breakfast. He dug deeper, enough to reach his hand under a shoulder to pull her forward and flip her over. Not that he needed to. He knew who it was. The only thing that surprised him was her eyes.

Sad eyes. For the first time in many years, Fuzzy McMahon didn't look like she wanted to kill someone.

CHAPTER 1

I'm sitting in a white wicker chair facing Margie-the-cafeteria-lady who saves all the carrot ends for my horse, Brenda Starr. Except now she says she's my therapist and this is an emergency appointment I've scheduled because Brenda started talking to me today.

"I think I'm going crazy," I say to her. "Remember I told you my father's whole family is nuts? His brother committed suicide, his sister might as well keep her finger jammed in a light socket—that's how many times she's had shock treatment—three other sisters have been on Lithium long enough to stabilize Attila the Hun, and my father's no poster child for stable behavior himself. Now *I* think my horse said 'Why?' when I wanted to go faster."

"And remember I told you," Margie-the-cafeteria-lady-therapist says to me lovingly, soothingly, caringly, "any genetic disorder would have presented itself to you by now? Besides, how do you know it's not true? How do you know your horse didn't talk to you?"

I look at her like she's talking Russian. I don't get it. Where's my old therapist, the Freudian with the bad toupee who reads to me session after session from his psychiatric texts, mangling the words he doesn't know? And where's my skirt? Why am I sitting here in my slip and panty hose? Margie says I switched to her, the reigning expert on the nonlocal mind and tomato canapés, because I kept falling asleep on the Freudian's couch. I remember now, I'd sleep away forty-five of the fifty minutes and he'd say, "Good session, you're working through your resistance." As for my missing skirt, Margie says we'll get to my disorganization/vulnerability issues next time.

"Talking horses," I say to Margie. "I stopped believing in that possibility when my brother pointed out that Mr. Ed's lip movements didn't match his words."

She looks at me and smiles, serenely, earth motherly, cosmic consciously. "A male ruined your openness to the wonders of the universe? I should have known." She sighs deeply and smiles even more serenely. "We all take such different paths. Men will get there eventually, it's important to keep remembering that. But tell me about the time when you had your dreams, when you could see with the eyes of a child, before your brother blinded you."

All I can think of is the fight I could have had with my brother over this one. I'd blamed him for plenty of things, and he certainly was a big jerk to grow up around, but this opened up a whole new realm of sibling combat. "Maaaaaaa," I'd have screamed, "Larry robbed me of my innocence, he took away my dreams and blinded me."

My mother would have heard only the last part and would have screamed back hysterically, "What's that about your eyes? Did he punch you in the head again? I'm gonna kill that kid."

"Nattie," Margie says, "dreams, what were your dreams?"

I tell her about the dead man I saw in the back of a car when I was nine, that I don't know if it was a dream or not. She tells me the corpse in the Cadillac was a red blanket and I'd seen it the day my father left.

"Not your bad dreams, my child, your good dreams, my child," she says. "Tell me of those."

My good dreams? They always came with four legs and a velvet muzzle, I say to her. Horses. My good dreams were always about horses. I was one of those horse-crazy girls psychiatrists love to analyze: big horse equals big penis, she puts it between her legs and has a big penis of her own.

I tell her I wonder if my obsession with horses is genetic stamping. My father loves horses, as did those who came before him. In the old country, in Lithuania, his father had a big, dappled gray to pull his peddler's cart by day. By night my father's father, my grandfather, would throw his legs across the horse's long back and gallop across the fields. The horse was the color of moonlight, and my father says my grandfather told him he felt like he was riding the sky.

"Good, good," Margie says. Her hair is the color of my horse's mane, coppery blond and stick straight. I want to weave it into little braids like I do before I take Brenda to a show. "More, more dreams."

"Well, when I was very young, before Larry made me see that Mr. Ed wasn't really talking, I believed that horses would talk, if they wanted to. To the right person, someone they loved enough. That's what I dreamed of: a horse, my horse, that would talk only to me."

Margie's still smiling beatifically, and I wonder if it doesn't make her jaw sore.

"Go back to the barn and see if she talks to you again. Our time is up now. Call me as soon as you hear something. And remember, be open to the wonders of the universe."

Next thing I know, I'm standing in front of the barn. It's a perfect riding day; cool enough to bring a sweet tingle to your cheeks on a gallop through the fields. A small wind is blowing and the flowers have just started their magic show; giggly yellow explosions of forsythia play chorus to the narcissus with their fluted lemon heads bobbing rakishly against the new grass. It's the hyacinth that catches me short, though, with their candy curlicues of deep magenta tickling and teasing my nose. Amidst such natural wonder, even talking horses seem possible.

Be open to the wonders of the universe, I chant to myself as I walk to Brenda's stall. She presses her nose into my hand, looking for a carrot. I kiss her above the eye and rub her face. "Pretty girl," I say. "Are you the prettiest horse in the world, or what?"

I said that to her every day, even before she started talking. I never really expected her to answer. It's more of a rhetorical question, like, How are you?

Brenda looks at me, and I look around to make sure I'm the only person in the barn. Then I say quietly, just in case someone's there I haven't seen, "It's okay, Brenda, you can talk to me if you want. My therapist says I should be open to the wonders of the universe."

Brenda rubs her mouth against my hand and I feel her lips move, like Mr. Ed's used to. Adrenaline shoots down my arms and pumps at my heart. I hold my breath and listen hard. She's a soft-spoken horse.

I put my ear close to her muzzle and wait. And wait. Nothing. Then I feel her tongue lick my hand. I feel very foolish, and grateful no one's in the barn but me and the horses. It must have been a crow cawing when I thought she talked to me before.

I saddle her and walk to the ring. Walk, trot, canter to the right. The same to the left. The jumps are set low, so I figure I'll pop her over a few. I point her toward a fence. Just as we get there I hear, "I really don't feel like doing this today, my back hurts." I look around. There's no one—no thing—anywhere around except me and Brenda. No cawing crows, no yapping dogs. No one but us.

"What?" I say.

"I said I don't feel like jumping today. I threw my back out last night."

Holy night, I think. I couldn't say it because I can't make my mouth work.

"Look," she says, "I don't want to be unpleasant about this, but could we do it another day?"

I get my mouth working again and say, "Sure, Brenda, whatever you want." I hop off her and ask her a million questions, all the questions I've been storing up for a talking horse. But she won't answer any of them. She just looks at me with her big, brown eyes and rubs her head against my hand.

I call Margie. "Don't panic," she says. "You're okay. See what unfolds and go with it."

Next thing I know, I'm back at the barn. Brenda doesn't say a word while I saddle her. I go deep into the woods, where it's dark and cool. The last light of the day is dancing through the leaves. Any thoughts of my impending mental illness are out, gone, forgotten. I'm in glory land again, that old horse magic has taken hold.

"I don't like to get my feet wet."

I almost fall off my saddle.

"I said I don't like to get my feet wet, it gives me the chills. Couldn't we go a different way so I don't have to cross this creek?"

I look ahead, and sure enough there's a creek. And Brenda's talking to me again. And again she refuses to answer any questions or elaborate on her request or speak to me in general. No matter what I say, she says no more. So I turn her around, avoiding the creek, and head home.

The same thing keeps happening again and again. In the barn she's as mute as Jane Wyman in *Johnny Belinda*, but when I'm on her back, it's a regular—one-way—gabfest. First it's, "Could you get me the stall near the door, the horse I'm next to makes too much noise when he eats." Then, "I don't care for my name, Brenda Starr, I want to change it to Seabreeze, okay?" Finally comes a long diatribe about how she's always really wanted to be a parade horse, that walking down Tyron Street in a sequined mermaid costume is her idea of a real career, not being a show horse where she has to jump fences and have her mane braided.

12

"I look ridiculous in those little braids, and besides, they pinch my neck."

As if that weren't enough, she launched into my riding: "How am I supposed to know what you want me to do, with you banging around on the saddle like that. Sit still, would you? And take off the spurs, for God's sake. While you're at it, cut back on those desserts. I'm the one that has to cart around your extra pounds. Another thing, lighten up on the reins. You try putting a metal bar in your mouth and have someone yanking at it like you do. See how that feels, why don'tcha?"

Brenda couldn't find anything nice to say, always a complaint. I was paying $375 a month in board to listen to her bitch about the barn, my fat thighs, and what she really wanted out of life.

I'm back in Margie's office, telling her all about it, how Brenda never answers my questions, how she's not the least bit interested in my life. And now I don't even have a slip on. Just a pair of ratty underwear.

Margie looks very interested and has that same Eureka! look on her face the Freudian used to get when I talked about seeing my father in the shower. "Has her behavior changed, other than the talking?"

"I don't know," I say. "I'm so worried I'm going to do something else to annoy her, that's all I can concentrate on. She doesn't buck me off or bite me, if that's what you mean. She's fine, until she opens her mouth."

Margie looks very serious. We sit silently, pondering. I'm sure she's pondering where to commit me. Finally I break the silence. "And I don't even like going to the barn anymore."

The smile, that sweet beatific smile, returns to her face. She gets up and walks over to me and brings her face close to mine. She wipes away the tears rolling down my cheeks.

"Confucius said it first, but Meryl Streep made it famous," she says so softly I have to strain to hear her.

"Meryl Streep?" I say loudly, angrily, finally fed up. "What could Meryl Streep know about talking horses and ruined lives? Horses have always been my salvation. I don't feel complete without them. Now I can't go to the barn anymore because I have a blabbermouth of a horse. She complains more than my editor. I wish to God she'd just shut up and go back to being a dumb animal. Don't give me that crap about Meryl Streep. I've had enough of your go-with-the-universe talk to last me a lifetime, maybe even three. I'm outta here."

I storm out the door and Margie just sits there smiling understandingly.

Next thing I know, I'm back at the barn. Brenda's standing in her stall, eating hay. I don't say a word to her. Nothing. Silently I brush her and saddle her. I take the reins in my hands, gently, because I don't want to yank her mouth anymore since she's told me countless times how it bothers her. I squeeze her softly with my heels—I've thrown out my spurs because those bother her too—and we head for the woods.

I don't hear, see, or smell anything wonderful. I'm too busy trying to sit still. We turn down a trail I don't know and there's a small creek in front of us. I brace myself for a complaint, but Brenda walks across with no hesitation—and no words. I keep riding and riding. Finally I take her back to the barn and put her in her stall with a flake of fresh hay. She rubs her head against my hand.

I go back to my apartment and there's my father, Lou. "Nattie," he says, "have you been meditating? I haven't seen you this relaxed in a while. I got this movie from the video store, it's almost over, want to watch the end with me?"

I sit on the folded-up futon and look at the TV screen. Meryl Streep in early Banana Republic. Robert Redford in the same. Both looking very beautiful and very pained. She's holding back tears. So's he. They're talking about their failed relationship. Slow cut to her face, her tortured-but-strong eyes, her proud aquiline nose, her firm, determined mouth.

"Be careful what you ask the gods for," she says, looking past Redford, past the sienna-brushed horizons of Kenya, past the prancing herds of antelope, zebra, giraffe. She looks out of Africa and into her future. She pauses, cinemagraphically, dramatically, profoundly. Then she says, "They just might be cruel enough to grant your wish."

CHAPTER 2

I feel a hand on my shoulder. Shaking me. "Margie," I mumble, "Meryl was right. . . ." The hand shakes me harder. A voice, definitely not Margie's, comes through.

"Nattie, it's ten of nine. Don't you have to be at work?"

I inch my right eye open and bring the scene into focus. Meryl and Robert and all their khaki safari gear is gone. It's Lou, my father, looking down on me, in a dirty white T-shirt and even dirtier sweat pants.

"Huh?"

"Work, Nattie. Your editor—Candace, right?—she called about ten minutes ago. I told her you were in the shower. I think she could use a little meditation. She sounded very unbalanced, too much yang."

"You've got the first part right," I said, and forced both my eyes open as I attempted to reel myself back into the real world.

"Man, Lou, I'm never taking any more of your colloidal mela-tonin again. Talk about side effects. I thought that warning on the side of the bottle was just a lot of hot air, something to make the FDA happy. But they weren't kidding when they said this stuff could cause strange dreams. I've been having strange dreams all my life, but last night's takes the cake, not just in weirdness, but in realness. It was like someone cranked up the color monitor in my brain to hyperintense and wouldn't let me out. No thanks, Lou, from now on I'll pace the floors before I mess with my serotonin levels."

16

Lou was jumping up and down on his rebounder, pounding his head with his fists. "Getting the chi going," he said. "You know, if you did this twenty minutes a day like I do, you'd sleep fine. I don't have any trouble sleeping."

"That's because you're narcoleptic. You slept through my high school and college graduations."

Lou was still jumping. With each downbeat he said a word. "I . . . was . . . just . . . resting . . . my . . . eyes."

"Whatever you say, Lou."

I looked at him bouncing up and down on his minitrampoline and wondered what new age toy he'd be bringing into my apartment next. Last week it was the magnetic spray heat lamp from Donq Hi, China. Six hundred fifty dollars for a lightbulb mounted to a hunk of gray metal. He made me sit under it for twenty-five minutes, swearing it would cure all that ailed me. What it did was give me a heat rash.

Lou and his vitamin bottles moved in a few months ago. It was either that or watch him wander from ashram to ashram or spend his days at Father Devine's rest stop for the homeless and weary. Aside from his snoring, so far it wasn't that bad. I actually even liked the acupressure reverse gravity shoes he brought home the week before the Donq Hi lamp.

"I'm taking a shower. If Candace calls back, tell her I drowned."

I slipped under the hot needles of water and tried to remember my dream. If I let it get away now, I'd never be able to retrieve it. Something about a talking horse, my talking horse. Then it hit me, why the dream:

Candace's Johnny-come-lately trend-story assignment she wants pronto. As if we're on to something new and hot here. It could've been worse, though. Far worse. She could have sent me hustling to SouthPark to see what Charlotteans are wearing to cruise the malls these days; or even worse, heading off to Gastonia or Shelby or wherever the advertising department deems our latest editorial penetration zone to be. As *The Charlotte Commercial Appeal*'s reluctant fashion writer, I'd have been obligated to write any and all of the above, with a smile on my face—or hear about it in my yearly review.

For once Candace had something else on her mind besides me and hemlines. Thank heavens for small miracles.

This small miracle came in the shape of a page from the *New York Times Book Review* section. After only 343 weeks on the best-seller list, and a major motion picture, *The Horse Whisperer*—known by my horse friends as "The Britches of Madison County"—had finally caught the attention of Candace. She'd summoned me to her office yesterday, with the best-seller chart in her hands. I saw a big, red circle around *The Horse Whisperer*.

"Any here?" I saw written in the margin. If I wasn't mistaken, it was our publisher-who-would-be-editor's handwriting.

"Nattie," Candace said, "there's a lot of talk about this book, and now the movie. Read it?"

I shook my head no. I didn't want to read the part about the horse getting mangled by a truck, and my friends who did read it said it was like spending the whole day in a Hallmark card store.

"Doesn't matter," she said. "You get the point. It's popular. People are reading it. Must be wondering if there're any horse whisperers here. Let's find one. We'll run it on Sunday."

Finally, after many years of therapy and a deal with God about my foul mouth, I'd started winning the struggle to hold my tongue and temper. What I wanted to say was, "I suggested that very same fucking story to you three years ago, and you told me, 'Once again you are overstretching the bounds of creativity,' and then assigned me to cover the JCPenney Spring Fling fashion show in Shelby."

What I said was, "Candace, that sounds like a great idea. I'll track down someone today."

She put a neat check mark through the red circle surrounding *The Horse Whisperer*. I'd been been-thered, done-thatted. Excused.

It was my time to leave. Candace moved on to her next piece of paper.

Just as I got to the door Candace said, "Nattie, I'll e-mail you your list of questions after I meet with the Team Captains."

I squeezed my hand around her doorknob, visualizing it to be her head. Team Captains, could things get much dumber? Then I remembered who was running the show these days at *The Charlotte Commercial Appeal*: the gray flannels in Miami, chain central. This journalism-by-committee baloney was a direct hit from them and the foundation for their latest reorganization of the newsroom, the third in as many years. Surely a result of their incessant readership surveys, it wiped away all the old department names like Features or Sports or Investigative and replaced them with silly third-grade cootie titles such as "The How We Live Team," "Batters Up for the Future Team," and "The Don't Do That Team."

In this latest incarnation, *The Charlotte Commercial Appeal* editors are no longer editors, but Team Captains. And now all the Team Captains and *their* Team Captains meet every day to "chart the direction of all upcoming story assignments." What that means in English is that the editors, I mean Team Captains—all of whom have never written, much less reported a story in their lives—preconceive, write, and edit the thing before the reporter gets a crack at it.

I gritted my teeth. "Great," I said. "I can't wait to see what you guys want me to ask."

Candace eyed me suspiciously. I knew she couldn't nail me for being sarcastic. I'd purposely made my voice as edgeless as a greased ball. My friend Mickey-Turner Burnett, the book columnist, has been working with me, teaching me how to navigate the tumultuous waters of *The Charlotte Commercial Appeal* newsroom without becoming food for the sharks, aka Team Captains.

Mickey-Turner, who grew up in Sewing Circle, Georgia, has made me rethink every notion I ever had about Southern womanhood. "Just because we talk slow and smile a lot, people think we're stupid," she'd said to me in Lesson One. Stupid as the fellow who started Microsoft, I'd learned by observing her in action. Mickey-Turner writes exactly which stories she wants and exactly how she wants to write them. While the rest of us get Cuisinarted by the Team Captains, she gets a kid-glove, hands-off edit I can imagine only Bob Woodward himself getting at *The Washington Post.*

I smiled my best Mickey-Turner smile—while wishing for a bolt of lightning to rip down from the heavens, smoting all the Team Captains flat—and left Candace's office.

CHAPTER 3

It didn't take long to set up an interview with a local horse whisperer. Like I told Candace three years ago, talking to animals is a growing—and at this point, overpublicized—business. God forbid, we at *The Charlotte Commercial Appeal,* the largest newspaper in the Carolinas, should go out on a journalistic limb and write about something before the rest of the world knows about it.

Every horse magazine I know has run a story about animal communicators. That's what they call themselves, and for anywhere from thirty to a hundred fifty bucks they'll ask your horse all the questions you've always wanted to ask yourself. Now, who the answers are coming from is another question entirely. For me, the jury's still out. Part of me really wants to believe someone with the gift can tap into a horse's mind, but a bigger part of me says, "Get a grip, Nattie."

I knew exactly the person to call. Sarah Jane Lowell. Talk about quotable. This woman was born to be a story. I met her a few months ago at the barn where I board my horse. She was there "talking" to a sulky gelding by the name of Rip Tide, whose owner wants in the worst way to ride at the big, indoor horse shows in the fall. Unfortunately for her, so does everyone else with a bankbook big enough to get there. Hard as it is to believe, there's no shortage of those bloated bankbooks; reams of competitors all across the country drop five to ten thousand bucks a month, going from horse show to horse show campaigning the you-know-what out of their horses to win the ribbons and earn the points that will qualify them for the grand finale: the Washington International, the Pennsylvania, and the National horse shows.

Rip Tide hadn't always been so recalcitrant. But now, for some reason, he wouldn't canter around a show ring without pinning his ears back in disgust and slamming on the brakes smack in front of the jumps. The owner must have blown a couple thousand dollars in vet bills, X-raying and ultrasounding every part of his body. Finally, when the horse doctors threw up their hands in surrender, my best friend Gail, the barn manager at February Farm, asked the owner if she wanted to enter the Twilight Zone and bring in a woman who claims she can talk to horses.

"What've I got to lose?" the owner said.

"About a hundred dollars," Gail said. "But a friend of mine says she's Dr. Dolittle. Her horse supposedly told this woman about an old hoof injury that was bothering him, one he'd gotten long before she'd bought him. Damn if the vet didn't come out and find it on the X ray, exactly where the horse said it would be."

So Sarah Jane came and talked to Rip Tide. And, among other things, here's what he had to say:

"I don't like going to horse shows, I feel like I'm always being judged."

Some women have greasy mechanic or muscly pool guy fantasies. My arrested development froze my fantastical realm in the talking horses category, so I, more than most people, wanted to believe it could happen. But when I heard that one, even I had to duck in my horse's stall to keep from laughing in her face.

My father, on the other hand, who finds the notion of talking horses as natural as aliens visiting Stonehenge, believed her hook, line, and sinker. It didn't hurt that she was everything he'd always gone for before he forsook sex to become a Brahman. Sarah Jane Lowell was a grown-up Heidi; yellow hair that looked like spun lemon glass; strong, assertive bones; and chicory-blue eyes. She wasn't tall and slim like most blond equestriennes; she was about five-four and had a body that looked like it could labor in the fields all day without breaking a sweat. "Honed" was the word. All that plus she bore an uncanny resemblance to his second wife, Hilde, the Nazi's daughter.

It's true, Lou had married a woman young enough to be my sister, whose father happened to die fighting in the same war my father fought in. Unfortunately, his future father-in-law's side was the one bent on annihilating my entire religion. File that marriage under the perishables column; its shelf life was shorter than a can of tomatoes, which is pretty long for a grocery item, but a ways short of till death do us part.

Not that he was pursuing Sarah Jane that way, or vice versa. She was at least thirty-some years younger than Lou. But they'd hit it off as friends the day I brought him out to the barn to watch her in action. Since then they'd been like Fric and Frac, going to Sai Baba meetings, angel gatherings, message circles, planet healings, sweat lodges, and the like. She'd become a regular guest at our dinner table, praying over every bite of tofu that went in her mouth. There was so much talk about white light, good energy, and godly paths, I wanted to shake them both and force them to scream all the curse words they knew.

And at the risk of being cynical, so far she hadn't hit him up for any dough—though I had my radar on alert. She seemed like she was for real, but I'm not known for my character assessment abilities. This can be a big liability in the news business, where you have to deal with professional liars day in and day out. That's why I don't report politics.

When I'm not chained to the fashion beat, I write features; for the most part, stories that contain fewer reasons for people to lie. That's not to say I haven't gotten snagged a few times, though. As has my father. It must be genetic, this believing-what-people-say thing.

Last time he hooked up with a beautiful, young blonde traveling the same spiritual highway to nirvana, it cost him $3,500—and I'm not talking tolls. I'm talking scams. She'd convinced him to "invest" in the Shamanic Goddess Transformational Center she said she was building in Jamaica. Trouble was, the only plans she had for the Caribbean involved a month-long stay at a fancy resort with my father's Rolfer, a startlingly handsome Dane ten years her junior.

"Nattie," Sarah Jane said when I called her yesterday, "I was just thinking about you. I think my angel must have a crush on your angel and tickled his ear to get you to call. How's that sweet horse of yours? Want me to ask her something for you?"

We'd been through this before. Of course, I'd plopped down my money, even after the comment from Rip Tide, who had worked out a deal with his owner—through Sarah Jane—that he'd quit pinning his ears and refusing fences if he got at least one weekend off a month and two extra flakes of hay a day.

According to Sarah Jane, my horse loved me, loved her life, but preferred the name Annie to Brenda Starr. She could take or leave Rob, my trainer, mostly leave him when he flew into a snit about how dirty she got. And no, she didn't think I was too fat to carry around.

"Not this time," I'd said, and explained the story I wanted to write, which would involve me tagging along with her.

Usually people jump at the opportunity to snag their fifteen minutes of fame. Sarah Jane was another story. At first she flat out said no.

"Don't take this personally, Nattie," Sarah Jane said, "but mainstream newspapers always slant things to make people like me look like total kooks. You either get misquoted, which I'm not saying will happen with you, or they take your picture through one of those strange fish-eye lenses. Sorry, but no thanks."

I didn't go into this line of work for nothing. I'm nothing if not persistent. After five minutes of swearing I'd get the quotes straight, keep the story on an even kilter, and check the lens the photographer was using, she agreed.

"You've worn me down, Nattie. Yes, okay, just stop asking," Sarah Jane said. "Tomorrow morning I've got three clients at Anyday Farms in Weddington, how would that work?"

"That's Fuzzy McMahon's place, right? Just off Route 16?"

Dead air filled the phone, and I thought I'd lost her. "Sarah Jane, you still there?"

After a second she said, "I'm here." But her voice sounded different, worried or scared or something.

"Sarah Jane, are you okay?"

Another pause.

"Sarah Jane?"

"Oh, sorry, Nattie. My mind slipped away from me for a second. I'm sorry. There must've been eggs in something I ate yesterday. I get spacey if I eat animal products. That's right, it's the McMahon place. I should be there around ten."

"See you then," I said, and hung up. Eggs making Sarah Jane spacey? It seemed to me it was the mention of Fuzzy McMahon that launched Sarah Jane into orbit, not some unidentified chicken by-product.

CHAPTER 4

A ten A.M. interview, that's why I hadn't been hustling into the newsroom this morning. I figured my gig with Sarah Jane would last three or four hours. Candace wanted to run the story Sunday, so I'd have to have it written by tomorrow morning, which meant the proverbial long day's journey into the night in front of my computer at *The Charlotte Commercial Appeal.*

"Lou," I yelled into the living room, "I'm leaving in five minutes. If you're coming, you'd better get dressed."

In my family, the parent-child roles have always been confused.

It was another twenty-five minutes before we actually left. First we couldn't find his shoes, then his hearing aid. When he asked if I knew where his glasses were, I slammed out the door.

"I'm leaving, Lou," I screamed, because he never did find his hearing aid. "I have a ten o'clock interview. I'm not showing up late because you can't find your head."

He hustled down the steps and joined me in my car, where I handed him his glasses. Found, under the passenger seat of my car, next to a pair of petrified carrots.

Even though I drive the same way every day to go to my barn, the development along Route 16 still startles me. I know I'm starting to sound like those old fogey geezers whose voices crackle when they say, "Why, I remember when gas was a nickel a gallon." But I do remember when I could go for long, breathless gallops around the Knights of Columbus horse show grounds off Tom

26

Short Road and then cool out with slow, easy walks around the endless stretches of cotton fields. Now, the only galloping being done is by the multitudes of toddlers on their stick horses who live cheek to jowl in their cedar shingle houses.

As I drove, my father was trying to convince me to go with him and Sarah Jane to hear a famous channeler channel messages from the Archangel Michael. If I didn't have to write the story, I'd have said yes. Not especially to hear what Michael had to say, but to watch the very Reverend Rowe Quarrels stage his demonstration against all the "devil worshipers"; that's what he calls anyone interested in new age stuff or anything the slightest bit tinkly. I wanted to see his hate show in action, not only because I love watching vivid people, but also because he'd gone after me and a story I'd written last October about five hundred witches celebrating Halloween in Asheville. I thought I did a fair job reporting the event. So did Lady Passion, the high priestess of the Asheville Coven. Even the ministers from the local churches thought I'd presented a balanced report. Not so Rowe.

He was hopping mad when the story came out and stormed into Fred Richards's office, ranting about *The Charlotte Commercial Appeal* being the devil's trumpet. What happened next is a perfect example of why Richards, our editor, is known about the newspaper chain as the Shoe Salesman. Rather than stand behind one of his reporters, Richards promised the venom-spewing hothead that to make it up to him, *The Appeal* would be honored to run a column by Quarrels every other Sunday and put it right next to the words of Charlotte's most famous son, Billy Graham.

I was so mad I wanted to quit and get Lady Passion to cast an impotence spell on Richards. But then I remembered the mouths—two of them, both equine—I had to feed, and that Lady Passion and her fellow Wicca witches only do good deeds. Suffice it to say, there was nothing good I wanted done to Richards. Besides, it wasn't as if Quarrels was singling me out personally, or that I'd been the first—or last—to be on his receiving end.

When I moved to Charlotte, the local public radio station ran a show called "New Age Saturday"; lots of floaty harps, pan pipes, and Native American chants, the kind of music that makes you want to go out and hug a few trees. Well, the Most Reverend Quarrels deemed the music to be Satan's sounds. He and his followers made such a fuss—demonstrations, letters to the editor, boycotts—that the radio station pulled the program. The funny part is, I'll bet dollars to doughnuts not one of his followers even listens, let alone donates, to public radio.

Then not too long ago, a dance troupe came to town and happened to flash a little flesh. The Reverend Quarrels must change his clothes in the dark, because the idea of a naked body so offended him he got a court order to stop the performances on religious grounds. Talk about tightening the Bible Belt. What I, as a Jew who's never read the New Testament, can't figure is which passage is it exactly where Jesus says, "Thou shalt see no nude bodies or listen to harp music"?

Intolerance like that always makes me wonder what secrets the intolerantee is so furiously trying to beat back in himself. Like that Maryland politician and his vicious antigay crusade years ago. It was no surprise to me when he got busted at a gay bar trying to pick up a boy minor. I couldn't help wondering why the Reverend Rowe protesteth so much.

Not that I had time to ponder that issue or any other. My father was going on and on about the channeler, talking nonstop and too loud, because he couldn't hear himself, because he couldn't find his hearing aid. It was so distracting, I missed the turn to Anyday Farms.

"Lou," I said, searching for a place to do a U-turn, "how about a deal? You be quiet and I get us there alive?"

"Yeah, Nat, just one more thing—"

I sliced my hand through the air and shot him the Look. Finally he was quiet. I found a driveway, turned around and headed back up Route 16, this time spotting the green and white sign announcing ANYDAY FARMS.

The entrance was a long crunchy ribbon of gray gravel. Flanking the sides were two rows of Bradford pear trees popped out in their full cotton-ball blossom glory. As if I needed another sign that I'd been on the fashion beat too long, the first thing that came to my mind was all the dotted Swiss fabric Geoffrey Beene draped his models in for his spring/summer collection.

The road forked at the end, one sign pointing to the barn, the other to the house. We veered left, toward the barn, an equestrian palace known in the horse world as Ashlee-ville, as in Ashlee, Fuzzy McMahon's daughter, who now owns most of the junior hunter and children's jumper divisions. Her mother basically stands at the in gate writing checks for every horse that comes out with a blue ribbon.

I'd been there a couple times for horse shows. It was a to-die-for show barn, something Aaron Spelling would've built if Tory liked horses instead of cheesy television shows. The aisles were wide enough for a Rockette kick number, the fourteen-by-fourteen stalls bedded knee-deep in fresh pine shavings, in front of which hung polished brass saddle racks and matchy-matchy brush and tack boxes all bearing the green and white barn colors and Anyday logo. A washer-dryer churned in the tack room, and there were enough saddle racks so no boarder would have to wait her turn to get at one. The heated and cooled rider's lounge came with a cushy striped sofa, matching club chairs, television, VCR, shower, john, stove, sink, and refrigerator.

I could have done without wall sconces and coordinating chandeliers, but the stadium-size indoor arena would have been nice on all those nasty, icy winter days when Rob insisted I ride or forget horse showing forever.

Money, money, money, this place shouted. And why not? Fuzzy McMahon, née Fuzzy Feldman of the Feldman Family

Value Stores, came from some very deep pockets. Almost as deep, a business reporter friend of mine told me, as any of Sam Walton's heirs. Apparently, Fuzzy's family's Family Value Stores were second only to Wal-Mart in revenue.

The barn was as spectacular as the board. Six hundred big ones a month for the honor to be an Anyday horse. But then you'd have to put up with the infamous Fuzzy McMahon, who, from what I've heard, is a true anomaly: a Jewish drunk. And it wasn't only from my friend Gail that I'd heard it. Fuzzy's known far and wide in the horse world for her wild, boozy temper tantrums.

Gail and Fuzzy had been longtime drinking buddies, starting way back in high school when they used to cut classes and steal whiskey from Gail's mother. Thankfully, Gail, who's been battling the demon rum her whole life, now twelve-steps like she's climbing to the moon on a souped-up StairMaster. But Fuzzy, from what Gail tells me, was never the least bit interested in AA, Al Anon, or any kind of help to dislodge her from what's become her best friend, booze. Some pal; the foul stuff has managed to eat up everything in her life: her looks, her smarts, her marriage—not that losing the schmuck she married would be such a major loss.

I have to hand it to Gail, she's maintained whatever shred of friendship she can manage with Fuzzy, despite the woman's explosive tirades against anyone in striking distance, including Gail. I, unlike Fuzzy, lucked out in the best buddy department. Gail is as loyal as they come; she would, and has, given up just about anything for me, including half her yearly vacation to play grief counselor, maid, cook, chauffeur, hand-holder, tissue-getter, whatever my mother and I needed the week after my stepfather died.

As I drove toward the barn my father started talking again. Five minutes had passed, the limit to his tongue-holding ability.

"Is this that Feldman woman's farm you were telling me about? I once did a deal with a Manny Feldman. German army hats. Maybe she's related to him. I'll ask if she—"

"Lou, if you see her, turn around and go the other way. If she is related to him, I'm sure he bilked her out of money the same way he did you. Seven thousand, wasn't it?"

"Yeah, but I got to keep the army helmets."

"Not to mention the celery salt," I said.

We both started laughing. A few years before the army helmets, he and his brother, who's even crazier than my father, invested in sixty thousand cases of celery salt.

I was about to remind him of his investment in bringing the London Bridge to Arizona, which, as far as I can tell, doesn't have enough water anywhere in the state to span a twig over, when I saw the flashing cop car lights. Lots of them.

"Holy cow," I said. "Who called out the cavalry?"

CHAPTER 5

Judging by the barn manager's face, which was grayer than a dirty dish towel, she must've been the one who made the call. She was standing by the front sliding doors, next to a tall, skinny man who didn't look much better.

I was pretty sure her name was Cathy something. When I'd gone there to show, she'd been running around the barn, making sure all the trash was being picked up as it was dropped. The same for the horse poop. She must've missed a few errant piles, because when I'd walked in the rider lounge to use the bathroom, I walked in on Fuzzy McMahon ripping another orifice into her.

That had put Candace in a new light for me.

I looked around for Sarah Jane, but didn't see her or her old gold Mercedes. I did see my good friend Tony Odom of the Union County sheriff's department walking down to the pasture. I'd recognize that cute butt anywhere.

I snuck up behind him and tapped him on the shoulder. He must have been on high alert, the same way my horse gets when she's sure a rock on the trail is really a bobcat in disguise, because he spun around fast enough to knock me over if I'd been standing any closer.

"Jeez-sus, Nattie, you'll get yourself killed that way. What in the good lord's name are you doing here anyway? You got murder radar wired into that sweet head of yours?"

That took the smile right off my face.

"Murder?" I said. "As in dead, willfully so?"

"Come on now, Nats. If you want to dance, let's go to Country City."

"Tony, I'm not dancing. I really don't know what you're talking about. I'm here for a story, but it's got nothing to do with murder. At least I didn't think so."

Tony looked at me suspiciously.

"It's the truth, I swear. You know I wouldn't lie to you."

We both knew that was true. He'd saved my life, and he knew I'd never return that favor with a lie. "I'm supposed to meet a woman here by the name of Sarah Jane Lowell for a story. She's a horse psychic."

He started to laugh at the notion of a horse psychic, then stopped. "Sarah Jane Lowell? Is that what you said her name was?"

"Why?"

He shook his head and smiled. "I ever tell you you're like a knife with no handle? Answering questions with questions like you do, never know what end to grab ahold. You must be driving that poor boy Henry crazy."

"Tony, neither of us is here to discuss my social life—which, since you've asked, is getting more and more interesting. Henry and I are going along fine at a slow, judicious Henry pace, and he hasn't locked himself up in the loony bin or started downing Zoloft yet. Why do you want to know about Sarah Jane? I'm not letting you take another step until you answer me."

I swung around and stood square in front of him.

"All right, all right. Don't get your fur raised. You're here, can't do much about that. And I don't guess it'll be another ten minutes before there're more reporters here than thirsty fleas on a sleeping dog, so I might as well tell you. That girl over there, the one that looks like she just choked up hair balls? She and that fella found a dead woman half buried in the manure pile at the bottom of this pasture."

"Anyone I know?" I said.

"I'm telling you this off the record. OFF THE RECORD. You

didn't get it from me, hear? It was Fuzzy McMahon, the woman who owns this place. She and that Sarah Jane Lowell psychic woman of yours had words the other day. Loud, killing kind of words. The kind you never should say to anyone just on the off chance that anyone turns up dead like Miz McMahon here."

"Who threatened whom?"

"I understand they were both going at it for all they were worth. Screaming and hollering at each other like two politicians right before an election. Looks like Miz Lowell might have gotten herself the last vote. Now, Nattie, if you'll excuse me, I've got to go gather me some evidence."

Tony put his hands on my shoulders and stepped me aside. As he started back down to the pasture, I said, "Tony, I'll give you a call later."

"I expect you will," he called back. And smiled.

It was the smile that made my heart do that flippy thing. Even though we were just friends and I was well on my way to being something more with Henry, I still felt a tingle in my innards every time I saw Tony. And it wasn't just that cute behind of his.

I may have shallow life goals—to get my name in *People* magazine and meet Robin Williams—but most times, with the exception of occasional forays of the lustful nature, I go for depth in my serious relationships. Which explains Henry, and all the Henrys that preceded Henry.

Tony wasn't only easy on the eyes, but fine on the mind. Much to my disappointment, it didn't look like we were destined to tango this time around, though we came mighty close this past summer. He was married, and that *is* where I draw the line. Maybe next life. Or last one.

Besides, it was an interesting turn of events, me, Nattie Gold, old hippie anarchist who thought police officer and fascist were one and the same, being *very* good friends with a cop. Not to mention, it was proving to be extremely helpful in my line of work.

For instance, I was now the first reporter in Charlotte to know that one of the Queen City's richest daughters had met an untimely and illegal end. What I really wanted to know was what Fuzzy and Sarah Jane had been fighting about. But it was pretty clear Tony had told me everything he was going to tell me—for now.

I know, I know, Fuzzy McMahon's death wouldn't be my story, not unless Candace wanted a report on what the well-dressed corpse was wearing. The chances of her cutting me loose to go work news-side again were about as good as me riding in the Olympics. But nothing said I couldn't help out my friend Les, the cops reporter, and dig around for him, seeing as I knew most of the players in the Charlotte horse game.

I'd headed to the barn to find Cathy when I heard the gravel crunching again. I looked up and saw Sarah Jane's Mercedes inching its way toward us. She was an infuriatingly slow driver, and whenever we went someplace, I made sure it was me behind the wheel. No matter how much or how often I repeat my TM mantra, poky drivers still make me feel like reaching my foot over and stomping the gas pedal. I waved to her, and I could've sworn she was looking directly at the barn. But she didn't wave back or smile or anything.

She did, however, do the oddest thing.

At the fork in the road she gunned the gas then floored the brakes, forcing her geriatric Mercedes into a very dramatic 180 degree spin. It was like Sarah Jane had mutated herself into some kind of female Burt Reynolds, spinning her car back around the other way so fast she sent half the gravel driveway flying into the Bradford pear trees. Then, with her wheels spinning faster than I'm sure they've ever gone before, she screeched out of my sight and into the horizon.

After I closed my mouth, I thought about it for a second. That's when it occurred to me: she'd done her automobile acrobatics at exactly the spot where Lou and I first spotted the police cars.

CHAPTER 6

I wasn't close enough to my car to hop in and chase her. Even if I had been, my car can barely run, let alone chase. Great. There went my interview, zooming out the driveway at 100 miles an hour. Tony was halfway down the pasture by now, and I didn't think it was my place as a journalist to tell him as a police officer that a possible suspect had just pulled away like she was Bonnie of Bonnie and Clyde.

Besides, I had my own problems. No interview. What was I going to tell Candace? I'd have to scramble up something quick.

And I had to get in touch with the photographer and tell him to get here pronto before they sealed the place up. I walked in the barn and would have headed directly for the office where there was hopefully a functional phone. But being equine obsessed I had to peek into each stall to see what all these big bucks had bought. It was one gorgeous piece of horseflesh after another. I was practically orgasmic by the time I reached the shimmering blood bay colt. He looked like a junior incarnation of Ruskie, the most beautiful horse God ever created, who used to live at the barn where I board my horse. Unfortunately, Ruskie also had a few personality problems and met his demise—the victim of an insurance scam deal—before he could tell a horse psychic his issues.

But was he ever something to look at. Just like this little guy. This one had a big white blaze running down his perfectly chiseled head, with just enough of a dish in his nose to whisper back to his

Arabian ancestors. Made me want to switch professions and become a horse thief.

Then I looked down at his legs; the front ones were wrapped in cottons and flannels. The card on his front door gave all the pertinent information; his name "Dubonnet," his owners' name, "J. and J. Sukon"; what vet to call in an emergency, "Doc Lockton"; and underneath that in big, capital letters: STALL REST, ABSOLUTELY NO TURN OUT. Wonder what happened to him? He looked kind of young to be stuck in a stall, wrapped from hoof to knee.

As I was meandering—window shopping, really—I found Cathy and the tall, skinny man standing by the stall of an agitated gray pony. I introduced myself to them and told them I was there to interview Sarah Jane. Cathy gave a half laugh and said, "I can't believe she had the balls to even think about showing up here today."

I'd been thinking the same thing. But "ballsy" wouldn't have been the word I'd have chosen. "Dumb" would've been, except I know Sarah Jane's no dummy. That's assuming she had something to do with Fuzzy McMahon taking her final samadhi—Lou-talk for kicking the bucket.

"You mean kill her and then show up at her place the next morning?" I said. "Hard to believe anyone would do something that brazen."

Cathy laughed again. "I guess you don't know Sarah Jane Lowell. Brazen, you say? That would be an understatement, like calling old Ebert here slim. Huh, Ebert? You know why Ms. McMahon was screaming so loud the other day when she came down to the barn and found Sarah Jane here? If I'd known, I'd have never told the boarders about Sarah Jane Lowell, saved myself one of Ms. McMahon's eruptions. I'll tell you why she was screaming so loud. A friend of Ms. McMahon's walked in on *Mr.* McMahon and Sarah Jane going at it in her barn while he was supposed to be shoeing the lady's horses. Some blacksmith he is. Sarah Jane was there supposedly talking to a bitchy chestnut mare. I guess the mare had nothing to say."

Sarah Jane and Bobby McMahon? Well, knock me over with a feather. Not on McMahon's account. He'd poke his stick at anything that moved. But sweet Sarah Jane of the white light?

"Imagine," Cathy said, "that woman and Mr. McMahon going at it right there in Ms. McMahon's friend's barn. You know anyone with a bigger set of balls?"

If I'd had time, I'd have told her about Candace, who, according to *The Appeal*'s managing editor, has the biggest cojones in the newsroom. But I didn't. I had to call the photographer. Relations were already strained enough between my department and Photography. I didn't want to pop up on their list of why they hate Features—I mean, The How We Live Team—so much.

"Can I use your phone?"

"Help yourself," Cathy said, and pointed toward the office.

I turned, but before I left I had to know what had happened to Ruskie Junior. "What's with the wraps and stall rest for that one?" I said, and pointed toward the gorgeous colt.

"Oh, you mean Dubie?" Cathy said. "Two bowed tendons. Too bad too, because he was about as correct a colt as I've ever seen. There goes his life as a conformation hunter."

Too bad was right. Barring a miracle or great advances in veterinary medicine, that colt would never step a hoof in a conformation ring, where judges count off for even the most minor of blemishes, let alone for such major faults as blown-out tendons. Two big, ugly bows running down the back of a horse's legs would be like ripping a slash through the Mona Lisa's smile.

"That's a heartbreak," I said.

"Yeah, especially considering what they paid for him."

I shook my head, went to the office and changed the photo mission. Then I went out to gather Lou.

"Yo, Lou," I called, "change in plans, we gotta go." He was wandering around the barn, looking at the fire extinguisher tags. Even though he'd sold his fire extinguisher business a few years back, he still couldn't walk by a unit without checking to see if it was expired.

"I thought you were interviewing Sarah Jane," Lou said as he got in my car.

"So did I, but it looks like something more important came up. Like fleeing from justice."

CHAPTER 7

I've got a shrink friend who swears there's an authority gene floating around the swimming pool of things that make us human. You have it and you like to follow the rules, believe the experts have something more than arrogance to back them up, and want the world to think you're a good girl. You don't have it and you're sentenced to a life of straddling yellow parking lines, automatically discounting anything anyone with a uniform, badge, or title says, and admiring Willie Nelson for his approach to taxes.

It's not hard to guess what gene's missing on my helix. And it's even less difficult to figure out from whom I didn't inherit it.

When I told Lou what Tony had to say about Sarah Jane and Fuzzy McMahon's cat fight, he waved his hand through the air, dismissing Tony and all his kind in one fell swoop.

"Cops, they always get things wrong," Lou said. "Arrest the wrong people, let the guilty ones go by mistake. Kill a few along the way. Just look at what they did in Philly, with those MOVE people. Burnt half the city down. Then did you read in the paper they have to pay more than two million dollars back to all the people they've falsely arrested? 'They,' you know who 'they' is? The taxpayers of Philadelphia—me, that's who—have to pay for the police screw-ups. I know he's your friend, but he's got it wrong. It can't be Sarah Jane. I've never heard her raise her voice, except when she's chanting. You know how these guys work. They want to get these cases wrapped up fast, so the minute they hear something, boom, even if it's not the right person, they make it the right person. You know what I mean?"

"Well," I said, deciding not to remind him they really weren't *his* tax dollars at work because he favored the Willie Nelson approach, "this particular officer of the law wouldn't lie. At least not to me. It doesn't sound as if Sarah Jane and Fuzzy McMahon were calling to a higher order the other day."

Then I told him what Cathy, who has no authority to abuse and/or discount, had to say. That silenced my father.

"Sarah Jane ever mention anything about the McMahons?"

Lou thought about it and shook his head no. He remained quiet the whole way home, so I knew he was as perplexed as I about Sarah Jane. I was having a difficult time jibing the Sarah Jane that Cathy described with the Sarah Jane I knew. The one I knew was practically a Jain, sweeping bugs out of her way because she didn't want to harm another living creature. The Sarah Jane I knew wouldn't knowingly eat meat, eggs, or dairy. She refused to wear leather or fur or feathers or anything that came from an animal. And she had the annoying habit of giving thanks to each and every plant that crossed her lips, thanking them for sharing their bounty with her. This, to me, was not the way a murderer behaved. But you never know what's going on underneath, in Sarah Jane's case, her seemingly serene walls.

I didn't have the luxury to ponder which was the real Sarah Jane. I had to hustle if I was going to scrape together anything resembling a Sunday story. I dropped Lou off at my apartment.

"Seitan stew for dinner okay?" he said to me.

"Don't forget the seaweed," I said. I laughed, but Lou didn't. Maybe he hadn't heard me. But my guess was, his mind was on Sarah Jane.

CHAPTER 8

I broke a few speed limits driving to work. Who really goes twenty-five miles an hour on Queens Road anyhow? Not anyone, that's who. And at the risk of sounding like my father, least of all the police. I've seen them zipping down roads like Queens like they were practice runs for the Charlotte Motor Speedway.

By the time I got to work, it was close to noon. Not much time to interview and write something. That was assuming I could find someone to interview. I was scanning my memory for another horse communicator with a Carolina connection as I ducked past Candace's office and headed to the department formerly known as Sports, which was mercifully out of her visual reach.

Luck was not on my side. Or as my Zen friends would say, I was choosing not to be successful. The three other horse communicators I called must have been out communicating, because all I got were their answering machines.

What to do? What to do? Knowing Candace, she'd already promised the story so there was no going back. I tried the Reach trick my father's ex-before-he-became-a-Brahman girlfriend taught me. You say "Reach" when you can't find something you've lost, and all of a sudden it swirls forward. Technically, I had lost something: Sarah Jane. I'd tried her number, but also got her machine.

"Reach," I muttered again.

"Reach what?" said one of the sports reporters.

It happened to be Robin Clark, the newest and cutest of the sports guys, maybe even of all the reporters at *The Appeal*. Imagine

Mel Gibson with just enough Michael J. Fox to make him sexy *and* cuddly at the same time—that's what Robin looked like. But it wasn't just his handsome puss that had all the women drooling, he was smart and funny and a terrific writer to boot. Even I, who cared nothing about basketball unless it had to do with my hero, Muggsy Bogues, read Robin's stories.

And he was good-natured, even in the face of utter stupidity like the time his Team Captain made him dress in green and yellow and pretend to be a Packers fan during the Packers-Panthers play-off. The poor guy had to parade around Ericsson, the-Swedish-phone-company, Stadium, see what kind of abuse he got, and then write about it. Three other reporters had turned down the assignment. Not only did Robin write a hilarious story, but he scored a date with a towering, blond Viking of a woman from Sheboygan.

I could easily be counted as one of the female droolees, though that's as far as it went for me. I wasn't in the market. Henry, the Henry I'd teamed up with for a couple stories, and I were slowly working into some kind of understanding. I didn't understand it yet myself, but it felt like it was heading in an interesting direction.

Despite my unavailability, I didn't want to make a total fool of myself and tell Mr. Cutie Clark I was speaking to spirit guides, asking for their help. These sports guys aren't exactly angel-talkers.

"Reach a decision," I said. "To tell or not tell Candace her Sunday front story has fallen through less than twenty-four hours before show time."

"Let me know when you do, I'll go downstairs for coffee. I can't stand the sight of bloodshed."

"Me neither," I said, "especially my own. What a day."

"I hate to see the innocent die young. Anything I can help you with?"

"I'm not that young anymore and no one's called me innocent since I was twelve. You wouldn't happen to know any local horse psychics, you know, someone who talks to horses, would you?"

43

He cocked his head and looked at me. I knew I was going out of his boundaries with that one.

"Yeah, of course I do, what do you think we are here, a bunch of closed-minded jock orangutans who've never channeled to Orca?"

"Very funny, excuse me while I prepare for my funeral," I said. No time like the present. Just tell her now and get it over with.

As I started to get up, Robin said, "No, I'm not kidding. About knowing someone who talks to horses. Actually, I do. Hang on a second." He spun around in his chair and rummaged through his desk. He pulled out a chewed reporter's notebook and leafed through it.

"It's right here, just give me a second. I heard about him at the Camden training track, a fellow who claims he can talk to horses. I thought it might make a funny column one day if I got stuck with nothing to write. Let's see, I'll find it, I'll find it. Just give me a minute. A couple of the trainers I know admitted they'd used him, more than once. You know as well as I do these old racetrack guys aren't kissy-faced, goo-goo-eyed girls about their horses. The only thing they care about is bottom line, will it make the horse run faster? They said this guy helped. Who knows? If I had that much money at stake, I'd be talking to Orca too. I know it's here, somewhere. . . . Bingo. Found it. William Holland. His number's 803-555-7014."

"Robin," I said, "I don't care what they say about you sports brutes. I'll never let them call you Neanderthal-couch-potato-wannabe-jocks again. I thank you and my mother thanks you. One funeral a year's enough for her."

He smiled and then bowed. I concentrated on allowing myself to be successful. And guess what, William Holland answered on the second ring. Not only that, he had plenty of time to spend with me on the telephone. I couldn't make it to Camden and back and then write the story, so a phoner would have to do. What the hay, most of my work as a reporter is done with a phone growing out of my left ear. Usually I can get a good enough word picture going in my mind and then crank it into a story that sets the reader right there with the interviewee.

William Holland turned out to be a winner. He talked and talked and talked as I tapped and tapped and tapped away at the keyboard. He had that smooth kind of caramel voice that dips up and down the mountains and valleys of his Southern accent. There's nothing better than a good Southern storyteller, it's like going to a concert—Appalachian opera. And William Holland was a master storyteller. As good as Bucky Reynolds, surely one of the most well-known horsemen in America and certainly the best storytelling one. Bucky not only can tell a story, but impersonate the person he's telling the story about.

I didn't know about William Holland's impersonating skills, because he was telling stories about horses. Who knows what they talk like? Do Southern horses say "y'all"? Do German horses *sprechen zie Deutsche*? How about those wild mustangs out West? Do they sound like John Wayne?

All questions I peppered William Holland with. He laughed.

"Not exactly John Wayne," he said, "more Gary Cooper at *High Noon*. Nah, just kidding. It's not like I see the horses' lips moving. Not like that at all. They don't actually speak to me in words, like you and I are doing right now. I see images, as if I'm looking through their eyes. I feel their feelings, hear their thoughts."

"Thoughts?" I said. "Horses stand around and think all day? What about, whether the horse in the next stall is getting more grain or his rider is too fat?"

"You're not far off. But lucky for us, horses aren't especially judgmental animals. They're domesticated animals, bred to work. And they enjoy it. They really do. For the most part they want a job, and feel just the same as us when they're good at what they do. They like pleasing 'their people.' That's how they think of us,

45

kind of like you'd say 'that's my horse,' well, they'd say, 'that's my person.' "

Even if it was made up, I liked that. I hate the idea of being thought of as anything's owner, it's far too imperialistic for me. I'd have never made a good missionary or conqueror, as if there's any difference. I also liked hearing that horses enjoy their work. I've always felt a little guilty imposing my will on a horse. Just because I feel like cantering or jumping a fence, doesn't mean the horse does. I've often wondered why my opinion should carry more weight.

"If they like what they do, then what's all this equine business of pinned-back ears and bucking and kicking and refusing fences? Not exactly good corporate citizenship behavior," I said, as one who's done the human equivalent of all of the above, and more.

"I didn't say they were robots," Holland said. "Couldn't get much further from the truth. Horses and cats. Pure emotion. Do something to make them mad and you'll hear about it. Hear about it big."

That explains my psychic link to equines far more than my father's age-regressor who said I was Catherine the Great a few lifetimes ago; horses and I were separated at emotional birth. Reflection before action isn't a connection my wiring can make either.

I could've talked away the day with this man. I didn't care if it was a lot of hooey, I liked the hooey he was shoveling. It played into all my fantasies, in fact it was the core of my personal mythology: talking horses. Plus he was a reporter's godsend. Articulate, funny, introspective, and highly quotable. I knew this story would just about write itself. Which it did. I had forty inches of copy in no time. Too bad forty inches is considered an opus these days, thanks to America's atrophied attention span and *USA Today.*

I'd be lucky to make it through the editing juggernaut with twenty-five inches intact. I pressed the send button on my computer. Next stop, to my Team Captain, Ron Riley, Candace's squirrelly little shadow. With any luck, he'd hand the edit off to my friend Jean because he'd be too busy doing what he does best and most: sucking up to the Big Kahuna Team Captain, Fred Richards.

I was about to get up and take a trip down to the cafeteria to stretch my legs when the telephone rang. Even a fashion question I could handle, after how much fun I'd just had interviewing Holland and then watching the story write itself. Almost as good a high as riding my horse.

"Nattie Gold, *Charlotte Commercial Appeal*. How can I help you?" I chirped into the phone.

"God, Gold, they put Prozac in the drinking water there? How come you're in such a good mood at work?"

It was Gail, who'd been on her own kind of high for the last three months since she married Torkesquist, our craziest shooter in the photo department. But her voice wasn't sounding too happy at the moment.

"Just happy to be alive," I said.

"Glad you are—alive, I mean. Have you heard? About Fuzzy McMahon?"

Oh man, in all my self-preoccupation about getting my story done, I'd forgotten to call Gail about Fuzzy McMahon. Of course she'd be upset, she'd been trying her damnedest to rescue her before something like this happened. I apologized to Gail and explained why I hadn't called. Not only is she loyal, but forgiving—for a price.

"Don't worry about it," Gail said. "Besides, now you'll feel too guilty to say no when I ask you to go to Fuzzy's mother's house with me. I can't bring Torkesquist, you know how he gets, he'd probably say something about how long it takes maggots to eat through a body. Besides, Nattie, you're Jewish. They're doing something called sitting shivers, and you'll know what to do."

"Gail, you're such a shiksa," I said. "It's sitting shiva. After a Jew dies, the family of the deceased is supposed to be surrounded by friends and relatives and lots of smoked fish for a week to help them through the shock. But I'm neither family nor friend nor smoked fish."

"You're *my* friend," Gail said, "and we're going tomorrow night."

Jews and guilt, the religious equivalent of soup and sandwich. Of course I said yes.

CHAPTER 9

I hung up the phone and looked at the clock. It wasn't even five yet and I was finished. My long day's journey into night had just been shortened to a quick trip to dusk. I e-mailed Les, the cops reporter, about Fuzzy McMahon. Since she was white, prominent, and very rich, her death would be a big story. Front-page, above the fold, with a two-column picture. Sad and unjust as it may be, had she been black and poor, she'd have been a small mention buried at the bottom of page 3B next to the Shelby Peach Blossom Festival news.

As it turns out, Les was grateful for anything I could give him. By the time he'd gotten to Anyday Farms, Cathy Sullivan and Ebert Darnell weren't so talkative. All he knew was that Fuzzy McMahon was found dead with a smashed-in skull. I told him what I'd heard, gave him Sarah Jane's telephone number, and offered to call my source at the Union County sheriff's department.

"I owe you one," he messaged back.

"Just as long as it's not a trip to that tattoo parlor where you took Henry," I wrote back. The night Henry's wife left him, Les took Henry drinking, not something Henry normally—or ever—does. He got drunk for the first time in his sheltered life, and the two of them wound up at Sunny's Tattoo Parlor on Independence Boulevard. The next day Henry woke up in Les's car with a rose on his butt.

I called the sheriff's office and asked for Tony. They know my voice. A Philadelphia accent is harder to shake loose than a Jack Russell with anything.

"Nattie," Tony said. "What took you so long to call? I was expecting to hear from you hours ago."

"I told you, I had a story to write. Just because the person I was supposed to interview may be wanted for murder doesn't mean I'm off the hook with Candace. Is she?"

"Is she what?"

"Talk about dancing. Tony Odom, you know exactly what I'm asking. You're just stalling for time, trying to think of a way to shut me up."

"Nattie, darlin', nothing short of a long roll of sticky duct tape and a sharp pair of scissors could shut you up. Not that I'd ever want to, 'course. You mean is she wanted for murder? Not yet. She's wanted for talking to. There's plenty of questions your Miz Sarah Jane Lowell needs to be answering."

"Such as?"

"Nattie, Nattie, Nattie. Lord, girl, you know I cain't tell you that. You here talking to me in your O-fficial capacity as a *Charlotte Commercial Appeal* reporter, I'd be half a sandwich shy of lunch if I answered your questions."

It was looking as if Les wasn't going to owe me anything.

"Tony, off the record, then, way off the record. No one will ever know it came from you. Just throw me a crumb, is there anything concrete to pin this thing on Sarah Jane? And what about the husband, aren't spouses always the prime suspects?"

A pause on the line. Tony was weighing his options. We both knew what he had about Sarah Jane was going to come out sooner or later. My guess was sooner, given how fat a cat the murder victim had been. I'm sure Tony was swatting at reporters every time he stepped outside.

"Come on, Tony, you know it's not going to stay a secret, whatever it is you've got. You might as well give it to me. Isn't there some wise Confucian saying that once you save a person's life you have to keep saving it?"

"Nattie, you dying there at *The Appeal*? I don't hear any gasping or coughing. Some silent killer getting you?"

"Nothing silent about Candace," I said. "I'm talking about metaphorical death. If I can even just get a little something about the McMahon story, the cops reporter will tell his editor and his editor will tell the big editor and that will be more ammunition in my war to get off fashion. Please, Tony, one more conversation about fanny sashes or bustiers or shoulder pads and I'm going to kill the next Belk's buyer who crosses my path."

Tony laughed, a good sign. "Well," he said, "I can't be responsible for a murder, and I've got to do something to get you to quit your hammering. Lord, Nattie, did you ever find the right profession. You're worse than a pack of hound dogs chasing a leaky coon. All right, all right, but this is going to cost you big. You've been promising me a real Jewish meal since I met you, and so far I'm the only one who's done the cooking."

"If you call red-eye gravy cooking," I said. "Okay, you name it. No, let me name it. I'm not making kishka for anybody. How about lox and bagels? I'll invite Henry, you bring the wife. It'll cost me a week's pay, but I guess you're worth it. Now start talking."

"I like those little seeds on the bagels, you know, the ones that pop around in your mouth like crunchy fire ants."

"I never ate fire ants, Tony. Must be some quaint Southern custom that never made it north of the Mason-Dixon line." I oozed the next line in my thickest South-speak: "Y'all sure strange down here, boy. No wonder you guys lost the war. You probably mean poppy seed bagels. I'll get them, but don't be taking any drug tests the next day. So talk, Tony. Sing to me, baby."

The wrong thing to say to an opera freak. He launched into the toreador song.

"Tony," I yelled into the phone. "Tony Pavarotti, enough. Enough. I give, I give. I'll add herring to the menu, just quit the concert and tell me what is."

Tony stopped singing and started talking. "That husband's got himself an alibi tighter than the green skin of a swollen tick after a week-long blood-drunk. Ever seen one of them? Not something you're likely to forget; a thirsty one'll get the size of a shooter marble. Oooh lord, step on one of those babies and you feel like you've stepped on a small animal."

I was getting sick to my stomach. Tony fancied himself a master metaphortician, so much so that before he wanted to be a cop—just like Daddy—he wanted to be the next Faulkner. I wasn't the only one who landed in the right profession.

Well, too bad, the hub had himself an alibi. But I grew up watching Perry Mason—when my brother didn't force me to watch the Three Stooges—and I knew you could poke a pin in even the most airtight of alibis.

"Tony," I said as I choked back my uprising veggie burger, "spare me the tick details. Though think what you'd have had to have done in your last life to come back as one—scary enough to make you a godly sort, huh? What about Sarah Jane, got anything concrete?"

I heard a low whistle and then a pause and then: "How's a shovel? Concrete enough for you, darlin'? Caked with something that looks an awful lot like dried blood and red clay. We found one just like that by the back door of your daddy's friend's house."

CHAPTER 10

Sarah Jane and a bloody shovel? Something was wrong. I didn't know her that well, but I knew her well enough to know she wasn't stupid. Ballsy I could work on accepting. But stupid enough to leave a murder weapon by her back door? Nope.

Not that where you went to college is an infallible IQ indicator, but Sarah Jane did tell me she'd graduated from the University of Chicago. As I recall, that's no place for dummies. Stretching my mind back twenty years, I'm fairly certain it was one of those "most selective in the country" schools in the Baron's guide, right up there with Harvard and Swarthmore. Three higher institutes of learning nothing short of a different last name—such as Rockefeller or Kennedy—could have gotten me into.

This was getting serious. Real serious. I called Lou. I knew he'd want to know about this latest and most troubling development. Apparently, I'd used up my allowance for success. No answer. If I got one more answering machine today, I'd throw the phone across the room.

"Lou," I shouted into the phone, "pick up. It's me, Nattie."

Dead air. And more dead air. Maybe he was in the bathroom. He likes to camp out in there doing God knows what. I hung up, waited fifteen minutes, and called again.

I cupped my hand over the mouthpiece and shouted even louder, "Lou, pick up the blasted phone. It's me. Nattie. Your daughter—in this life. Come on. It's important, it's about Sarah Jane."

Nothing except the whir of my answering machine recording the empty space around my screaming.

He was probably asleep. That's always a sure bet with Lou. Well, I guess the latest news about Sarah Jane would have to wait until I got home. I looked at the clock. Five forty-seven. Thirteen more minutes before I could leave with impunity.

When I first started working at *The Commercial Appeal* almost four years ago, reporters came and went as they wished. Like grown-ups. That was before the productivity studies came down from corporate headquarters. Now, along with story quotas, we've got "work-time performance goals," management-speak for punch-the-nine-to-six-clock or no raise for you, sister.

Both Candace and her shadow were in a meeting. Because all the offices had glass walls, I couldn't sneak out unobserved. So I cleaned my desk. I didn't have to, I mean it wasn't a requirement like it was at the last paper where I worked. The owner of that chain considered our paper his flagship, and he was quite the clean sailor. Every night he'd walk through the newsroom, leaving behind little yellow Post-It notes on all the desks that weren't left a blank Formica slate.

I busied myself some more, and when the big hand finally reached the twelve and the little hand was on the six, I gathered my stuff and left.

This was March. This was North Carolina. This was *southern* North Carolina. So what was I doing shaking like a kid who'd been in the pool too long? I was freezing, and freezing after February is not in my contract. I'd moved south for short winters and early springs. That means T-shirts and flowers in March. It doesn't mean goose bumps and shivers.

Something was blowing in and I didn't like it one bit. The temperature must've dropped twenty degrees since I'd been outside this morning. I was shivering and my denim jacket wasn't helping. I got to my car, prayed the heater was working today and cranked it to high. It was working, but I wasn't.

I couldn't get warm. The goose bumps on my arms stood as stubbornly full-mast as a classful of eighth-grade boys in sex ed class. Something more than the weather was wrong. My body knew it. Now if it only would let my mind in on the secret.

I hate this feeling. Hate it. Hate it. I hate knowing things before I'm technically supposed to. It's been happening to me my whole life, and next life I'm coming back without it, thank you very much to whatever Great One gave me this ability.

I knew my best friend's grandmother was dead before they found her. I knew my father had left us before my mother told me, and I knew when a beautiful colt hung himself on his halter in the middle of the night. The problem, other than the obvious one of who really wants to know these things anyway, is that I'm not always right. If there's an authority gene, then there's also a worry gene, which I have in triplicate thanks to my mother who didn't let me cross the street until I was sixteen. So I never know when it's worry or real.

By the time I got home, I'd stopped shivering. But the goose bumps were still standing at full attention. I rubbed my hands up and down my arms, trying to coax my skin back to something resembling human flesh. My body wasn't buying it.

I parked next to Lou's junker, a car he bought from the repo man. Why anyone ever bothered to repossess a 1981 Cougar with no inside door panels, a missing rear seat, and an engine that complained more than a reporter, I'll never know.

Hard to believe, but it had gotten even colder outside in the ten minutes it took to drive home. Something bad was blowing our way, no doubt about it. I dashed upstairs to my apartment, hoping that the something was just weather. I slid the key in the lock and let myself in, expecting the worst.

CHAPTER 11

So much for being a worrier. What I got was a soft pillow of cumin-laced air. Mmm, something smelled good. Seitan stew. Lou must've spiced up the fermented soy blocks into an edible form.

"Yo, Lou," I called out, "good job on dinner."

No answer. Maybe he'd lost his hearing aid again.

"Lou," I screamed as loud as I could without getting my downstairs neighbor banging his broom handle on his ceiling again.

Still no answer. I looked around my living room. His futon was closed up for the day. Maybe he'd decided to catch a snooze on my bed rather than mess with unfolding the thing.

"Wake up, Lou," I yelled, now loud enough to make all my neighbors start banging my walls. "Let's eat. You don't have that much time before Sarah Jane picks you up to go hear Ramu the channeler."

No answer. No rustling in the bedroom.

"Lou," I shouted. "Get up."

No answer still. Where else could he have been? My father likes the cold even less than I do. He'd rather eat raw meat than take a walk in weather like this.

My heart started slamming against my chest. Despite Lou's vitamin, herbal, and colonic quest for the fountain of youth, he's had—literally—a dizzying array of health problems. Starting with colon cancer eleven years ago, continuing with a quadruple bypass a few years back, then right after he moved in, something called a TIA—short for transcient-ischemic attack—which left his left arm paralyzed for an hour. Between the TIA and his persistent equilibrium problems, the doctor's warned him he's a perfect candidate for a stroke.

So I had reason to worry. And that wasn't even factoring in his mental stability.

I rushed to my bedroom, praying I wouldn't find a stiff lump in my bed. After burying my stepfather last year, I didn't think my battered soul could take another emotional assault of that magnitude so soon.

The lights were out, the curtain closed. I couldn't see my hand, let alone my bed. Another bad sign. No noise. My father could cure a narcoleptic with his snoring.

I walked three strides to my bed—it's a small apartment—and fished around. Nothing, just a set of rumpled sheets I hadn't straightened out this morning. I reached over and flipped on the light on the table. The bed was empty all right.

I cocked my head to the left and sniffed. That mmm-mmm good smell had turned into uh-oh burnt. I hotfooted it back into the kitchen, grabbed a long wooden spoon and tried to stir the stew. Tried to. It wasn't going anywhere. The heat had superglued the stuff together into one large black clump stuck to the bottom of the pot.

This wasn't the first time my father had almost burned down my apartment. Last week he set two pieces of sprouted kamut bread on fire in my toaster and came hollering and screaming at me for what to do. That from a man who serviced fire extinguishers for more than thirty years. Then there was the infamous sweat lodge incident that almost got my father thrown in jail. But that's another story.

My father is forgetful, but leaving the apartment with the stove on goes beyond his normal spaciness. I didn't know what was up. Maybe he and Mrs. Flock, my next door neighbor and his ex-girlfriend, had reconvened. I never really bought his Brahman shtick for one minute, certainly not from a man who's ruddered his entire life with his sexual organ.

Lou and Mrs. Flock hadn't parted company on great terms, so I was hesitant to call. I busied myself in the kitchen while I waited for a what-to-do answer to come to me. That's when I found the note, under the bottle of tamari sauce. Given my father's indecipherable hieroglyphics and the brown splatters of tamari, it was nearly impossible to read what he wrote. All I could make out was something about he didn't know when he'd be back.

Lou and I have had this conversation many times. He knows I, and the rest of the reading world, can't understand his writing. So I've trained him that if he leaves a note he's got to back it up with a phone message if there's something important he wants me to know. I picked up the phone and dialed my office number, hoping the training stuck.

"You have three messages," the miniature man in my phone told me. The first one was from Gail, my best friend. The second from Denise, my shrink friend and Candace's sister. Amazing to think one womb could give birth to a human being—Denise—after delivering a robot. You'd think all those wires and hard edges would've torn things up in there. The third message started, another female voice. Dang, where was my father?

Then I listened closer:

". . . This is Sarah Jane. Lou asked me to call you because he can't find his hearing aid and you know he can't hear anything over the phone without it. Anyway, he's with me, helping me out. I've just got some things to work out, then I'll be back. I'm a little out of alignment right now, must be Mars squaring my Uranus. Once my planets ease up, things should be better. I'll be in touch."

She'll be in touch, how considerate of her. A bloody shovel shows up by her back door, a rich woman whose philandering husband she just happened to be bopping becomes one with the earth not of her accord, and half the police in Union County are trying to track down a Miss Sarah Jane Lowell. And she'll be in touch once her planets ease up.

My father was on the lam with a possible murderess who thought her Uranus was squared. I knew something bad was blowing our way, and it had nothing to do with cold fronts.

CHAPTER 12

What to do? Darned if I knew. What would any reasonable person do if her father started playing Clyde to a misaligned Bonnie?

I couldn't call Tony. Even after all these years I still remember Faye Dunaway and Warren Beatty bouncing around like epileptic rag dolls as the camera zoomed in tight on the nauseating spray of bullets ripping away at their blood-spurting bodies. By the time the credits rolled around, they looked like a couple of stomped ripe tomatoes. Given my father's disdain for members of law enforcement, and Sarah Jane's precarious legal situation, I'd be asking for tomato sauce if I set the police on their trail.

I thought about calling Henry, and almost did. But I didn't. I'm tired of putting men in the oh-save-me-please role. It's a tired old song for me and needs to be pitched. Just because I've played mother to my father all my life doesn't mean I've got to keep looking for Daddy to take care of me. Dr. Freud aside, Henry and I need to be on equal footing if whatever we've got going is going to work, and there's nothing equal about me running to him for help all the time.

I'd already gone womano a womano with two murderers. What's a missing father after that? Cake. Not to mention he is a big boy and whether he needed rescuing was still questionable at this point. Maybe there was a reasonable explanation for Sarah Jane's sudden departure. Maybe her Uranus really was out of whack.

That was it. Sarah Jane. Start with her. Go the Henry route: amass information. My old editor, who actually had been a reporter at one time so he knew what he was doing, once told me if you get stuck writing a story, it's not your writing skills you need to question. It's your reporting. It takes facts to build a story, and if you don't have them, you've got nothing.

Which is exactly what I had with Sarah Jane. Nothing. The only something I had was her name.

Or so I thought.

CHAPTER 13

It turns out Miss Sarah Jane Lowell was an aka, many times over. I found that out the next morning when I went to work. Les, the cops reporter, had done some digging after I'd left and e-mailed me what he found out.

But that's getting ahead of myself.

I'd done my own digging last night at Ramu the channeler's lecture, the one my father and Sarah Jane had planned on going to before she decided to do her David Janssen/Fugitive impression.

And okay, the channeler's name's not really Ramu. It's Faye Cope when she's not in trance; when she is—out in the ozone receiving messages from Michael—that's when she becomes Aranor, an ancient warrior spirit come back to help humanity make it through the millennium. But only those members of humanity who can afford it. Twenty-five bucks to the big show or $175 an hour for private channel counseling. Apparently Ms. Cope had been a hard-driving Washington, D.C., lawyer before the angels started whispering in her ears, telling her there was a higher judicial system that needed her services—and paid more.

I didn't go to hear what the Archangel had to say, but what the attendees had to say about Sarah Jane. Surely someone there would know or at least have heard of the Heidi-girl who talks to horses. How many of them could there be?

Ms. Cope/Aranor were speaking at the Unitarian church, a modern under-parking-lotted building set in a little patch of forest just off Sharon Amity Road. I'd been there before to cover a Sierra

Club meeting for *The Appeal*. Because this is Charlotte, a city that razes its history—and vegetation—at the blink of a hungry developer, there hadn't been a huge turnout that night. But even at that, parking was tight. I'd had to wedge my little car in between a tall pine and a short Honda.

There was no wedging last night. I couldn't have parked a roller skate in that lot, not that my Rabbit's much bigger. It was packed tighter than an anal retentive's dresser drawer, and a lot less neatly. I had to park a good half mile away and hoof it down the shoulder of one of Charlotte's busiest roads.

I stupidly was wearing a black dress under my dark brown coat. Yes, I know black is out—I wrote the stop-the-presses news flash myself—but this was the only clean thing in my closet, and I don't give a hoot what the ninnies of Seventh Avenue say anyway. Not only was this dress clean, but it was cut in such a flattering way that only my most intimate acquaintances knew what figure flaws lay beneath.

Hard to believe a channeler, even one who'd channeled for Shirley MacLaine, could attract a crowd big enough to warrant overflow parking of this magnitude. The Queen City isn't exactly North Carolina's new age Mecca. You want crystals and communes and tantric sex gurus, go to Asheville. You want banks, brick colonials, and concert halls with such lyrical names as Nations-Bank Performance Place, stay in Charlotte.

As I walked to the church I was concentrating on not getting killed by the steady stream of cars zooming by. It's a busy road where people—including myself—always add at least another ten to fifteen miles an hour to the speed limit. It's funny how being on the pedestrian end of things changes your perspective. Suddenly, thirty-five miles an hour seemed a reasonable speed for this road. I raised my fist to a shiny black Beemer whooshing way too close and way too fast. "SPEED LIMIT!!!!!!" I screamed after him. Where were the cops and their big radar guns when you needed them?

Between the cars outside and my prayers for safe deliverance inside, I didn't hear anything else. It wasn't until I saw the church that I heard the noise. Some kind of chanting. Were they astral projecting to a higher plane?

I turned the corner and it all became clear. The crowd, the chants. I'd completely forgotten about the Reverend Rowe Quarrels's traveling hate show. They were there in full rancor.

"New Age is Satan's Age. Jesus says death to the devil." Louder and louder they chanted.

There were about thirty of them: red-faced, shouting, and wearing such harsh and ungodly grimaces of hatred I felt sorry for the man whose name they were invoking. If Jesus was watching, I'm sure he was watching in sorrow. I know I was.

Being the child of Saturday matinee movies that I am, my mind flashed to Jeff Chandler's chiseled face, his parched lips whispering, "Forgive them Father for they know not what they do."

Ditto.

The placards were more of the same. "Satan's calling, his name is New Age." "Heaven awaits Christians. Hell awaits New Agers. You will burn for eternity."

At the center of it was the reverend himself, with his big preacher pompadour that poufed high into the sky like a curvy capital letter N. He probably stood six feet or a little better, but it was hard to tell given his hat of hair. He had a big geological face on him that looked like assembled land masses: Canada for a forehead, tall and broad; Rocky Mountain cheekbones jutting into the next person's space; and protruding cliffs of eyebrows that looked like shaggy fallen trees. You could tell he was the kind of man who thought he was handsome, and maybe he was to women who liked that neo-Neanderthal look. To me he looked too much like a malevolent Fred Flintstone.

But the women liked him, that was for sure. I could tell by their adoring glances in between their hateful chants. And he ate it up. I wondered how many Jessica Hahns he had in his flock.

A few of the new agers were trying to talk to the protesters, trying to convince them that their way was God's way too, that there were many paths to the same place. They were about as effective as me trying to explain to my Team Captain that no matter how many editors plan the direction of a story, you can't know what it's about until you report it.

I stood back and watched. I knew the outcome, they knew the outcome. Why waste the words? Neither side was going to walk away any less certain of its righteousness.

As I was watching, I caught the reverend's eye. I'm no bosomy beauty queen by any stretch of the imagination, but I'm not dog ugly either. I've got long, red hair that some may see as flashy, and as I said, this dress flatters the best of what I've got. Sometimes men glance my way and, yes, I admit it, it feels nice to be looked at. Except this time. Having the reverend's eyes scan me up and down like he was the laser machine at the Harris Teeter and I was a box of tomatoes gave me the heebie-jeebies. This man was inventorying my body parts—especially the top shelf—and I didn't like it one bit.

I stared straight at him, mouthed the words, "God's watching you," and pointed skyward. Then I turned around and walked to a group of women standing by the entrance to the church.

They were trying their best to ignore the Quarrels bunch. Given the noise level, it was difficult, something akin to having a discussion on the nature of God at a Metallica concert. I'm pretty sure they were talking about Feng Shui, the ancient Asian approach to interior design that's got new agers doing everything from throwing out all their electric clocks to relocating toilets to western walls, thereby freeing up their chakras to allow them to become the millionaires they were destined to be. This woman was telling the group how since she switched her bed to an east-west axis she doesn't wake up with headaches anymore.

"Or go to bed with them," she laughed. "And that makes my

husband a very happy man. He thought I was crazy moving all the stuff around. Now he says I can move the furniture anywhere I want it."

They all laughed, and I took that empty space between the sentences to introduce myself. I almost went on autopilot and launched into my Nattie-Gold-I-work-for-*The-Charlotte-Commercial-Appeal* spiel, but then remembered I was flying solo. Not working. Though I wished I had been. Being a reporter is the same as being a waitress—my career before journalism—you've got a professional reason to be brazen.

I apologized for interrupting their conversation and then said, "Do any of you know a young woman by the name of Sarah Jane Lowell? She's an animal communicator."

The Feng Shui lady spoke. "That name sounds familiar. Sarah Jane Lowell. Sarah Jane Lowell. Hmmmm, how do I know that name? A friend of mine called someone who talks to dogs, but it was a man. Another person I know had her cats talked to. That was a woman. But I'm sure her name wasn't Sarah Jane. Then I know of another animal communicator, but her hair is red. And someone else told me about a woman who does talk to horses. I think she was an older woman. You said this Sarah Jane Lowell was young, so it wouldn't be her. I've heard of a couple more, let me think for a second."

Animal communicators were coming out of the woodwork, the nineties answer to MBAs. So much for my Sunday story and any hope of me telling the readers something they didn't already know about. That's what you get when you have to wait for a roomful of Team Captains to decide what's new and happening.

"What's she look like?" she said.

"Picture Heidi all grown up," I said. "Without a ripple of fat."

That sparked something in the woman. I could tell by the look on her face she'd suddenly remembered how she knew Sarah Jane. Judging by the flash of a scowl, it wasn't because Sarah Jane was translating messages of love from the woman's darling dog.

But she didn't say anything.

"You know her?" I asked again.

The woman nodded. "You're not with the police, are you?"

Before I could assure her I was no Joe Friday, one of the other women said, "God, Joanne, don't you know who that is? She writes that fashion column in the Sunday paper."

I looked at her and smiled. "Guilty as charged," I said. "I'm really here as the fashion police to arrest the Reverend Rowe Quarrels for breaking the six-inch-hair rule."

Since I wasn't covering a story, I could have opinions. They laughed and I again reassured Ms. Feng Shui I wasn't there to lock up Sarah Jane. Not at least until I found my father.

She seemed reassured enough to start talking. "I don't like to say bad things about anyone. It makes for negative energy and we've got enough here tonight. Once you said not a ripple of fat, I remembered where I knew that name. I'm a masseuse. I had her as a client. Once. Her check bounced and I had to keep calling her. My husband says I shouldn't take checks, but honestly, this kind of thing never happens. I never did get the money. I called a few times and she apologized and told me to redeposit it. It kept bouncing. Finally I gave the check to my husband, he's got a hardware store and has a telephone number he can call to approve checks. I probably should've done that first. I'd have never taken her check. She was on the under-no-circumstances-take-a-check list, and my husband said there's a warrant out for her in Pennsylvania.

"That's why I asked if you were from the police. I didn't want to be responsible for her going to jail. It was only sixty dollars, and who knows, maybe there's a good explanation."

"Yeah, maybe," I said, hoping more than believing.

This wasn't going the way I wanted it to go. Like I said, it's impossible to write the story before you report it, but in this case it would have been nice. I'd have written myself a tidy little piece about a beatific blond Dr. Dolittle who talks to the animals, thanks the vegetables before she eats them, and just happened to be journeying on a soul renewal trip with a dear old friend, my father.

But that would be fiction and I am a journalist. And we journalists worship the god Accuracy. It was no longer accurate to think of Sarah Jane Lowell as a tinkly new age surfer shrouded in white light. There was most certainly a dark shadow converging on her aura. I know bouncing checks is a long way from smashing someone's head in with a shovel, and it's not as if I'm virginal in that territory myself—bouncing checks, not bashing heads. The difference is I'm not wanted in Pennsylvania, I'm not the prime suspect in my lover's wife's murder, and I didn't do a gravel-spitting spin when I eyeballed a fleet of police cars at the murder scene.

CHAPTER 14

Things went from bad to worse the next morning in the form of Les's e-mail.

"Nattie, your Sarah Jane Lowell has many names for herself. Where should I start? In Pennsylvania? New Jersey? Connecticut? The list is kind of long, it might crash the system."

Oh man, by the time Les had gotten to investigating her, it was too late to check the courthouse for lawsuits. So there was only one other way he could have found out about her aliases. Not good, not good at all. It had to be police records.

If she had a list of aliases longer than an elephant's trunk, that must mean she had a list of arrests of equal elephantine proportions. Les has sources up the wazoo at the Charlotte city police, and I was willing to bet that one of them ran a computer search of my father's latest folly.

I scanned the rest of my e-mail. Nothing urgent, a few messages from Candace "suggesting" fashion column ideas for me, no doubt "suggested" to her from the publisher that were "suggested" to him from his rich buddies whose families owned the clothing conglomerates. And a message from my Team Captain, Ron Riley. I didn't even open up that one. My morning was bad enough without his sniping.

Instead I walked over to Les's desk. All right, so it wasn't only to look at the list of the many Sarah Janes. He does happen to sit next to Henry.

Henry looked up as I walked toward him. He was in his usual pose: head craned to the right, ear planted to the phone, fingers tap dancing across the keyboard. He smiled, I smiled, he smiled, and so on. We both had a case of the eighth-grade giggles around each other. That's because the big IT hadn't happened yet.

Between his kids—two boisterous boys ages seven and ten—and my father, we'd have to rent a room at the Motel 6 to get more than two minutes alone together. The only time we'd been by ourselves in the last few months was in the office or his car. I'm way too old for a backseat tryst, and Henry's way too tall. As for the office, everything has glass walls, enough said. So for now, the big IT was in a holding pattern. It was okay, though. I liked taking this slow approach; it made me feel very 1950s.

Lack of opportunity wasn't the only thing holding us back. Henry's not one to rush into anything too quickly without considering all the possible ramifications, of which there were plenty, given the fact that he's a single dad. Thinking before acting is not my normal approach to anything in life, but it did seem prudent in this area. These are the nineties we're living in, not the sixties. All you have to do is turn to the obit page to see what that means.

As I walked by, I unobtrusively skimmed my fingers across his back. Nothing said I couldn't torment him—and me. I lingered for a second more than I needed to pass by his desk. I liked having my hands on him, even if it was only a quick skim. Reluctantly I turned my thoughts back to Les and his list. He was sitting at the next desk, looking through a notebook.

That's when I heard Henry say something about Quarrels, the Reverend Rowe Quarrels. Was Henry on his way to felling another fallen minister? If so, there was a God. Someone needed to put an end to Quarrels's hate mongering, and all the better if it were Henry. I made a mental note to drag him downstairs for coffee later and pick his brain.

I mouthed "Later" to Henry and turned toward Les, or more accurately, the back of Les.

"Les, my dear," I said to a headful of frizzy brown hair, "let me guess. Ms. Sarah Jane Lowell is the featured guest on this week's *America's Most Wanted*?"

He spun around in his chair. Did they get this guy out of central casting or what? Rumpled blue oxford tracked up the front with coffee dribbles and lord knew what else, shirttails sticking out of what were many moons ago black corduroy pants before he'd worn the wales off, scuffed deck shoes split up the sides, no socks, and little toes falling through the cracks.

He had a cigarette behind his ear and brought it to his mouth. When smoking was allowed in the building, he'd flick his ashes in the pencil holder of his top drawer. I'd put money they were still there, every last ash.

Les was a character all right, and sad but true, one of the remaining two who'd survived the character cleansing pogroms at *The Charlotte Commercial Appeal*. When I first started working there, the place was rife with the eccentric. It was one of the things that gave *The Appeal* an edge. Back then, we had a bite to us, something that distinguished us from all the other mid-size papers in the country. We had a columnist who routinely skewered Charlotte's sacred cows and served them up for barbecue; another columnist who wrote in her own strange and wonderful Southern pidgin English; and we had one of the best editorial cartoonists in the country, who could make you guffaw one day and sob the next, not to mention capture the essence of Jesse Helms with just a set of goofy but malevolent googly eyes. We had. Past tense.

What we have now is a reflection of corporate headquarters, a bunch of gray flannel suits running the place who could just as easily be selling shoes as newspapers. God forbid reporters should show some spunk or creative spirit. Which is why I have to watch my p's and q's if I want to keep paying board on my horse.

Our chain doesn't like big personalities or reporters thinking they're anything but worker bees. If there's any question about that, go down to the lobby and see whose name's on the Pulitzer

Prize display for the Jim Bakker/PTL story. Or more accurately, whose name's not. You won't find word one about Henry Goode, the reporter who spent two years researching, reporting, and writing the award-winning stories.

Les took a bite out of his cigarette and swirled it around his mouth.

"On *America's Most Wanted?*" he said. "Not this week, my little fashion fraulein."

He spit the slimy brown leaves into an ancient plastic coffee cup. "But who knows what next week will bring. She's a real piece of work, though. Grifting her way up and down the East Coast. Did she hit your old man up for any dough yet?"

I shook my head. "At least not that I know of. Show me what you've got."

Les pulled up a nearby chair and motioned for me to sit. He slid his notebook over my way. "Take a look," he said.

I scanned down the page. Sarah Jane Lowell. Susan James Lester. Samantha Josephine Light. And so forth. Many variations on the SJL theme. She obviously wanted to keep her monogram intact, and I don't know which disappointed me more, her criminal tendencies or her prep leanings. Ever since my traumatic ninth grade year at Bala Cynwyd Junior High School, where all the rich Jewish girls with surgically altered noses and closets full of monogrammed LadyBug sweaters made fun of me because I couldn't afford either, any accouterments of prep style raise my ire. Sarah Jane hadn't seemed the monogram type, but then again she hadn't seemed the check-bouncing, skull-smashing type either.

"Okay, Les," I said, "don't be gentle, tell me how, where, and what. I'll supply the whys when I get my hands on her."

For the next ten minutes Les ran down Sarah Jane's aliases. I'd been right, he'd gotten his information from the cops. She was quite the scam artist, working one community until she could no longer write checks or bilk "believers" out of their life savings, then moving on to the next. He showed me a few of her ads that ran in various new age newspapers. She promised she could do everything from contact your departed loved ones to shifting the universe to a more lucrative position for you. It appears the only shifting she'd been doing was bank account shifting: from theirs to hers. And worse yet, she seemed to prey on old guys. She'd done time in both Pennsylvania and Maryland for bad checks. And, the big "And," she was wanted in Pennsylvania for bilking an old geezer out of his life savings.

"Not pretty," I said. "Not pretty at all. Jeez, Les, I know I'm not great in the character judgment category, but this is ridiculous. I haven't been this fooled by someone since I made an ass of myself over a redneck blacksmith I thought was Damon Runyon with dirty fingernails. The only earthy thing about him was the bull excrement that came out of his mouth. I guess the same goes for Sarah Jane. I thought she was for real. I bought her peace, love, and white light routine hook, line, and sinker. Maybe I am in the wrong line of work."

Les laughed. He had a snorty kind of sneer laugh. "Gold, lighten up. This girl's good. Real good, according to my sources. She's been fooling people her whole life. I guarantee you, you won't be the last one. Especially if they get her for the murder of that McMahon woman. She'll have the press lapping at her hands. Mark my words, she'll be conducting interviews with *People* magazine from her jail cell. Hell, I'll bet they put her smiling face and big hooters on the cover. Tell you what, I wouldn't turn her down. I don't care what she's wanted for. Take a look."

Les slid me a fax copy of a picture. I did a double take.

"Huh? This isn't Sarah Jane," I said.

"That's her, believe me," Les said.

I looked again. Maybe it was some version of Sarah Jane Lowell. But it sure as anything wasn't the Sarah Jane Lowell who used to show up in my apartment for Tofu Surprise in her Birkenstocks, baggy dropped-crotch yoga pants, and all-cotton jerseys in an assortment of boring but naturally dyed colors.

This was a babe. Big-time. In big-time babe clothes. Black mini, tasteful but tight enough to show off well-honed cheeks; black hose, black high heels we commonly refer to in the fashion writing business as Joan Crawford Fuck-me pumps (though I've yet to get that exact wording in the paper), and a drapey white silk blouse draping over the abundant heave of her chest. Here was the weirdest part: the hair. Black as a lonely night, which made her pale skin seem even whiter. She was a study in black and white, a regular architect's wet dream.

"So," Les said, "how big of an ass did you make of yourself around the redneck? You Ivy League high-toned Jewesses love those primitive types—for a night. Then you always come back to class, which explains Henry. So did you do him? Did it make you feel like he Tarzan, you Jane?"

"Les, you're such a butt hole. I'd call you worse but I've sort of sworn off cursing. You like everyone to think you're one of the Working People. Give me a break, we both know you're a blue-blooded high-toned Wasp in raggedy clothes. Hotchkiss, wasn't it? Daddy still living in Westport? And for your information, I went to the agricultural school at Cornell—Moo U—not the endowed Ivy League high-toned Jewess part. Since I stupidly brought it up, yes, I made a Class A fool of myself, but no, I didn't, as you so poetically put it, 'do' him. But that, sweetie pie, is a long and stupid story I'll tell you over a bottle of wine sometime. Now, can I have a copy of Sarah Jane's sordid life story or do I tell everyone which eating club you belonged to at Princeton?"

Les punched the print button on his computer. "It's yours for the taking."

I thanked him and headed to the printer, but before I could get a step away, Les started pounding his chest and doing a Johnny Weissmuller: *"Ahhhh aha, ahaha."*

Me and my big mouth. I had to go tell him about the redneck. Someday I'll learn to shut up and keep my boundaries clear. In the meantime, I'd have liked to shoot him the bird, but I couldn't decide if that would be breaking my ban on cursing.

CHAPTER 15

I could no longer ignore Ron Riley's e-mail, because he was standing right over me, or as over me as a five-foot-five-inch little man could.

"Nattie," he said, "I told you I wanted to edit that horse whisperer story first thing before the ten o'clock meeting. And I also told you to leave a note on your computer when you walk away from your desk."

"What about a bathroom pass?" I muttered.

It was a good thing Riley had the mid-level editor's ear, which is just about deaf to anyone below him and all about tin to anything written. "Oh," he said, "you were in the bathroom. Well, next time read your e-mail. I just have a few questions and a couple changes we thought will help the story."

Ahhhh, a dagger to the heart. A few questions and a couple changes with the dreaded "we" word after means an upcoming gang bang by Riley and the rest of his fellow Team Captains, who could no more string a sentence together with any sense of grace than Pat Buchanan could seem human. I could feel the blood ricocheting around my veins and arteries like sky-rocketing pinballs hopped up on supersonic fuel. I was about to tilt out fast if I didn't do something.

"Ron," I said, and forced my lips to turn up in some semblance of a smile, "I have to run back to the rest room for a second. Sorry, it's a bad time of the month."

That would shut him up. No man likes to discuss menstruation issues with a woman.

I ducked into a stall, locked it, and sat down. I scanned my available list of coping tools: the first one from the Good Doctor Greene, unofficial *Appeal* psychiatrist who's got three-quarters of the reporters going to him to learn how to cope with management. His goal was to make me waterfowl: "Let it roll off your back, just like water on a duck." But since he was a psychiatrist, it wasn't a goal we were even close to reaching after three years of therapy. Next my thoughts moved to tears, hissy fits, and threats, my usual course of action. I can hardly categorize those under coping skills, because they accomplish the opposite. The only thing left was Lou's Om-Nahamah-Shee-Viya chant. It had worked when I thought Henry was bopping a murderess, so it was worth a shot now.

I closed my eyes and ran the chant through my brain, hoping for a miracle; the miracle that I could smile my way through the gang bang no matter what clunkers they edited in. I take writing seriously and give every story my all, so it's painful when things get rewritten and end up reading like bad press releases from two-bit flacks. Or worse yet, make no sense at all, e.g., the time an editor changed my lead to, "Eureka, out of the pages of the *Progressive Farmer* . . ." It was a story about Ralph Lauren's new collection and the understated country elegance of his clothes.

I know in the long run my story ends up lining some cat's litter box. But it's the short run that gets me. In the cosmic scheme, I'm sure this is all part of the choosing-my-battles lesson. It's just that some lessons are hard to learn.

A few minutes passed and so did my terror. I took a deep breath, kept my mind occupied with the chant, and walked back to my chair. Riley was tap, tap, tapping away at my computer, no doubt hack, hack, hacking away at my story.

Kitty litter, I forced myself to think. The next day's litter box.

"Just a few changes," Riley said. He was biting his fingernails again and stacking the droppings on my desk. "Tell me what you think."

Of course, he didn't really want to know what I thought. If I told him, it would show up on my annual review as uncooperative. He swung the computer to face me. Half the damn story was in bold—his changes.

I surprised even myself by the calm tone in my voice. "Ron," I said, "why don't you give me a few minutes to read over what you've done. How's that sound?"

It didn't sound like me, that's how it sounded. Being the corporate bad girl, this new me also surprised him. I'm sure he was waiting for me to plunge a pencil through his hand. He gave me a funny what's-wrong-with-you-look and said, "Sure, I'll be back in ten minutes. All right?"

"Perfect," I purred, thinking how proud Mickey-Turner, my coach in manipulation, would have been of me; maybe even enough to make me an honorary Southern Belle.

His changes were worse than horrible, and his questions inane. Who cares how many veterinarians there are in North and South Carolina and what percentage of them got their degrees from Carolina vet schools? That was one of his questions following this quote from Bill Holland, the horse psychic: "Even some of the vets are now telling their clients to call me."

I saw Riley walking back my way and I swear I heard someone whisper in my ear, "Choose your battles carefully, Nattie." I felt like Luke Skywalker going into a blind laser fight with Darth Vader.

"Okay, Obi-Wan Kenobi," I said.

Riley sat down. I smiled. He sort of smiled. "Some good changes there, Ron," I said. "Want to start with those?"

I offered him up four or five I could live with, and it threw him for such a loop that by the time I got to the rest, which were absolutely ridiculous, he was a melted marshmallow in my hand. Taffy; stretchable, manipulable taffy.

I even axed the vet question. So, Obi-Wan, does that mean I find out next that Darth Vader is really my father?

"Okay, Nattie, let's go through the story one last time," Riley said. "I need to finish it before the ten o'clock."

Just then my telephone rang. Riley shot the innocent piece of electronics a scowl. "Nattie, take a message. I told Candace it'd be ready for the meeting."

"Nattie Gold, *Charlotte Commercial Appeal*, how can I help you?"

It was a mouthful for sure, and by the time I got it out, the last thing I felt like doing was advising some confused reader about what to wear to her niece's debut. But if we got caught answering the telephone any other way, there went our performance ratings. As someone who always flunked citizenship in elementary school, I didn't like it one bit. But back then I had the luxury of being rebellious, I didn't have two hungry horses to feed.

"Nattie, it's Sarah Jane. Something's wrong with your father."

CHAPTER 16

I motioned to Ron that I couldn't take a message, and he motioned to me that I had no choice. Back to being the bad girl. I ignored his banging his watch with his stubby little index finger. I ignored the contortions of his squirrelley little face mouthing the words "Ten o'clock meeting." I even ignored the changes he was making to my story, the ones we'd agreed he'd leave alone.

"What do you mean there's something wrong with Lou? And where the hell are you, Miss Sarah Jane Lowell, Susan James Lester, or Sally Jessy Raphael, or whatever name it is you're going by today?"

"Oh," she said. "You know."

"Of course I know. What'd you think I was going to do, wait until you got your celestial road map squared up? We'll get to your Uranus later. First tell me, what's wrong with Lou? Is he in the hospital? Was it a stroke?"

"Nattie, don't even say that. Just thinking those thoughts sends ripples of negativity through the universe and to Lou. We have to be positive, if not we'll—"

"Sarah Jane," I cut in, "can the Nancy New Age bit. We both know what you are. Just tell me about Lou."

I thought I heard a sigh on the other end, or maybe it was Riley, who was waving his arms wildly my way. I turned my back to him.

"He won't talk," Sarah Jane said. "I mean he'll answer yes or no if I ask him something, but that's it. And something's wrong with his voice. He sounds lifeless."

"Like someone let the air out of him?" I said.

"Yeah, how'd you know?"

"I know because he's my father. I know because I've seen it before. In him. His sister. His brother. Practically his whole damn family. He's been wrestling with manic depression his whole life. I don't know what flips the switch, but something inside of him shuts down. Sarah Jane, where are you?"

I heard something from the other end. This time I was sure it was coming from her end; you don't generally hear cars screeching across the fifth floor of the *Charlotte Commercial Appeal* building.

"Nattie, I can't talk anymore. I've got to go right now. I'll do something with Lou, I'll take him to a healer or something. And you're wrong about the other stuff. I've changed."

Click. Before I had a chance to register what happened, Riley rapped the desk with his fingers.

"Nattie," he said, "I told you to take a message. It's 9:57. We've still got more work to do. How do you expect me to make the ten o'clock meeting and finish editing the story?"

All the lessons I'd learned from Mickey-Turner evaporated from my brain that very instant. I spun around and speared him with my eyes. Then my mouth:

"I don't give a flying you-know-what about your meeting. Do whatever you want with the story, you always do. And by the way, do your personal grooming at home, not my desk, okay?"

I slammed my arm across the desk and shot his pile of dirty nail crescents into his lap. No amount of chanting could rein me in now. I did the only thing I could do to stop myself from popping him, as they say down here, upside the head. I stormed away.

Okay, so score one for Darth Vader. Sorry, Obi-Wan.

CHAPTER 17

"You said what to Riley?"

I repeated the whole sorry tale to Henry, who had that concerned Daddy look on his face, the one that makes me want to curl up in his lap, the one that makes me feel everything's going to be okay no matter how badly I just screwed up.

"Nattie, Nattie," he said, "they hate it when you get emotional. You know that. But we'll deal with that later. It's hard to believe Lou would run off with Sarah Jane—and troubling. Very troubling. How come you didn't tell me sooner?"

"I didn't want to come running to you for help, I want us to be on equal footing."

Henry shook his head and put his hand over mine. "If we can't come to each other for anything, then something's wrong. Nattie, stop worrying about equal footing, it's never going to happen because . . ."

I started to get in a huff when I saw the smile spread across his face and he finished his sentence.

". . . I'm fourteen inches taller than you."

"Cute, Goode, real cute," I said. "Just wait till the end of the world, which according to Lou's friends should be rolling around with the millennium. It'll be me and the rest of the little people who inherit the earth, we fuel-efficiency-size folk who take half the energy to operate than you tall mutants. Mark my words, you and your basketball brethren will be dinosaurs, just like those big gas hogs they can't give away today."

"Oh?" Henry said. "I'd check my facts if I were you, Gold. Last week, *The Wall Street Journal* ran a story about how Chevrolet can't make enough Suburbans to keep up with the demand. If I remember correctly, they get about ten miles to the gallon. That puts them in the big 'big gas hog' category, don't you think?"

I slipped into my deepest, treacliest Scarlett O'Hara-ese. "I do declare, Mr. Henry, once again you've gotten me on the accuracy issue, but I pray to the great heavens above, one day—before I return to Tara—you'll learn the difference between accuracy and truth."

Then I smiled by best beauty queen smile and poked him in the ribs with my index finger.

He laughed, I laughed, and I'm sure we were both thinking the same thing: Where's the closest ten square feet of private space?

Two people can't keep looking at each other in that google-eyed way forever. After who knows how long, Henry sobered up and asked for details about Lou and Sarah Jane. I told him all I knew, including the really incriminating stuff from Tony and Les—and that I had no plans and only one crazy thought of where to go from here.

"How crazy?" Henry said.

"More impossible than crazy," I said. "I was thinking I could probably get my hands on Lou's credit card numbers, assuming I can find some crumpled receipts of his around my apartment. Knowing Lou—and now Sarah Jane's true nature—no doubt she's got him footing the bill for their little escapade. But even if I lower my voice and pretend to be him, no bank's going to tell me where he's been spending his money. And don't even ask: No, I don't have his PIN number. You don't happen to know Mr. Master at MasterCard do you?"

I could tell by his smile that I'd struck pay dirt. "You do?" I said.

"More like Ms. Master," he said. "I actually do have a source at Wachovia whom I could tap for a favor. But that's assuming Lou's credit card is through that bank. Is it?"

I scanned my mind and tried to visualize his credit card. I came

82

up with orange circles and a funny little hologram of a leafed-out tree. For the life of me, I couldn't remember the bank logo.

"I'll let you know when I go home. Maybe I'll slip out for lunch and see what I can find around the apartment. Want to come with? No one's there . . ."

Henry's face was working. I could just about hear him weighing all the factors. When his lips turned downward ever so slightly, I knew I'd be going home alone. Which was just as well; a lunchtime quickie wasn't the way I wanted to consummate our relationship either.

"Nattie, you know I'd like nothing more. But I've got an interview scheduled at eleven that will probably run two to three hours. I can't cancel this one, it could be a hell of a story."

I arched an eyebrow and quieted my voice. "Anything to do with the Reverend Rowe Quarrels?"

He did a quick double take. "Nattie, between you and Hankie, you're going to get me to believe in psychic phenomenon. How did you know?"

"Henry," I said, "your son Hankie is psychic, you've seen that yourself. You just don't want to admit it because it isn't rational to you. As for me, it's only flashes here and there. And I can hardly tell the here from there. The only extraperceptory ability I harnessed for that one was my bird-dog ears. I heard you mention Quarrels's name on the phone and then made a guess."

"Good guess," Henry said.

"So spill it, what's the reverend been doing? Something that can land him in Jim Bakker's old jail cell?"

Henry's face was doing that working thing again, weighing his options, probably deciding whether he could tell a blabbermouth like me. I can keep a secret, if it's so labeled. However, if it's not, you might as well consider putting what you tell me on a billboard on the corner of Trade and Tryon Streets.

"Quit worrying yourself into an ulcer," I said. "I won't tell anyone, even if they pull out my nails from my fingers, or worse, cut off my legs so I could never ride again. Come on, Henry, let me in on this. I saw Quarrels and his despicable group last night and I'd consider it proof of God if he's done something bad enough to silence his vitriol."

"Nattie, I'm not kidding that you can't talk about this to anyone. No one."

I shook my head and said, "Duly labeled as a secret. So what'd he do, steal from the collection plate? Run a salvation scam business someplace else?"

The look on his face said I hadn't even gotten close.

"Worse than that?" I said. "How bad can it be?"

Henry looked me square in the eye—singular—which is the only thing anyone can do, since my left eye is usually wandering the outfield playing a game unto itself. I used to hate my walleye; it was one more thing for the other kids to make fun of me about. Until I met Lady Passion, the Asheville witch with an inward right eye. The second she saw me, she smiled, called me "Sister," and told me my walleye was the witch's mark. "A hundred years ago," she'd said, "you'd have been burned at the stake for that eye."

I'd been called a witch before. But never by a real one, and only when I'd gone for more than a week without riding my horse.

"Come on, Henry," I said. "You've covered plenty of slimeballs. It can't be any worse than what you've already seen."

Henry had a strained look on his face, way beyond the percolator expression he normally wears when he's weighing, measuring, and predicting events.

"As the father of two boys," Henry said, "I'd say it's worse. Far worse. I spoke to a woman who says she has proof Quarrels has been molesting little boys. *Little* boys. Ten and under."

CHAPTER 18

There are two things in life I'd have sworn I'd go to my grave without doing. Number one: eat Spam. Number two: defend a hate-spewing religious intolerant the likes of the Reverend Rowe Quarrels.

Looks like I'm down to one now. And though today I say I swear I'll never let that pink stuff cross my lips, you never know what curveballs life throws at you. Who knows, maybe scientists will discover Spam to be an anticarcinogen, like they did Cheez Whiz a few years back.

"He didn't do it," I said. "No way. It's as simple as that, Henry. Quarrels just didn't do it. As much as I'd love nothing better than to see that supercilious smile knocked right off his smug face, I'd bet something big on it. Not my life, but my collection of plastic horses. How's that? And I'd rather go without eating than lose those."

Henry cocked an eyebrow and looked at me like I'd just flown in from Venus. "A few seconds ago you were ready to lock him up—and that's the kindest thing I've ever heard you say about him. Now you're coming to his defense. Which one is it, Nattie?"

I polished off the dregs of my coffee—if I was to go back upstairs and face Riley again in this lifetime, I'd need to be drugged. In this case, caffeine and sugar.

"Yuck," I said. "Man, who taught them to make coffee here? The North Carolina prison system? I can't believe I still drink this

85

stuff. Henry, it's both. You know I'd love to see that sanctimonious slimeball find himself a new ministry behind bars, but I think he should be guilty of something first, other than hateful self-righteousness. You're going to think this is crazy, but as a woman, believe me, I can tell you Rowe Quarrels isn't the least bit interested in little boys. It's big girls he likes. And given where his eyes come in for a landing, I'd say the bigger the better, at least up top."

"How do you know that?" Henry said. "Did he make a pass at you last night? I thought he was leading an anti-new-age rally."

"He didn't make a pass," I said. "But it was the way he looked at me and the way the women in his flock looked at *him*. I'm sure he knows at least half of them—in the biblical sense. I've met womanizers like him before in my life, and you've got to believe me, he's one of the best. They do this thing with their eyes, where they lock their high-beams onto a woman and don't let go until she screams, 'Yes, yes, please yes.' "

This wasn't computing with Henry. I could tell by the way he was looking at me. He had nice eyes; soft blue, kind eyes. But not laser eyes. I knew from such eyes. They were the eyes that can break a woman's heart in eighteen different pieces. A woman, this woman. I once came perilously close to succumbing to that high-beam lock, and I'm sure it would've landed me square into the crying suite of Heartbreak Hotel.

It was the blacksmith I'd told Les about. This man knew exactly what kind of power he had, and he even told me he could scan a crowd, pick out the women—plural—he wanted and then get them. I must've been one of them, because he locked onto me with the ferocity of an alien spaceship beam, and I was as powerless to resist as one of those Arizona abductees. But as luck—my luck, not his—would have it, he got kicked by a horse. And just to show there is a God, it was a mare in teeth-grinding, tail-lifting raging season who smashed him flat in the back with a flying left hind hoof. She put him out of commission, any kind of commission—

shoeing, eyeball-locking, body-locking, whatever—for a solid six months, and by that time I'd come to my senses.

"So," Henry said, "just because Rowe Quarrels found you attractive, you're telling me that exonerates him of anything else? Nattie, of course he looked at you. Lots of men look at you."

"How do you know?" I smiled, probably bigger than I should have. Was that a tinge of possible jealousy in his voice? I hadn't seen this side of Henry before, and I guess if I'd been further along in my evolutionary path, I wouldn't have enjoyed it so much.

"I've seen them," Henry said. "And I don't blame them for looking at you, for your information. I'm glad you find this so funny, but back to Quarrels. So he looks at women, he could be omnivorous for all you know. The person who called me said she has evidence."

My intuition was screaming Henry was wrong, but I let it drop. It would have served no purpose to pursue this topic. Henry wasn't one to factor in intuition easily; mine, his, or anyone's. Henry lived in his mind and took few visits to his heart. That's what made him such an unquestionably fair reporter. Besides, I'd have chased this Quarrels stuff down myself, no matter what my sixth sense was telling me. If I was wrong and the reverend did have a taste for little boys, it would be the story of the year.

"Keep me posted, would you?" I said. "I'd love to hear what that evidence could be. I've got to go. If I don't get back to the newsroom soon and fix some broken fences, I'll have two starving horses on my hands."

I started to get up and Henry took my hand. "Wait one second, Nattie. I think you should have a plan on how you're going to deal with Riley. Be prepared. Know what you're going to say, anticipate his reaction, and at all costs, control yours. Remember, your big emotions scare them."

For the next ten minutes Henry and I worked out my fence-fixing strategy. I was queasy in the stomach at the prospect of going back upstairs, but I had to do it. Had to eat crow. Yes, part of my repair job included an apology for hotheading out into orbit. Henry made me swear I wouldn't tell him about the missing Lou. "Remember, they don't want to hear—and they don't care—about your personal problems."

We got up from the table in the cafeteria and Henry squeezed my hand.

"You can do it, Nattie. I know it'll be unpleasant for a few minutes, just get it over with quickly and then it'll be finished."

I squeezed his hand back and forced a smile. "It or me?"

CHAPTER 19

Henry was right, though I wouldn't have used the word unpleasant. More like major ouch of the tetanus booster kind inflicted on me every year by the evil Dr. Julian. Each June, the sadistic and bald pediatrician of my youth used to lay me facedown on his clammy green vinyl examining table, pull down my white cotton Carters and ram my flesh with a dull needle no doubt used on all the other helpless kids who came before me, getting ready for summer camp.

Like the shot, my apology hurt like hell for a few seconds—those seconds being when I first went up to Riley and started groveling. Then it just out and smarted every time I thought about it. But at least it was over and I still had my job.

Not only that, but Riley was actually smiling by the time I finished my mea-culpa-it'll-never-happen-again shtick. Mid-level editors like nothing better than when reporters prostrate themselves in abject submission. Especially short mid-levelers like Riley. I'm sure it made him feel like the big man, something in short supply in his little life.

Lest anyone think I have a thing against short men, some of the most truly powerful men I know are short in stature. My departed stepfather David, the biggest man I've ever met, stood only five feet eight inches tall. But he knew height, real height, is as much a state of mind as a state of being.

Unfortunately, that was a lesson that hadn't yet visited itself upon Riley. And wasn't he ever the magnanimous one after I'd apologized up every side and down when he told me not to worry. "Forgotten," he said, holding up his right hand as if he were stopping traffic. Yeah, sure. Forgotten, my nose. Forgotten like Nixon's missing eighteen seconds of tape. I'd wager a week's salary that this morning's explosion popped up on my next review as an example of how I'm uncooperative, hotheaded, and, the biggest sin of all, not a team player.

"Let's wrap this up, so I can ship it to Candace," Riley said.

"Right," I said, and gulped silently.

We settled back into my story and the changes he wanted. By this point I had little bargaining power, so I was forced to do all his adds, including the number of Carolina veterinarians. Worse than the adds were the cuts. By the time Riley wrapped things up, the story was eviscerated by one-third. Our Sunday pages, which when I first started working at *The Appeal* ran stories you could sink your teeth into, now looked like *USA Today*'s baby brother. It was sound-bite journalism at its worst: lots of graphics, microminiskirt-size stories, and more bullets—those big dots at the start of each new heading—than the Israeli arsenal.

After I'd groveled and let him maul my story without a peep, Riley stood up to leave.

"I think it's a good read now, Nattie," he said.

I forced a smile, and when I did, I noticed an unpleasant, metallic taste in my mouth. Blood, it was blood. Then I noticed my teeth had a vice clamp hold to the inside of my lip, and I'd cranked it so tight to keep from responding to Riley's last zing that I'd bitten clear through.

"Jesus, Joseph, and Mary, what's this job doing to me? You've got to draw the line at self-mutilation, Nattie-girl," I said to no one in particular. I reached for my coffee cup and spat. Sure enough, what came out of my mouth was redder than a freshly painted barn.

I spat again and ran my tongue over the gash. Soon it would

probably swell and I'd look like Muhammad Ali. I made a mental note to bring up this shooting myself in the foot—or more accurately, mouth—with the Good Doctor Greene during our next session. At least that would stop him from reading passages about hysterics from his psychiatric text.

It was moving on toward lunch, one of the few times of the day I could leave my desk without having to clock-in with an editor and tell him where I was going and when I'd be back. Time to track down Lou's credit card slips. With any luck, he'd be a happy Wachovia banker.

After my morning, that's exactly what I could have used—a bit of luck.

CHAPTER 20

Talk about a bit, how about a bucketful? I found three crumpled credit card slips with just a sideways glance at his corner of my apartment. For the first time in my life I was thankful my father defines the word "slob."

And the luck bucket kept getting bigger. Right above the trademark MasterCard circles was the name "Wachovia," pronounced the first time by all transplanted Yankees as Watch-o-veeya. The correct pronunciation, which you'll be told faster than a Joan Didion sentence, is Wok-oveea.

I grabbed the phone and punched in Henry's number. By the second ring I could tell it was rolling over to voice mail. I'd forgotten about the Reverend Quarrels inquisition.

"Henry," I said to the empty phone at the other end, "glory hallelujah!!! I must've had a direct connection last night when I said my prayers, because guess what? I've struck pay dirt. Lou's a Wachovia man! How's that for luck? Here's his credit card number. I'll be your best friend for life if your gal at Wachovia can track down where Sarah Jane's spending my father's money."

After that there was nothing to do but eat and go back to work. I broiled myself a quick veggie burger and sprinted down to my car. I'd have slipped south on Providence Road for a fast trip to the barn, but given *The Appeal*'s new lock-in policy, it looked like my afternoon quickies were a thing of the past. All I needed to do was get caught on my horse when I should have been chained to my desk, and I'd join the growing ranks of unemployed journalists.

Besides, it wasn't as if I'd be going horseless for the day. Denise, my new buddy at the barn, and I were going trail riding as soon as I got off work. Just six short hours from now I'd be back in glory land atop the girl of my heart, Brenda Starr. I'd slide the reins to the buckle and tell her to do with me what she pleased, which was usually a long, slow caress of a ride deep through the woods. Lou, Sarah Jane, Ron Riley—they'd all be shoved into the cotton-covered corner of my mind, inaccessible on horseback.

Hard as it was for me to believe, Denise and I had clicked right off. I mean she is Candace's sister, and I still can hardly believe I'm actually friends with the enemy's blood kin. Not only is she nothing like her older sister, but she's a shrink, so I thought she'd be constantly analyzing her sister's behavior from a clinical perspective. I was a little worried our trail rides would be rife with psychiatric text talk, with lots of obsessive/compulsive thises and dominate control issues thats. But given my sessions with Dr. Greene, I figured I could take it.

"She's an overbearing bitch," was Denise's opening gambit on our first trail ride together, and she hasn't slipped in a "shibboleth" or "folie à deux" since.

"Shrinks don't talk like that," she'd said to me when I told her what I'd been expecting. "Let me rephrase that. The shrinks I know don't. You sure your guy went to med school?"

I made another mental note to really look at the diploma hanging on the Good Doctor's wall, directly above his tangerine-and-lime-flecked shag carpet.

The funny thing about Denise was she seemed quiet at first. The more I got to know her, the more I realized what a hoot she is. That's not to say I don't miss the long rides Gail and I used to take. But she upped and married our crazy photographer a few months ago and they haven't come up for air yet.

I'd barely seen her since the nuptials, and I missed her. I couldn't believe she was taking a night off from their quest for full-body rug burns. Truth be told, that's the real reason I agreed to go to the Feldman family palace, to get some time in with Gail. Also, more than a little part of me was curious about the lifestyles of the rich and Jewish, Southern style. I wondered which heritage had claimed them.

If there was foil wallpaper shining anywhere in the house, I'd have my answer.

In addition to my sociological study of Jews below the Mason-Dixon line, I also figured I'd be able to poke around Chez Feldman and come up with at least a theory about other possible suspects. Despite Sarah Jane's criminal tendencies and her hysterical dash out of town, I still had a hard time believing she'd taken a shovel to Fuzzy's head. But then again, I am character-assessment challenged.

For living proof of that missing component of my personality, all I have to do is remember the womanizing blacksmith I went gaga over. I haven't yet mentioned a few key parts to the story. He was nothing like Damon Runyon, not a drop of poetry in his soul. What he was, was a pugnacious giant-size banty cock of a man with a mean streak wider than the outer beltway that's gobbled up all my old riding trails. And according to a female friend of mine who did succumb, he was a real lie-back, do ME kind of guy, despite all his crowing about his lotharion skills. So what had I seen in him? Got me.

Maybe Les was right: I was looking to be Jane for a night.

Speaking of Les, he was standing by my desk, writing me a note when I walked back in.

"Computers down?" I said. "Haven't you heard of e-mail?"

"Already sent you three," he said. "Figured you weren't available electronically. Possibly hiding out from an editor? Tell me what you know about the husband. The *blacksmith* husband. From what I hear, he's a redneck. Redneck, blacksmith . . . hmmmm, Ms. Gold, could two and two add up to four here? Could we possibly be talking about *your* redneck blacksmith, perchance?"

I know my face turned redder than my hair. I could feel the blood rush upward like there was a blue light special in my cheeks and all the corpuscles were stampeding Kmart shoppers.

Oh yeah—the other *BIG* key part to the blacksmith story. His name is Bobby McMahon. That's right, McMahon, as in the widower McMahon.

CHAPTER 21

Okay, okay, so I almost bopped that stiff's hub. This is not something I'm proud of. File that debacle under the part of my past I'd like never to have happened, along with half the drugs I did in my foolish youth. At least then I'd had age—the lack of it—to blame stupid behavior on. More than three years ago, when I'd swooned into a tailspin for McMahon, I was firmly rooted in my mid-thirties. Old enough to know better.

Not to excuse myself too much, but I was out of my league from the nanosecond I set eyes on him. I'd never tangled with a professional womanizer before, and Bobby McMahon, though never advanced beyond his voc. ed high school degree, could easily be awarded an honorary Ph.D. in schmuckology. He'd spent an entire lifetime honing his ladykilling skills to lethal sharp precision, while I'd spent an entire lifetime leaping from one responsible nice-guy father figure to another, with the exception of one out of character detour that cost me a broken heart.

But the man who broke my heart was no skilled womanizer, just a plain old confused schmo like the rest of us. I was still smarting from that breakup when McMahon swaggered into the picture. So add vulnerability and your basic rebound bounce to the whys of how I could've fallen for the likes of Bobby McMahon, a redneck blacksmith who, from this historical vantage point, had no redeeming qualities other than being able to patch a hoof back together fairly well.

I met him the day Brenda arrived in Charlotte. She'd torn off her front shoe during the van ride down from upstate New York, and I needed to get her feet fixed pronto or risk a lame horse for the next six months. The only bad thing I could ever find to say about Brenda concerns her feet. They're the worst a horse could have: shelly, flat, and constantly sore without pads. She's living testimony to the little ditty practically every horseman can repeat in his or her sleep:

> One white sock, buy him.
> Two white socks, try him.
> Three white socks, deny him.
> Four white socks and a white nose,
> Take off his hide and throw him to the crows.

This old saying presumes a white hoof, which is always at the end of a white sock, is weaker than a black hoof. Brenda, the owner of three white socks and a huge white blaze down her face, falls somewhere just shy of crow feed when it comes to the tenacity of her feet. So I was pretty desperate to get her foot patched up before the whole thing split down to an excruciating nub.

Gerry, the barn's regular blacksmith, was out of town, shoeing horses on the Florida circuit. I'd only met Gail once before the van pulled in, and I guess she felt she didn't know me well enough to say, "I'll call this other blacksmith named McMahon for you, but watch out, he's a lying prick who's felled half the women in Charlotte."

Instead, she told me not to worry, that she'd get Brenda's feet fixed by day's end. She beelined it to the office to call McMahon. Apparently all she had to do was mention that the owner of the horse with the torn-up foot was a new woman boarder. McMahon was there in twenty minutes.

I was standing in Brenda's new stall, brushing her copper coat and worrying about her foot. It looked pretty bad to me. I figured this blacksmith was going to have to work magic plus use half a can of liquid plastic to make her walk without crutches.

The stall door slid open and in walked Bobby McMahon. It's not that he's dangerously handsome like Sean Connery or Daniel Day Lewis. He's a moderately good-looking guy. All right, he does have nice hair, I'll give him that: swirly sable stuff that croons around his face like a Tony Bennett ballad. And he does have those goyish straight, even features that make Jewish girls swoon. But it wasn't the bumpless nose—been there, done that many times, in fact all the time—that got to me.

Like I said earlier, it's his eyes and what he can do with them. It didn't hurt that they were so blue they looked like two hunks of electric turquoise he'd plugged into the nearest wall socket. The second I looked at him, he locked those orbs on me, ratcheted up the wattage and stared at me harder than I'd ever been stared at in my life. Stared at me as if no matter how hard and how long he looked, he could never get enough.

There's something to be said for raw, wanton, primal, bottom-less desire. A lot to be said, especially from a woman who's just been dumped by a man who's told her the spark is gone.

Then the Smile seeped across his face. Slow and easy, edging from one corner of his mouth to the other. It was the you're-what-I've-been-looking-for-all-my-life-and-I'm-what-you've-always-needed grin.

Being the articulate wordsmith I am in times of high stress, I performed true to tradition and really wowed him with my verbal prowess.

"Hi, you're here to fix my feet? I'm mean fix my horse's eyes, feet. I mean, feet. Oh, you know what I mean." Then I sputtered an introduction of the lamest kind and went to shake his hand. Except I'd forgotten I'd left my grooming box in front of my feet.

Add graceful to articulate wordsmith. I tripped over the box and would've landed face first in pine shavings had McMahon's two big, strong arms not caught me mid-fall.

"Long trip down for you from up North?" McMahon said. He kept his hands on my arms and his eyes on my eyes. I had no desire to remove either.

"Well, sort of," I said, and forced myself to shut up. I knew I wasn't capable of making sense, or worse, not giggling. He didn't have to know I've arrived in Charlotte two weeks earlier.

"That foot's torn up something bad," McMahon said, finally noticing my horse. "But I can fix it."

Modesty obviously wasn't on his checklist of virtues. But in all fairness to McMahon, I challenge anyone to name a blacksmith with even a smidgen of humility. I'm convinced that to join the society of professional hoof-nailers, you have to swear to the following oath: "Thou shalt always find fault with the blacksmith who came before you and assure/boast to the horse's owner you can right the horrible wrongs perpetrated on her darling's hooves."

"Bring her on out," McMahon said. "She'll be good as new in a few minutes. Better, in fact."

Brenda limped out of the stall, and that brought me back to reality. Nothing like a hurting horse to bring things into focus for me. I regained some of my verbal ability, enough to take me past the eighth-grade giggles. We talked while he filed, rasped, and patched. Besides his nice, swirly hair, I'll give him something else: he's funny and tells a good story. And I do like a good storyteller. Since I'd only been in the South two weeks, I found his low-country accent—*wahr* for wire, *rahd* for ride—charmingly exotic.

Of course, he had great stories to tell; he was a blacksmith, and blacksmiths are the horse world's equivalent of hairdressers. Owners tell them things they wouldn't tell their best friends, and what they're not told, they hear. Blacksmiths are the proverbial flies on the wall, privy to most everything that goes on in the horse show world, which is plenty. Like the story he told about a pony mother who tried to hire her groom's felon brother to whomp some kid's head.

"Not kill her exactly," McMahon said. "Just put the little pigtails out of commission long enough for her daughter to win enough points so the other kid could never catch up for the year-end awards."

Apparently even convicted felons draw the line at children.

"Well, that boy said no to the mama," McMahon said, "and damn if she didn't turn around and ask him to get the kid's mama instead, thinking the kid'd be too broke up to ride. That boy was quick on his feet. He put a gun to the mama's head and stole the diamonds off her fingers and ears—and her money. The mama never could report it to the police."

I was dying to know who it was, but McMahon was mum. All right, I'll give him something else, he was sort of discreet. It didn't really matter who it was anyway. Over the years, I'd run into any number of horse show mothers capable of such behavior—and worse.

By that story's end, he had Brenda's foot looking almost like normal again. And he'd asked me out for dinner that night. Like the fool I am, I said yes, even though the little man in my head was banging every pot and pan he could find, screaming, "Trouble, trouble, trouble."

Five hours later Bobby McMahon was standing at my door with that same high-beam eye lock and grin. Given how my hormones were ricocheting off every surface inside me, I'd have been happy with takeout.

"Know a good Chinese place that delivers?" The words slid past my lips before I could stop them.

He smiled wider. Bobby McMahon taught me plenty about womanizers, the first being their most powerful weapon: the old double W. Wait and Withhold.

"Next time," McMahon said. "Let's go to Gus's Sir Beef."

I thought he was taking me to a romantic steak house with smoky candles and dark booths where we could slide our hands up and down each other's legs. The only hand sliding going on at Gus's was of the kid-with-no-napkin kind: hands sliding up and down clothes to wipe off gravy, ketchup, or whatever else didn't make it all the way to their mouths. Gus's is as family a family place as you can find, with tables full of screaming babies and kids running crazy through the aisles. But it does have good food—a plateful of steak for him, an assortment of vegetables for me—and it's cheap. At the time, I figured his frugality was due to his profession. I didn't know he was married to one of the richest women in Charlotte, who had him on a tight financial leash.

After the best banana pudding I've ever tasted and a steady stream of funny stories in his then-exotic-to-my-Yankee-ear drawl, we headed back to my place. He walked me to my front door and slid his arm around my neck. He kissed me, and had I been a pinball machine, I'd have been jolted into full tilt. Just as I was about to drag him inside he said, "I'll call you," and turned around into the night.

If rule number one is the double W, rule number two is the big T: Tantalize. He called the next night and our talk quickly turned to what else?

"I just might have to pack me a picnic lunch when I get to you," he said, "that's how long it might take me to finish."

It sounds not only double yucky to me now, but funny in light of my friend's less than satisfying experience with him. "His idea of foreplay is to turn off the lights," she told me. However, at the time, I bought it, just like Lou did with Sarah Jane. Talk about the apple not falling far from the tree.

I didn't see McMahon for another couple of nights—remember Wait and Withhold—he kept telling me how busy he was. I'm convinced it was the Great Divine's way of protecting me, along with a little assistance from Mother Nature. Because when he did show up at my door carrying three bags of Chinese takeout and a walletful of Trojans, I'd moved into a time of my womanly cycle that's not conducive to the activities he'd described in detail on the telephone.

That's not to say it was a totally chaste evening. We were active enough for me to get a peek at some of the ugliest bruises I'd seen in a while. Big, purpley blotches up his right arm and down his back.

"That's the last time I mess with an unbroke stallion," he said.

I steered clear of his injuries and he steered clear of certain parts of me. So technically speaking, Bobby McMahon and I do not know each other in the biblical sense. Technically speaking.

Thank God. Because the next day when Gail asked me if I wanted to go on a trail ride, even that old horse magic couldn't fix what I found out. About fifteen minutes into the woods she turned to me and said, "Did that asshole McMahon hit on you? I'd have asked you sooner, but I haven't seen you since then."

Before I could get the "Yes" out, she shook her head.

"Jesus Christ, I knew it. Someone should cut it off, just sheer it right off his body."

"So what if he hit on me?" I said. "Okay, he's not the smartest guy around, I'll grant you that. In fact he's kind of dumb, but you know how it is with horses, you never want one that's too smart. Every once in a while I like that in a man. I mean it's not like I'm looking to marry him."

Gail snorted. "Good thing, Nattie, 'cause he already is."

That stopped me dead in my smugness. "Is what?"

"Married, you fool. He's married as shit. Married to Fuzzy McMahon. Oh, I forgot you're new to town, let me tell you who Fuzzy McMahon is."

"Don't bother," I said. "I read the *Chronicle of the Horse*. Her name's all over the magazine. She sponsors half the classes at the Washington International Horse Show and the other half at the National Horse Show. She's bought every famous pony and horse in America and Europe just so her little princess can win blue ribbons. Spare me the details. That's Bobby's wife? I swear I didn't know he was married."

"Same last name, my dear."

"Oh man, I never made the connection. Why would I? What would a millionairess see in an uneducated blacksmith who's dumber than dirt?"

Gail gave me her best do-what look and said, "You tell me."

CHAPTER 22

"Well Ms. Gold? Speak up, is *her* redneck blacksmith *your* redneck blacksmith? And why the withholding act? How come you didn't tell me right off?"

I was so lost in my memories, I barely heard Les speaking to me. Not one to be dismissed or ignored, he stepped into my personal space and poked a finger my way when I didn't respond.

"You there, Gold? Or we taking a stroll down memory lane? Tell me, was McMahon a golden oldie?"

The finger in my shoulder brought me back to the newsroom real quick.

"Back off, Rover," I said, and removed his digit from my body. "I was working on a need-to-know basis. As in, I didn't think you needed to know as of yet. But since you asked, yes, those redneck blacksmiths are one and the same. I didn't tell you because he's a jerk and I'm not exactly proud of myself about that. Thankfully 'that' wasn't much except in my mind—and on the telephone. The only good thing that came out of the whole sorry episode was I discovered if things don't work out in journalism, I probably could make a pretty good living telephonically—if you get my drift. Even if he hadn't got kicked by a horse the day I found out he was married, I was starting to hear the little alarm bells going off in my head. Whether I'd have listened to them is anybody's guess. But when I found out he was married, that was it for me. I, unlike some people, draw the line at wedding vows."

Les looked me square in the eye without flinching. He was either the best poker player in the galaxy or the rumors that he was seeing the editor's big-breasted secretary, the editor's *married* big-breasted secretary, were untrue.

"Seen him lately?" he asked.

"Not in a couple years," I said. "And darn if that schmuck didn't try to eye-lock me again. But it didn't work, thank God. He's like smallpox, one small dose of him was enough to vaccinate me. What else do you want to know besides he's a womanizer? That's a given. Whether he's a murderer, I don't know. He did tell me he likes a good fight and doesn't mind fighting dirty. Not that he needs to. He's a big, tall guy who could flatten just about anybody. He's also a Republican *and* a card-carrying member of the NRA whose idea of fun is to shoot the whiskers off a groundhog and watch it freeze in terror before he pops it right between the eyes with another bullet."

Dredging up this stuff was making my stomach turn. "I must've been out of my mind at the time. Anyway, you got anything good on him that can take the spotlight off Sarah Jane? I thought Tony said McMahon had an alibi tighter than a swollen tick's skin."

Les was smirking like a ninth grader who'd just seen the girls change for gym class. "One more thing," he said, "define 'not a lot,' as in 'not a lot happened.' "

I stepped forward into his personal space and poked my finger at him. "Listen Les-*ter*, I'll drag your sorry butt back to Sonny's and have your ex-wife's name tattooed on your you-know-what if you don't drop it. I've said all I'm ever going to say—uninebriated. Now can we get past this, please? Haven't your hormones ever short-circuited your brain before?"

Les squinched his legs together and crossed his hands over his privates in feigned horror. Then he flashed a peace sign and said, "I've been known to flip the old breaker box on occasion myself."

"So," I said, "what about McMahon? What do you have on him? And just how tight is that alibi?"

"His kid," Les said. "He's got his kid swearing they spent the whole day and night playing darling daughter and doting father capped off by dinner at Gus's Sir Beef and a late movie."

Another blue light special for my blood corpuscles. They swarmed to my face and turned me bright red again.

"Something about Gus's?"

"Forget it," I said. "Maybe the kid's lying to protect Daddy. I'm heading to Fuzzy's house tonight, maybe I can feel things out for you, ask a few discreet questions."

Les flipped his head back and laughed, if that's what you call the gargly growl that rumbles up from his throat when he finds something funny.

"That's a good one, Nattie. Ask a few *discreet* questions. What're you going to do, gag yourself?"

CHAPTER 23

So I almost bopped the stiff's hub, *and* I'm not known for discretion. While I'm enumerating my personality flaws, let me throw in subtlety and good taste. The lack of. They don't seem to be anywhere inside me, try as I might. But there's a reason.

I know I'm not sounding like the est graduate I am; the one who had pummeled into her battered psyche that "getting it" meant I am responsible for EVERYTHING in the universe, from the destruction of the rain forest to Al Gore's growing bald spot. Sometimes—forgive me, Werner Erhart—I slip and look for blame elsewhere.

Like at the top of my head. A while back an Israeli behaviorist did a study on redheads, and—big surprise—found a definite redhead personality. Aggressive, loud, assertive, no discretion, you get the picture. It doesn't take a psychiatrist to figure out why. Since the consuming drive in childhood is to fit in, when you grow up with something different growing out of your scalp, you automatically don't. So you do whatever you can to find your place. You become aggressive, assertive, etc.: You become a redhead not in hair only.

If subtle and discreet fall outside the parameters of redheadness, maybe that's why I'm not the kind of reporter who can stand back, disappear into the curtains and watch the story unfold. My night at the late Fuzzy McMahon's was no exception. Les was right, I'd have needed to gag myself.

But I didn't get thrown out. On the contrary, I almost had to give out numbers to all the people who couldn't wait to add their two cents about Fuzzy, her life and her death. The only one not talking was Fuzzy's father, Mo Feldman, and that's because his wife Bootsie seemed to be his official mouthpiece. Every time he opened his mouth, she jumped in with both feet, trampling the first syllable to pass through his lips. After a while he gave up and made himself happy with a plateful of whitefish.

The culinary clues only confirmed my anthropological investigation as to which heritage claimed the Feldman family. There was no contest. The minute I saw the concentric circles of illuminated Lucite hanging in the foyer and the cherry-red lacquered wall units shining brighter than a new set of fake nails on the counter girl at Dunkin' Donuts, I knew their Jewish roots tapped down deep into their collective soil. The only surprise was where the house was located: in the Eastover section of Charlotte, an old money, oh-so-tony neighborhood of rolling-hilled, multi-acred lots crowned with commanding, though incredibly boring, brick colonials. I'd have pictured the Feldmans in something with a little more flash and pizzazz; one of those faux stuccoed McMansions, sandwiched between other faux stuccoed McMansions in a gated community way south and east of Trade and Tryon Streets.

"Nattie Gold? Right? The fashion editor?"

I started to shake my head no and explain I was just the fashion writer, a small distinction I'm starting to realize is important only to me. Writer, editor, I still cover the rag trade.

"Sort of," I said, and offered my hand to the woman standing in front of me. She was shorter than me, which could make her eligible to be an official member of the Little People of America, sported a pricey-looking modern take on the old pixie do, and was a bit on the hefty side but camouflaged it well with straight Donna Karan from the tip of her overpriced black turtleneck to the hem of her equally overpriced black trumpet skirt. Her brown hair was either kissed by the sun's rays to make delicate flecks of gold here and there, or she had a true artist for a beautician. Probably a combo of both, given her skin, which was darker than Rutger Pearson's, our publisher who, rumor had it, slept in a tanning parlor on Tuesday and Thursday nights. She also had the worst nose job I'd ever seen. The truncated appendage on the front of her face, once recognizable as a nose, was so whittled down it made Michael Jackson's shaved nozzle look human by comparison. Time to switch plastic guys, if you asked me.

"You couldn't be here on business," she said. "I mean *The Appeal*'s done some awful, just awful, stories. But I can't believe even they could sink to something so low as sending the fashion editor to a wake."

This obviously wasn't one of Fuzzy's Jewish friends. I didn't know which to correct first, my purpose or the correct name of the evening's event.

"I knew Fuzzy through horses," I said. Not a total lie; I didn't deny I was there on business, and it was more my business than *The Appeal*'s anyway. Though I planned to pass along any information to Les, I was really looking for a way to take the heat off Sarah Jane so my father didn't end up a fugitive. "You know, it's not actually a wake. It's called sitting shiva. There you have it, one of the three things I know about being Jewish—and I'm of the faith."

The woman gave me a funny look. I didn't know if I offended her, she was uncomfortable around Jews, or just plain grieving. I went for the third option and tried to offer my condolences.

"I can't believe she's dead," I said. "It's horrible what happened to her."

The woman gave me an even funnier look.

"Horrible what happened to her?" she said, and then of all things, started to laugh. Loud. "Then you didn't know Fuzzy from the horse world, that's for sure. Give me a break, it's perfect what happened to her. As far as I'm concerned, Fuzzy's death is enough to make me start going to church again. It proves God's up there watching us, because I can't think of anyone more deserving to wind up in the poop pile than Fuzzy McMahon."

Now it was my turn to give funny looks. The left side of my mouth slid up as my left eye squinched down.

"Watch out, you'll give yourself wrinkles doing that," the woman said.

I didn't feel like going into the virtues of Lou's latest: emu oil, guaranteed, he was told by the shyster who sold him seven cases, to wipe the age right off your face. Wrinkles, crinkles, sun spots, even the half-moon puffs below your eyes on water-retaining days would be gone, vanished, obliterated by the ancient healing powers of the great walking bird. "It'll bring back your freshness, Nats," he'd told me. He'd already told me I, as well as my mother, had lost our freshness years ago.

I let my lip drop and unlocked my squinched eye. Emu cream or no emu cream, I didn't need any more wrinkles than I already had from twenty years of riding horses in the sun with a face more unprotected than a couple of teenagers in the backseat of Dad's car.

"I'll take that last comment to mean you and Fuzzy weren't on great terms," I said.

She laughed again. "You could say that, and you could say that about almost everyone here and anyone who's ever been within three feet of her. What were you expecting, a roomful of people in tears? Let's put it this way, Kimberly-Clark won't be making a lot of money on this shiva. Shiva, right?"

I nodded, trying to digest what was happening. Even I, the used-to-be queen of inappropriate comments, would have held my tongue a little harder.

"A witch on wheels was what she was. I'm not the only one who thought so. Look at her daughter. Does that look like the face of deep mourning?"

I followed her finger to a clot of preteen girls standing by a large platter of lox. The tumescent mound of shiny pink fish flesh was piled double-D cup high, and I'd bet my bottom dollar— which is what a platter like that must've cost—there were at least two more of those babies waiting on what I predict would be runway-long stretches of Corian countertops grained to look like granite. Not to be judgmental about my people, but I've noticed that except for all but the highest of German Jews, many of my kind seem to be allergic to all naturally occurring building, furniture, or lighting materials.

"She's the one on the end," the woman said.

I didn't need to have her pointed out. I'd seen her face too many times in the *Chronicle*. Now that I looked closely and in person, I saw that she did favor her father an awful lot. Same thick, wavy dark brown hair, same straight nose, and since I was seeing her in color for the first time—the *Chronicle* is mostly a black and white publication with agate print and postage-stamp-size pictures— darn, if she didn't have Daddy's bad-boy-blue eyes.

The woman was right about young Ashlee McMahon. She didn't look too broken up about her mother's departure. She and her girlfriends had their heads together, whispering about something. However, I didn't find that as damning as the woman standing next to me. Kids handle grief in funny ways. A friend of mine lost her mother when she was Ashlee's age and spent the day of the funeral with me at City Line Lanes, bowling, eating greasy fries, and sneaking the smokes we'd stolen from my mother's pack of Luckys into the smelly ladies' room where we made ourselves sick. It took her years of therapy to finally work through her grief after nearly screwing up her life with drugs and sex.

I didn't want to get into that kind of discussion with this woman, whoever she was. She'd been so busy talking, I was having a difficult time getting in any questions. Finally I charged in.

"By the way," I said, "what's your name? And if you weren't a friend of Fuzzy's, what brings you here tonight?"

She eyed me like I was a Monday piece of perch at the Harris Teeter fish counter. "Is this going in the paper or something?"

I held up my hand. "No, nothing like that. It's just that after living in the South for more than three years, I gotta say it's refreshing to find someone who says what she thinks and doesn't drip honey when she talks—or as the case may be sometimes, saccharine."

She smiled and extended her hand. "Carter Evans, and I'm here because of her."

Again I followed her finger to the girls by the lox. "The tiny one with the long brown hair standing next to Ashlee. That's my daughter, Ralston. They started riding ponies together when they were both in kindergarten."

"Ralston Evans? The one who rides Wishbone?"

If there was a puffometer on the market that measured pride-swelling in centimeters, kind of like a woman's cervix in labor, Carter Evans would have been fully dilated.

"Second in the country last year," she said, beaming as bright as a set of those halogen fog lights that blind oncoming drivers. "First so far this year. She was champion at all five Ocala shows this winter."

Now it clicked. The Rutger Pearson tan on the faces of half the people in the room. Of course, the Florida circuit. Not too fast on your feet that time, Nattie girl. Keep missing them like that, and you'll be stuck writing about fishnet panty hose the rest of your life.

Here's how it goes—the really rich horse show people don't spend many days shivering. When the mercury drops, so does their location. Everyone with enough bucks and no job relocates to one of two places in the sunshine state: Ocala for the Hits Ocala Winter Circuit, or Palm Beach for the Winter Equestrian Festival. Palm Beach being Palm Beach is the more prestigious of the two series of horse shows. Which is why Ralston won all those Ocala championships.

Since Carter Evans was a possible source, and a good one given her loose lips, I didn't want to alienate her. More importantly, there was no reason to be unkind and remind her that we both knew why her daughter's pony won all those Ocala championships: Ashlee

112

McMahon doesn't even stop in Ocala. Her custom air-ride eighteen-wheeler zooms straight on through to Palm Beach, where it deposits her stableful of pricey horseflesh.

Furthermore, the reason why Ralston's pony was finally number one in the country is because the Feldman Family Value heir doesn't compete in that division anymore. Ponies are a thing of the past for Ashlee McMahon. She's moved on to horses, big expensive horses. Five of them alone in the junior hunter division, including Can-Do, a huge bay gelding who looks like a Leonardo da Vinci painting come to life. Can-Do, who can and did do it all last year, including dethroning Rox-Dene from her long reign as Horse of the Year, set Mo Feldman back a half-million dollars—and that's just in yearly lease fees. They don't even own the horse.

Plus young Ms. McMahon started riding jumpers, where the only thing that counts is how high and how fast the horse can jump; as opposed to the hunter divisions, where horses are judged on artistic merit. So far she'd ridden four jumpers, but the list had been growing exponentially when Fuzzy was alive. A friend of mine heard Fuzzy ranting to Ashlee's personal trainers that she didn't want her daughter standing around horse shows for even thirty minutes with nothing to do.

Since Ashlee's never lifted a brush or hoof pick in her life and wouldn't know which end of the saddle goes where, occupying her time would only involve riding. And since she doesn't train, tune, or prepare the horses in any way, filling up her day would only involve moving from one groomed, braided, trained, and tuned horse to another.

The most famous of her jumpers is a little chestnut mare called Kiss-Me, who captured not only a gold medal for the U.S. equestrian team, but the hearts of the viewing public with her small stature and giant will. When Fuzzy lured this horse away from its owner—with a check for one million dollars—the *Chronicle of the Horse* bemoaned the sale in an editorial, whining about the raiding of all the grand prix jumpers. The editorial We complained that the most talented horses were ending up in the junior or amateur jumper divisions, leaving little left behind for the professionals to ride in international competitions. As if the richest-rider-wins concept was new to the horse world.

And in Kiss-Me's case it was even worse. The kid showed the mare in the *low children*'s jumper division; not even the high, let alone the junior division, which is a step up from children's. That would be like taking Rox-Dene, plopping a squirmy three-year-old kid in pigtails on her back, and plodding her around the ring in the lead-line classes. Kiss-Me's an Olympic gold medal horse who can practically jump the moon—those grand prix competition fences can get as large as five and a half feet high and wide. Instead she was being asked to jump fences sometimes not even half that size. So far the answer had been a resounding no. The kid had yet to complete a course without the horse slamming on the brakes in front of most, if not all, the fences.

The only reason I knew all about Ashlee's fleet of horses was because Mommy took out two double page ads in the *Chronicle* four weeks in a row, congratulating little Ashlee on the purchases of her new horses and their victories together.

These are the people I had to compete against. I was just starting to feel sorry for myself when I heard the front door open. The buzz in the room stopped short and it got so quiet I could hear Mo Feldman chomping his cigar.

Just as I was about to turn around I saw a set of arms reach for Carter Evans.

"Damn, Carter, if you're not the last person I'd have expected to see here. It sure is *goooood* to see you."

She looked past me and smiled. It wasn't the same smile she'd given me earlier. And I knew why. I'd been on the receiving end of that drawled innuendo before.

"Bobby McMahon," she said in a voice that sashayed slow and easy across the syllables, "I could say the same about you."

CHAPTER 24

This was a night of religious importance, all right. God had scored two new foot soldiers: me and Carter Evans. Though truth be told, I'd sort of enlisted before this latest display that She not only exists, but is keeping count of who does what to whom and then turns it all around on you: the New Jersey take on karma.

In Bobby McMahon's case, She got him good, right where it hurts—his packaging. I hadn't seen him in a couple of years, and those weren't a couple of kind years. All those Budweisers he'd been chugging had finally caught up with him. He had a big, old double chin, puffed-out cheeks, a web of icky purple spider veins on the sides of his reddened nose, and the brownish-purple remains of a shiner on his right eye. Then there was his gut pouring out over his belt.

Man oh man, what had Sarah Jane seen in him? At least when I threw my body his way, he'd been attractive. Now his face and body were as bloated as his ego.

McMahon was hugging Carter and trying to eye-lock me at the same time. I gave him a get-real look and said, "How you doing, Bobby?"

His voice slid back to its sleazy roots. "I'm doing just fine now," he oozed. "Now that I'm standing next to the two sexiest women in the world."

Carter was puffing up again and I was ready to pop McMahon upside the head. Except I had some questions to ask him. I forced myself to be nice, remembered his IQ was half the size of my horse's, and figured a few insincere but well-placed words could get me some important information.

"It's good to see you too, Bobby. Been a while, hasn't it? Carter, would you excuse me while I steal Bobby away for a few minutes? I haven't seen him for years, and we've got some catching up to do."

Carter Evans reluctantly dislodged herself. "Just as long as you return him in one piece."

She winked McMahon's way. "I'll be right here, waiting. Don't make it too long . . . this time."

Wait and withhold, was there anyone in the room he hadn't used that trick on?

"That looks like it was some shiner, Bobby," I said. "Another wild stallion?"

He looked at me and I knew he didn't know what I was talking about. Given that he'd probably had 459 women since me, I'm sure my almost-night with him was long gone in his memory.

"Do what?" he said.

"Last time I saw you, you'd been on the losing end of words with an uppity stallion, remember? Bruises on your arm and back?"

A slow click in McMahon's eyes. "Oh yeah, right. No, this time it was a mare. Damn if it wasn't a chestnut mare, just like you."

"Ha ha, very funny," I said. I was watching Gail eyeing me from the other side of the room. She knew what I was up to, I'd discussed my plan with her on the way over. It was good to have someone to bounce my ideas off. I'd have talked to Henry too, but all I got was his answering machine. First I thought his interview with Reverend Quarrels's accusers must've gone into double over-time, then I remembered this was his busy dad night. From school, to tennis, to swimming, to cello. Somewhere in between it all, tacos at Taco Bell. He and the boys wouldn't be home until at least nine-thirty. And by then Henry'd be so worn out, the only three words he'd be able to string together would be "Go to bed."

Gail wasn't sure whether McMahon would even show up tonight. He and the Feldmans weren't exactly chummy. Far from it. Gail told me they came close to disinheriting Fuzzy when she brought home the blacksmith and announced him as her intended. It didn't help matters that she'd been in the family way.

"He's got a bigger set of balls than your editor's if he does come," Gail had said. "Just as well if he doesn't, Nattie."

Gail wasn't keen on me spending time, any amount of it, with McMahon. "He could suck you right back in," she'd said. "I've seen him in action a lot longer than you have. Just be careful, okay? You've got something good starting with Henry, don't go screwing it up, like you almost did with Tony."

Gail had taken an instant dislike to Tony, and being the Capricorn she is, never got over it. Even after the guy saved my life, she still can barely manage a hello. I was starting to regret I'd told her my heart still flutters when I see him.

"They're not in the same league," I'd said. "The only thing my heart does when I think about Bobby McMahon is feel sick."

I smiled at Gail and gave her a how-could-you-even-think-I'd-fall-for-him-again look. The best thing about best friends is the telepathy thing that develops. Our connection tonight was better than Bell Atlantic's. I could tell by the look on her face she got my message loud and clear, she knew I wasn't about to be sucked back into Bobby McMahon's lascivious lock. Though try as he might.

"Damn, Nattie," he said as we walked to an unoccupied sofa, "you sure are looking good. We never did finish what we started. What are you doing after this anyway?"

This guy defined no shame. He was actually hitting on me at his wife's shiva. I don't know why I was surprised, though. I found out later that the night he came toting three bags of Chinese take-out had been his and Fuzzy's tenth wedding anniversary.

I smiled and forced myself not to say, "Get yourself a mirror, McMahon." Instead I said, "Can't tonight, Bobby. I've got to track down my father. It turns out he's run off with a friend of yours. Sarah Jane Lowell. That name ring a bell?"

McMahon shook his head. Not in a no, but more in a go-figure-it kind of way.

"You and your daddy know her too?"

"Apparently not as well as you," I said.

"Yeah, well, that was a mistake. I should have stayed myself way clear of her. She's crazy. Got a temper like the worst kind of crazy mare. You say she left town, with your daddy?"

"Yup, and in a big hurry," I said. "Seems she and Fuzzy got into it and she's now the number one suspect. Before the police could ask her any questions, she ups and takes off with my father. Makes her look plenty guilty to them."

"Well, I'll be damned, the police think she murdered Fuzzy? I knew she had temper to her, but murder? I guess I should be happy it wasn't me she started swinging at," McMahon said. He was acting surprised by the news, and I knew he wasn't. I was sure Tony and his boys grilled him good about his connection with Sarah Jane, and even Bobby McMahon wasn't so stupid that he couldn't put two and two together. So he was lying. But lying was such a natural activity for him, it was difficult to tell whether he was lying for a reason or just out of habit.

"Do you think Sarah Jane could've killed Fuzzy?" I said.

"Sure she could've, especially if what they were fighting over made them mad enough." He looked at me and smiled. "Though I'd have figured Fuzzy'd be on the winning end of things. Sarah Jane had a temper, but nothing like Fuzzy's. You didn't want to be nowhere near Fuzzy when she got herself worked up. I may not have been the best husband, but she was a hard woman to be married to, picking fights wherever she was at. After a while, I couldn't stand it no more."

"Anymore," I said. Speaking of not being able to stand something anymore, a person can only listen to such an assault on the English language for so long.

"Huh?"

"I mean any more thoughts on any other possible suspects? Sarah Jane didn't seem the murdering type to me."

McMahon laughed. "People ain't always what they seem, Nattie. Down deep, I mean. Who else could've killed Fuzzy? Almost anyone in this room, 'cepting maybe her mama and daddy. Fuzzy made everyone mad. Real mad. Anyone who ever worked for her like to take a shovel to her head. Anyone who ever had a kid ride against Ashlee wouldn't have liked her too good neither, and her daddy's sister's boy—Sukon's his name, he's that ugly-looking man standing by her daddy right now, he's the biggest suck-up you ever want to meet—he hates her worse than all of them put together. What I can't figure is how'd he get that wife with the nice ass? Must've been the size of his checkbook because I bet his pecker ain't the size of this little pretzel here. That enough for you, or you wanting me to go on? You can't be thinking about finding Fuzzy's murderer yourself, are you?"

Bootsie Feldman answered the question for me. She'd come up behind us and must've heard at least the last part of our conversation.

"She wouldn't have to look far, would she, Bobby? Mo told me you were here. I couldn't believe you had the audacity to show your face. You haven't been welcome here since the day you ruined my daughter's life. And you're certainly not welcome now. Leave."

McMahon didn't move. "How could I've killed your daughter when I was with Ashlee? Come on, Bootsie, an educated woman like you should know better."

"I'm smart enough to know you're nothing but trash. Always have been. You may not have struck my daughter down with your own dirty hands, but it's your fault she's dead. Ashlee's staying here with us, and don't even try to fight me on that. Now get out, or do I have to call the police?"

She pivoted and marched up to the closest phone.

McMahon tried to whisper something in my ear. I leaned away.

"You're crazy if you stay here, Bobby."

"You might be right. But it'd be worth it, seeing you again."

He squeezed my hand. Once that would have sent a shock through me, now all it did was make me want to go the bathroom and look for a bar of Lava.

CHAPTER 25

"Where'd Bobby go?"

It was Carter Evans. I met her coming out of the bathroom.

"Fuzzy's mother threw him out," I said. "And accused him of murder while she was at it. Think he did it?"

She looked around for him, as if I were lying and had stashed him someplace so I could keep him all to myself. This woman had it bad; must be he'd been waiting and withholding on her for a while. "I'm sure he wanted to," she said, still scanning the room, "but then again, who didn't? I've thought about it myself more than once."

Then she brought her eyes back my way and watched me looking at her. A smile spread across her face. "So if you are here writing a story, which you say you're not, put me on your list of suspects. By the way, you haven't seen Ralston, have you? I told her we could stay thirty minutes and that was it."

If this woman did off Fuzzy, she was either very smart or very stupid. Or the third possibility: she just had a very big mouth with no cruise control option. As the owner of that model myself, those exact words could—and have—come through my lips pertaining to my editor, Candace the Horrible. For the first time in my life I was happy Candace was still breathing, because if she wound up face first in a manure pile, I'd be sitting in jail looking guiltier than Jeffrey McDonald.

"Haven't seen her for a while," I said, and we both looked around the room for the tiny equestrienne. Neither Ralston nor the rest of the prepubescent bunch was to be found.

"They're probably in the bowling alley or the miniature golf course or whatever it is that old moneybag Feldman's got in his basement. I guess I'd better go look for her. See you at a horse show sometime, Nattie, or call me if you want to know more about Fuzzy. The number's in the book, under my name. The husband's a doctor, doesn't want hysterical patients calling him at home at three in the morning."

Evans, Dr. Evans, I knew that name sounded familiar. Now I remembered. All the models I've used for fashion shoots practically have his number tattooed on their lipo'ed thighs. He's the Queen City's king of plastic surgery, known throughout the Carolinas for his steady hand, flawless face-lifts, and Rodinlike body sculpturing. What in God's name happened to his wife's nose? Talk about passive aggressive—or not so passive. Now I understood why she was so hot for McMahon; she was wearing on her face what kind of marriage she had.

Gail was deep in conversation with someone I didn't know. To bide my time, I walked up to the food area. I've never been able to resist lox, especially when it's free. Just as I was spearing a few slabs of it, Ashlee McMahon walked by, alone.

The small, petty side of me—those parts ruled by what traces of Virgo I unfortunately have in my astrological makeup—kept screaming that this kid had everything I'd ever wanted, with the exception of her dumb name. Horses, the Florida circuit, two world-renowned horse trainers at her personal beck and call, a straight nose, and, just to show that life is truly not fair, long, thin thighs. I wanted to push her face first into the creamed herring and slide her down the rest of her rich grandfather's deli spread.

Then the dominant force in my personality—my Aquarius sun sign and Leo ascendant—kept whispering to me gently, but insistently, this kid also had a murdered mother. And if anyone knows loss, it's me. I turned toward her, introduced myself and told her how sorry I was.

She looked at me. I recognized that blank stare. I'd seen it gazing at me from the other side of the mirror after my stepfather David died.

Aquarius and Leo stormed the gates, obliterating all traces of Virgo. I was flooded with such deep sorrow for this girl I had to stop myself from wrapping my arms around her slim shoulders and "there-thereing" her like I was some kind of manic Mother Teresa. She looked unbearably lonely and lost standing there in her grief.

I started talking to her, mostly about horses, because any horse-crazed female will tell you that's the safe and comforting place to go when you're hurting so bad inside you feel like something broke that can never be fixed.

I asked her about her new horses, especially Can-Do, and she perked up a little. But it wasn't until she got to talking about her pony, Blue By You, that the living dead look left her pretty face. She got downright animated as she talked about him, and darn if she didn't look even more like her daddy when her eyes started going high-voltage. I knew she'd gone back to a happy place when I counted eleven "likes" in three sentences.

As in: "Blue was like the best pony anywhere. Like he'd do anything for me and he knew my moods. It was like crazy the way he knew me and would do anything for me. He'd jump from the other side of the ring if I asked him. I wish I could take him to the Culpeper show next week, but Mom keeps sayings 'no more ponies.' "

Her mother's presence hadn't slipped into the past tense yet. No surprise there. It took me almost six months to talk about David that way, and even now when I do, it's still hard to make the words pass by the lump in my throat. I was, however, surprised that this kid was going giddy about her pony. You don't find too many kids on the A-show circuit who've kept that kind of Misty of Chincoteague love blazing. Usually by the time they get to Ashlee's level, it's more about points and ribbons than equine adoration.

"You want to see Blue sometime? I taught him to bow."

"Sure," I said, figuring it would never come to pass. I'd been in the South long enough to know that Sometime was just west of Never-Never Land. Not that I would have minded meeting her bowing pony, but I had plenty of other things to do, such as earn a living, find my father, and ride my own horse.

She was quiet for a few seconds, and I took it as an opportunity to scarf down a couple bites of lox. Silky, smooth, and salty, yum. I was lost in my culinary reverie when Ashlee spoke.

"How about Sunday? I don't have a show this weekend."

Ashlee had such a needy look on her face, I didn't want to say no. My heart hurt for the kid, rich as she was. She had a dead mother who probably hadn't been much of one when she was alive. But no matter how wretched Fuzzy McMahon had been, she was still her mother. And some mother was better than no mother. At least there's always the hope things might change.

Excuse me for playing amateur shrink, but my guess was that along with mourning her mother, Ashlee was also mourning the death of a life that could never be: namely one where Fuzzy McMahon miraculously turns into Donna Reed, with a perky little flip at the end of her perky yellow hair and a perky, sweet smile that's always spread across her what-can-I-do-to-make-you-happy face. I knew what it felt like to ache for a childhood you'll never have. This kid needed someone who understood.

But I didn't know if I could be that person this weekend. Where I was going to be depended on where my father's credit card slips were coming in from, within reason. If he and Sarah Jane had taken off for Tahiti, then I'd probably be in Waxhaw watching Blue By You take a bow.

"It's a deal," I said, "if I'm in town. I might have to take a quick trip—family problems—but I'll call you as soon as I know. Okay?

I didn't think it was appropriate to tell her right now my family problems were her family problems; as in tracking down my father, who was with the person police suspected had killed her mother.

She must've figured she was getting the brush-off. "Yeah, sure. Whatever." She started to walk away, and I took her arm in my hand.

"Ashlee," I said, "not only do I want to see your pony, but I want you to show me how to make Brenda bow. Think you can do it?"

"Maybe," she said, and started to walk away when Gail intercepted her.

"Hey sweetie," Gail said, and tried give the kid a hug. Ashlee met Gail's advance with as much enthusiasm as if it were full frontal contact with an oozing leper. Gail ignored the recoil and continued to talk. "How you doing? If there's anything you need, call, okay? Your mom would have wanted it that way. And listen, whoever did this to her won't get away with it. One way or another, that person will be caught. I promise. Not only is the Union County sheriff's department trying to find out what happened, but so is Nattie. Or didn't she tell you that?"

I hadn't. I didn't think it was right to bring it up and/or pump the kid for information. Some reporters have their limits. And pumping bereaved kids is mine.

CHAPTER 26

I was mid-bite into a bagel stacked Dagwood-sandwich high when Gail joined me back at the table. She'd been talking to Ashlee, or at least trying to.

"Did you tame the lion or what?" she said.

I tempted the wrinkle gods and squinched my face again. "Huh?" I said, because my mouth was otherwise occupied.

"I watched you with Ashlee. I couldn't believe (a) she was talking, and (b) she was almost smiling. No matter how nice I try to be to the kid, I've never seen anything but a snarl on her face. You sure do have a way with surly thirteen-year-olds."

I swallowed slowly. There are some things in life even I, the reincarnation of Speedy Gonzales, won't rush. "Firsthand knowledge," I said. "Remember, they didn't come any surlier at that age than yours truly."

She nodded. After more than three years of long trail rides, there wasn't much we didn't know about each other. Gail knew I wrote the book on prepubescent snarls, specializing in nasty, hateful, and, above all, terrified thirteen-year-olds. That was the year only two words could come out of my mouth. The first one started with F and the second with Y.

It was the year my mother met David, and even though he practically staged a dog and pony show for my brother and me every time he was around us, I was scared that if my mother married this big, boisterous man she wouldn't have enough time or love left over for me. Nothing could have been further from the truth, but go tell anything to a snarly thirteen-year-old girl.

The only person who could get past my armor of anger was a counselor at Camp Reeta, the Jewish Y summer camp I'd been going to every year since I was nine. Ellie was her name. She had waist-skimming, wavy brown hair and wore flowing Indian print dresses with beat-up water buffalo sandals. She wasn't even the counselor for my bunk, but for some reason she took an interest in the little redheaded girl with a scowl on her face and a growl in her voice. During her free periods she'd take me on walks or just lie next to me on the grass, naming the clouds as they passed.

"Doesn't that one look like Mr. Potato Head doing the twist?" she'd say.

We never talked about my mother's marriage or my anger or my loneliness, it was enough just to have someone who cared. Seeing Ashlee standing there must've tugged in me what had tugged in Ellie all those years ago.

"She's an all right kid," I said to Gail. "I know, I've heard the stories about what a brat she is, but maybe it's just that she's misunderstood. It couldn't have been easy having someone like Fuzzy for your mother."

Gail rolled her eyes. "You've got that right. More on that subject later. But we need to get rolling, so let me introduce you to some people before we leave. I'm hoping that's soon. I promised Torkesquist I wouldn't be late."

"God, Gail," I said, "can't you guys stand to keep your hands off each other for more than twenty minutes?"

Her face started to flush, and it wasn't the red fury spots that erupt when she gets angry.

"Jealous," she said, and smiled.

"That and very, very happy for you. Now let's go talk to more of the bereaved. Maybe I can catch me a killer."

"One more, Nattie, and I'm buying you a belt to start putting notches on."

Gail led me around and made the introductions. There weren't a lot of tears flowing, or for that matter even many nice words about the deceased. Gail told me most of the people had come to make nicey-nice to the Feldmans.

"They're not a family you want to be on the wrong side of," Gail said.

I steered clear of the matriarch, Bootsie. No matter how rotten Fuzzy had been, it still must've hurt something awful losing a daughter.

Gail was just about breaking out in a rash to get back to her Prince Charming. Well, good for her. If anyone deserved happiness, it was Gail. God knows she'd had plenty of unhappiness in her life, starting with a souse for a mother.

We made our adieus and exited. I could almost hear the tulips shivering, cursing the day they'd listened to the daffodils' promises of a new, sunny world. The flowers weren't the only things shivering and swearing under their breath.

"Hate this God-blessed cold," I muttered as Gail and I headed down the hill to my little blue Rabbit, which for some reason looked littler. Must have been the juxtaposition of my minuscule car and the battalion of Mercedes, Lexuses, and Range Rovers. Like one of those optical illusion cartoons on a Stuckey's paper place mat; you guess which arrow is bigger, but they're both the same. It's the juxtapositioning that makes one seem smaller. Line my Rabbit against a car lot full of automotive Goliaths, and my little David looks even smaller.

Or so I thought.

"Holy Mother of Night," I screamed as I kicked my wounded car.

It *was* smaller. Nothing optically illusionary about four slashed tires.

CHAPTER 27

It was getting harder and harder to keep my promise to the Great One. A slew of curse words were leaping at the front of my mouth like Mexican jumping beans on steroids. But a pact is a pact and I'd sworn I'd be the Pat Boone of language skills if my old boyfriend John pulled through a night in intensive care after a nasty dose of nicotine poisoning.

He's fine now, which leaves me permanently muzzled.

"I can't believe it," I was screaming. "Those ffffffu . . . tires were new. Three hundred dollars and now look at them. Ahhhhhh!!!!"

I kicked the car again. I'd made no promises about violence, especially to inanimate objects. Perhaps I should have; another searing pain shot up my leg. I just hoped the aluminum bolt holding my leg together from a recent riding accident was stronger than my temper.

"Take it easy, Nats," Gail said. "It's just a car, no one's dead. Though it does look like you've done it again, made someone mad enough to wish you were dead. Nattie, I can't take people going at you all the time like this. Is fashion that bad? I mean, the worst those assholes have ever done to you is lie about hemlines so you got it wrong in the paper."

I looked at her and started laughing. The alternative was crying, and I was too angry for that.

Angry that I had a set of four slashed tires, and angrier that I was driving around with vanity tags that announced what I drive to all the crazed psychopathic murderers I'd been coming across lately. It'd be difficult for even the most stupid murderer not to figure out that the blue Rabbit with *The Charlotte Commercial Appeal* sticker in the back window above the North Carolina plates that say NATTIE belongs to the same Nattie Gold, reporter for *The Commercial Appeal,* who'd been asking all those who-done-it questions.

The funny thing is, I hate vanity tags. The only reason I was driving around with them was because of David. He got them for me and was so excited that he'd convinced the woman at the DMV to bump someone else's request for "Nattie" over his, I couldn't bear to tell him how much I hated them. Then he died, and looking at the tags reminded me of him, so I couldn't get rid of them. And now this.

At least I knew I was on the right track. My questions were making someone squirm. But who?

CHAPTER 28

We called the cops, they came, they filed, and they went, leaving me with little hope my slashed tires would fortify their solved crimes rate.

"Vandalism," one of the blues said. "Even in this neighborhood. Kids with nothing to do. I don't care how many video games they have, they're bored. We'll call you if we hear anything."

Yup, right after I hear from the other McMahon—Ed, telling me I'd won Publisher's Clearinghouse. In the meantime, Gail called Torkesquist to come pick us up. While we waited, we talked about the night's events, spending way too much time on what a horse's ass the first McMahon—Bobby—is, was, and always will be.

"He was talking about Fuzzy's cousin's wife's nice rear end at his own wife's shiva," I said. "And that was after he'd hit on me *and* his daughter's best friend's mother. What a sleaze."

"Didn't I tell you he'd nail anything remotely female?" Gail said. "I bet you anything both those women spent more time in the sack with him than Fuzzy."

"You think?" I said.

Gail gave me a get real look and we moved on to the subject at hand: my slashed tires and the likelihood that the person was as nimble with a knife as he or she was with a shovel—as in bashing Fuzzy's head.

So we started to make a list of all the people I could've pissed off enough to hurt my car and send me a message to shut up. We decided to limit it to the Fuzzy McMahon case. With my mouth, if I'd opened the possibilities to the general public, we'd be there for days writing.

There was also the fashion community to consider, which could throw a monkey wrench into my tire-slasher-equals-head-basher theory. While the reading public seemed to appreciate my who-would-ever-wear-something-that-ugly fashion coverage, I was not beloved by the trade. However, if I opened that Pandora's box, we'd be chasing down Charlotte's entire retail clothing industry, starting with Mark Donner, owner of Donner's, a small chain of stores that specializes in rich white lady clothing.

I'd made the mistake of bringing an African-American woman to Donner's beauty salon for our annual before and after make-over article. Donner scurried up to me so fast you'd have thought I was bringing in the late Princess Di. But rolling out the red carpet wasn't on his agenda. In a voice dripping unctuousness, he told me his stylists weren't trained to do ethnic hair. So sorry, but we'd have to find another place to make over our lucky reader.

Guess what? To get a cosmetology license in the Tar Heel state, beauticians must demonstrate knowledge about the styling and care of *ethnic*—read that African-American—hair. Either he was breaking the law and employing renegade, unlicensed cosmetologists, or he was a racist jerk. I wanted to let the readers decide but our fearless leader Fred Richards, not known as the Shoe Salesman for nothing, wouldn't let me run the story, wouldn't want to alienate the owner of the store that runs weekly quarter-page ads. So I leaked it to a friend at *Creative Loafing*, Charlotte's alternative paper that routinely butts horns with the establishment and doesn't seem to care about annoying anyone.

"You know," I said, "maybe we shouldn't cut Donner off the list so fast. I saw him there tonight, sleazing up to Bootsie. And he saw me too, though he made pretend he didn't. I'm sure he's mad as hell about Jerry Klein's column in *Creative Loafing*, and it wouldn't take a genius to figure out how Jerry found out."

Gail reluctantly agreed, probably for the sake of killing time before her sweetie arrived. "Okay, he's on the list. The B list. But I can't really see him slashing your tires. You know, Nattie, you probably did him a favor. He's probably happy as a pig in shit about that column, hoping Charlotte's black community will boycott his stores."

I hadn't thought about it that way, and now that I did, it riled me even more. I'd wanted to shake the little jerk at the time, but our make-over subject, a very gracious and savvy guidance counselor from West Charlotte High, calmed me down, said not to worry, this wasn't the first time something like that had happened to her nor would it be the last. She was obviously used to dealing with stupid and infantile behavior; the difference being her students' heads were swirling with hormones and there was always the hope that someday they'd grow up into decent adults, something that clearly escaped Donner.

"Where do you think you're living, Miss Yankee girl?" she'd said to me. "This is the state where Harvey Gantt lost not once, but twice to Jesse Helms."

I couldn't argue with her about that, nor with Gail about Donner's hope to eliminate all but the fairest from his dressing rooms.

"You're probably right," I said to Gail, "but you never know, maybe it embarrassed him last Sunday at Myers Park Baptist where he was masquerading as a good Christian."

Gail, who hasn't been to church since she was christened or baptized or whatever it is Episcopalians do to newborns, nodded. "Yeah right, him and all those ass-kissing hypocrites here tonight pretending to be upset about Fuzzy."

She wiped the back of her hand across her eyes. In my zeal to find suspects, I'd forgotten that Gail had lost one of her oldest friends and tonight's event was no picnic for her.

"I'm sorry about Fuzzy, Gail," I said, and with that the floodgates opened. She started crying hard, shoulders heaving as she tried to choke out words between sobs.

"She . . . was . . . so . . . unhappy . . . I . . . wish . . . I . . . could've . . . done . . . something . . ."

What a sight we must've been. The tall blonde bawling like a baby, wrapped in the little redhead's arms; both of us leaning on my poor, deflated Rabbit.

That's how Torkesquist found us.

"Jeez, Louise, what'd they do that's got Gail so worked up? Have Fuzzy skinned, stuffed, and propped upright in the living room? What's a matter, didn't she look natural?"

Most people's reaction to Torkesquist and his warped sense of everything is not positive. It's a miracle he's still shooting pictures for *The Appeal*, given the paper's ongoing personality pogroms. But it's hard to fire talent like his. He's been Southern Photographer of the Year more times than he can count on his fingers, which is only nine since he's missing one. His right index finger got caught in a garbage disposal and he will tell anyone all the gory details if you even glance that way.

Gail found him beyond charming. She loved everything about him, from the shaggy bowl of blond hair that kept falling into his eyes to his pink plastic glasses to his Minnesota accent which was so thick it was a wonder words could even squeeze out. Happily she slipped from my arms to her honey's. One thing led to another and within seconds they were just about to break some laws in North Carolina.

"Come on you guys," I said. "This is embarrassing and probably illegal. Just drop me off at my apartment, then go park on Queens Road if you can't wait. It'd shake up those Myers Park biddies real good to hear you two going at it."

They unlocked from each other and we all got back in Torkesquist's truck, the three of us and his three unruly dogs. It was a tight squeeze, but it was a ride home. I wasn't going to deal with a tow truck until the morning.

We continued making our list, zeroing in on all the people I'd grilled in my subtle—"so who killed her?"—way. Carter Evans could've easily been up there in the number one spot of suspected tire slashers/Fuzzy murderers. But just like you don't buy the first horse you look at, unless you're stupid like I am, you don't usually catch your killer first time out. After finding two of them myself, I can attest to that. What I've learned in my brief career as a fashion-writing private detective of sorts is that solving murders is a meta-phor for living life; both are full of curveballs, red herrings, wrong turns, missed opportunities, and, most of all, foolish assumptions. But if you're real lucky, you work hard, say your prayers, and your karma's right, the guy in the white hat kicks butt.

As for the black hats, we put Bobby McMahon on the list, right under Carter Evans, where she's probably spent many a night, either in reality or her imagination. I don't care if he had a good alibi—maybe the kid was lying to protect Daddy—he sure as any-thing had motive. Lots of them, according to Fuzzy's cousin, Jason Sukon.

Sukon had told me Fuzzy was worth at least ninety million dol-lars, and for some unknown reason her philandering hubby was featured prominently in her will. He wouldn't tell me how he knew, but assured me in an exceedingly patronizing way that he did. He did everything in an exceedingly patronizing way. That's because he was a towering, arrogant you-know-what hole, with squinty lit-tle banker's eyes, squinty little banker's glasses, and a big beak to rest them upon. Not only that, but he had some kind of skin condi-tion or rash around his neck. So between his long, jutting nose, rangy limbs, and red throat, he looked like he should be swooping down on roadkill for dinner.

He was Fuzzy's father's sister's boy, the one McMahon told me hated her worse than anyone. McMahon wouldn't tell me why the bad blood, or who knows, maybe he was lying about the whole thing.

I put Sukon on my list just the same. He gave me the creeps.

McMahon wasn't lying about one thing: the guy was a champion suck-up. I could practically hear slurping noises when he got around Mo Feldman, kissing up to the rich geezer about how sorry he was for his tremendous loss of such a fine, decent, wonderful daughter, then turning around to me and spewing venom about his dead cousin. Yuck.

I also didn't like the predatory way he was eyeing the Feldman house, as if he were a roving inventory taker, and I especially didn't like the predatory way he was eyeing Ashlee. There wasn't a shred of the avuncular in his nasty, little, beady eyes. No wonder he looked just like a vulture. Jason Sukon, number three on my list.

"What about the wife? You know, the one with the nice butt?" Gail said. "Didn't you see how she had his little filberts in a vice grip?"

Forgot about the lovely Jeannie Sukon and her inviting posterior. She could easily rake in the dough with a dominatrix business going on the side. Little bit of leather, a few whips, some chains, and I bet she could—or does—get old Jason and any other banker-who's-been-bad barking up a storm. It's not that she looked like Elvira or any other flashy skin queen. On the contrary, from the nose up, with her thyroid eyes popping out, she bore a startling re-semblance to Kermit the Frog. From the neck down, in her faux English country clothes, she was the picture of suburban propri-ety: the Myers Park matron who'd just slipped onto the taupe gloveskin seats of her 550 DL, heading off to the Morrocroft Har-ris Teeter and then Charlotte Latin School to pick up the kiddies. But it wasn't the way *she* looked, it was the way she *looked*.

You could tell exactly what she had hubby by three sentences into a conversation with them. She stood by his side like a fourth grade teacher, poised and waiting to whack the knuckles of her un-ruly pupil with a sharp rap from a hard ruler. When he spoke, he tried to surreptitiously peek her way. But because he was on the dark side of dense, his try at the surreptitious looked an awful lot like a Peter Sellers in the Pink Panther impersonation.

These days, arrogant, dim, and male is an especially annoying combination to me, or maybe my tolerance for that particular personality cocktail has been strained, given whom I have to deal with at *The Appeal*. Nevertheless, Sukon was all of the above and more. But was he a murderer? Did he have the smarts to pull it off and then frame Sarah Jane? I didn't think he had the brain power to find the men's room at Ericsson Stadium.

The wife, however, was plenty smart. She was clearly something to watch out for. I wouldn't want to stand between her and whatever she wanted, especially a lot of it, such as large amounts of Family Value dollars or whatever it was that caused the bad blood. I hadn't considered a two-man operation before, but now that I did, it seemed logical. She was the brains, he was the brawn, in a manner of speaking. I mean how much brawn does a six-foot-five-inch man need to slam a small woman into eternity?

There was no doubt Jeannie Sukon could make her husband do whatever she wanted. Any tighter hold and his voice would have been an octave higher.

Jason and Jeannie Sukon: numbers 3a and 3b.

Fuzzy's maid, Grace Williams, made the number four spot. Unfortunately. I was hoping she wouldn't turn out to be my murderer/car mutilator because she seemed okay, except that she hated Fuzzy more than the Ayatollah hated Salman Rushdie. She was yet another person who couldn't find a good word to say about the departed Family Value Store heiress. She found plenty of others, though: stingy, mean, drunk, and so on.

"I wouldn't be here tonight if I didn't love Ashlee like she were my own," the woman said. "That poor child, rich as she is, I wouldn't take her life for nothing. Nothing. You should've seen how her mother used to treat her, especially when she got drinking. She was mean like that to everyone who crossed her path, but to her own flesh and blood? Anyone who got near her on her bad days, got a piece of her mind. It didn't matter who or what: Ashlee, Ashlee's friends, Mr. McMahon, anyone. Didn't matter if it was an adult, child, dog, or cat. Just horses. That's the only thing she never got mean to."

Finally evidence that Fuzzy McMahon hadn't been totally despicable. That and the few kind words from the tall, skinny man who worked at Anyday. Ebert Darnell.

"I'm hoping she's found her peace now," Darnell'd said. "She was awful troubled, but good underneath. You had to know where to look—and when to stay away from her."

Not exactly words to chisel on a tombstone.

I added a few more peripheral names to the list, mostly employees and a couple of other horse show mothers. Any more and we'd have enough to sing the full choral arrangement of "Ding, Dong, the Witch Is Dead." My head was starting to reel with all the possible suspects. At least I'd accomplished my mission.

I guess I was satisfied, except now it looked as if I'd be spending every spare second either working my list or finding my father.

CHAPTER 29

Asheville. Of course that's where Sarah Jane had whisked Lou to. Where else but the East Coast Mecca for new age nomads, the only place in the universe that not only has a Chamber of Commerce, but a Chamber of Consciousness?

Asheville's been getting a lot of press lately for the lemminglike march of searchers in search of meaning. Supposedly, the surrounding mountains are studded with trillions of tons of quartz, which also supposedly send out the perfect vibrational pitch for spiritual awakening, as long as you've got the perfect vibrational bucks to pay your guru. Pardon my cynicism, but I've never gotten the concept of paying for God, be it a Jewish, Christian, or Swami Pootchacadukas deity.

It's not only the quartz that new agers claim lures them to Asheville, but all the vortexes in the surrounding peaks. Apparently our bodies aren't the only things with electrical energy points. In humans, they're called chakras. In Mother Earth, they're called vortexes, and for some reason, Asheville's got a bunch of them.

So, between the quartz, the vortexes, and the five thousand nearby witches, Asheville's gotten itself quite a bit of notoriety on the subject. *Sixty Minutes, Vanity Fair,* even a Rush Limbaugh type radio guy made mention of this mountain city and its appeal to what he called granola-crunching, underwearless flakes who never pay taxes.

Henry was the one who found Lou in Asheville. Or more accurately, his money. He'd come through with the MasterCard trace and found the last receipt from something called The Third Eye. I don't know why I didn't think of Asheville right off. First I miss the Florida circuit tans, now this. How could I be so dense?

I was starting to think like a man. Time to stop taking the DHEA Lou just bought me and shelve it right next to his melatonin, which made me dream of kvetching horses. This latest find of Lou's is some kind of natural testosterone precursor that supposedly revs up your engine and does everything from increase your sex drive to turn gray hair black.

I don't know about his sex drive, but Lou's rpm's started running rampant. He got so hepped up he spent a day racing around my apartment chirping, "I'm flying without wings, Nats, flying without wings." Then he went to the army-navy store and bought himself full combat fatigues, complete with shiny new medals. That was when I called Denise, my new buddy at the barn who's a shrink.

"Get him off the Zoloft right away," she said. "He'll give himself a stroke. Who knows what the DHEA is doing, but I do know what the Zoloft does. I can't believe his doctor put him on it. That's bad medicine. I knew it would flip him into a manic state."

That, however, was better than the previous alternative: depression. After he split with my neighbor, Mrs. Flock, and had that TIA the doctors told him could be a harbinger of a stroke, Lou spiraled down into a near-catatonic state. He didn't shower, shave, brush his hair, or change his clothes. His voice was completely flat and his eyes dead. Being around him was like handling powdered lime—you felt like all the moisture was being sucked out of you.

I forced him to put away his Saint-John's-wort and all the other herbs his acupuncturist swore would cure depression and made him see a shrink with a real degree from a medical school not in the Caribbean. He must've been feeling pretty bad, because he agreed and for the first time in his life went on drugs. Zoloft. Denise had warned me that he should start first on Lithium, a mood stabilizer, then Zoloft. I knew my father would never go for that; he had a couple of siblings who'd been off and on Lithium their entire lives and still wound up getting periodically juiced with enough electrical voltage to light up the NationsBank Towers *and* the Wachovia Center.

Denise had been right. Between the DHEA and the Zoloft, Lou flipped into as manic a stage as I'd ever seen him, or any of his equally bipolared kin, in. So I hid his bottles, every last one of them; the Zoloft, the DHEA, the Evening Primrose oil, the shark cartilage, even the emu lotion, everything. I told him to consider the next few days as time to purify his body and soul, like when he spent a week in a cave with Ms. Celestial Wild Wombmyn, steaming out his spiritual demons.

"Just think of it as an Indian sweat lodge, minus the heat," I'd said.

He bought it. Except I hadn't counted on the residual effect of whatever drugs and herbs had overcharged him in the first place. I made the mistake of leaving him alone in my apartment with Henry's kids. Henry had an emergency assignment and asked me to watch the boys. I didn't have any milk in the house and they wanted to dunk their Fig Newtons in the worst way. I thought it would be safe to make a quick run to the closest Harris Teeter. What could happen in twenty minutes?

Plenty. When I got back, half of the Queen City's fire department was parked by my door, sirens blaring, lights whirling, and rubber-suited firemen bounding up the steps. You can imagine what my heart was doing at that point. It was a miracle I didn't expire on the spot. Being the daughter of a woman whose life mission it was to make sure I knew of every possible calamity that could befall me, I imagined the worst: all three of them charred, broiled, or incinerated. Dead, dead, and dead.

Even though I raced up the stairs faster than I've ever run in my life, it was all in sickening slow-mo, the same way it goes when I'm toppling off my horse's back. It takes about five hours before I finally hear that all too familiar and nauseating thud of my body smashing to the ground. It was taking the same amount of time to reach my door, so I had plenty of time to vacillate between marrow-quivering fear and extreme self-flagellation, as in how could I be so stupid as to leave Lou alone with two children?

I barged into my apartment and, to my utter glee, saw Lou and the boys standing near my bathroom looking not the least bit charred. My bathroom was another matter. Smoke was billowing out from the little room in great gray heaves.

"Sweat lodge, Nattie," Lou said. "I was just trying to show Hankie and Chet how a sweat lodge worked."

Lou had made a campfire in my bathtub and tried to cover himself, the smoking embers, and Henry's kids under my down comforter, all the while chanting, "Om Nahamah-Shee-Viya" at the top of his lungs. It was the noise that first alerted the neighbors to call for help.

I threw away all his bottles after that.

"You should've seen it, Dad, it was totally cool," Chet said to Henry later that night. I don't think Henry will be asking me any-time soon to watch his kids again.

Lou settled down after that and even put away his fatigues and medals. He'd seemed fine since then. But now apparently he was back to despair. I'd have to find him, because before the Zoloft/sweat lodge incident he was mumbling he was too scared to live and too scared to die. Suicide is not a foreign notion for the Gold children. His eldest brother did it thirty years ago.

I'd have preferred a few long trail rides this weekend—as planned—but it seemed my daughterly duty, which in my family plays out to being the parent, was to try to find my father before he got cachectic again, or worse. So that's how I found myself heading west on US 74, after I'd wiped out my savings account on four new tires.

CHAPTER 30

Before I left, I called Ashlee about seeing her bowing pony another time. With surly kids it pays to be as specific as possible so they don't think you're blowing them off. I told her I was going to Asheville to find my father because I was worried about him. I prudently left out the part about Sarah Jane. She asked why I was worried, and I told her: My father was bipolar, the new buzz term for manic-depressive, and followed that with the thirty second explanation. Ten years ago I might not have told her or anyone else. It's hard to get comfortable with the notion that manic depression is an illness with no blame other than some bad circuitry, just the same as diabetes or multiple sclerosis. Most people still don't get that.

"I hope you find him," she said.

"Yeah, me too," I said. "So how about next weekend? Can I see Blue take a bow then?"

"Next weekend?" Ashlee said. "That's Culpeper. Aren't you going?"

I wasn't and I assumed neither was she. Not with her mother barely cold in the grave. My reason was more along economic lines. Culpeper, a huge show grounds just north of Charlottesville, Virginia, was a good seven hours away. Just the vanning charge to get Brenda up there was out of my financial reach. That wasn't taking into account my lodging at sixty dollars a night, my trainer's lodging at another sixty a night, my horse's lodging at ninety dollars, which did not include bedding so add another twenty-five dollars in bagged shavings, trainer fee at fifty dollars a day, entry fees— easily a good two hundred dollars—and you can't forget those ridiculous extra fees the greedy show managers tack on these days: a twenty-dollar late fee because who knows two months in advance what they're doing, fifteen dollar office fee, fifteen dollar grounds fee, eight dollar American Horse Show Association drug-testing fee, eight dollar Hunter Jumper association fee, and the twenty-five-dollar I-can-charge-you-whatever-I-want-since-the-ASHA-doesn't-allow-any-other-shows-nearby fee. All that and then you've got to eat. So does your trainer, who never reaches in his pocket during a show. Go to one of these big A-3 shows like Culpeper and it's obscenely easy to drop $1,500 in less than forty-eight hours.

"No Culpeper for me unless I win the lottery," I said. But truth be told, even if I'd had the bucks to blow, I'd have felt a little uneasy jumping my horse there. That's where Christopher Reeve was catapulted head first into a log jump, leaving him a paraplegic. Classy man that he is, he never blamed the horse. This is a person who's in my prayers every night.

"How about Wednesday, right after I get off work?" I said. "Say sevenish?"

"Okay," Ashlee said. "I'll call down to the barn right now and tell Cathy she can let Blue out and that you're coming Wednesday night." I think I even heard some enthusiasm in her voice.

"Sounds like a plan," I said. "Look, if you're feeling down or you teach Blue a new trick and want to tell someone about it or just feel like talking, I'll be at the Motel 6 on Tunnel Road. You can call me anytime, okay?"

"Motel 6?" Ashlee said.

The kid had probably never stayed in anything with less than three stars. To her the Holiday Inn would be slumming, to me a night there would be about as likely as a stay at the Plaza.

"Yup," I said, "the towels are probably thinner than toilet paper, but the price's right. See you next week."

Next I called Gail and asked her to keep an eye on Brenda, especially her hooves, which, despite the heroic efforts of Gerry the blacksmith, were chipping away like crumbling sand castles. Her right front shoe was barely clinging to what remained of her foot.

"You know Gerry's out of town again," Gail said. "Should I call the slimeball if she throws that shoe? Or do you want her to limp until he gets back?"

No choice there. "Can't have her go barefoot, she'll rip the bejesus out of her feet," I said. "Do what you have to do. Do me a favor, write this number down on the board: 704-555-6700. Motel 6—it's where I can be reached if anything's wrong with Brenda."

Having a horse is a lot like having a kid. You can't step a foot out of town without making sure 150 people know where you'll be every second.

I also had to call Henry, thank him for his trace and tell him I was headed out of town. Surprise of surprises, he was worried about me going to Asheville myself. This from the man who not a year ago thought a life-threatening phone call to me was the act of an anonymous coward and nothing about which to be concerned. After a few bodies turned up, myself almost one of them, Henry reconsidered. Now he's practically like a mother hen worrying about me. He wanted to go with me, but he'd already made soccer-birthday party-swimming lessons-music recital plans with his kids.

"Stop worrying," I said to him. "It was only my tires. If someone wanted to hurt me, they easily could have. I'll call you when I get there. And then we'll figure out exactly how I can repay you for tracking down Lou's credit card slips—just remember, I hate chocolate, so think of something else you want smeared all over you."

"Whipped cream," he said, and I heard a little voice echoing his, "Whipped cream, I want whipped cream too. Tell Nattie not to forget me."

I laughed, Henry laughed, and Hankie laughed, though he didn't know what he was laughing at. Or did he? Never underestimate a Goode kid.

From whipped cream we moved on to the Reverend Quarrels. I was dying to know about his interview, and this was the first opportunity I'd had to speak to Henry since then. Being the fractious colts they were, his children wouldn't let Henry finish a sentence without a who, where, what, or when. This much I did piece together from our fragmented conversation:

Henry met with the mother of a nine-year-old boy who she said started acting out in ways he'd never done before. Talking back, screaming, calling names—things that seemed pretty normal to me after being around the Goode boys. But apparently this child had been a model citizen, one of those scarily well-behaved miniature adults who addresses all men as sir and all women as ma'am. When his behavior changed, the mother did all the things she could think of, short of whacking the kid with the back of her hand. She sent him to his room, took away television, Nintendo, desserts. She ran through her entire parental arsenal, to no avail. The kid, inexplicably, had turned into a junior Damian. Then one morning the mother said she walked into the bathroom and found him trying to molest his five-year-old brother. Somehow she got it out of him that he was just doing to his brother what the Reverend Quarrels had done to him. "He told me God wouldn't be mad if I let him," the boy said.

It didn't ring any truer to me now than it had before. Not after seeing Quarrels—and his many ladies in waiting—in action the other night. I know some people are simply sexual predators, omnivorous in their appetites. I'm not saying Quarrels isn't ravenous, I'm just guessing his menu selections stick pretty close to the adult female entrée variety.

Not that this proves anything, but he does that same Bobby McMahon eye-lock thing. And I'm sure he's got the Smile down pat too. My gut told me this man was a womanizer, not a childizer. I had no proof, just that same uncomfortable feeling of certainty I get when I know things I have no way of knowing.

As for the things I have a way of knowing, such as that kids supposedly don't lie about these kinds of things, it makes me wonder. I know I'm stepping outside the arena of political correctness, but who's to say some don't? When I was a kid, I could've sworn I'd seen a dead body in the backseat of a car. I wasn't intending on lying, and who knows what it was that I really did see, but one thing was for sure: I didn't mind all the attention it caused, and it stopped me from thinking about my parents splitting up for a while.

"One more thing, Nattie," Henry said. "The mother says she knows you."

CHAPTER 31

"**N**o way, too obvious. It sounds like she watched a made for television movie about child molesters."

Denise was talking to me. I'd sworn to Henry I wouldn't tell anyone about the reverend and his accusers, and I wasn't—exactly. I had one last call to make before I hit the road to Asheville, and that was to Denise to cancel our riding plans. Plus I wanted to run by her what Lou's shrink had told me to do if I found him and he was, in fact, doing the Zombie. Somehow the talk turned to kids and lying and I asked her the old hypothetical question. No names, just a "made-up" situation about a mother saying her kid started acting out and ended doing to his brother what he said had been done to him.

"Maybe way down the road the boy would do that," Denise said. "But not right away, not so abruptly. At first he might start bed-wetting or having nightmares or being afraid to be left alone. But he wouldn't turn into the bad seed overnight. That's Hollywood, Nattie. Working on an incest story? If that's your source, I think you should find another."

So Denise didn't buy my hypothetical story and wanted to know who it was. I couldn't and didn't spill the beans, and she didn't press me on the subject. Had situations been reversed, I'd have been pretty obnoxious, asking the who question every ten seconds. I guess that's one of the reasons we went into our respective fields.

"Some people might believe the child," I said.

"I'll bet those 'some people' have kids," Denise said. "Parents are never objective about this. Don't get me wrong. It's horrible, and if the man did do it, he should be locked up forever. But this kind of explosive and emotionally charged situation has the potential of turning into a witch hunt. If you want any evidence of that just read your own paper. Hard to believe, but half of all the child abuse cases filed—I think it was somewhere between 1.6 and 1.7 million a year—are false. People lie, kids lie, it happens all the time. Come on, Nattie, who is it, anyone I know?"

Maybe Denise should have gone into journalism after all. So much for not pressing me. She'd have known the accused, that's for sure. The Reverend Quarrels was a high profile preacher, and not in hair only. He had a big congregation, and a big castle of a church to hold them all. And don't forget his Sunday column, the one he got after I wrote that witches story and the Shoe Salesman wanted to show Quarrels that *The Appeal* isn't the liberal, godless, Jewish-controlled rag the right-wingers think it is.

Though no one at the paper appreciates the humor in this, occasionally I, the only Jew in the department, get stuck with editing duty and have to shorten the reverend's verbosity when the news hole is tight. Which is always. So it's slice and dice and get those windbags down to a quick six inches of God-talk. I not only nip and tuck here and there, but change all mentions of Jesus to God. This way, Jews, Buddhists, Muslims, Baha'is, whatever, we can all get something out of it.

"You know if I could tell you who it is, I would," I said to Denise. "But you yourself just said this kind of thing could easily turn into a witch hunt. So I gotta keep a tight lip on it."

"Tell me when you can," she said. "What about the mother? Is she a secret too?"

I could've told her who the finger pointer was, for all the good it would have done her. Denise had no way of knowing the woman. I barely knew her, despite what she'd told Henry. It took a few minutes for my synapses to start snapping before I could connect the mother's name to a face. But finally it came.

149

I'd met the woman a few years back; it was one of my first non-fashion assignments for *The Appeal*. Lillyane—wrap me in Saran Wrap—Litton was coming to town to shill her "Total Female" book. Of all things, Quarrels's church was bringing her to speak to his church's ladies group. Apparently, the Total Female's totalized husband had gone to Bible school with the reverend many moons ago. The accuser had been assigned official escort/protector to Ms. Litton when the reporter from the big, bad *Charlotte Commercial Appeal* came to do what they were sure was going to be a smear job.

Surprise. I didn't smear anyone and I even kind of liked Lillyane Litton. Why shouldn't I? Making nicey-nice was what she did for a living. In fact, it was the premise of her life: get people, particularly those with an extra appendage, to like you. "Someone's got to take the first step," she'd said to me. "So what if it's the woman? Why should you keep score?"

Her message was basically the golden rule, with a few R-rated how-to detours of the "greet him at the door wearing only Saran Wrap" kind. And I have to say, her husband couldn't do enough for her. Getting her tea, water, rubbing her sore feet. He was a geisha boy in navy pinstripe. Plus he looked at her with those same I-can't-get-enough-of-you eyes that once made my knees turn to jelly when Bobby McMahon looked at me that way.

Much as I thought I'd hate the woman's politics from a feminist point of view, I had to admit, from a humanist point of view, her do unto others way of thinking made sense.

Not everyone in Quarrels's congregation was amused by her new use for Saran Wrap. Including the accuser. As I recall, she was a bit on the mousy side and had a hard time even saying the word "naked" when she told me she thought Litton's plastic wrap idea wouldn't go over well with the ladies of the United Evangelical Church of Southeast Charlotte.

She told me that while we were waiting for the Total Female to finish her total makeup. I guess it takes a lot of time to totalize yourself, because after talking about Saran Wrap, it was still just me and the accuser waiting for Ms. Litton to make her appearance. Somehow with me most conversations end with horses. This time, I swear, it was she who brought me there.

She'd read a Sunday fashion column of mine about jodhpurs being fashionable and me being a rider. At the time, her ten-year-old daughter Jennifer just started riding lessons, and she asked me for equipment advice. My standard line to all is make sure the kid wears an ASTM approved helmet. Not that you'd find one junior rider on the circuit who does.

That was it, the extent of our deep friendship. She'd politely sneered about the Saran Wrap, we'd talked a little horses, I did my interview, the photographer shot his pictures, and we all said good-bye. Nothing more.

Something was tugging at my brain about this woman and I was once again regretting the drugs I'd done in my youth. I used to have an almost photographic memory. Past tense—that was before my years in Boulder, Colorado.

"Reach," I said to myself. Nothing was coming up except where I'd left my turquoise suede ankle boots. That was okay too. Because at this moment—rushing around, trying to get my stuff together for the trip to Asheville—I didn't really care about that woman, who she was, or why she had such an urge to nail her minister. That, I figured, was between her, her God, and Henry Goode. My turquoise boots, on the other hand, I did care about. What else could I wear with the purple paisley mini?

CHAPTER 32

My turquoise boots and I made it to Asheville in record time, just over two hours. Another day I'd have gone easy, drinking in the mountain views like steamy cups of lacy chamomile tea. But I was on the coffee run this time. Get there and get there fast.

Even in my jangled state I was still swept away by the beauty of the place. Asheville nuzzles itself right smack into the welcoming belly of where the Great Smokies link their time-worn arms with the Blue Ridge Mountains. Say what you will about the new age mumbo-jumbo of the magnetic pull or celestial alignment or harmonic convergence of the world's oldest mountains, but when the deep lavender mist hangs low in the Smokies and creates an echo of peaks and valleys, it's a pretty stirring sight that can churn up spiritual rumblings in the most skeptical of souls.

I was stirred, no question about it. I pulled my car to the shoulder and, defying the zooming vehicles, opened my door and walked to the side of the road. There I stood, who knows for how long, just looking. Not wanting to sound too much like Lou, but something about the mountains tugs at my soul, makes me feel like I've come home. I felt it the instant I drove into Boulder all those years ago, and I feel it whenever I drive into Asheville.

Even for those not so karmically inclined to big rocks, what's not to like about Asheville? Commanding views of two spectacular mountain ranges with peaks jutting so close you want to reach out, grab hold and yodel; a thriving town dotted with all sorts of interesting cafés, shops, museums, and castles, plus the best currant rye rolls that'll ever slide down your throat. It's easy to see why Asheville's a must-stop place on any Carolina tourist's map.

I checked into the Motel 6, which wouldn't be categorized as a must-stop place on anyone's but a pauper's tourist map. As suspected, the towels were on the thin side, but the sheets were clean. That's the first thing I checked. I can put up with almost anything in cheap motels, and God knows I've stayed in an assortment of them doing the big bucks horse show circuit on a little bucks budget. But dirty sheets? That's when I ask the guy behind the counter for my money back.

I had a plan, sort of. I mean as much as I'm capable of planning. I'd cruised the Web before I left, zeroing in on the Asheville sites. I made my way from the Chamber of Commerce to the granola-eaters-cum-computer-nerd pages that linked me to all sorts of interesting new-agey Asheville events.

I could see why Sarah Jane had practically airlifted her greedy self and my father here. The possibilities for new age scammers were limitless. Everyone had a shtick—and an outstretched hand. In any given week, the financially well-endowed soul searcher could explore the following: Rebirthing Breathwork; Huna, the ancient Hawaiian way to clear your life path; Goddesses of the Four Nations Dreamshops; Shustah Meditation Symbols; Agni Fire Yoga; Mayan Calendar Workshops; Psychosynthesis; Shamanic Trance Dancing; Grof Holotropic Breathing to access nonordinary states of consciousness; and Pan-Eu Rhythmy with Global Citizen Ardella Nathanael.

And that was just from the top half of the calendar listing. Seeing as Lou had done most if not all of the above, it was this entry that caught my eye:

Swami Zerostra Elijah takes for his bride the truly magnificent Kadishka, a woman, an enlightened ancient soul, fulfilling her final earthly incarnation, a beauty whose physical beauty he will not have gazed upon until Saturday when they are rejoined in blessed matrimony by the Reverend Howard Steinberg, author of the best-selling book, *The Leopard Runs with the Stars and So Can You.* Swami and Kadishka, the half to their whole, have been searching the cosmos for each other for many lifetimes. They finally found one another at the dawn of the millennium on America Online. Come celebrate as the universe celebrates this joyous reunion at the trinity of the afternoon on the fourth vortex of Mt. Mitchell.

So Swami was getting himself hitched to a woman he'd never seen. How could that be? This was the guy who'd posted in the AOL New Age folder that he soul-travels to women's bedrooms for connubial visits. Maybe those weird dreams I was having had nothing to do with Lou's melatonin.

If the swami and his new missus were planning a big nuptial bash open to all, it'd be a reasonable guess that Sarah Jane would drag her pumped-up butt there looking for fresh meat, since her current meal ticket—my father—was warping out on her. That wasn't until three, at least I thought that's what the trinity of the afternoon meant. So I had some time to scour around town looking for Lou.

Since it's already been established my motel was no Holiday Inn, I had to assume voice mail wasn't on the list of amenities.

"Hey, Mr. Patel," I said to the man behind the counter. We'd gotten pretty chummy when I checked in. "If anyone calls me, would you mind telling them I'll be in and out this afternoon, so just leave a message and I'll get back to them?"

"Sure, sure, Miss Gold," he said. "Not to worry. I'll take messages. Good luck finding your father."

Like I said, we'd gotten pretty chummy. By the time he handed over my room key, I knew half his life story; his prearranged astrologically sanctioned marriage to the lovely Mrs. Patel, who bore him three daughters, which was something of a problem for a not-so-rich shopkeeper in Delhi, but two of the girls insisted on love marriages which involved no dowries, so after they were locked into matrimony he moved his bride, his mother, her mother, and their remaining daughter to Asheville, where he dropped every penny of his life's savings, buffered by a big loan from First Carolina, into the purchase of the Motel 6. The remaining daughter completed her Ph.D. in astrophysics and enlisted in the Air Force with the hopes of becoming an astronaut, making her the first Indian woman to go into orbit.

"Thanks, Mr. Patel," I said. "And tell Mrs. Patel I'd love to try her samosas."

Even if I didn't have a passion for Indian food, I'd have said yes to his earlier offer. Given my financial picture, I was in no position to turn down a free meal. The tire incident left my savings account and me severely wanting for horse show dollars. The new show season was just gearing up, and if I had any hopes of being part of it, it meant major cutbacks.

"You will be loving them, I promise," he said. "I'll leave them in your room, waiting for you when you come back."

The cutbacks also included no in-room phone calls at a buck a pop. Instead I fished around the bottom of my purse and found a quarter. I dropped it in the pay phone and called Lady Passion, the Asheville witch I'd written about last Halloween, the one who told me I had the witch's mark. We'd gotten friendly since then, and I was hoping to find time to see her. However, between her nurse's hours at the hospital and my father-finding mission, I might have to settle for a telephone chat.

I don't know what I hate more, answering machines or Call Waiting. I got her machine.

"My Lady of Passion, it's me, Nattie Gold," I said. "I'm in town trying to find my father. But that's a long and stupid story.

Hope all's well with you and the hub. I'm at the Motel 6, give me a call if you're not off on your broom someplace flying to parts unknown."

Nothing to do now, except start my search. Like Henry says, follow the money, which I did, straight to the Third Eye. That was the last place Lou's MasterCard was used.

Now here was an opportunity to update my wardrobe and really annoy Candace at the same time. The latter appealed to me much more, since I could hardly afford the former. Racks and racks of scratchy cotton shmatas with Neiman Marcus price tags swam before my eyes. I held up one dress—$275, more than half a week's pay—and looked in the mirror. Whoever made this got his inspiration from Harris Teeter, and I say *his* inspiration because no woman would think another woman would ever wear something so ugly. This garment could double as a shopping bag. Same texture, same shape, same color. In fact, the store was awash in those awful yawn colors with ridiculous names like Ennui, Ecumenical, Bliss, and Celestial: grayish, gray, grayer, and grayest, if you ask me.

"Can I help you?"

I hadn't seen her approaching. The salesgirl, a tall, washed-out blonde in and of the Ennui, ran her eyes down my outfit, starting at the orange turtleneck, scanning to the purple paisley mini, sliding past the black tights and screeching to a halt at my turquoise suede ankle boots. I guess in the context of this store, I did look like a flashing neon Eat-at-Joe's sign. Okay, okay, maybe not only in the context of this store.

"Bakers," I said, pointing to the boots, "nineteen ninety-five. My drag queen friends love them. And yes, you can help me. Or I hope you can."

I reached in my purse and pulled out a picture of Lou. Unfortunately, it was of Lou with a German army helmet on his head, one of the 75,000 he and his buddy Manny Feldman had imported from the Motherland to turn into flower pots. It was the only picture I had of him, except for the auragraph he had taken when he went manic from the Zoloft. He was so high then that the ring of fuchsia shooting every which way from his head—what the aura-grapher called his energy field—completely engulfed his face like he was on fire from the inside out.

"I think this man came in here the other day," I said. "He was with a blond woman, about five-fourish, real pretty, good figure. He might've been on the quiet side. Ring any bells?"

She was still looking at my boots. I ducked my head down, to meet her gaze with my eye.

"It's important," I said. "That man's my father and I need to find him for a medical reason."

"The boots are cool," she said. "Do they come in orange?"

"Yeah, but I don't think it's the right statement with the Ennui, do you?" I said, and pointed to her shmata.

She looked down at her dress like it was road kill. "This? I hate this crap. We have to wear it at work. I wouldn't be caught dead in it."

Now that she mentioned it, it did look an awful lot like the shroud my stepfather David was buried in; the yard of cheap mus-lin that the funeral home ganef with the fake smile and bad caps charged us five hundred dollars for. To that man, who so adroitly exploits the mind-mush of the bereaved, I offer my grandmother's most famous line, "May your wife become a widow," or on a gen-tler, more evolved note: "May you get everything you deserve."

I held up the picture again. "My father, seen him?"

She was nodding her head. "Yes I did. They were in the other day. I remember thinking they must've been father and daughter, you know, because of the age difference. But then the way she was trying on clothes and showing them off to him—it wasn't too father-daughterly, if you know what I mean. That was *your* father? Wow. What's wrong with him, anyway? She could barely get him to talk. And he looked a little lost."

This woman I owed no explanation. She didn't need to know my family history of depression, and since I wasn't Tipper Gore campaigning for the cause of mental illness, I just said this:

"His heart medicine needs changing." So what if it was a total lie, it's not as if come Judgment Day I'm going straight to hell for that one. I'm sure there'll be plenty of other infractions cited for the big trip down south, namely my murderous thoughts toward Candace and Ron Riley.

"Heart, that's serious," she said. "You should take him to my healer, Manuel Teeta. He's from the Philippines. The healers there are amazing, they operate without knives or scalpels. They go inside you with their hands, you don't feel anything and there's no scar afterward or any sign of surgery. Manuel doesn't do that here, even in Asheville, he'd get deported. But he did fix my shoulder. The surgeon at the hospital wanted to operate, with knives and scalpels and pins. I didn't want anything metal left in me. As it is, I'm halfway through getting all the silver fillings out of my teeth. A friend of mine told me about Manuel, and not only did he fix my shoulder, but I have this sore knee from when I was—"

She was about to launch, I could tell. Get a person talking about his or her infirmities and you're looking at least at a twenty minute monologue. That's assuming it's just the routine stuff— bike injuries, measles, stitches. If they've veered off into the medically exotic, say polio, meningitis, or tsetse fly disease, add another forty-five to sixty minutes. Normally I'd have listened. I love life stories, and it is amazing what people tell me. But I didn't have the time to spare if I wanted to continue my search through Asheville and make it to the swami's big bash.

"Manuel Teeta?" I said. "I'll write that down, it's a great idea about taking my father to him. I don't think he's done the Philippine healer thing yet. He got kind of stuck on the Lemon Grass Institute, a place in San Diego that's heavy into internal irrigation. The healer sounds good, though. But I can't take him anywhere unless I find him. Did the woman he was with mention anything about where they were staying or going? Anything you can think of that could help me track him down?"

The salesgirl was rubbing her shoulder, right where she said it had been healed.

"Let me think a second . . . Yeah, now that I think about it, the woman told your father she'd take him back to the Blue Moon Bakery. That's usually good for a smile from anyone who's been there. Not him. He just sort of gave a little nod and followed behind her."

Things were bad. My father lives to eat, especially if it involves anything sweet on someone else's plate. He won't actually order something made with the demon white sugar, but watch out if you do. After his lecture on the evils of dextrose, half of your sweet whatever will be gone before you've had one sip of coffee, and that's not only because he's snitched most of your dessert. He's also commandeered your caffeinated hot drink—another nutritional God-forbid he'd never order on his own and chastise you for doing so—to dunk and drink.

"Come to think of it, it was just about this time of day they came in. Maybe that's a regular thing with them. I'd head over to the bakery."

My thoughts exactly.

CHAPTER 33

No Sarah Jane. No Lou. No luck.

But it wasn't a total loss. There are worse places to strike out than the best bakery in North Carolina, possibly the Southeast. I ordered a half dozen currant rye rolls, a cup of coffee, and sat myself down at a table by the plate-glass window. At least I could eat in peace without Lou raiding my cup and plate.

The Blue Moon Bakery is one busy place. I've never been there when there hasn't been a line snaking out the door. So it was no surprise the cute bakery boys behind the counter couldn't remember seeing Sarah Jane or my father. They barely had time to look at Lou's picture.

Talk about a harebrained plan anyway. Who was I, the Jewish Lone Ranger, thinking I'd drive to Asheville, miraculously locate my father after saying "Reach" a few times, and then lasso him and his scam-running harlot and haul them back home to make her face justice and him medication? Get real, Nattie. Once again, case in point of the apple not falling far from the tree, and more evidence for the naturalists in the great nature vs. nurture debate.

That said, it's not as if Lou and I haven't done this dance before and done it successfully. When I was seventeen, we hitchhiked through Europe together. In Israel, we split up. He went to Turkey, I stayed in the homeland because of a certain handsome Sabra I'd met. "Meet you in Amsterdam in three days," were our parting words. Nothing more precise than that, no exact time or location. And darn if we didn't pull it off. Three days later I was two bites into a slab of briny herring when I heard, "Nattie G!!!!!" It was Lou, standing on the other side of the fish cart, three bites into his herring.

I lingered at the Blue Moon for a few more minutes, polishing off two of the rolls. The remaining four and Mrs. Patel's samosas would be dinner and possibly breakfast. Easy on the wallet—and the hips. Short women don't take much fuel to run. Cap off my tank a few too many times and I start looking like an upside down mushroom, which presents a big problem given my chosen sport.

There's no disguising below-the-belt figure flaws in skintight britches, which isn't a problem for ninety-seven percent of the other riders who are six feet seven inches tall and weigh thirty-nine pounds. So why didn't I choose another wish-I-were-a-Wasp sport like tennis, where you get to wear jaunty little skirty things and terry-lined sun visors? Probably because I have the eye-hand coordination of a mole, those furry little guys who can't see.

I meandered around the city, stopping in bookstores, galleries, and something I hadn't seen for twenty years: head shops. Lots of head shops. I couldn't believe my eyes—and nose. I didn't even know they still make incense. Where'd they get this stuff from, Sonny Bono's old wardrobe? Tie-dye shirts with Jerry Garcia's loopy grin, floor-size bongs, Day-Glo incense holders, roach clips, hash pipes, Zig-Zag wrappers—someone pushed me through a break in the time-space continuum.

I flashed my picture of Lou to everyone I encountered. A few people thought they'd seen him. One guy swore he did. That was at The Mythic Enchanter/ress, a store that specialized in gauzy shirts with little mirror appliqués, Sherpa jackets, and chakra jewelry. The problem was nailing down the specifics. Not only was he a little loose on concrete details, but the longer I stayed in the store, the mushier I got. By the time I left, I could hardly say my name. My poor brain hadn't been bombarded with that kind of smoky illegal stimulation since Boulder, and it was becoming very clear why I stopped.

It turned my brain to oatmeal.

I sat down on the sidewalk, waiting for the fog to lift. When I was reasonably sure I wouldn't crash my car, I headed back to the motel, where I stopped by the front desk to collect my messages. This time Mrs. Patel was there.

Mr. Patel must've had himself a set of lucky starts to score an astrological match like that. Not to be totally superficial, but his missus was a beauty. Her thick hair was wrapped in a bun at the nape of her neck, and it looked like a shiny, black snake sleeping in the afternoon sun. That may not seem like a compliment, unless you've seen the iridescent glory of a black snake up close, the way the tiny flecks of jeweled greens and blues tingle in and out of one another, dancing and snapping and whirling to some kind of crazy cosmic beat. That's what her hair looked like to me, and it framed a face of delicately carved features with wide-set eyes so deep and dark you could dive into them and never hit bottom.

"Ah, Miss Gold," she said, "it is a pleasure to meet you. My husband was telling me about the lovely young woman checking into room number four. He asked me to give these messages to you."

Mr. Patel must've graduated from the same school of hand-writing as my father. My phone messages were close to indecipherable. Even this woman, his partner of twenty-seven years this incarnation, couldn't make sense of who called me and what they had to say.

"My husband has many virtues," Mrs. Patel said, "unfortunately, penmanship is not being one of them. He will be back in an hour and we will then ask him what he has written. I am very sorry."

"Not to worry," I said. "My writing's not much better, and besides, I'm sure I can figure out most of it."

Here's who I thought called: Henry, Gail, and was that really Ron Riley with the message to call immediately? Could that possibly be and not just a bad read on Mr. Patel's writing? I could feel

162

the resurrection of the rolls rising back up my throat. Thank God I, like horses, don't have the power to regurgitate. I'd have lost it right then, all over Mrs. Patel's nice rug. Then there was something about a mother. Mine? That's all I needed was Mother worrying about me tracking down her crazy ex-husband. The last message took me for a loop. Someone whose name started with a D and looked like it had an X in it, followed by several words, two of which I could just make out: lying and child.

As I was walking back to room number four, it clicked. D and X, put an I and an IE in and what do you get? Dixie. It stumped me because she usually goes by her witch name, Lady Passion; except, it seems, when she leaves telephone messages. I wondered what the lying child business was about. Maybe her psychic connections had zoomed in on me thinking about Henry's story. How else would she know about the Reverend Quarrels's accuser? I now had two bits of evidence to present to Henry, who would discount both. On the more scientific note, there was Denise's professional and skeptical assessment of the veracity of the mother's story. And now Lady Passion's celestial insight. I decided to tell Henry, who was still processing the notion of witches' blood coursing through my veins, only the first.

But tell him later. Now, I was going to taste Mrs. Patel's samosas. It was becoming even clearer why I'd stopped smoking pot. Not only did it make stupider than normal things come out of my mouth, but stupider than normal things go in as well. Basically anything that wasn't nailed down was prey to my grabby hands during an attack of the Munchies. At my worst I'd actually mixed together flour, sugar, butter, and cinnamon and gobbled that down. Who had time to bake, under the influence? I'm not known for patience when all my wits are about me. Throw a smoke bomb in my head and the Ms. Instant Gratification inside me Gozilladizes what little reservoir of reasoning I've got.

It was no coincidence I'd gained twenty-five pounds during my freshman year at the University of Colorado.

I found the room key, a feat in itself, and slid it into the lock. That, like the towels, was on the flimsy side of cheap. Even in the most secure motels, I always push a chair against the door when I go to sleep. I am, after all, my mother's daughter, waiting for the worst to happen.

I didn't have to wait long. Here we go again. Was this some kind of bad joke?

Well, I wasn't laughing. There's nothing funny about a smashed up motel room. Someone had gone through all my things—notes, clothes, newspapers—and flung them around like a gorilla in heat. Worst of all—in my state of hunger—the samosas were ruined, rubbed to a pulp into the formerly clean sheets. Bits of peas and potatoes dotted in and out of smeary yellow tracks of chickpea dough, making the whole bed look like a piece of Jackson Pollock performance art, had he done performance art.

There were no ominous messages written in lipstick on the bathroom mirror. Been there, done that, last murder. My plastic horse collection, glued back together from a previous assault by a crazed killer, was safe at home, and no one was trying to run me over with a big white truck. So compared to others, this offense scored a 3.5 in technical on the scare-the-crap-out-of-Nattie scale. However, on artistic merit, I'd have to give it a 9.5 just on the bed alone.

I was clearly making someone jumpy. And that someone either wanted Sarah Jane to stay hidden, making her look guiltier than O.J., if that was possible, or wanted to catch up with her before I did. It was also pretty clear my tire slasher/samosa smasher meant me no physical harm—yet—just an emotional rassle or two, enough to scare me off my mission.

That someone obviously hadn't accounted for my Jack Russell personality. I'd give up on this baby when hell froze over or, even less likely, *The Charlotte Commercial Appeal* went off contingency budget.

CHAPTER 34

I set to work, gathering my stuff and trying to clean up the Jackson Pollock as best as I could, while trying to figure out who knew where I was.

How about half of Charlotte? I'd told just about everyone, and then some. The only thing I didn't do was post a notice in *The Appeal*. Almost everyone on my suspect list had a way of knowing my travel plans. Everyone except Mark Donner, the little racist squirt who'd thrown me and my make-over out of his store. Reluctantly, I stopped thinking of him as a murderer.

That left everyone else. Great. My head was starting to pound and my eyes starting to droop. First you eat, then you sleep—what a wonder drug; wonder as in I wonder why people still smoke it. Maybe it was really Nixon's plot to tranquilize America's rebellious youth.

I'd have to get horizontal if I had any hope of stringing together a coherent sentence. My head hit the pillow and out I went. Sometime after that the phone jangled into my dreams. Half awake, I flung my arm, searching for the noisy intruder.

"Hello, hello," I said. No answer. Must be my twisted funster playing another funny prank on me. Ho ho, phony phone calls, how droll. What was I going to hear next, "Is your refrigerator running?" or, "I know what you're wearing"?

"Are you there or what?" I demanded. More moments of silence passed. "You've got ten seconds to say something before I pop open your eardrum with the loudest scream you've ever heard." Okay, so I was a little cranky between my slashed tires, trashed room, and rude summons from dreamland. It didn't help that I was PMSing up a storm and left my homeopathic fixer-uppers in Charlotte.

"Ten, nine, eight . . ." I started. Then I looked down at my hand—I was holding the hearing end of the phone by my mouth. Ooops. I sliced my count off at seven, flipped the receiver around right side up and counted my blessings that I was alone.

"Hello," I said into the correct end.

"Hey sweetie, it's me, Gail. What were you doing, wrestling with the phone or something?"

"Something like that," I said. "Is Brenda okay?"

I could cut to the chase with Gail and she'd understand the preemption of any social graces like how are you or what's new. We both know that when you leave your horse in someone else's care, a long distance call isn't to chat. Something was wrong, and being my mother's daughter, I assumed the worst. Brenda was dead.

"She's alive," said Gail, who after more than three years knew my pathology well. "Calm down, start breathing."

My heart stopped slamming against my ribs and I let out the air I'd been holding.

"But she did throw that right front shoe and tore off part of her hoof with it," Gail said. "Maybe it's better you're not here to see it. You know how ugly her feet can look. Gerry's out of town and I left a message on the slimeball's machine. He must be hanging out in the lingerie section at Dillard's—or knowing his level of class, Kmart. I'm doing my best to find a blacksmith, but until I do, it's stall rest for Brenda."

"Shi—ooot," I said, catching myself mid-syllable. A promise is a promise, even in times as desperate as these. "That's all I need, for her to rip the tar out of her foot now. Why couldn't she have done this in the winter, when there was nothing to do but dream about horse shows? How does she seem on it? A little ouchy?"

Stupid question and I knew the answer. Brenda, the horse of three white legs, was blessed with everything except good feet. Looking at them cross-eyed is enough to make her gimpy.

"Sure you want to know?" Gail said. "You being three hours away and on that dumb rescue mission of yours."

"Lay it on me. My day couldn't get much worse."

"Well, she's not quite three-legging it. But close. She's not happy about putting weight on it, so I gave her a Bute. I'll give her another one later tonight. You asked, Nattie."

"I know, I know." Could having kids be this much trouble? Another stupid question; I'd been around Henry and his boys enough to know the answer.

A shoeless horse with a hoof that must've looked like it'd gone through a paper shredder, and no blacksmith around. What a day. At least there was better living through modern chemistry: the Bute—short for Phenylbutazone, a sort of horse aspirin—would ease my poor girl's pain.

I obsessed about Brenda's foot to Gail until I happened to look at the clock. If I didn't hustle my buns, the swami and his swamette would be astral-projecting themselves to honeymoonville by the time I found wherever and whatever the fourth vortex of Mount Mitchell was.

"What do you mean your day couldn't get worse?" Gail said as I tried to say good-bye.

I quickly told her about the room trashing, which was a mistake since she's been taking worry lessons from my mother.

"Nattie," she said, "so what that this jerk hasn't hurt you *yet*. That doesn't mean anything. Come home now. Lou'll find his way back. He always does."

We both knew she was talking to deaf ears—metaphorically speaking, since Lou was nowhere in sight.

I promised I'd call the second I got back, and she knew I would. She held the trump card: the condition of my lame horse.

I crammed the rest of the messages in my pocket, rushed out

the door and into my little blue car. After listening to Gail, I half
expected the engine to blow up when I cranked the key. Instead all
I heard was just the usual rumble of complaints from my senior
citizen of an automobile. A lot of "Oy, my aching backs" and "Take
it easy, wouldjas?" but no explosion.

What I had to do now was find the fourth vortex of Mount
Mitchell. You can bet there's no street sign labeled as such. However, I'd done my homework when I was in Asheville this morning.
Not only had I flashed Lou's picture around town, but I'd also
asked everyone I'd talked to where and what the fourth vortex is. A
few people looked at me as if I might be off my medication. A couple others sort of pointed west and said, "That way." The guy at
The Mythic Enchanter/ress was even more vague: "It's in the
mountains," he'd said. Thank you, Albert Einstein.

It was the owner of Malaprops who knew. She, like her book-
store, was quite the resource. I'd lingered there longer and spent
more money than I should have, but it's hard to find these kinds of
real bookstores anymore. The ones where the people who work
there actually know and love books. Like Quail Ridge in Raleigh
and the Little Professor in Charlotte. Who knows how long they'll
last in the shadow of the looming superstores? My favorite book-
store in Greensboro, Atticus, switched to selling tchotchke then
finally closed after one of the book-selling Goliaths opened its
Wal-Mart-size store in the same mall.

This woman knew exactly whom and what I was talking about.

"Of course, the swami," she'd said, and then drew me a map
after a puzzled look washed across my face when she tried to give
me oral directions.

I held the map in my hand as I navigated myself toward the
peaks in front of me. I had to give it to the swami, he knew beauty
of the geographical kind. I don't know if this is everyone's idea of
heaven, but it sure is mine. I was swaying in and out of soft green
valleys with curvy black satin ribbons of creek. I was rocking up

and down the climbs and falls of these old hills like a pinball riding a sine curve, my head swiveling from side to side to make sure I caught every flash of spring's razzle-dazzle show. Charlotte was a good ten days ahead, blossomwise, so it was like catching Mother Nature's opening movement twice.

I was so smitten with the budding landscape I drove right past the big yellow sign with the rainbow colored letters announcing: RE-UNITED AT LAST!! COME CELEBRATE!!! and an arrow pointing down a narrow dirt road.

I veered to the shoulder, threw my car in reverse, and backed up until I reached the sign. Now would have been a good time to have the vehicle of my dreams, a Hummer. "Hold on," I said to my little blue Rabbit and pointed it nose first down the rutted path. When I have kids of my own, I know they'll have mouths the size of the Grand Canyon, talking back from the second they learn how to say no. Until then, I've got my car, the drama queen, to badger me. As it bounced from bump to gully, it let me know in no un-certain terms what assault I was inflicting on its poor, aged body. Its normal rattles—the quiet, innocuous ones asking politely for a little drink of WD-40—turned into metal-grinding shrieks of "What the hell are you doing to me?" interspersed with unsettlingly loud clangs of "No amount of WD-40 will ever make this right again between us, sister."

I was practicing for motherhood: I ignored everything and pressed my foot to the gas pedal. A mission is a mission, and some-thing strong inside me told me I was getting close to pay dirt. Be-sides, being one who chooses form over function any day, this ride was worth it, even if my hunch was wrong and Sarah Jane and my father were on their way to Sedona by now.

As if Nature's Spring Collection wasn't enough of a sensory treat with her baby leaves of sheer, feathery green and the sweet clamor of boisterous peepers singing their little hearts out, the swami's party had long, fetching fingers. Bits and pieces of music played hide and seek with my ears as the floaty notes drifted off the mountain toward me. Blue and yellow balloons were tied to tree branches, and forever chains of colored paper loops scalloped in and out of the woods.

If you were going to get married, this was the way to do it. However, meeting your soulmate in cyberspace and tying the eternal knot sight unseen wouldn't have been my top choice for openers.

The closer I got, the more notes reached my ears, until I could make out a melody. It was aging hippie music: flutes, guitars, and tambourines spiraling around the lilty trills of a Joni-Mitchell-on-a-happy-day kind of singer. Directly ahead was a gathering of cars, not exactly the old hippie cars of my youth. My compatriots had traded in the Bugs and painted vans of our past for sportier—and pricier—models. I scanned the lot of them—BMWs, Acuras, Volvos—undoubtedly for the parents in the crowd—a few Lexuses here and there, and the obligatory raft of sport utility vehicles for the boomers who thought they could four-wheel-drive themselves across the rocky terrain of time, back to their glory days when nothing but the cheap mattresses in their group houses sagged.

I was looking for Sarah Jane's old gold Mercedes. And hot damn if I didn't find it.

CHAPTER 35

There it sat, sandwiched between two black Expeditions and one red Blazer, making her gold Mercedes look like the mustard lining of a rare roast beef on pumpernickel.

I just about kicked my heels in glee as I dashed over to her car. Now if the gods were really on my side, Lou'd be asleep inside, sprawled and snoring across the cracked leather seats. It wouldn't be the first time I'd found him asleep at the wheel.

I peeked in. So much for my divine luck. But at least they were here. Somewhere. It was her Mercedes, no doubt about it. No one can trash a car like Lou. His clothes were strewn all over the backseat, mixed in with vitamin bottles, little Baggies of what I hoped were Chinese herbs, an old loofah, a couple tubes of Tom's Natural Teaberry Toothpaste, and his jar of magnets, each one strong enough to hold up two elephants.

Uh-oh, he wasn't wearing his magnets. Another bad sign. Usually he's got them strung around his neck to keep his electromagnetic flow flying. When he stops wearing them, that means he's also stopped taking showers, stopped changing clothes, and about stopped living. This put Brenda's little toenail problem in a different perspective.

Although Denise strongly urged me not to let Lou anywhere near a hit of Zoloft ever in this lifetime, Lou's shrink was of a different medical mind—after I nixed his top choices: commitment and/or shock therapy. I told the doctor I wasn't even going to discuss either of those, so think of something else to bring my father back.

Reluctantly he suggested trying Zoloft again, since my father wouldn't consider Lithium, and given his siblings' failure on the drug, it was probably just as well. And if things were really dire, he said, I should consider kick-starting Lou out of the blackness by twinning his meds with Ritalin until he started talking again. Both bottles were rolling around the bottom of my purse.

I was armed and ready to rescue. Hi-ho, Silver, away.

I followed the music down a small wooded path that opened up to the sweetest little meadow imaginable, festooned in frilly party clothes like a Laura Ashley girl. Balloons, streamers, wind socks; I half expected to see Martha Stewart standing there doing a television special on quaint country weddings.

Though I'm not much better at crowd estimates than the National Park Police, I'd have put the count between three and four hundred. I know I should have been scurrying around, looking for Lou, but I came in the only way out, so I knew he wasn't going anywhere without me catching him. I was dying to see how close I'd come to imagining what the swami looked like. It's a dumb game I've been playing ever since I can remember; I close my eyes and get a picture in my head of someone I haven't yet met. Sometimes I'm dead wrong, but more often than not, I'm right on the money, down to eye color.

Here's what I pictured: Before the swami became a swami I was figuring him to be an Ira Rosenstein or Gary Gluckman or Steven Lipschitz or some variety thereof; one of the many Jew-Boos of my generation who dropped the Jew in favor of the Boo— as in Buddhist. I was seeing him just under six feet and on the wiry side; long dark hair, corkscrew curly; dark, dark, intense follow-me eyes; orthodontically corrected teeth half slipped back to their original sins; and that new-age-cosmic-come-on-brother-let's-get-together-smile which is a first cousin facial contortion to what happens below the nose of funeral home directors.

I started scanning the meadow looking for my version of the swami, and of course Sarah Jane and Lou. Seeing as how I worship at the altar of color, my eyes were listening to my brain's instructions about as well as a two-year-old whose mother keeps telling her not to touch the little doggie. It was the swirls of fuchsia, turquoise, and saffron playing loop-de-loop with each other on a billowy piece of silk that shanghaied my eyes. Not only that, but it was edged in purple fringe and tied to four cobalt-blue poles. It was the visual equivalent of a six-course meal at a five-star restaurant.

If eyes can have orgasms, I was having one. Amidst my ocular ecstasy I realized what it was I was looking at: a huppa, the mini-tent thing that the bride and groom in a Jewish wedding stand under. So maybe I'd been right about the swami's maiden name.

Sure enough, taking his place under the kaleidoscopic huppa was the swami of my mind. I wasn't close enough to see if I'd gotten the teeth right, but everything else was on the mark. The music stopped and someone banged a loud gong three times. That must've been the signal to gather, because everyone started walking toward the huppa. Including me.

My eyes had their color fix and started listening to me again. I surveyed each grouplet of wedding goers for white hair—my father—or yellow hair—possibly Sarah Jane, assuming she hadn't hit the Miss Clairol again. Or maybe the blonde was the Miss Clairol.

Just as my eyes zoomed in on a shock of white hair, I nearly jumped out of my skin.

BAM!!BAM!!BAM!!BAM!!

Those God-blessed gongs were going at it again. And they weren't stopping. This time I wasn't perched up on the hill, I was standing five feet away, close enough for the noise to rattle the silver fillings in my teeth.

I put my hands over my ears and sighted in again on the white hair. There he was. And there she was. Yellow hair and all.

I broke into a run and, never taking my eyes off my quarry, sprinted toward Lou. He looked up and saw me. On a high day he'd have screamed out, "Nattie G! Welcome aboard." On a medium day he'd have swept his hand across the sky, arcing out a hello wave.

This was a low day. He just looked at me.

I ran faster. Sarah Jane caught sight of me and started to edge away. That's when I really spurted. I felt like I was back in sixth grade trying to beat Randy Spilks in the fifty-yard dash. I never did.

And I wouldn't have caught Sarah Jane either had she broken into a run. She was walking briskly, trying to be inconspicuous in her escape. I, on the other hand, have never been or cared about being inconspicuous—those loud redheaded genes of mine—so I was careening through the crowds like an out of control bowling ball ricocheting off the gutters.

Just as she was about to hit the path, I made a leap for her and grabbed the hem of her ugly aubergine natural fiber shirt. That stopped her short.

"Going someplace, Sarah Jane?" I said between gasps of air.

CHAPTER 36

With the gongs still gonging full blast, it was a little on the loud side to have the conversation I'd been planning to have with Ms. Sarah Jane Grifter. She started to talk, but neither of us could hear anything over the BAM, BAM, BAM-ing of the gong.

I pointed to the crowd, wrapped my fingers around her wrist and led her back to where I hoped Lou was still standing. She followed behind like a recalcitrant dog who'd just messed in the house.

Lou was exactly where I'd left him. I don't think he'd even blinked. I wrapped the fingers of my other hand around his wrist and started to pull them both back to the parking lot where we could begin to sort things out—and get away from that horrible noise.

I didn't get the spiritual significance of the banging gongs. Maybe it was the auditory version of what the dervishes do: whirl themselves to oneness. Maybe this was how the swami and his followers catapulted themselves to nirvana. It wasn't working for me. Each time the big guy with the big stick banged the big gong, the outlines of my head jumped out two feet and came crashing back in on me. Thanks, but no thanks, Swami, the only oneness with anything I was feeling right now was the oneness I wanted to have with a big bottle of Bayer.

I pulled Sarah Jane and Lou faster. I didn't know how much longer my head could stand each explosion. I was sorry I wasn't going to see the swami see his bride for the first time, but if I didn't get out of there soon, I'd have to grab the stick out of the gonger's hand and gong him. Except that I had no hands left at this point for physical assault since I had Sarah Jane in one and Lou in the other.

I turned my head around to them and mouthed "Hurry, please." That's when something even louder than the gong crashed by my ears. I didn't have time to register the confusion starting to swirl my brain. Something wasn't right. The sound was coming from the wrong place. Three more crashes thundered past my head.

"Holy shit," I screamed, "that's no damn gong!"

I dove to the ground and pulled them down with me. Those were shots—gunshots—tearing by us. Before I had a chance to turn my head and see who was dead, another one ripped right next to me, within singeing distance of my hair.

So the bad news was someone was trying to kill me, Sarah Jane, or, least likely, Lou. The good news was that damned gonging finally stopped.

I know, I know. I backslid into the land of bad-words big-time. Two verbal slip-ups in less than a minute, if you count damn as a curse word. But surely God, being the merciful God I choose to believe in, would cut me some slack on this. I mean five bullets did just whiz by my head.

I pressed my face into the ground, not only for protection from flying lead, but for comfort. The damp, soothing earth was a poultice for my rattled soul and pounding head.

"Nattie?" A hand shook my shoulder. "Are you okay?"

Reluctantly I lifted my face from the cool dirt and looked up into Sarah Jane's eyes. Here I go again, impaired by my character-assessment handicap, but she did look concerned. That, however, wasn't enough for me to make nicey-nice with her.

"Sarah Jane," I said, "how would you think I am? I've been chasing you halfway across North Carolina, some idiot's slashed my tires, trashed my room, and now invaded my personal space with bullets. My father's near catatonic, and I have to drag your sorry butt back to Charlotte. So all in all, I'm not okay. Okay?"

She recoiled from my verbal assault and actually looked surprised.

"Nattie, all this negative energy, it's not good for anyone. Here, let me help you."

Sarah Jane started rubbing her hands together just like my crazy aunt; the one who thinks she's the reincarnation of Edgar Cayce, never mind that she was thirty-eight years old when he died; the one who thinks she's got healing hands; the one who snuck into the cardiac intensive care unit when my father was losing too much blood after his quadruple bypass operation. The nurses found her crouched over her brother—my father—swooping her arms across his body, knocking out wires and tubes and anything else in the path of her hysterical flight.

"Hands off, sister," I said, and intercepted hers with mine as they came my way. "I'd say you've done enough."

By this time there was quite the crowd watching the Nattie–Sarah Jane show. Even the swami was there. He knelt down to my level.

I don't like being shot at and I'm not ready to take my final samadhi. Besides, when I do, I want to go there on horseback. So I was pretty shaky and I knew my legs would never hold me up. Lying face first on the ground, I extended my hand to him, introduced myself and apologized for the ruckus, if that's what you call a round of gunshots interrupting your wedding.

"I knew this was going to be an exciting day," he said, and smiled at me. It was a smile so warm, so forgiving, and so welcoming, that given my wobbly—both physically and psychically—state, I wanted to ditch Sarah Jane, forget the white-haired man with the dead expression, and turn over all my earthly possessions to the swami so I could frolic through the woods with him and his followers.

Shock has a way of scrambling my circuitry, making me want to jump into the nearest security blanket available. It happened to me after David died: I found myself eyeing an overweight male mourner, thinking how good it would be to be in his arms. Thank God I couldn't stop crying, because I'd have probably propositioned him, right there in the middle of the mourner's Kaddish, between the first two Yis-kah-davs. Then when my friend and podmate Jeff was killed, I hurled myself into the arms of Tony-the-cop and practically shimmied myself up and down his adorable body. Once again the hand of God reached right down and protected me, not that I wanted the protection, thank you very much Your Nosy Holiness. Because despite my acrobatics, Tony's "dawg"—as he so colloquially put it—wouldn't hunt that night, or any other night, so he says, with anyone but his yo-yo of a wife.

I sank my face back into the coolness, praying that I'd taken too much melatonin again and this was all a dream. I closed my eyes hard and tried to summon up a talking horse.

Instead I got another shake on the shoulder.

"Nattie, are you shot or something?"

It wasn't Brenda talking. It was Sarah Jane again, and she sounded very worried. Back to reality. I gathered my legs under me and forced myself to stand up.

"I'm not shot, I'm not shot, calm down," I said. "What about you?"

"I'm fine. Protected by the angels. Lou's fine too."

He was vertical now with that same blank look on his face. You'd think almost being killed would rattle some kind of reaction out of you. It's easy to forget how formidable a foe depression is.

"Lou," I said as gently as possible, "it's time to go home now. We'll get you fixed up, I promise."

I put my arm around his shoulder to lead him away. Before we left, I made my apologies again to the swami and wished him many lifetimes of happiness with his soulmate. I figured it was reasonably safe to go to the car since the gunshots had stopped a while ago and one of the swami's followers had run into the woods right after the shots were fired and found nothing or no one.

Given that most of us there were old hippies, calling the police was never mentioned. That was just as well by me. The last thing I wanted to do was spend three hours with a bunch of blues answering questions.

As we walked back to the car, Sarah Jane started sputtering explanations, apologies, and never-again promises.

"I know I shouldn't have left Charlotte so fast," she said, "but when I saw those police cars at that farm, I couldn't think of anything else to do. And I know I shouldn't have gotten Lou involved, but he told me if I ever needed anything—'anything at all,' he'd said—to just ask him. He said he'd give me the shirt off his back."

I looked at the shirt on her back. The ugly aubergine number. It'd looked familiar when I made a grab for it and now I remembered why. The Third Eye, I'd seen it hanging there, it was the one with the three-digit price tag.

"I'll just bet he did," I said. "But I guess you didn't like what he was wearing, so you took him on a little shopping spree, huh?"

She blushed darker than a dogwood in the fall.

"I didn't bring enough clothes with me, that's all. It's not like it looks, Nattie, I swear. I told Lou I'd pay him back. And I will. I've changed, I know it sounds like a lie, but I really have. People change, they do and I have. I don't want the life I had. And I can't go back to jail. All that negative energy. That's why I flipped when I saw those police cars. I mean what was I to think? You'd have done the same thing."

"Really?" I said. "Which part? Kidnapped a seventy-two-year-old manic-depressive? Taken a slew of old geezers for their life savings? Bopped a dumb blacksmith in his wife's friend's barn? Or killed the aforementioned wife when she went nuclear after finding out about your little love tryst?"

Sarah Jane looked at me like I was talking Russian.

"Which part would that be, Sarah Jane? Maybe you can channel me an answer, or why don't you just ask your spirit guides?"

Sarah Jane put her hand on my arm to stop me from walking. The high blush had fled her face. She was leaning now toward a lighter shade of pale. "What did you mean, 'kill the wife'?"

I peeled her fingers from my arm. "Oh, can it," I said. "You should've been an actress. But I guess you are, aren't you? You've just redefined the parameters of the stage. You know exactly what I mean. Either from firsthand knowledge, which is looking more and more like a possibility, or from Lou. I'm sure he told you."

"Told me what, for Christ's sake?" This was the first time I'd heard Sarah Jane's voice leave the confines of the go-with-the-flow range. I'd have put the above sentence in the near-shriek category.

"Fuzzy's dead," I said. "Or maybe that's not clear enough for you. Let me put it to you in language you can get: Someone—and the police think you're just that someone because they found a bloody shovel by your door—decided it was time for Ms. McMahon to leave this body behind and soul-travel her way to her next incarnation."

Sarah Jane's skin was now approaching the color of a sycamore tree in the dead of winter. I call them ghost trees, if that's any indication of her pallor. "Fuzzy's dead? Murdered? When? What shovel? I don't own a shovel."

She was sputtering now and doing a very convincing job of it. She was either channeling Meryl Streep's spirit or maybe she really didn't know. Who could tell? Surely not me. I told her the hows and whens of Fuzzy's demise and asked her the whos.

"I didn't kill Fuzzy," she said. "I'd never physically hurt anyone. Never. Nattie, I'd never do something like that. I've done some awful things in my life, but kill another human being? Never. I swear. I swear. I swear to God I'd never hurt anyone. Besides, why would someone be shooting at me if I was the murderer?"

She had a point, if in fact the shots had been meant for her. But maybe she was in cahoots with a co-murderer, say someone such as her lover-boy Bobby McMahon, and just maybe he was starting to get jumpy that she couldn't keep a secret. Who knew? Not me, that was for sure. I was still working on accepting that she wasn't Sarah Sweetness and Light. However, I've gotta say, she looked pretty darn sincere standing there with tears tracking down her perfectly chiseled cheeks.

"You mean Lou never mentioned anything about Fuzzy?" I said.

Sarah Jane started shaking her head back and forth. "When I got to your apartment to talk to him, I was really upset. I thought the police had found me, you know for that other thing in Pennsylvania, and that's why they were there. Lou had his hands full trying to calm me down about that. I told him everything, *everything* about my life. It's the first time I've ever been totally honest with someone. It felt so wonderful; so enlightening; so—so—so—I don't know how to say it, it was just so right, like I'd been lost my whole life and I was ready to start a new path."

"So was that path an HOV lane?" I said. "Did you think the New Life Patrol was going to give you a ticket for only having one person in your car? Did you have to drag along my father?"

Sarah Jane looked at Lou standing there, lost in his despair. That's when the waterworks really started. Between sobs—real or fake, I still didn't know—she kept apologizing for ruining his life. I'm a softee, what can I say? I reached my arms around her.

"Sarah Jane, stop. Stop. You didn't ruin his life. This isn't something you caused, this is something he's been wrestling all his life. His brain chemicals are out of whack, no one knows what throws the levels off. So stop crying, okay?"

She took in deep, jagged gulps of air, trying to steady herself, and I was patting her back wondering if I'd been hoodwinked once again. When she was calm enough to start talking, she did.

"Your father was so terrific when I told him all those horrible things. Not the least bit judgmental. He didn't hold any of it against me. He's a very evolved, forgiving soul. I swear he didn't say anything about Fuzzy, I swear it. I guess he didn't want to upset me any more than I already was. When I told him I was going to Asheville, he's the one who asked to come along. He remembered that bakery. Funny, huh? That's the first place we went. Then all of a sudden he just stopped talking. I had no way of knowing about Fuzzy."

"What about the news? Newspapers? Television?" I said.

"Nattie, you know as well as I do, Lou doesn't read the paper or watch the six o'clock news. He can't stand to hear about the bad things happening in the world, and neither can I. I swear to you, *I swear to you on my mother's life*, I didn't know about Fuzzy."

She was still in my arms with me there-thereing her. And I was just about to believe her when I remembered something she'd told me over a dinner of tempeh bacon and tofu eggs. I'd been talking about mothers—mine specifically, and what a pain she can be, especially when it came to choices in men. Sarah Jane's face got all sad like some kind of sleepy-eyed hound dog. And her voice got real low and whispery.

"At least you've got a mother," she'd said as tears spilled into her tofu, turning its bright turmeric coat into a sickly yellow mess, "mine died when I was seven years old."

CHAPTER 37

We're standing in the lobby of the Motel 6. Mr. Patel is trying not to eavesdrop, but even a monk would have a difficult time ignoring us. Words like murderer, grifter, scammer, and fugitive have a way of piquing anyone's interest.

Needless to say, we didn't get much settled in the parking lot at the swami's wedding. Except I did get Lou to his meds. He was still mute, but hopefully that would change as soon as the Ritalin kicked in.

Of course, Sarah Jane had had a ready answer about her dead/alive mother. It was: "I meant *if* my mother were alive I'd swear on her life that I knew nothing about Fuzzy."

Right. I may be character-assessment impaired, but I'm not an idiot, although it was seeming more and more as if I were approaching that state. Consider this: I actually watched Sarah Jane drive away from the swami's bash after she promised to meet me at the Motel 6. Drive away as if she were a normal person; as if she were someone you could count on to do what she said. Really, though, I had no choice. Two cars, three people. I sure as anything wasn't going to leave Lou with her as security.

Imagine my surprise when I saw her old gold Mercedes creep onto the blacktop. It had been a while, and I'd already checked out of my room, packed my car, and figured she was halfway to Altoona. But no, she was back like a bad check, something she was all too familiar with.

And now here we were discussing her return to the Queen City. She was looking forward to that about as much as I look forward to my yearly pap smears.

"Sarah Jane," I said. "You don't have a choice. You're the one who's been swearing up one side and down the other about your innocence and that you've changed and you want to right all your wrongs. How are you going to do that while you're fleeing from the police?"

She'd already run through a slew of reasons why she couldn't go back to Charlotte, all of which fell into the I-have-to-wash-my-hair category.

"I know you're right," she started again. I could just about see her brain scouring every remaining crevice of its twisted gray matter for a believable excuse. "I know I should go back and talk to the police. I just don't think my car will make it all the way there. Something's wrong with it. That's the reason I was late getting here. I'm sure you thought I was running away again. I wasn't even thinking of that. It took me so long because I had to stop in two gas stations to add oil. Every time I turn around the oil light goes on."

Mr. Patel, who'd by this point given up all pretense of not listening, officially joined the conversation.

"You could leave your car here," he said. "It will be safe with me, and when you are ready to come back and get it, it will be here waiting. If you like I could have my nephew look at it. He knows something about cars."

Was that a dirty look Sarah Jane was leveling that nice man's way?

"That's very generous of you, Mr. Patel," I said. "Sounds like a plan to me. How about to you, Sarah Jane?"

She had nowhere to go but east—to Charlotte. "I guess so," she said. "Let me just get my things and put them in your car. I'll be right back."

I said I was approaching idiot. I hadn't gotten there yet.

"Here," I said, "let me give you a hand."

I wasn't about to let her out of arm's reach. Like Fric and Frac, we walked to her car. Crammed into her trunk was enough stuff to start a new life, which is probably what she'd been planning. "I can't fit everything in my car," I said. "Choose."

The rice cooker stayed behind, as did the Acme juicer, the electronic shiatsu machine, and two suitcases. She whittled herself down to three large bags. Two of them I stuffed in my trunk, the other in the backseat.

"It'll be a little cramped for you back there, unless you want to leave more here," I said. She shook her head no. "Your choice. Let's go get Lou."

Lou was sitting in a chair, staring into space. I waved my hand in front of him. "Time to head back to the Queen City," I said. The front desk was empty, so I called out, "Hey, Mr. Patel, thanks for everything. See you next time I'm in Asheville."

Just as Lou, Sarah Jane, and I were walking out, Mr. Patel rushed into the lobby. "Miss Gold, wait please, one second, if you are not minding. While you were outside you received a telephone call from a person named Gail. She said you would know who she was and where to reach her. She said it is very, very urgent."

The elevator shaft cable inside me snapped, plummeting my heart to a slamming crash at the bottom of my feet. Gail. Long distance telephone call. Very, *very* urgent. This was not good.

"Miss Gold, are you all right?" Mr. Patel said. "You are very pale."

I took a deep breath. "No, I don't know, I mean I won't know until I call. Lou, Sarah Jane, wait right here."

I rushed to the pay phone and credit-carded my way to Gail. Twelve rings. Where in God's name was she? Finally, on the fourteenth, she answered, huffing and puffing as if she'd just run a race.

"Nattie," she said between breaths, "I knew it'd be you. I was in

Brenda's stall. Calm down, she's not dead. But she is pretty damn lame, and I don't think it has anything to do with that torn foot. It fooled me at first because it's the same leg, right front. I never could find Bobby McMahon, but I got another blacksmith out here who did a decent enough job. Even with how much she tore it up, she shouldn't be this lame, especially with the shoe back on. Something's wrong, Nats."

"How bad is it?" I said.

"Bad enough that she's lying down. When she gets up, she won't put any weight on it and she looks like she's hurting. You know how she gets that 'woe is me' look? Well, she's got it now. Doc Loc said he'd be here in a couple hours, he's right in the middle of an emergency call. I just wanted to let you know what's happening and find out when you're coming home. That guy at the motel said you'd checked out. Did you find Lou?"

"Yeah, I found him and Sarah Jane," I said. "Do you think she needs some Banamine until the vet comes?"

I knew she knew the drill, but I had to ask. Banamine's an analgesic. You give it to horses in distress so they won't colic from the pain; because colic, a regular old stomachache for any other creature, can be a killer for a horse.

"Already done, my dear," Gail said. "Now don't you be driving back here like a maniac. I know you're upset, but getting dead isn't going to do anyone any good. Least of all Brenda. Okay?"

I knew she was right, but I also knew that wouldn't slow me down. I hustled Lou and Sarah Jane into the car and zoomed off into the day with little explanation to my riders.

Not that they were asking. Lou was still silent and Sarah Jane was working her fingernails to bloody crescents. One can only rip at oneself for so long, and after about twenty miles Sarah Jane tapped a torn finger on my shoulder.

"Nattie, are you okay?" she said. "Your aura's bright red. What was the telephone call about anyway?"

I didn't know what color my aura was supposed to be. Probably not bright red.

"I've been better," I said. "A lot better. The call was about Brenda. She's done something to herself and I think it's bad."

I could feel the tears start to pull at the back of my throat. If I didn't clamp myself down fast, I'd be thunderstorming inside. Not exactly the best way to be negotiating an old, crotchety car at eighty miles an hour.

Sarah Jane placed both hands on the back of my head, and just as I was about to tell her to get them off, darn if it didn't feel as if I were being pumped full of some kind of sparkly yellow light. I didn't say anything and neither did she.

After a while she took her hands away, and then we rode in silence for another five minutes or so. Even though I was filled with that strange sparkly light and I did feel a lot less anxious, that didn't stop the chatter in my head. Try as I might to force myself toward the positive point of view—that Brenda's lameness was probably only a bad bruise—the doomsday man inside me was louder. He countered with, Yeah, dream on, girlie, you're looking at least at a life-threatening infection, a broken leg, or a mysterious equine-eating bacteria that starts at the hoof. If not those, then—

Sarah Jane interrupted me at my most horribly imaginative. "Nattie, I'm talking to Brenda. She wants you to stop worrying."

"What?" I said. "What are you talking about?"

"I'm talking about and to your horse, Brenda Starr. Remember, I *am* an animal communicator. I may be a lying and sometimes thieving you-know-what, but I can talk to animals."

Given everything that had happened, I'd completely forgotten about her Dr. Dolittlian claims.

"I'm talking to Brenda. She's in her stall lying down because she says her front right leg hurts. But she wants you to stop worrying. She knows how you get when she even gets a scratch."

I hadn't told Sarah Jane anything. Not which leg or that she was lying in her stall. Nothing beyond that she'd done something bad. Okay, she had my interest.

"Tell her to hang on till I get there," I said.

Sarah Jane was quiet for a few seconds and then started to chuckle.

"What's so funny?" I said.

"Brenda's the one who laughed first," Sarah Jane said. "She says her leg's a long way from her heart and she'll be fine until you get there. She thinks she might have done something to one of those ligaments near her cannon bone when she was running around in the pasture. She thinks that's it because the same thing happened to her friend, the horse in the stall next to hers at the barn where she used to live before you and she hooked up. She remembers him describing how it felt and she says her leg feels the exact same way. That's why she's not too worried. Her friend was fine after some stall rest, and she says she could use the time off from Rob because he's starting to get on her nerves. You, she loves."

Talking horses, was I dreaming again? Who cared, at least she loved me.

CHAPTER 38

B y the time we got back to Charlotte, Lou was talking again. The problem was, he wasn't stopping. I was starting to wish I hadn't given him the Ritalin and just let the Zoloft slowly bring him back.

He was chattering about everything from how happy he was to even feel like talking to what Sarah Jane's plan should be. Given my father's take on the police, it didn't involve calling Tony or any of his brethren.

"Lou," I said, "we're not discussing this. Sarah Jane has no choice. You've got to be a grown-up here and encourage her to be one too."

The irony of me—the person who hasn't been to the dentist for three years because it hurts and who has bounced enough checks to finance a separate wing on Hugh McColl's Myers Park mansion—giving advice on how to be a grown-up made me smile.

Meanwhile Sarah Jane and Lou had just about switched roles. The closer we got to Charlotte, the less she talked, until she was as mute as he'd been in Asheville. On her part, however, it was more a case of abject terror than clinical depression.

No one, least of all Sarah Jane, objected to going directly to the barn before returning to my apartment to call Tony. Even if either had, it wasn't negotiable. I was just about half nuts with worry because other than Sarah Jane's "message" from Brenda, I had no idea what was happening with my horse. I'd called Gail several times from the road, but gotten no answer. So when the gravel road to February Farm appeared before me, I disregarded all old man Clark's reprimands about me driving too fast down the driveway. I gunned the engine and hightailed it to my ailing girl, spitting chunks of stone every which way and hoping the geriatric owner was home sipping some sherry in his Eastover living room. The car had barely come to a stop when I jumped out and sprinted to Brenda's stall.

She was lying down, and did she ever have that woe-is-me look on her face. I dropped to my knees and wrapped my arms around her neck, then blew softly in her nose. She pressed her head on my leg and I stroked her white blaze. I buried my face into hers and rubbed my forehead on the spot above her eye she loved me to scratch.

"Oh, pretty girl," I murmured, "what have you done to yourself? Please, please don't let it be anything bad."

I knew I should've gotten up to find Gail and see what the vet had to say, but I didn't know who was getting more comfort from our embrace, me or Brenda. She was leaning into me and I into her.

"Mind if I break you two lovebirds up?" It was the booming voice of Doc Lockton, a pink-skinned, white haired man who could've passed for Captain Kangaroo's brother. Doc Loc was the kind of veterinarian who cared about his patients as much as their owners did, sometimes even more. Many times, I'd seen him wipe the tears from his cheeks when things went the wrong way.

"Oh, hey, Doc," I said. My voice was quivery and I didn't try to mask it. If anyone understood this kind of sadness it was he. "She looks bad, huh?"

"It's not great, Nattie," he said. "She doesn't want to stand up and she can barely walk. Here, run your hand down the back of her leg. It's warmer than the other. What do you say we get some use out of my new ultrasound machine and see what's going on in there?"

I'd say I'm looking at a big vet bill, that's what I'd say. And stupidly, I didn't get medical insurance for her. But I've lived in a dirt-floored basement with no plumbing to support my horse habit in the past, so I said what I always say when it comes to the care of my equines: "Do whatever it takes, Doc."

Brenda wanted nothing to do with standing up. Finally we cajoled her to the vertical, albeit the three-legged vertical. Doc Loc wanted to ultrasound her in the aisle, but I couldn't stand to see her hobble one step farther. I convinced him to zap her right there in the stall.

Meanwhile Gail had come by with Lou and Sarah Jane in tow. She put her arms around me. "Don't worry, sweetie," she said to me.

Doc Loc busied himself gelling up her right front leg. When it was gooey enough, he bounced the ultrasound into where she was lame. Sure enough, on the screen was a dark spot running down her suspensory ligament.

I looked at his face. Doc Loc's easier to read than a Dick and Jane book. He was right, things weren't great.

"Well, Nattie, it's what I thought. She's torn her suspensory."

I looked at Sarah Jane. Had I been her, I'd be standing there like a puffed-out rooster, oozing I-told-you-so's through every pore in my body. She was looking down, kind of sheepishly.

A torn suspensory. I hadn't believed Sarah Jane in the car, not only because I didn't know yet whether I believe in horse communicators, but because I didn't want to. Blown suspensories are serious injuries that take time and luck to heal. Despite the doomsday man in my head, I'd still been hoping for a simple stone bruise.

So much for hope. "How bad a tear? And what are we looking at in recovery time?"

"This is the part you're not going to like, Nattie," he said. "We could send her to Apex, where they've got all that fancy equipment that can tell you exactly how severe the suspensory's torn. But I'd advise you to save your money, for right now. Judging by what I see here, it could be a lot worse. If we treat her aggressively—keep her leg wrapped, inject it with hyaluranic acid—I'd say a month to six weeks in the stall, followed by another four months of limited turnout. Six months—at the least."

I felt myself take a sharp grab of air. Oh man, the perfect end to a day that included having my hotel room ransacked and bullets slicing even more split ends into my already frayed hair.

"That's the bad news," he said. "The good news, I've seen worse tears with the horse coming back completely sound."

I hate this good news/bad news stuff. It makes me feel like a total selfish ingrate. I know I should've been happy Brenda would probably be as good as new, given the horrible possibilities, but *at least* six months without my fix?

I felt even more awful when Brenda plopped back down on the sawdust with that sorry look on her face, the same one I was now wearing on mine. "You hear that, girl?" I said. "At least six months. You wanted time off from Rob? You've got it. You could've just asked, we could've arranged it without all this drama."

Gail looked at me like I was nuts. And maybe I was. But the first part of what Sarah Jane had told me Brenda said turned out to be true, so why not the other part?

"I'll explain later," I said. I had lots of questions to ask the doc about Brenda's condition and treatment, and I wanted to get them in before he got beeped to some colicking horse somewhere in Waxhaw or Weddington. Gail left about halfway through. She had to start feeding, and Lou and Sarah Jane decided to take a walk now that Lou had rejoined the living.

I'd gotten most of the answers I needed when Gail came back carrying the mobile phone. "It's for you," she said to the doc. "Jeannie Sukon. She said it couldn't wait."

Jeannie Sukon. The dominatrix married to Fuzzy's vulturine cousin. Interesting. I was sure it was business, because I knew Doc Loc was too sweet a man to get tangled in her formidable web. I hadn't realized she had an equine connection.

He put the phone to his ear and I heard his end of the conversation: "Swollen even more? Really? Right. Okay, I'll be there as soon as I finish here."

He handed the phone to me and started to leave. "Nattie, my dear, anything else I can tell you? As much as I'd prefer to stay here and talk to you, if I don't get to Anyday Farms soon that woman will beep me every three minutes."

"Anyday? That's Fuzzy's place, is that where you're going?" I said. "What's wrong there?"

"The Sukon woman and her husband's colt. Too bad about the little fellow. He's one gorgeous young lad. Bowed both front tendons and now she says it's getting worse."

I closed my eyes and pulled back the memory of the exquisite colt with the bandaged legs I'd seen the day of Fuzzy's murder. I focused on the card by the front of his stall. Now I remembered why Jason and Jeannie's name seemed familiar. Of course, they owned Dubonnet, the junior Ruskie.

"What happened to him anyway?" I said. "Isn't he kind of young to bow both tendons?"

"You bet'cha," Doc Loc said. "It doesn't happen often. I can't even think right off of the last time I saw something this severe in something so young. But, sad to say, it does happen. Who knows why, bad luck, a bad turn, weak conformation? I don't know. But to hear this woman talk, luck played no role in it whatsoever. It's always easier to look for someone to blame than accept the fact that rotten things happen for no reason."

"What do you mean?" I said. "I mean I know what you mean about rotten things happening for no reason, just look at Brenda. But what do you mean about Jeannie Sukon?"

Doc Loc shook his head. "That woman's convinced someone bowed her colt's tendons."

I know my eyebrows must've shot clear up to my hairline. "The only way to do that's with wraps, isn't it? She thinks someone wrapped her colt's legs tight enough to bow them?"

"Bingo, Nattie," Doc Loc said. "You know as well as I you can do more harm than good wrapping a horse's legs if you don't know what you're doing. But Cathy, the girl who manages Anyday, knows as much about wrapping as anyone. Besides, she swears the colt had nothing on its legs the night before they found him with the bows."

"It's kind of hard to bow a horse with no wraps," I said. "What does Jeannie Sukon think happened, the colt wrapped himself and then took them off before anyone could see?"

"Not far off," Doc Loc said. "She was pretty angry that day and wasn't hiding it. She was throwing around blame like crazy. That colt had cost them a lot of money. But it wasn't even the money she was so upset about. It was his destiny—a big word, for a little guy. They'd bought him as a junior hunter prospect for their daughter. They thought they'd move him up through the green conformation classes, get a name for himself, and then have him ready just in time for Becca's—that's their daughter—final junior year of showing. Thought they'd finally found a way to beat Fuzzy at her own game. Which is pretty hard to do these days because you know Fuzzy's been buying up the top horses in the country. I suppose they figured the only way to beat her was to make a top horse of their own, one that Fuzzy could never buy. And this colt was very, very fancy. If any horse could do it, this was the one."

"They bought a yearling for their daughter to eventually show in the junior division so she could beat Ashlee?"

"That's right. Becca Sukon and Ashlee have been riding to-gether since they were toddlers."

"Doc, what are you saying here?" I said. "That Jeannie Sukon thinks someone hurt the colt because that someone knew it would grow up fancy enough to knock Ashlee and her fleet out of the blue ribbons?"

He was nodding.

"That someone, might it have been Fuzzy McMahon?"

"Bingo," Doc Loc said.

CHAPTER 39

Jeannie and Jason Sukon, step right up to the top of my suspect list.

And to think I figured it was Family Value Store money that had the cousins in such a tiff. Little did I know it was something bigger, older, and far more primal than the pull of currency: the need to whomp someone's butt, the consuming hunger to be victorious, the thrill of the conquest.

Which is all to say Jeannie and Jason Sukon wanted their little Becca to throw Ashlee McMahon out of the winner's circle once and for all. They wanted *their* little girl collecting the blue ribbons, getting her photos in the *Chronicle of the Horse* and riding the victory gallop at Madison Square Garden. Apparently they wanted her there badly enough to do something as stupid as buying a yearling. There's only one thing riskier in the horse world than buying young stock with the expectation of getting a competitive horse, and that's breeding. Either way, you're headed for a heartbreak unless you're real lucky or your horse karma's real good.

It seemed the Sukons needed a karma-wash. The question was, if Fuzzy had bowed the colt's tendons, was that enough to drive someone to murder? Any reasoning person would automatically say no way; however, let me remind all reasoned souls of the Texas cheerleader mother who tried to pay someone to kill her kid's competition.

Times like this make it hard for me to have any hope for my kind. I remembered what Sarah Jane once told me a horse told her:

that way back when horses could have refused domestication and continued to run wild, they chose to serve humanity out of love and respect. Love and respect for what? A species of creatures that can't love or respect each other? Suspending disbelief for a minute, I bet there's many a horse today cursing his ancestors.

To bow a baby horse's tendons on purpose, now that's downright cruel. Whether it was heinous enough to warrant the death penalty could be debated. What Jeannie should've done was cracked Fuzzy good in the shins with a steel pipe. That's how that poor little colt must've felt. However, this was all still speculation on my part. It's possible, though highly unlikely, the colt bowed his own self by running around the pasture like an idiot. I didn't know, and Fuzzy sure wasn't going to be fessing up, at least not to my ears. Who's to say what happened on her judgment day?

Doc Loc didn't know if Jeannie Sukon had any proof that Fuzzy or one of Fuzzy's emissaries had wrapped her colt into a double bow. It looked as if Jeannie and I would be having ourselves a little chat.

Later, though. Right now we had other things to do. The call to Tony. Not only was it time for Sarah Jane to report in, but I thought Tony should know that someone was trying to scare me off by trashing my room and playing target practice with my head.

I got Brenda tucked in, wrapped, and medicated for the night, and then kissed her good-bye. Was that a nicker I heard as I shut her stall door? Get a grip, Nattie. This talking horses stuff was going to my head.

We drove home with Lou doing most of the talking. Every time I thought about telling him to stop, I forced myself to shut up and think of Meryl Streep in early Banana Republic. File this under Be Careful What You Ask the Gods For, chapter two.

To my surprise, Sarah Jane marched herself right up to my telephone. "What's his number, Nattie?" she said.

Maybe she really was turning over a new leaf. Maybe she and

McMahon didn't kill Fuzzy. The world tonight was filled with lots of maybes. I took the phone from her and dialed Tony's home number.

"Tony Maroni?" I said to his hello. His wife didn't answer. I wondered if she decided she wanted to be single this week.

"Nattie darlin', where you been keeping yourself, girl? I'm not even going to ask what you've been up to, 'cause I'm sure it's about as legal as a blind man driving an eighteen-wheeler down Tryon Street in an ice storm."

"I haven't broken any laws for a long time, if you don't count speeding," I said. "But I do have someone standing next to me I think you'll be right interested in talking to. How'd you like to have a chat with Sarah Jane Lowell?"

"You mean the Sarah Jane Lowell wanted by the police for questioning in the murder of one Fuzzy McMahon? That wouldn't be the same Sarah Jane Lowell who left town with one Louis Gold, father of Natalie Gold, reporter for *The Charlotte Commercial Appeal*? The same Natalie Gold who herself left town to find her father and the possible fugitive from justice, Sarah Jane Lowell?"

If I could have reached through the wires to shake him, I would have.

"How'd you know all that?" I said. "What do you guys do there, employ a psychic?"

"Nattie, don't take this wrong, sweetheart, but even a half-dead dog learns from his mistakes, and I know you're smarter than a half-dead dog. Way smarter and a bunch cuter. But girl, you keep making the same dang fool mistake: assuming we're idiots down here just 'cause we talk slow and our grammar ain't as good as yours. I'd be twenty points shy of West Virginia normal not to keep track of you when we're working the same case."

I started laughing. It was good to talk to Tony, even if he'd outfoxed me, again. He was a darn good cop.

"Okay sweetie patootie," I said, "what don't you know, then?

I'll say three things, tell me if any ring a bell. Slashed tires. Trashed hotel room. Bullets whizzing by my head."

"Yes, no, and no," he said. "Lord, Nattie, it sounds like you've gotten someone real riled again. You sure do have a knack for that. Tell me what happened this time."

I filled him in on my Asheville adventures, and he did the telephone equivalent of nodding; he said uh-huh at each break. I couldn't ask him if he still considered Sarah Jane a prime suspect, since she was standing right next to me.

"Let me talk to her," he said.

I handed her the phone, and you bet I listened. She explained where she was at the time of Fuzzy's death—unfortunately, at home alone, meditating—and admitted to a liaison with Bobby Mc-Mahon. She also fessed up to her priors and said she'd be turning herself in to the Pennsylvania authorities once she cleared up things here. Then I heard her promise to stay at my place for the night.

She gave me the phone and went into the bathroom.

"Nattie," Tony said, "I'll be over first thing in the morning to talk to her. She says she'll stay put. Make sure she does, hear? I can't force her to stay. Don't tell her this, but those charges in Pennsylvania have been dropped. The old fool she bilked changed his story."

"But what about the shovel you found by her door?" I whispered. "You sure intimated it had Fuzzy's blood all over it."

"It had blood, all right, just not the kind of blood anyone but the SPCA would be interested in," Tony said, "Besides, now it's looking like it wasn't a shovel that killed her anyway."

"Really?" I said. "What'd you do, find some kind of mark on Fuzzy that didn't look like a shovel?"

Tony laughed. "Lord, I should've known better than to say anything but hello to you. I guess it won't hurt anything, me telling you, since that wild-haired nutty guy from your paper's putting it in his story tomorrow. They sent Fuzzy McMahon's body to the

M.E. in Chapel Hill. It was definitely a blow to the head that killed her, but whoever done the killing used something kind of funny to hit her. It left a flat circle mark on her."

"Guess you guys'll be busy looking for a flat-circled tool," I said. "Wonder what it could be?"

"Stop wondering, that's what keeps getting you in trouble, all your wondering this and wondering that," Tony said. "You call me right away if anything funny happens there tonight. I mean anything, any strange noises or any of them weird feelings you get. And make sure your door is locked good and tight. You do have a way of shaking people up, and it's looking like you're shaking someone pretty good. Just because this person missed the first time doesn't mean there won't be a second time. Want me to bring Rin over?"

Just what I needed: an old, arthritic, near deaf dog who thought I was his soulmate. As much as I loved the old boy and was very grateful to him for helping Tony find me in the woods many moons ago, thereby saving my life, the last thing I wanted to do was share my already overcrowded apartment with a snoring and, I'm sorry Rin, smelly dog. I politely declined Tony's offer and promised to wriggle-chain the three of us in.

I hated to hang up, but I couldn't sleep on the telephone with him. Though it was an intriguing idea. Intriguing, but stupid and self-destructive to even go near that thought. If I didn't get it through my hormone-infected brain once and for all that Tony was married and that was that, I was in real danger of screwing up things with Henry.

And it's not that I didn't have the hots for the tall boy. I did and do, but whenever Tony came into the picture with his slow drawl and dark eyes, I just wanted to run my fingers through his hair and feel myself bounce around his curls.

Can a woman carry a torch for two men? I'll probably get that answer when I hear the sound of one hand clapping.

Right now, however, I barely had the energy to brush my teeth let alone ponder the whys of the universe. Apparently neither did Lou and Sarah Jane, who were settling in for the night. He on his futon, she on the couch. I was also looking forward to taking the express train to dreamland, but speaking of Henry, I'd promised to call him when I got home. A little voice answered the phone.

"Hey, Hanksters, it's Nattie, whatcha doing?" I said.

"*X-Files*," he said. I took that to mean he'd forced his father to let him watch a tape of the show.

"Okay, Fox," I said, "this is Scully, put the smoking man on the phone."

That got a laugh out of him. "She wants the smoking man" I heard him say. Henry came to the phone, chuckling.

"You're back sooner than I thought," he said. "Things must've gone well."

Now it was my turn to chuckle. "That," I said, "depends on your definition of well."

For the second time in less than five minutes, I told my tale of Asheville. And for the second time in five minutes I was again offered bodily protection.

"Want me to come over?" Henry said.

All this male concern was starting to make me giddy. I politely refused. Three Goodes, two Golds, and one Lowell in my apartment would not make for a happy night.

"*Et tu?*" I said, reaching the limits of my French. The only other thing I remember clearly from ninth-grade French class was Mademoiselle Duchette squinting her eyes behind her black Harlequin glasses and constantly saying, "*Nat-ah-LEE, fermez la grande bouche.*"

I switched to my native tongue. "Anything new on Quarrels? Oh, before I forget, you'll love this: my witch buddy in Asheville left a weird message for me. She told me to watch out for a lying child. One can only assume, *mon petit*, that's your lying child. And I don't mean the ones you've spawned. I'm talking about your accuser. I'm sure Lady Passion would go on record if you want to quote her directly."

"Maybe I could also consult your Ouija board," Henry said. "You do have one, don't you?"

"Right next to my Magic 8 ball. I use it to talk to David."

Henry laughed. He thought I was joking. I wasn't, about either statement.

"So?" I said, "what about Quarrels? What happens next?"

"Check out the mother, see what I can find out about her. Interview other parishioners. Talk to some experts in the field of molestation. See if the boy's teacher will talk to me. I hate to do it, but talk to the boy and then make an appointment to talk to Quarrels."

"Sounds dicey, Henry," I said. "Watch out on this one. My radar's screaming, 'Alert, alert.' I know you don't believe in any of this woo-woo stuff, but something's wrong with the picture."

"Possibly so," he said. "But I'm not rushing into print, you know that."

Was that the understatement of the year. Henry's never rushed into anything in his life, whereas I've never gone slower than a blur. If things should proceed between us, we would be the ultimate odd couple, and not just in height.

"Any other thoughts on the mother?" he said.

I'd already filled him in on how I knew her, that she was the Total Female's official escort during my interview.

"Just that she seemed so squirrelly, kind of like she was waiting to get hurt," I said. "You know that look? The one that's sort of a half question with a slight veneer of cower? You see it on women with no self-esteem, the ones batted all around by what people— men people—think of them. Okay, okay, I'll stop. I know, I'm starting to sound like Betty Friedan."

"It's all right," Henry said, "I like a woman with an add-DEEE-tood."

That was Philadelphia speak for attitude. He'd never heard a thick Philadelphia accent until my healing hands aunt came cruising down the East Coast on her Palm Beach run. She winters there every year in her all-white trailer with her all-white carpet and her all-white furniture, where she eats pomegranates by the white moonlight. Aside from thinking she was a total, but charming, loony tune—the only baggage she carried with her was three crates of pomegranates—he was intrigued by the twists and turns her words took.

"That's interesting about the mother," he said. "I don't know if it has anything to do with my story, but I'll keep it in mind. Anything else?"

I still couldn't remember what it was that had been tugging at my mind about her.

"Nope," I said. "I'm headed off to dreamland. I've got to put an end to this day before something worse happens, if that's possible."

CHAPTER 40

I t was.

Despite Tony's and Henry's concern, nothing more dramatic happened during the night than the crashing peal of the telephone followed by a wad of thick, dead air. Another hang-up. I didn't even bother to press *69 anymore. What was the point? I'd just waste seventy-five cents to find some giggly preteen or heavy-breathing jerk with a stiff pecker who thought it was sport to annoy newspaper columnists.

Since my picture's in the paper every Sunday, I get lots of weird calls. I used to hear regularly from Mr. Holiday Inn. I call him that because he'd telephone me every so often, swearing we'd danced away the night at the Holiday Inn in Gastonia.

Tony was on his way over and Sarah Jane was scrambling up some tofu. I was standing in the kitchen, drinking my morning caffeine fix and talking to her. I didn't know if any of what she was telling me was true, but it was interesting.

I'd asked her flat out how and why she became what she did.

"On one hand you're talking all this peace, love, and white light stuff," I said, "and on the other you're taking old guys for everything they've got. What gives, Sarah Jane? Then there's the way you look and sound and carry yourself, like you're straight out of Updike country; tennis lessons at the club, barbecues by the backyard pool, sailing in the Sound. They don't teach grifting at Miss Porter's, do they?"

In the last two days, not much could make Sarah Jane laugh. I guess pondering your future behind bars evaporates a sense of humor pretty quickly. I know I'd told Tony I wouldn't tell her she wasn't going to jail, at least not for her pre–North Carolina exploits, but I couldn't stand to see that mopey face of hers. I didn't tell her exactly that the geezer dropped the charges, just hinted that things wouldn't be as dire as she thought, assuming she really didn't kill Fuzzy—an assumption I hadn't completely bought. That lightened her mind a little, at least enough to get a small chuckle out of her.

"I didn't go to Miss Porter's, Nattie," Sarah Jane said. "And I didn't go to the University of Chicago like I told you."

"I know that," I said. After Les unloaded her rap sheet on me, the first thing I did was place a call to the registrar at the U of C. The closest they could come to a Sarah Jane Lowell was Sarah Johnson Lowell, class of 1951. Even the best plastic surgery couldn't erase that many years.

"Of course you would by now," she said. "I went to Einstein High in Wheaton, Maryland, just outside Washington. We didn't belong to a country club, I never took tennis lessons, and we swam at the county pools with the rest of the suburban middle class. I come from a totally unremarkable, boring family, house, neighborhood, life. Both my parents worked for the government, we lived in a three-bedroom split-level, I have a little brother named John who works at the Library of Congress. The only thing of note in my growing up was I probably shoplifted twenty thousand dollars worth of tapes, clothes, shoes, whatever, without getting caught. I was very good at it. That and I was Queen of the Prom."

I bet she was. Looks are something you can't manufacture. At least not easily. As for her shoplifting tendencies, I put that up there with her God-given appearance—something she was born with. I'm sure they'll find a sticky fingers gene someday, maybe two rungs down from my personal favorite—Mr. DRD4—the adventure gene. How else can you explain why one kid in a family turns out to be a grifter, the other a librarian?

It's the old nature versus nurture issue again, and there was no question to me which makes us what we are.

Sarah Jane was on a roll and kept talking. I guess it felt good to unload, or maybe it was just another piece of her performance art. Whatever, here's what she says happened: after high school, she commuted to the University of Maryland, had no idea what she wanted to do with her life, so she took English lit classes.

"I was so bored, I thought I'd die," she said.

One afternoon she and a few girlfriends cut Contemporary American Drama and cruised up Route 1 looking for something more fun to do than read about George and Martha's problems in *Who's Afraid of Virginia Woolf?* On Sarah Jane's dare, they pulled into Madame Teresa's parking lot and went in to see the palm reader.

"She predicted stupid things, that I would meet a short man with lots of money, that I'd have three kids, things like that. But her presence fascinated me. Everything about her fascinated me, from her dyed black hair to the raised blue veins on her hands."

"Was she for real?" I asked. "I mean, did she have any kind of gift?"

This time Sarah Jane didn't just chuckle, she out and out laughed.

"You've got to be kidding," she said. "A gift? Sure she had a gift. The gift of grift. She wasn't honest, of course she wasn't honest. She wasn't boring, was what she was. I went by to see her every day and badgered the you-know-what out of her just to let me hang out there. You can imagine how thrilled my parents were to find out I was spending all my time with a Puerto Rican convict pretending to be a Gypsy fortune-teller. But I threatened to drop out of college, so they let me alone."

As it turns out, Sarah Jane did graduate with a degree in English literature, which left her a few employment options: Hardee's, McDonald's, or KFC. Instead she chose Madame Teresa's, calling herself Sister Sarah.

"The interesting thing was, lots of the time I wasn't making it up like Teresa was doing. One of the reasons I'd been so attracted to Teresa was because all my life I've heard voices, had imaginary friends, known things before they happened."

Under the influence of someone other than Madame Teresa, Sarah Jane might've gone another way. Though probably not, given whatever undiscovered genes were rattling around inside her. With Teresa's help and guidance, she flourished at bilking the unfortunate, became an expert at getting easy, quick money from people looking for something they'd never have. Teresa wound up getting busted for a particularly nasty scam involving an old, arthritic woman in a wheelchair. Luckily for Sarah Jane, who'd helped her, she'd been out shopping and just pulled into the parking lot when she saw the police cars there.

"I pointed my car north and never went back. So there it is, Nattie. The sorry but true tale of Sarah Jane Lowell."

I raised my eyebrows. "Ever considered writing fiction?"

She laughed again, and so did I. "I don't blame you for not believing me," she said. "I wouldn't either. Ready for breakfast? Hey, Lou, let's eat."

Lou didn't hear since he was jumping on his rebounder, pounding his fists against his skull and chanting some guttural Celtic prayer he'd learned at Finnhorn, a spiritual retreat near Stonehenge he and my neighbor Mrs. Flock had gone to. I walked over, tapped him on the shoulder and pointed to the table.

I looked at the clock. It was still only eight-thirty on a Sunday morning, too early to call the Sukon home. We had time for a quick bite before we headed over to Anyday Farms. If I was lucky, maybe I'd catch up with Jason or Jeannie there.

I'd arranged with Cathy, Anyday's barn manager, for all of us to come out right after breakfast. When I told her why, first she laughed and then said, "Why not?"

Even I, the daughter of the biggest flake east of the Lemon Grass Institute, couldn't believe we were doing this. And the funniest part was, it was Tony's idea.

He'd called at seven-thirty, wondering if I was still alive and if Sarah Jane was still with me or had slipped out into the night, stealing my father again.

"Oh come on, Tony," I said, "I think there's a good side to her. I saw it yesterday on the way home from Asheville."

"Oh yeah?" he said. "What'd she do, poke a Piggly Wiggly checkout girl in the head with a gun to get money for gas?"

"Tony, where's your generosity of spirit, boy? People can change—if they want to."

Then I told him about Sarah Jane doing that weird thing with her hands and how it really did calm me down. He didn't start laughing until I got to the part about Brenda telling Sarah Jane she didn't want me to worry about her.

"Nattie, darlin', did that girl put something in your tea? Or you been smoking it? What are you gonna tell me next, she's getting messages from Mr. Ed? Tell her to ask him from me how they got his mouth to move. I got me a twenty dollar bet riding on it with a buddy of mine. I say they sprinkled his lips with pepper, he says they used strings. Talking horses, huh? If that's the case why don't we just take ourselves on down to that barn and ask that pony who did it. Far as I can tell, he's the only living witness to the murder, excepting the one who did the murdering."

Well, hit me upside the hay-ad with a two by four. Why hadn't I thought of that?

"Anthony D'Angeles Odom," I said. "Your mama sure done born herself one smart little colt. That's exactly what we should do. I'll get everything arranged by the time you get here. 'Bye."

I hung up before he had a chance to laugh.

Why not ask Blue By You? Fuzzy was found in *his* pasture. Surely he saw who brought her there.

I ran this idea by Sarah Jane, who was now serving us her scrambled Tofu Tumble. She'd offered to wait for Tony, but I told her he was more a grits and red-eye gravy man.

"Sure I'll give it a try," she said. "But you know as well as I do, whatever I hear from that pony, your policeman friend is going to think I'm making it up."

She was probably right, but it would give me something to go on. And should it come to pass that the pony did finger Fuzzy's murderer, it would make one terrific story, one that I could convince Candace to let me write. I'd pitch it as a follow-up to my horse whisperer story.

The horse whisperer story. Darn, in all the hysteria I'd forgotten my story was running today. If I was lucky—and Candace had thrown her weight around—they'd be promo-ing it on the front page.

Chalk it up more to her weight than my luck. On the top of the front page: "Carolinas' Own Horse Whisperer. Nattie Gold talks to the man who talks to the animals. Page 1D, Carolina Living."

Even after all these years in the newspaper business, it's still a rush to see my name in print, especially on the top of a front page that goes to 300,000 people. And you can bet the boys in the chain count on that rush; that way they can get away with paying us what they do. While seeing my name is pretty terrific, seeing my words come to life is even better. I flipped to our section front and there she was, the story that practically wrote itself. I didn't read it. I knew what it said, when it said it better, before Ron Riley's twitchy fingers wrecked it.

There was a small knock at the door and I looked up to see Tony letting himself in.

"Dang, girl, I thought you said you keep your door locked. I coulda been a murderer," he said.

"Maybe you are," I said, and reached my arm around his

shoulder to give him a hug. He seemed kind of deflated. Only one thing does that to him. "How's things with the missus?"

"Don't ask and I'll keep my sad stories to myself," he said. "I'm tired of sounding like a bad George Jones song. We shoulda written ourselves a living will along with our vows, swearing we'd be smart enough to know when to pull the plug before one of us got to where there was nothing but empty space left. Enough of that, so you want to go talk to the pony? Just don't tell anyone at the sheriff's office I did this. Deal?"

"Deal," I said and shook his hand.

Before we left, Lou offered Tony a glass of his power drink. Despite his mother's Italian roots, Tony was Southern enough to be polite at all costs, including drinking what looked like pool scum, which wasn't far from what it was. If he'd been a woman, he'd not only have taken the drink graciously, but added in the sweetest magnolia voice possible, "Idn't this interesting?"

Lou watched him drink it, and when he finished said, "In twenty minutes you'll feel it kick in."

Tony laughed. "I expect I will. Nattie, how come you're not drinking it?"

" 'Cause I'm not Southern. I can tell Lou exactly what I think."

CHAPTER 41

We piled in Tony's red Blazer, the only automotive choice. My car was too small to cram in four grown-ups, and Lou's hardly ran. On the way, Sarah Jane told Tony how it works for her. First she closes her eyes, then says a prayer asking for protection from nuisance spirits. After that she clears her mind to get rid of all the chatter so she can hear what the horse is trying to say to her.

"Sometimes they talk in words," she said. "Sometimes images."

I could see a smile start to seep across Tony's face. He stopped short of laughing—those Southern roots of his again.

"Well," he said, "I guess they thought Alexander Graham Bell was nuttier than a Baby Ruth when he started talking about sending voices through wires."

Ever the Dixie gentleman, putting even possible murder suspects at ease.

I ran by the idea of stopping at my barn on the way but was vetoed before I even finished the sentence. I'd already talked to Gail twice this morning to make sure Brenda was okay, plus I'd asked Sarah Jane to ring her up psychically and ask her how she was feeling. Even though I'm not sure I believe, I thought I'd cover all the bases, just in case.

"She said her leg is throbbing a little, but it's nothing she can't handle," Sarah Jane said. "She wants you to stop worrying and she also wants you to know Rob came into her stall last night and couldn't have been nicer. Gave her some hay, brushed her face, even kissed her. Now she's feeling bad about saying those things about him."

Guilt, she was feeling guilt. She was definitely my horse.

We got to Anyday Farms and found Cathy and Ebert standing by the front of the barn to greet us. And to my surprise, so was Ashlee.

"Ashlee Feldman McMahon," I said, "what's a thirteen-year-old doing out of bed before noon on a Sunday non-horse-show morning?"

"Jeannie told me you were coming," she said. "And bringing a horse psychic. I want to talk to Blue, so I got Daddy to drive me here from Gram's."

Sure enough, there was McMahon's truck. I hadn't noticed it when we drove up because it was parked around the side. Just as I was about to ask where Daddy was, I heard the gravel crunching. Two cars were coming our way, a taupe Lexus and a silver Mercedes.

Jeannie Sukon emerged from the Lexus, Carter and Ralston Evans from the Mercedes. Ralston ran up to Ashlee and the two thirteen-year-olds burst into giggles. Great, we had practically my entire suspect list gathered to hear the pony say who done it. The only one missing was the maid, and I'd have bet my plastic horse collection she didn't do it. Not exactly the quiet chat with Blue By You I'd intended.

"Cathy," I said, "do I have you to thank for making this a party?"

"You didn't say not to," she said.

She had a point.

McMahon sauntered out from inside the barn. Poor guy, he didn't know who to eye-lock first, me or Sarah Jane or Jeannie, in black jeans tight enough for me to see what he'd been ogling at, or Carter, who already had her eyes riveted on him. I could've sworn I started to smell his brain short-circuit.

Before he completely fried, I, being the hostess of sorts, made the introductions. Talk about the tangled webs we weave. Standing within ten feet of one another were one set of current lovers—Sarah Jane and Bobby McMahon; one set of possible former/current lovers—Jeannie and Bobby McMahon; one set of wannabe lovers, at least on one side—Carter and Bobby McMahon; one almost set of lovers—myself and the often mentioned McMahon; four possible murder suspects—McMahon, Sarah Jane, Carter, and Jeannie; one cute cop—Tony; one deaf guy—Lou; and two pubescent, giggly girls, one of whom was the murder victim's daughter.

Hold a fluorescent tube up and it would have lit, that's how charged the air was.

McMahon looked at Sarah Jane and I saw something more than hello pass between them. Sarah Jane had told me her relationship with him was purely carnal and one she'd told him she didn't plan to continue. But Sarah Jane had told me many things, most of which turned out to be lies.

Was that a meet-you-later look of two lovers who couldn't wait to get their hands on one another again? Or a don't-say-anything-I've-got-it-handled look from one murderer to another? Darned if I knew.

McMahon walked over to Ashlee and slid his arm around her shoulder. "Hey, Ash-peeps, you wanting me to stay, or come back and pick you up after you talk to your pony?"

She slipped under his arm, looking very comfortable there. Both of them did, actually, and I was seeing a new, better side of the sleazeball. He stroked her hair and kissed the top of her head.

"Ralston and I are gonna ride afterward," Ashlee said, "so if you've got something to do, you can come back later. Unless you've got something to ask Blue. That's the lady who says she can talk to horses," she added, and pointed to Sarah Jane.

"So I've heard," McMahon said, or rather, oozed. Then the Smile seeped across his face and he was definitely flashing it Sarah

Jane's way. I guess he hadn't gotten Sarah Jane's termination notice—or maybe it had never been sent.

While McMahon was busy eye-locking and smiling up Sarah Jane, Jeannie Sukon was getting hotter by the nanosecond. Her jaw tightened, her lips squinched, and her eyes slitted. She was doing her own dominatrix spin on the eye lock, aimed directly at Mc-Mahon. It wouldn't take a psychic to figure out she was not happy not to be the object of McMahon's attention. And she was clearly a woman who didn't like not getting what she wanted.

Carter Evans wasn't a happy camper either. She'd switched her stare Sarah Jane's way, and as one woman who's felt inadequate many times in her life, I could easily guess what she was doing—comparing herself to the competition, and not faring well. It's a difficult lesson to learn, and not one I've completely assimilated, but this comparison stuff is poison to your psyche. Use another person as a yardstick and you're bound to come up short, it's the very nature of comparison. There has to be a loser, and it's almost always the measurer because there will always be someone taller, thinner, smarter, or prettier. In Sarah Jane's case, she was all of the above, plus blonder.

"So you talk to horses, do you?" Carter Evans said.

There was a mean edge in her voice, and I didn't like where this was headed. Before Carter could continue I clapped my hands together, making pretend I was Lauren Tewes on *The Love Boat*. "All right," I said, with such a chirp in my voice I made even myself sick, "are we ready to start?"

I looked at Sarah Jane. She was remarkably unruffled.

"Sure," she said. "Let's see what Blue says happened."

That stopped everyone in their tracks. Ashlee turned toward me and said, "What'd she mean, 'see what Blue says happened'?"

"Didn't Jeannie tell you?" I said.

"Tell me what? She told me a woman who could talk to horses was coming to the barn with a newspaper reporter."

213

Oh lord, it was up to me to tell the kid we were trying to find her mother's murderer. When I did, she blanched, and I didn't blame her one bit.

"Maybe we should do this another time," I said.

Ashlee looked at her father. He squeezed her shoulder and whispered something in her ear.

"No, that's okay. I want to hear," she said. "I mean *as if* horses could talk anyway."

"Yeah, this oughta be good for a laugh," Carter said, and did— laugh.

Meanwhile, Jeannie had walked over to McMahon and pulled him to the side. I heard her say, "Bobby, I need to talk to you for a second."

Tony was hanging back, taking it all in. Lou was talking to Ebert, trying to get him to give up fatty foods. Not that he needed to. If the man stood sideways and stuck out his tongue, he'd be mistaken for a zipper. Cathy was smirking and Ralston was splitting her ends.

That left me and Ashlee standing by the front door. "Sure you want to do this?" I said. "I could just as easily come back another time with Sarah Jane if this makes you feel uncomfortable."

She stood there for a second, rubbing the toe of her paddock boot in the dust. "Nah," she said. "That'd be stupid for you to come back with her. She's probably making it all up anyway. She's real pretty, she's one of Dad's girlfriends, isn't she? I can tell by the way he looks at her."

This was turning from bad to worse. I didn't answer right away. What would I say?—yes, she along with half of southeast Charlotte?

"You don't have to answer that," Ashlee said. "I know all about it, everyone does. I mean everyone in screaming distance of Mom knew about Dad's girlfriends. That's what she used to yell about. I mean like it wasn't the only thing she used to yell about, but it was the big thing. Don't take this wrong, but I didn't blame him, like who'd have wanted to be married to someone like her anyway? All she ever did was scream and drink. Everyone thinks I'm so lucky 'cause I have all these horses and everything, but they didn't have to have her for a mother."

I didn't have much to say to that either. I couldn't exactly agree with her and say, "Yeah, Ashlee, I hear she was a real turbowitch."

I thought about going the Lou route and offering some new age platitude like, "There's a lesson in everything, our job is to figure out what it is." But then I remembered what it felt like to be thirteen, so I said:

"You know, Ashlee, life sucks sometimes. Maybe next time around you'll get a better mother. Of course you could also wind up short and fat and poor."

It was nice to see her smile.

"You're not like any other grown-up I know," she said.

"That's because I'm still trying to figure out how to grow up. If you've got any tips, pass them my way. Okay, kiddo, what do you say we go talk to your pony now—or watch Sarah Jane make it all up? Whatever you want to believe is fine by me."

We walked to Blue's stall, where the party had gathered. All of them. Lou, Sarah Jane, Tony, Cathy, Ebert, Jeannie, Carter, Ralston, and Bobby. Blue was pacing like a wild lion in a cage for the first time. Ashlee slid open the door and stepped in. That calmed him down.

"He hates being inside," she said. He nuzzled at her hand, and I saw why—she was feeding him those swirly red and white mint restaurant candies. He continued to nuzzle at her, even after her candy supply ran out.

"Ready, Sarah Jane?" I said.

"Any time you are," she said.

"Let's do it," I said.

Sarah Jane closed her eyes and stood silent for a few minutes.

This must have been the praying-for-protection-from-nuisance-spirits phase. I wondered if it would work with nuisance editors.

"Hi Blue," I heard Sarah Jane murmur to him as she stroked his neck. Her eyes were still closed and she started to smile.

"He says he loves the peppermint candies and wants to know if Ashlee has any more," Sarah Jane started.

That brought more than a few eye rolls and a snort from Carter Evans. Well what was everyone expecting, he'd say right off who whacked his human's mother?

"He wants me to tell Ashlee he misses going to shows with her and he plans to have a little talk with her new jumper, Kiss-Me, that Olympic mare with the holier-than-thou attitude. He says he doesn't care how many gold medals she's won, he's going to tell her if she refuses a jump one more time with Ashlee on her back, he's going to kick her in those world champion legs of hers. Ashlee, he wants you to know he doesn't blame you, he knows it was your mother who wanted you to stop showing in the pony division. And you're right, he says he does hate being in a stall. He wants to be outside. But he wants me to ask Cathy to switch pastures. He doesn't like his anymore."

Here we go. I felt a jolt of adrenaline.

"Sarah Jane," I said, "ask him why he doesn't like his pasture anymore."

She was silent for a moment.

"He says, you know why."

A coy pony. "Ask him if it's because that's where Fuzzy was."

Again Sarah Jane was quiet. This time for longer. Finally she said, "He won't answer me."

"Tell him to do it for Ashlee," I said.

More time passed. "He still won't answer," she said. "All he'll tell me is that he wants to go out in the front pasture by the road, instead of the one near the creek."

A recalcitrant interviewee. I applied the same principle I would if I were interviewing a human: ask the question again, with different words. This time I went for the straightforward approach.

"Ask Blue if he saw who buried Fuzzy," I said.

I know this sounds ridiculous, but I swear I saw the pony's ears pin back. Sarah Jane was quiet even longer.

"He won't answer and he says to stop asking the same question, he's not stupid. He says he's finished talking."

"Just ask him one more time," I said. "See if you can't get an image instead of words."

Sarah Jane started shaking her head. "Nattie, sorry, it doesn't work that way. He doesn't want to talk anymore. I can't force him, I can't invade his thoughts or feelings or drop in his brain to see what he's seeing. It's a conversation, same as I'd have with you or anyone else. I don't know why he won't talk anymore. He just won't. Sorry, I did the best I could."

I looked at Tony and gave him an oh-well look. "I guess it's back to regular detective work," I said.

Tony was smiling. He didn't have to tell me he'd just come along to indulge my genetically set whacko tendencies. I knew it, and even though nothing happened, I was grateful he'd come. I walked over to him and squeezed his hand.

"Thanks anyway," I said. "Ready to head out?"

"You betcha," Tony said. "Just one more thing. Sarah Jane, would you ask the pony how they got Mr. Ed's lips to move."

Now Sarah Jane looked annoyed. "Tony," she said, "I don't make fun of your work and I wish you wouldn't make fun of mine."

Tony held up his hand. "Whoa now," he said. "I'm not making fun of you. I got me a bet riding on this and I don't care how I get the answer."

Sarah Jane turned from Tony back toward Blue. "Huh?" she said. "Oh, okay, I'll tell him. He says he'll answer that if you tell him how Jesse Helms gets his eyes to go in different directions."

Tony did a double take. He didn't know whether to laugh or be shocked. That's when Sarah Jane started laughing.

"Just kidding," Sarah Jane said. "Blue didn't say anything about Jesse Helms or Mr. Ed. How would he know about either of them? He's never watched TV or read a newspaper. I just wanted to see how Tony liked being on the receiving end. What Blue really said was he wanted to know if anyone had any more of those mints."

CHAPTER 42

I can't say Sarah Jane bowled everyone over with her psychic abilities. She did, however, make Jeannie Sukon happy, or as happy as she could be with McMahon looking at Sarah Jane instead of her.

After Blue quit talking, Jeannie asked Sarah Jane to come to her colt's stall and ask him who did what to his tendons. I knew what she suspected and I didn't think it was anything for Ashlee to hear. Thinking of your mother as a drunken shrew is one thing, thinking of her as a cruel-hearted horse maimer is another.

"Hey, Bobby," I said to McMahon, who was edging Sarah Jane's way, "why don't you take Ashlee and Ralston out to the Circle K and get them some Chee•tos or something."

I leaned over to him and whispered why. He nodded and actually thanked me for thinking of Ashlee.

"Girls, y'all come on with me," he said. "Let's go get us something real bad to eat."

Carter Evans seized the moment. She looped a girl under each arm and walked toward McMahon's truck. "We'll all go," she said.

The four of them squeezed into McMahon's truck, and you can guess where Carter positioned herself—practically in his lap.

The rest of us went over to the gorgeous colt's stall. Was he ever something to look at. William Holland, the horse communicator I'd interviewed for the story I'd written, told me horses love inhabiting horse bodies. When I asked him why, he'd laughed and said, "Just look at them, wouldn't you?"

Another stupid question on my part. While most kids wanted to be doctors or lawyers or actors or something reasonable like that when they grew up, I'm the woman who used to be the girl who, when some towering grown-up leaned down to ask what I wanted to be, the answer was always the same: a horse.

By my way of looking at things, you'd be hard pressed to find a more majestic, breathtaking creature in all of creaturedom. With necks that slide into an arch of perfect harmony, you can hear the music of the curve if you're horse-crazy enough; and their heads chiseled and carved like the great canyons out west punctuated with those eyes, deep, brown wells that look like they'd forgive anyone anything; and their bodies of taut muscles, curved and stretched over a frame that melds power with beauty; yes sir, I'd say it's easy to see why horses like being horses. They won the genetic beauty lottery. And when you get one that looks like this fellow, it's hard to imagine a more perfect-looking collection of DNA.

"Jeannie," I said, "that's one magnificent colt you've got there."

She looked mad enough to double as an air-gun nail spitter.

"Magnificent—if his goddamned tendons weren't bowed," she said.

"Even with that," I said, "he's still pretty magnificent to me. I'd keep him just to be able to look at him."

If she could've growled, she would have. Instead she turned to Sarah Jane and said, "Not that I believe any of this, but since you're here, ask him what happened to his legs."

"Sure," she said, "I'd be happy to."

Sarah Jane was being downright magnanimous, under the circumstances. Not only was Jeannie Sukon being unpleasant, but it didn't look as if she'd be coughing up any dough. This was Sarah Jane's business after all, at least her more legitimate business. She usually got a hundred bucks a pop for a consult, and Jeannie Sukon hadn't even asked nicely.

She walked in the little guy's stall and rubbed his neck. Then she closed her eyes and went through the same spirit protection procedure as before. After a few minutes she opened her eyes.

"He's a very sweet little boy," Sarah Jane said. "He says he doesn't like what happened to his legs any better than you do. Not only do they hurt, but he says they make him look funny. He's a little on the vain side, not that I can blame him. He says from the second he was born, humans have been going crazy about his looks. And now that he's got these funny-looking things on his legs, he's worried that no one will like him."

Sarah Jane rubbed his neck again and cooed into his ear. "Don't worry, Dubie," she whispered, "everything will turn out fine."

Then she turned to us and said, "You know, he's a lot like a beautiful woman who's told every time she turns around how beautiful she is. After a while she starts believing that's all she's got, because that's all she ever hears about. Lots of people think beauty is a blessing, but it's more of a curse, if you ask me. Sure, it can open some doors, but sometimes it's better those doors stay closed."

Jeannie Sukon was looking at her like she was nuts. If I had to guess what she was thinking, I bet it went along the lines of, Easy for you to say, with that face of yours. However, she had other things on her agenda than the perils of great beauty.

"Okay, okay," she said. "Just ask him how it happened. Ask him if someone did this to him."

Sarah Jane closed her eyes again. A few moments passed. She opened her eyes and shook her head.

"I may have done some rotten things in my life," she said, "but this is—" She shook her head again and tears filled her eyes. "—this is . . . It's hard to believe someone could be so cruel."

Jeannie Sukon was almost jumping up and down. "Who, Sarah Jane? Who did what?"

"Fuzzy," Sarah Jane said. "Dubie says Fuzzy came into his stall after Cathy left for the night and wrapped some things around his front legs really tight and bumpy. The next morning, he says, it felt like his legs were on fire and he could hardly walk."

Jeannie slammed her hands together. "Dammit to hell," she said. "I knew it. I knew that woman couldn't stand the thought of me having a better horse. I knew it, I just knew. I told Jason it was Fuzzy, and he kept saying, 'Even Fuzzy wouldn't do something like that.' I knew it."

So now Jeannie Sukon was a believer. Funny, just five minutes ago she was rolling her eyes with the rest of the bunch. I didn't point out that there was a better than fifty-fifty chance that Sarah Jane was lying, again.

If nothing else, Sarah Jane was one smart cookie, and I'm sure she realized making Fuzzy a horse maimer put Jeannie Sukon square in the suspect seat.

This was about as much horse mumbo-jumbo as Tony could take. Though he was too polite to roll his eyes during Dubie's time to talk, I could see him trying to hold back his smile.

"Well, ladies," he said, because by this time it was just me and Sarah Jane and Jeannie. Cathy and Ebert had gone back to work, and who knows where Lou had wandered to. "I'm thinking it's just about time for me to be getting on, if you don't mind. I got some errands to run. Hey, Sarah Jane, would you mind telling that young fella we got to be going now. Oh yeah, and tell him not to worry about those legs of his looking funny. Tell him females like it when males have some foibles to them, makes 'em feel like they got something they can work on fixing."

By this point Sarah Jane couldn't tell if Tony was joking or not. Either way, she'd have probably ignored him. Unlike me, she wasn't charmed one bit by his down-home humor. And that was just fine by me. Like I said earlier, the hazard of measuring is not a lesson that's completely assimilated into my core. Even though I have nothing but friendship going with Tony, I could easily have found myself in Carter Evans's shoes, comparing myself—unfavorably—to Sarah Jane, had there been any spark of mutual admiration between the two.

This being female is complicated stuff. Next time I'm coming back as a eunuch.

CHAPTER 43

I was pretty itchy myself to get home. Not exactly home, but to my barn, February Farm. Not only did I want to check in on Brenda in the flesh, but I wanted to talk to Rob and find out if he had any horses I could ride in the meantime, the six-month meantime while Brenda's suspensories healed.

As anyone who knows me knows, if I went even half that long without sitting atop a horse, there wouldn't be enough Prozac in the world to fix me.

Tony was on the quiet side riding back into town. Now that the talking horse diversion was gone, it probably gave him plenty of time to think about what was bothering him—his marriage. I didn't probe because Sarah Jane and Lou were sitting in the backseat. I knew something was off because he just said, "I'll take that into consideration," when I laid out my why-Jeannie-Sukon-was-the-murderer theory.

"You have to admit," I said, "Jeannie had the perfect reason to kill Fuzzy, and she certainly had the emotional motivation—rage, with a capital R. Did you see how mad she was back there? She was madder than a Charlotte developer whose zoning permit was denied—not that that would ever happen."

Even my bad simile or slam at the Queen City's building fervor didn't raise a smile. Poor Tony.

When he dropped us off, I told him to call me anytime he was in need of a big ear. He just smiled, sort of, and drove off.

I didn't know what Lou or Sarah Jane had planned. Myself, I didn't even bother going back to my apartment. I hopped in my car and headed straight back the way I'd just come; down Highway 16, past the teal-roofed suburban sprawl I'd galloped across when it was green grass.

Oddly enough, no one was at the barn. Rob, I knew, wouldn't be there for a little bit. Sunday mornings were his time to commune with whatever or whomever's upstairs, though I don't know why. Since I've known him, his religion has brought him nothing but anguish. He's been going to the same Southern Baptist church since they dunked his head in water or whatever it is they do to marry your soul to their savior. And by my way of thinking, he's been hearing the same line of hooey all that time—that being gay and Christian are mutually exclusive in their God's eye. If there were any cosmic justice, Jesus would come back as a drag queen and all the so-called Christians of the world would miss his return.

To my surprise, Gail wasn't there either. And I knew she wasn't at church. The only temple she worshiped at was the Temple of Torkesquist. Besides, she always worked Sunday mornings, specifically because Rob was never there then. No boarders were around either. My buddy Denise was probably sleeping in—with her latest bad-boy boy-toy. She had the bod of a Barbie doll and a face to match, so her dance card was always jammed. What I couldn't figure out is why it was always jammed with jerks.

Being alone in the barn didn't happen often, but it was great when it did. Just me and a barnful of horses. I moseyed my way over to Brenda's stall. From across the way I could see a note hanging by her door, probably from Gail, telling me where she'd gone. As I got closer I saw something hanging next to it, a black cord. Strange, I hadn't left anything there, and it wasn't like Gail to leave one wisp of hay out of place, let alone dangly things a horse could get tangled up in.

When I reached Brenda's stall, I saw what it was. This was no longer funny, mildly amusing, or even plain annoying. I'd entered the terror zone, which makes me mad. Really mad. I kicked the wall and startled poor Brenda out of her morning nap.

I rushed into her stall just as she was scrambling to all fours. "Easy girl, easy girl," I said as I ran my hands over her to make sure she wasn't harmed. She was fine, but I wasn't.

"Jesus H. Christ," I said, and ripped the note off the wall. I had a pretty good idea what it would say before I even read it. My terrorist had done a fine job of communicating his or her intent with the little gift on the stall door.

I looked at the writing. Big block letters in black Magic Marker: WHAT DO I HAVE TO DO TO GET YOU TO STOP ASKING QUESTIONS AND MIND YOUR OWN BUSINESS? NEXT TIME, I'LL PLUG HER IN.

Plug her in à la Tommy Burns, aka the Sandman. Burns, a prime example of pond scum disguising himself as human, was the horse hit man for hire who killed his overinsured victims by that very method—by plugging them into the wall and frying them from the inside out. Here's how it worked: he attached an alligator clip to the horse's lip and another one to its rectum; the clips were connected together with an electrical cord which he then plugged into the wall.

The thing hanging on Brenda's stall was exactly that, an electrical cord with two alligator clips. You can mess with me, my car, my hotel room, even my plastic horse collection, and I can probably find some forgiveness in my heart, eventually. For instance, I'd actually been feeling a bit of compassion toward Jeannie Sukon if she in fact had offed Fuzzy, if Fuzzy had in fact done that despicable deed to Dubie. But start messing with my horse and it's war with no prisoners.

I was feeling nothing but fury toward the person who did this. I didn't care what his or her reason was, it'd never be good enough to threaten my horse's life. The problem was, I didn't know who to be mad at: Jeannie Sukon, Carter Evans, Bobby McMahon, or even Sarah Jane. That's right, Sarah Jane. I know she'd been with me all morning and couldn't have had the time to leave me this little surprise package. But I also remembered the conspiratorial look Bobby McMahon had shot her way at Anyday Farms. Maybe she and the sleaze were in cahoots. Maybe this was his handiwork, by her instruction. Or maybe Jeannie, Carter, or someone I hadn't even considered slipped by.

I didn't have a clue and I didn't like the direction this was going one bit. I rubbed Brenda's neck, kissed her nose, and marched myself to the office to call Tony. It was time to bring in the troops. Except he wasn't there and his missus wasn't up for talking. She wasn't exactly rude on the phone, but pretty darn close.

"Well, just tell him I called and it's important," I said.

"Fine," she said, and click went the line.

I was pacing, and that's how Rob found me.

"Want to ride?" he said. No hello, no I'm sorry about Brenda, no how have you been. But after three and a half years I didn't expect any of the above or anything else. He was a hell of a trainer and not much of a talker, at least not to me.

The offer to ride cut a path straight through my fury. "Is the Pope Catholic?" I said.

No smile. No ha-ha, just, "I got in a new two-year-old filly. Get on her."

I didn't dare ask questions, such as, "Will she kill me?" I had to assume Rob wouldn't let me ride anything totally nuts. And I purposefully didn't tell him about the cord and note I'd found. He'd find some way to blame it on me. This was something I'd have to work on out of his earshot.

"Great, thanks, this is terrific . . ." I started to blather, which is what I always do around quiet people. "Oh yeah, and thanks for giving Brenda that extra hay last night. She really appreciated it, but not as much as the kiss on the nose."

That buzzed his head around toward me. Had he been anyone

227

else, he would've asked either how I knew or what I was talking about, then I'd have told him about Sarah Jane's alleged conversation with Brenda. But he was Rob. He collected himself and said:

"Nattie, just get on the mare. She's in the third stall from the end. Her name's Grace, Amazing Grace."

My favorite song. Proof this was a meant-to-be collaboration. I found her munching hay, but when I walked in her stall, she came right over to me. I blew in her nose, she blew in mine—horse talk for "Hi, how are you, name's Nattie."

She was a bright chestnut, about the same color as Brenda, though she didn't have as much chrome on her. Chrome—horse people talk for white. Brenda has that giant blaze running down her face and the aforementioned three white socks, all of which make for a very flashy picture in the show ring. Grace had only a snip of white trickling down her nose, but you could tell she'd eventually grow into an elegant-looking horse in an old English hunting print kind of way.

That old horse magic took hold the second I swung my right leg over her back. Thoughts of someone threatening to kill my girl flew from my head. The only thing occupying my brain was trying to keep this little filly on a straight line. She was like riding a noodle, but she was only two and she was sweet and quiet and was trying her little heart out to figure out what I was asking her to do.

Gail drove up while I was in the ring on Grace. I waved her over and told her what I'd found on Brenda's stall.

"So that explains it," Gail said. "Damn, I had a feeling there was something weird going on."

"Weird?" I said. "Leaving an executioner's cord next to Brenda goes beyond weird. More like sick."

"No, no, I meant something weird at the barn," Gail said. "About an hour ago I got a call from the girl behind the counter at that convenience store on 16 telling me someone found old man Clark's February Farm credit card by the gas pump and I better come by and pick it up right away. When I got there, she handed me an envelope with nothing inside but a piece of cardboard. She told me someone had given it to the girl whose shift just ended. Someone wanted me out of the barn and knew exactly how to do it. Nattie, you better watch out, this person's smart. I hate your playing Dick Tracy. Don't you have enough problems with Brenda's suspensories? Why go asking for more trouble? For what? Fuzzy McMahon? Much as I loved her, she wasn't worth it. Nothing is if your horse gets hurt in the cross fire. For once in your life, take a warning. Stop asking all your damn questions."

Boy, was Gail hot. Since I was now loose as a piece of melted taffy from my ride on Grace, I calmly assured her I had everything under control.

Ha.

CHAPTER 44

H a is right. I had, have, and will never have anything under control. Not my professional life, my crime-solving life, or, most especially, my personal life.

The next twenty-four hours proved that.

It started with Tony's call. I thought he was returning mine, but as it turns out his wife never even gave him the message.

He called around eight. I was reading *Dreaming in Cuban*, trying my best to let the author whisk me away to her magical land of coconut ice cream dreams, spell-casting santeras, and irresponsible but charming Latin men. No matter how lyrical her words, my mind kept bouncing back to Brenda and her vulnerability. I was about to call Tony again, when the phone rang.

"Nattie, whatcha doing? I sure could use a good ear and a kind face. Rin's got the second part down, but he's lacking in the first area and his breath's a bit on the poor side. Feel like taking a drive someplace?"

Pretty easy to tell he hadn't gotten my very-important-call-me message. He sounded horrible.

My problems could wait, and besides, I could never turn Tony down. It had nothing to do with my hormonally swollen brain. He's always been there for me, even when I wasn't doing any asking. The least I could do was be an ear to his troubles. As for the most, well, that remained to be seen. For once the little man in my head was silent in my possible descent to stupidity. I guess he kind of liked Tony too.

"Sure, sweetie, I'll listen all night if you want me to."

We agreed to meet at my barn, halfway between his house and mine. The real reason I suggested it was to give me another chance to peek in on Brenda, see how she was feeling, and make sure there were no more little surprises waiting there for me. I would've dashed right out, but I did what any woman would've done: I made darn sure I looked as good as I could make myself look short of plastic surgery.

I washed my face and started fresh. Since I'd rather be caught dead than without concealer, which is how I look without it, that's always the first to go on. After that it's just a matter of a quick hit of blush, some mascara, and a healthy slathering of Picasso body cream. That's it, my entire beauty regime. I was ready to roll, once I figured out what to wear.

I couldn't call the fashion editor for advice, since I am it. So I followed the very same words I've uttered to many a confused caller: wear what makes you feel comfortable. That would be jeans. But this occasion called for a little more. A jeans mini. And clogs. Tony once told me he can't keep his hands off a woman in clogs. Maybe he wanted to relive the sixties.

I slipped mine on and clomped out into what? A mistake? Maybe so, but it was one I'd been fantasizing about more nights than I cared to admit. I forced myself not to think about Henry as I drove to the barn. Given the turbulence of my childhood, I'm very good at Scarlett-O'Hara-ing out unpleasant thoughts until tomorrow.

Tony's red Blazer was by the barn when I pulled up.

"Let me just run in and check on Brenda," I said.

"Already done," he said. "I think I woke her up. I thought horses sleep standing up."

"They do most times," I said, "except when they've pulled a suspensory ligament. Figure out where you want to go and I'll be back by the time you know."

I squeezed his shoulder and dashed into the barn. Brenda was lying down and she did seem startled to see me. But at least she wasn't wearing her woe-is-me look anymore and there was nothing on my stall door this time. I wrapped my arms around her neck and kissed her nose. Then, since no one was around, I leaned closer to her, tried to empty my mind of the chatter, asked for protection from nuisance spirits, and tried even harder to be open to her thoughts, the way Sarah Jane told me to do it.

This was truly a weekend for weirdness between Sarah Jane's inter-chakra light transfusion, Brenda's guilt feelings about Rob and Blue By You's recalcitrance, so I wasn't even shocked when I thought I heard someone say, "Have fun."

"I plan to," I said to Brenda as I rubbed her face and then left. Tony's car was running and I climbed in.

For once in all the time I'd known him, he was silent. No down-home witticisms about blood-swollen insects, no run-on sentences that stretched into pages about his Daddy's Daddy's Daddy, no jokes about me moving too fast through life. Just the dark blue air of a moonless night.

We were heading south on 16 toward Waxhaw. He turned left by the railroad tracks, past the antique stores, around the bend. I knew this road well. I was sure we were headed toward Cane Creek Park. We drove and I let him be still. I figured I'd tell him about my terrorist later, after he'd unburdened. He'd talk when he was ready; besides, I was feeling a bit contemplative myself.

The last time I'd been this way was with my good friend Fran. Her horse, Cappy, and Brenda were in the trailer and we were going to Cane Creek Park for a day of trail riding. We'd galloped across the clipped green fields, jumped the snaking split rail fences, done serpentines up and down the hills, and finally given our horses their heads as they stretched their long necks and carried us through the cool, wooded paths. All in all, as near perfect as a day could get.

The next week, Fran was diagnosed with bone cancer and it wasn't too long after that our rides stopped. She came to me in my dreams not too long ago, atop Atticus, the big brown Tennessee Walking horse of her girlhood who'd carried her through the cotton fields of Clover, South Carolina. I told her I missed her and our rides together. I couldn't hear what she said back to me.

"So I guess you're wondering why I'm not talking since I told you I could use an ear."

"Huh?" I said. I was still trail riding with Fran when Tony's words caught up with me. "I'm sorry, Tony, I was thinking about a friend of mine who died."

"Boy, we're just a couple of happy-go-luckies tonight, aren't we. I'm sorry about your friend. Tell me about her, maybe it'll make me stop feeling sorry for myself."

It'd be hard not to. It had taken her a long time to die and it hadn't been an easy way to go. I put Fran's slow and painful death on my list of complaints I planned to lodge against the Great Whomever when I got a chance to chat with him or her. Fran had been a kind woman who didn't deserve what she went through.

I told Tony this and more. "Hey, wait a minute," I said. "You're the one that's supposed to be doing the talking. So talk. What happened with Sharon? I assume that's what's got you so blue."

"What happened with Sharon?" he said. "What always happens with Sharon? Says she doesn't want to be married anymore. Says I'm too ethnic, too volatile, too Southern, too whatever it is that's bothering her that day. I'm not saying I didn't contribute to our problems, but I'm starting to realize we're just too damn broke to be fixed. We probably should've never gotten married, run the other way when we met each other."

He talked more about his marriage that night than I'd heard in the seven months we'd known each other. I heard how they met—in sociology class at Carolina; when they married—fourteen years this coming July; what his mother thought of her—thumbs down; and when things started sliding in the wrong direction—eight years ago.

"That's a long time to be holding on to hope," I said.

He nodded his head. "You got that right."

We reached Cane Creek and he pulled into one of the parking lots. I looked out at the inky sky and across the fields Fran and I had galloped across. It's not only hormones that bring people to-gether; sadness is a powerful aphrodisiac.

Tony was gazing out his window, silent again.

I must've been an alpha male in my last life, because I've never been one to wait around for the first move. I leaned across my seat and skimmed my fingertips across his cheeks. I'd forgotten how soft his skin was.

"I'm sorry you're going through this," I said.

Then I leaned over farther and lightly touched my cheek to his. I whispered into his ear, "Wanna see if we can't get that old dawg of yours to hunt tonight?"

I expected him to protest, say something like, "Nattie, this isn't fair to you."

Was I ever wrong. He turned his head to me and what I saw in those midnight eyes of his was anything but protest. I don't recall ever being looked at like that in my life. It was far different from Bobby McMahon's calculated eye lock.

This was so raw and primal, I swear for that moment I knew what it felt like to be a wild animal. He grabbed my head with his hands and pulled me to him. He kissed me hard, he bit my lips; his hands, his tongue, his mouth, they were all over me.

"Let's get in the back," he whispered.

I know this makes me un-American, but I'd never done it in a car before. I guess this was my night to become a full citizen. We tumbled onto the backseat, our legs and arms tangled in one another's.

We were breathing so hard, I couldn't tell where his stopped and mine started. We were two creatures, crazy in lust, our hands flying across each other's bodies. My skirt was up around my waist when I reached for his pants and started to slide them down his legs.

"Slow down, girl," he said so softly I could barely hear him. It was more like a coo than words. "Slow, let's go real slow."

The beat changed dramatically. His hands slowed down our

rhythm, and my body turned to a stream of silk, catching slow rides on slow, hot air waves.

"Slow, that's right, nice and slow," he whispered.

I could've gone on like this all night. I move so fast through life, having someone slow me down was not only the biggest turn-on I'd ever imagined, but a gift of abundant luxury.

His fingers circled across, around, and in my body. Soft and slow and gentle, finding spots I'd never known existed. He brushed his lips across my face, down my neck, to my nipples, to my stomach and below.

"Slow," I heard him say. "Let's take it real slow."

Slow is nice. Slow is great. Slow is luxurious. However, there comes a time when slow is no longer possible. And that time was coming. I laced my fingers into his hair, through his curls, to his head, and pulled him to me. Hard and fast.

Thank God there was no one in hearing distance. I've been vocal about everything my whole life, and this was no exception.

It was one of those multiple blast-offs. By the time I was finished, I was panting like I'd run the fifty-yard dash—and finally beaten Randy Spilks.

"God, Tony," I said. "For the first time in my life, I don't know what to say."

"Nothing," he said, and made sure I didn't. We went on like this for what seemed hours or seconds or years.

But once again, history repeated itself. Not on Tony's part. His dawg was ready, willing, and able. And, I might add, appropriately clothed in the necessary outerwear. It was I who called off the hunt. When push came to shove, so to speak, I did the unthinkable: the unthinkable that is, to a man.

"Tony," I said, as I wriggled away from him. "Don't kill me, but I just can't do this. For some stupid reason, I think I'll feel less guilty if we stop now."

"*Now?*" Tony said, between pants. "You want to stop *now?* Lord, Nattie, two people couldn't know each other much more than we do now. Don't you think the horse is already out of the barn, and in your case, whinnying up a storm?"

I'm glad it was dark so he didn't see me blush. "Not completely," I said. "I mean not technically. If we stop now, then in my twisted mind, we haven't done IT. And I'm hoping that will make me feel a little less guilty when I see Henry. I know this is hard for you, but I just need a little time to figure things out."

I heard a zip and then a deep breath. "Nattie," Tony said, "you *are* the most confusing woman I have ever met. But also the most interesting."

Poor Tony was doing his best to be understanding and I as a woman can only guess at his discomfort. Any other man would've put the key in the ignition and said, "Let's go."

But Tony's not any other man. He reached over and put his arm around my shoulder, pulling me close to his side. "If it's time you want, darlin', it's time you've got. Now tell me what's really eating at you."

I lay in his arms and told him what I'd found on Brenda's stall.

"I'm scared, Tony," I said. "I know you don't think so, but I feel like I can protect myself. Brenda's another matter. She's a sitting duck. If anything ever happened to her, I don't know what I'd do. I mean I know what I'd do if they caught the person who did it, and that scares me even more. I'd be facing a murder charge myself."

Tony was stroking my hair. How'd he know that second to riding, that was my calming drug of choice?

"Nothing's gonna happen to her," he said, "because you're gonna take that person's advice and stop asking questions. You're gonna tell me everything you know about Fuzzy's death, and I mean everything, and then you're gonna let me do my job and find her murderer. Aren't you?"

For once I had to agree. This person was smart, all right. He or she knew exactly how to stop me dead in my tracks.

"Yes," I said, and thought I meant it.

CHAPTER 45

J ust about bopping Tony. Now that certainly does muddy the waters of my personal life. Here I was, thinking Henry and I were on our way to extreme coupledom, and then this thing with the cop happens.

Has someone up there reshuffled my cards?

I didn't know whether to feel guilty or happy, so I settled on confused, a state of life I spend much of my time in.

I got home late that night, or early that morning, to be more accurate. Henry had called and left a message on my machine. Ouch, be still my guilty heart. Because we didn't technically do it, doesn't mean I didn't have plenty to feel guilty about. Just less. Gail had called too. I'd asked her to stop by the convenience store on her way home and try to find out who'd left the envelope. She agreed, reluctantly. I had tried, but when I got there, a man was behind the counter and he had no idea what I was talking about.

"I can't believe I'm doing this," Gail said to my machine, "but I found out something about that credit card thing that might interest you. But I still think you should just drop it."

I'd just promised Tony my detecting days were over, and now Gail had a clue for me. What timing.

I went to sleep and dreamed about my friend Fran during what was left of the darkness. I was so agitated I half expected my stepfather David to make a cameo appearance, joining the chorus

237

telling me to stop asking questions and wanting to know why I was such a meshuggeneh when it came to men.

He didn't, and once again I couldn't hear what Fran had to say when I told her I missed her.

So that's my personal life: completely out of control, kilter, whack—whatever you want to call it. As if that weren't enough for my aching brain to process, my professional life followed suit.

Monday morning I dragged my sorry self out of bed, forcing my brain not to list the ways I'd just screwed up my life, even think the R word—REBOUND—or figure out how I'd look Henry in the eyes later today.

I was alone in the apartment, another large luxury in life these days. I hadn't seen Sarah Jane since I'd found the cord by Brenda's stall, and that was fine by me. Given how gifted a liar she was, she remained a suspect. She and Lou were nowhere to be found when I woke up, but I was reasonably confident they hadn't ricocheted themselves back to the City of Magic Vortexes and Sublime Currant Rye Rolls because the rice cooker was cooking and Lou's car was in the parking lot. The air was warm—finally—so I assumed they must've been out for a walk, communing with the spring blossoms—or stealing them.

I threw together some kind of outfit, drank my morning colloidal vitamins—Lou's latest kick before the algae drink—and got in my little Rabbit, who didn't feel like getting out of bed.

"Wake up," I said as I throttled her choke. She coughed and sputtered and sounded an awful lot like she'd been smoking three packs of Luckys every day for the past twenty years. Finally she cranked over into a rumble somewhat resembling engine noise but closer to an old man clearing his throat of phlegm.

At least I didn't run into Henry in the parking lot. His car wasn't there yet; he must've been running a Chet or Hank errand. That was very fortuitous because I hadn't formulated a plan for either the bigger picture—Tony or Henry?—or the little one—what I could possibly say to Henry when I saw him? But who was I kidding?

I've never had a plan for anything, I've been a buoy in the ocean of life since I was a seedling.

I nodded to the guard in *The Appeal* lobby and slowly climbed the four sets of moving stairs. It was Monday; I was in no hurry, considering this is my least favorite day at work. That's when I have to write the dreaded fashion column, which usually involves talking to the dreaded fashion ninnies about some stupid trend that hasn't trickled down to the Queen City yet.

I didn't have a clue what major sartorial issue I'd be tackling today, and that was what I was thinking about as I walked through the newsroom, making my way back to the bowels of the building where they stashed Carolina Living, the features department now known as The How We Live Team.

All the offices at *The Appeal* are walled with glass, and we won't go into the metaphorical ramifications of that. The literal particulars are funny enough. What it means is no one can have a private discussion because even with the drapes pulled you can still see in. Whoever did the decorating chose a fabric with such a loose weave, it provided as much cover as a gauze skirt without a slip in the full sun.

Even though I was furiously trying to come up with something to write about, my eyes still skimmed across the glass walls to see who was doing what to whom. My brain slammed on the brakes at Fred Richards's office, our shoe salesman/editor's office. Something was definitely wrong with that picture, and it didn't take me more than a millisecond to figure out what it was.

The Reverend Rowe Quarrels was what it was. He was holding a page from *The Appeal* in one of his big, grimy hands, while the index finger from the other was repeatedly jamming at the headline. And, that was no look of Christian love on his face.

A sick feeling settled in my stomach, and I was sure it wasn't the colloidal vitamins. I'd already worked through the week of nausea/detoxification from those. It was the headline his index finger was assaulting: *CAROLINA'S OWN HORSE WHISPERER WHISPERS HERE.*

I looked at Richards. Uh-oh, trouble. He was wearing his most concerned we'll-find-a-shoe-to-fit-you look.

I ducked my head and scooted.

Not soon enough.

"Nattie, could you step into my office."

What a way to start the week.

"Sure," I said, "what's up?"

"Just want to discuss your Sunday story, see if we can't find some middle ground."

Oh God. Major I'm-going-to-get-screwed alert. He was dropping pronouns, slipping into the team talk spoken by *Appeal* editors of all levels when they're about to shove a new mission down someone's throat, which always involves (1) upping reporters' productivity by cranking out at least twice as many stories, (2) more group-think assignments with the originality of a housedress from Kmart, and (3) tailoring the news coverage to serve the community, aka never stepping on advertisers' overreaching toes.

I walked in, and this time preacher boy wasn't eyeing my body parts. He was looking far too piously righteous for that. If I really had guts, now would have been the perfect opportunity to do what made Sharon Stone famous and see if that didn't color his holier-than-thou cheeks a little.

"Miss Gold," he said. "Good to see you again."

I nodded and clamped my lips shut before "I'll just bet it is" snapped out.

He'd protested tinkly music, a channeler bringing messages from Michael, some dancers flashing a little flesh, and my Asheville witches story, so why was I surprised he was here this morning hammering my latest venture with his index finger?

"How are you, Mr. Quarrels?" I said, resurrecting the edgeless-as-a-greased-ball voice I'd learned from Mickey-Turner Burnett, book editor and mentor of the Southern-get-what-you-want method.

"I'm glad you asked that," Quarrels began as he puffed up his chest and assumed the position of pulpit pomposity. "Not very well, thank you. Not very well indeed. I came in this morning to talk to Mr. Richards about that story you wrote. The one about the man who says he can talk to horses."

"Oh, you did? Boy, that man was a delight to interview. Is there something else I can tell you about him?" I said, and smiled sweetly. Mickey-Turner would be proud.

"That man is no Christian, but I say everyone is entitled to his own belief. That's what's written in our constitution and I would be the last person to argue with that."

Yeah, right. Despite my inner dialogue, I forced the smile to stay on my face.

"It's when the media starts proselytizing, I get upset. That's where the argument comes in. Mr. Richards and I have gone around and around about this issue and I've found him to be a reasonable man. You, on the other hand, Miss Gold, continue to write these ridiculous stories about witches and so forth. People are vulnerable; they're looking for answers, and when they open the morning paper and start reading about a man who claims he can talk to animals, claims that animals can not only talk back but reincarnate to other lives, claims that spirits guide him, claims that he is a godly man when he is in fact closer to the devil than to Jesus Christ, that, Miss Gold, is when I get upset. I read in your story no words from the Christian point of view speaking to the dangers of the new age, or what I like to call the devil's age. Satan is an alluring foe, Miss Gold, and he uses his charms in many ways, including making people think they can communicate with dumb animals. You here are supposed to represent everyone's point of view. Not just the pagans'."

That did it. That wiped the fake smile right off my face. Mickey-Turner's lessons were evaporating faster than expensive perfume. I clamped down on the calming point on my hand as hard as I could, and I think that's what kept me from pushing the pouf out of his pompadour.

"*Mister* Quarrels," I said, "first off, William Holland is not a pagan. For the record, he's actually a member of the Camden Presbyterian Church. And furthermore, for your information, I did ask him if his spirit guides and horse-communicating stuff conflicts with his religion. He told me he was merely following in the footsteps of the original animal communicator, St. Francis of Assisi. By my way of thinking, that is soliciting the Christian viewpoint. I didn't, however, call a rabbi, monk, Sufi master, or sensei—because none of those guys have ever taken exception to anything I've written."

He did not look appeased. "Asking a Presbyterian hardly represents the entire Christian point of view. As for those others, I suggest you remember your readership. This is a Christian country—just read your dollar bill, 'In God We Trust'—and this part of the country particularly so. To serve up blasphemy like that on, of all days, Sunday, that's beyond comprehension."

I pinched the fleshy part of my hand between my index finger and thumb as hard as I could, wondering if I wasn't mixing up the toothache point for the emotional distress point.

"You know what's beyond comprehension?" I said. "Your take on America. A Christian country? What does that make me? A visitor? I was born here, just the same as you. I pay taxes, probably more than you do. As for blasphemy, show me one line in the story that even comes close."

Richards still hadn't said anything. Nothing like supporting your staff.

"I'm glad you asked, *Miss* Gold." Quarrels pulled a pair of bifocals from his inside pocket and balanced them on his nose. He scanned the copy, looking for the offending passage.

"Right here you say, 'You have to believe that animals and humans are equal beings if you want to talk to them. Then there's no language barrier, because the divine force translates.' "

"Whoa, wait a minute," I said, "*I* don't say that. Notice those two funny squiggly lines by the first Y and the last s? Those are quote marks. William Holland is saying that. Besides, what's wrong with that anyway?"

He shot me a look somewhere between wither and pity. *"Animals and humans equal beings?* Animals are primitive creatures. They don't know the difference between right and wrong, they're ruled by their primal urges, and they have no communication system to speak of—certainly not in words."

I couldn't help it, but a laugh escaped. "Sounds a lot like men to me."

"Nattie," Richards snapped, "I don't find that funny, and I'm sure the reverend doesn't either. Let's see if the three of us can't find a solution to this problem."

I didn't see any problem other than the blinders constricting Quarrels's soul. He had the compassion of a Roman about to throw food to the lions—in the squirming form of a living Jew, which is exactly how I was feeling now. However, what I thought or how I felt was less than incidental to Richards. So for the next ten minutes I sat there as the two of them figured out a solution to "our" problem.

This is where the turmoil of my professional life actually nosed out the turmoil of my personal life.

"Over my dead body" was my answer to Quarrels's insistence *The Appeal* run a We Were Wrong about my story. We Were Wrongs are acknowledgments of errors that appear printed prominently on the front page. Whoever's responsible for said error must write the We Were Wrong, along with an explanation of how it happened and what plans you've got to avoid such happenings in the future. They're also ammunition for editors at a reporter's yearly review. I take pride in my accuracy rate; I'd had only two WWW's in three and a half years. Plus it was the one thing they couldn't spear me on, though they always seemed to find others. Last year they cut my raise because I "stretched the bounds of creativity."

I was not going to admit to a mistake when there was none. I'd have liked to end the above dead body sentence with, "you pedophiliac hypocrite, you." But I didn't because I still didn't believe it—much as I wanted to—and I didn't want to wreck Henry's story.

Also, it surely would have meant an end to my weakly, and I do mean *weakly*, paycheck, assuming I hadn't already done that, given Richards's career platform: being polite to readers. No doubt that's the way he thinks he'll get noticed by the gray flannels in Miami and that'll be his leg up the corporate ladder.

Telling a reader, no matter how obnoxious, "over my dead body," doesn't fall into the parameters of politeness. Richards's face reddened. "Nattie," he said, "we don't talk to our readers that way. I think the Reverend Quarrels has made some good points about representation. I think a Clarification is in order. Why don't you go to your computer and write something up along those lines."

A Clarification, a baby-step below a We Were (read that "reporter was") Wrong. I stormed out of the office and would've slammed the door but my hand slipped.

CHAPTER 46

You can bet there'd be hell to pay later with Richards for my behavior, doubly so if the Clarification I was about to write smacked of anything but extreme mea culp-itudes. It took me many tries and many bile gulp-downs to finally come up with the following:

"*The Appeal* regrets any misunderstanding in the Sunday Carolina Living story concerning animal communicators. It is not an editorial belief that horses can talk, can reincarnate, or that William Holland receives divine translations. The story did not mean to imply that such things have been scientifically proven to be possible."

I pushed the send button on my keypad and buzzed it through cyberspace to Richards. Repugnant task number one completed. On to number two, scouring my brain for a fashion idea. Given the way my day was shaping up, a major front of self-pity was moving across my horizon. Then I remembered what my horse-trailer-selling Buddhist friend Tom from Southern Pines told me about suffering: to know the reason for suffering, I'd have to meditate on the reason for joy, as in how would I know black without white? As in, my morning sucked so far, but last night was pretty good; as in . . . I was just starting to get lost in my Deep Thoughts of the Day when I was saved by the bell. Alexander Graham Bell.

"Nattie Gold, *Charlotte Commercial Appeal,* how can I help you?"

"You've already done just that, darlin'—and mighty more. Yes sir, I've been thinking about a night like that with you, even if we didn't have a full hunt, for longer than a cheap race horse's back. I hope you're not sitting there stewing and regretting."

"Tony Maroni, hey, sweetie pie," I said. "Stewing yes, regretting no. And the slow cook has nothing to do with you. Though that slow cook of yours last night was pretty darn nice."

I filled him in on my tangle with Quarrels and then told him about the message from Gail. I hadn't had a chance to return her call, so I didn't know what new information she'd gotten about the bogus credit card run to get her out of the barn.

"I know, I know, I promised," I said, heading his protest off at the pass. "And this time I mean it. I'm not messing around with Brenda's life. For what? My curiosity? It isn't worth it. So I'll just call Gail, find out what she found out, and pass it right along to you. Okay?"

"Not okay. You don't need to be asking on my account. I got me a mouth that works fine and two ears that hear pretty good most times. I'll call her."

"Good luck," I said. "No offense, but she hates you. She'd sooner talk to Lucy Bladstone, and do I have to remind you where Lucy is? In prison for killing my buddy—and Gail's near-fatal attraction—Jeff."

"Is that why she looks like a cross-eyed cat whenever she sees me?" Tony said. "I never could figure why she won't say more than two words at a time. So that's it, she hates me? For any particular reason?"

"You're a cop; you know about her horse testing positive for swamp fever; you almost sent Rob away to prison forever; and you're a major distraction in my life, one she thinks will do nothing but hurt me. Choose any of the above, they'll all work."

Tony let out a low whistle. "Women, as long as I'm still breathing and still interested, I'll never figure y'all out. Lord have mercy on my poor, tortured soul. Okay, then you ask her. But don't you be going one step more and one step more after that. I know how you get. One thing leads to another, and next thing you know you're tumbling around the hay with someone ramming a gun down that mouth of yours, wonderful as it is—in many ways."

I laughed, and it felt good for my face to be something besides scowling, which is what it'd been doing since my morning visit to the principal's office. "That exact scenario hasn't happened yet, if you'll recall. And I promise, it won't happen this time either. I'm through playing Dick Tracy. I promise. It's hemlines and necklines for me from here on out."

We talked a little more, and before we hung up, made plans to meet later at February Farm after I rode. Deeper and deeper I was sinking, yet still no shrieks from the little man in my head or visits from the beyond with David telling me I was meshuga. Could I possibly be on the right romantic track?

Just as I was about to call Gail, the phone rang. My voice was more chipper this time around as I went through my introductory hello-how-can-I-help-you-perhaps-clean-your-house-on-Thursdays spiel all *Appeal* reporters are required to give when a member of the reading public rings our telephone. Sometimes Richards even gets his wife's friends to call reporters just to make sure we're Suzy Sunshine when we answer.

"Boy, Nattie, you sure sound happy." It was a young girl's voice pulling at my memory wires. But my remember synapses weren't snapping so fast. Then it clicked. Maybe the brain can regenerate the lost cells of unbridled youth.

"Ashlee," I said. "Well, things could be worse, I suppose. How's bout you, my dear?"

"Awesome," she said. "Guess what? Blue's going with me to the Culpeper show this weekend. I'm showing him in Large Pony. Eli and Jackson said it was okay with them. Isn't that great?"

Eli and Jackson were Ashlee's full-time trainers. They were an anomaly in the horse show world on two counts: they'd been together both professionally and personally for fourteen years, and more importantly, they were kind to their clients. Especially Eli. A long stretch of a man who always had a smile on his face, he'd easily get everyone's vote for Mr. Congeniality. I've never heard a bad word said about Eli Peters, which is saying a lot given the circles he moves in.

I've known people who've trained with Eli and Jackson—before they went exclusive to Ashlee. With these guys there's no yelling, cursing, public humiliation, or accusing riders of having meat axes for hands—all of which I've experienced repeatedly with a variety of trainers in my twenty years of horse showing. Now that I thought about it, it was no wonder Ashlee not only still liked riding, but still loved horses.

"That *is* terrific," I said. "I hope you have a great time, you deserve some happiness right now, kiddo."

"I had a great idea," Ashlee said. "Daddy told me about Brenda's leg. I'm really sorry, I had a horse do the same thing once. He's fine now. Anyway, like, why don't you come to Culpeper with me? You can ride Fritz. I already asked Eli, he says it's a great idea. Fritzy needs the work and I have too many to ride anyway. What do you say, Nattie, come on, it'll be fun."

How do you explain to a thirteen-year-old gadzillionaire you don't have the bucks to travel in her league. Hotel, training, braiding, stalls, entry fees—I was looking at a fast five hundred dollars slipping through my fingers before I even got in the ring.

"That's very sweet of you to offer, but—"

Before I could finish the sentence, she did. "Oh yeah, like don't take this wrong or anything, but it won't cost you anything. I'm going up anyway, all the horses are going up anyway, and the same goes for Eli and Jackson. So it's no big deal. You can stay in my room. Come on, Nattie, what do you say?"

I was about to say how could I refuse such an offer? Fritz was the leading children's hunter in the country, a point and shoot air ride of an animal who'd taken all his riders—even the ones who should've switched to bowling—to the top. It'd be like the calorie gods telling me they'd look the other way while I downed my weight in Ben and Jerry's Cherry Garcia.

"You're making it impossible for me to say no," I said.

"Then don't," Ashlee said. "You've been really nice to me, trying to find out what happened to Mom and all. You know, bringing that lady to talk to Blue and asking people questions. I know you're trying hard and it's not even your job. How's it going anyway? Sorry the thing with Blue didn't work. Have any ideas or clues?"

I couldn't tell her I'd given up. And not just because she was about to take me on an all-expenses-paid trip of my dreams. For some reason, I didn't want the kid to be disappointed in me. Maybe on a subterranean level I was trying to be the parent we'd both needed, or maybe my attempt to fix her childhood hurts was a way to fix my own. There were any number of neurotic possibilities, which was good because it would give me something to do besides sleep my way through sessions with Dr. Greene.

"I've got lots of ideas," I said. "The problem is, not too many clues. But some. Gail might be on to something. I'll keep you posted. While I have you on the phone, let me ask you something. How into horse showing is Jeannie Sukon's daughter?"

"You mean Becca? She used to be a lot. But that was before Richie."

Attack of the hormones. I wondered when it would happen to Ashlee or if she'd be like me, horse-crazy enough for the hormones to bounce off the armor of equine ardor.

"Hmmm, boys," I said. "Understandable, I guess. Okay then, let me ask you another question. Does that mean she doesn't care that much about riding in the junior hunter division, about getting to the Garden?"

Ashlee giggled. "Only if Richie were there. He's all she can talk about. She doesn't really care about horses anymore. Hasn't for a while. She'd probably stop riding if she could."

I didn't have to ask what that meant. It was another case of kid outgrows obsession long before mother. It happens all the time. Sometimes the kid never has the obsession to start with.

"What about Ralston Evans?" I said. "Who cares more about showing? Her mother or her?"

"Both," Ashlee said. "They're like both nuts about it."

"You and Ralston are good friends, right?" I said.

"Ralston's my best friend. I mean we fight and everything sometimes, but we're still best friends. Sometimes it's hard 'cause we show against each other, and then when Mom went around buying so many horses, Ralston's mom got kind of angry. I think it bothers Mrs. Evans more than it does Ralston—you know, me winning more than she does."

"How do you know?"

"How could I not know?" Ashlee said. "Ralston's mom can scream louder than mine. They had like a major fight at the indoor Raleigh show. Jackson had to stop them. And the only way he could do that was by getting his cell phone and telling them he was going to call the police if they didn't quit. I was like totally humiliated, so was Ralston. I mean they weren't just screaming, they were hitting each other too."

My parents were starting to look like Ozzie and Harriet.

"That does sound pretty horrible," I said. "Horse shows can bring out the worst in people, can't they?"

"I guess," Ashlee said. "But it wasn't like she was much different any other time."

I shouldn't have asked the next question. It was none of my business, but that's never stopped me before. "Ashlee, do you have any good memories of your mother?"

There was a long pause. Finally she spoke, and her voice seemed even smaller.

"I don't know," she said. "All I can remember right now is her screaming and hitting and going off into these major fits. Telling me I was just like my father; that I was an idiot like him or she couldn't trust me the same as she couldn't trust him, that I'd leave her alone the same as he did. Nothing I did was ever good enough or right. Nothing."

She stopped talking and I could hear her choking back the tears. Me and my big mouth and my stupid questions.

"Ashlee, I'm sorry. I'm sorry I asked. It was none of my business."

"No, that's okay," she said. "It's not like I'm telling you anything everyone didn't already know. Becca's mom once even called the Department of Social Services to report my mom."

"What happened?"

"Oh, some dumb lady came out to talk to me and Mom, that's all. Then she was nice for a couple days."

I wondered had Fuzzy not been a Feldman would they have yanked Ashlee out of her house. I made a note to call my social worker friend and see if she could find out more.

Enough tears and sad memories. Time to move her off the mother subject. "Are you and Becca Sukon good friends?" I asked.

"We're cousins," Ashlee said. "She's all right, I guess. Her mom's always been really nice to me. She's the kind of mom who does things with her kid. It's like she's really interested in Becca's life, even the things outside of horses. Aunt Jeannie used to take Becca out for a special dinner every Wednesday night, she called it their girls' night out. Then they'd go to SouthPark and shop, or a couple times they even went bowling together. 'Course that was before Richie. Now you can't peel Becca off the telephone unless it's to sign on her computer to send messages to you-know-who. How come you're asking these questions anyway? Does it have something to do with what happened to Mom?"

Stretch the truth, try not to lie—a good motto to take me through life. "Probably not," I stretched. "I'm just curious about the horse world's Generation Next. By the way, you shooting for the Olympics?"

"Mom was, that's for sure," Ashlee said.

"What about you? You want to be the next Margie Goldstein-Engle?"

"Sometimes I think I do. Then sometimes I think I want to be a normal kid, you know like hang out at SouthPark on Saturdays instead of going to horse shows every weekend."

Sometimes life has a way of smashing your face in lessons. Like now for me. All I had ever wanted to do when I was a kid was be around horses. I'd have traded all my mall hours in a heartbeat just to smell a dirty curry comb, as long as I'd gotten it that way from rubbing a horse.

"Hey," I said, "I have an idea. What're you doing tonight?"

Pause. "Nothing really."

"Let's go bowling," I said. "We can put on those cute shoes and I can show you just how a champion gutter ball-er works. How about if I pick you up at seven?"

"Cool," she said.

Bowling with Ashlee. It'd mean I wouldn't ride that little filly and have to tell Rob. Not good, but I could handle it. And it would also mean no after-ride tryst with Tony. Possibly good because as I looked up from the telephone I saw the tall boy striding my way.

"Hey, Henry," I said, and jammed my brain into superdrive trying to figure what in God's name I'd say to him.

CHAPTER 47

I was sure there was another Kmart special stampede of blood cells to my face, the question was, was there a Busby Berkeley corpuscle in charge, forming his zipping minions into the pulsating letter A on my forehead?

Not that I was married to Henry, or even in any kind of mutually agreed upon exclusive arrangement. Still, that didn't stop my guilt. Probably nothing short of a new heritage could. However, despite my flushed face, tapping fingers, and general air of what-have-I-done, Henry didn't seem to notice. So for all the times I've cursed the big difference between men and women—males come with a density gene—now I was thanking the genetic engineer who designed our prototype.

"Hi, Nattie," he said. "How's everything with Lou?"

"Much better," I said. "He's off the Ritalin and sailing smoothly on Zoloft, though I'm keeping my eyes on him to make sure we have no more sweat lodge incidents. Maybe it is bad medicine, giving him Zoloft, but it worked. He won't take Lithium or check himself into a loony bin, so I'm glad something helped him. I'm just thankful he responds to the Zoloft. Lots of manic-depressives don't respond to anything. I think Denise told me thirty percent."

We chitchatted for a few minutes and the reasonable side of myself took over. Last night was last night, and really no one's business but my own. Now to get my whole self believing that.

"I saw Quarrels walking out of Richards's office," Henry said. "I'm curious what that was about."

"Wonder no more," I said, and told him what happened.

"He's not the most open-minded person," Henry said. "But that should be no surprise."

"Open-minded?" I said. "The man defines the word intolerance, not to mention a few other ones I've sworn off saying. So how goes your story? Still think there's any there there?"

"Possibly," Henry said. "The mother tells a convincing story, but so far it's just her word. I did go to Quarrels's service yesterday morning. You were right about how women react to him. They were looking at him as if he were Robert Redford."

"He's more like Fred Flintstone to me," I said. "I just don't get it, the attraction he holds for women. Maybe it's got something to do with him being The Man, the one in charge, the one with the authority. Maybe it's just another spin on trying to get Daddy's love. Go figure. Any intimations or inklings of something amiss with the reverend's sexual taste buds?"

Henry shook his head. "Not a one. But I didn't expect anything along those lines. I primarily went to see him preach and ask around about the mother."

"Well?" I said.

"He's quite the orator," Henry said. "And she's how you described her, on the mousy, quiet side, and doesn't make much of an impression. Most of the people I spoke to didn't even know her, not that that in itself is so unusual. Quarrels has one of the biggest congregations in Charlotte."

It wasn't shaping up as too much of a story so far. But then again, he'd just started. He had his work cut out for him. We both knew *The Appeal* would never run anything close to accusations of a sexual nature unless he crossed every t and dotted every i— fifteen times. Then they still might not run the blasted thing, given their track record.

They'd made poor Henry jump through smaller and smaller hoops on the Jim Bakker–Jessica Hahn story, until he'd gotten it so airtight it was as close to the words from God as he could get short of growing his hair long and climbing Mount Sinai. The final time they pulled the story—it had been scheduled to run, and once again at the last minute the editors got cold feet—Henry was about to charge into Richards's office and quit. However, someone had leaked to Bakker that *The Charlotte Commercial Appeal* was finally printing the definitive story that detailed the whole sordid mess about his roll on the hotel bed with the big-haired church secretary from Long-Guyland and the $260,000 payoff from church funds. Thinking he was beating *The Appeal* to the punch, Bakker resigned and put Jerry Falwell in charge of his empire. Henry's story finally ran, but only because Bakker quit first.

"Did you ever remember what it was about the daughter?" Henry said.

"Nope," I said. "But whatever it is, I don't think it's that big of a deal. It'll come to me."

Henry was giving me an odd look. "You seem preoccupied. Anything wrong?"

So he hadn't seen the red letter A vibrating on my forehead, but he was picking up on something. I hadn't planned on telling him about the cord dangling by Brenda's stall because I didn't want one more person telling me I'd gotten in over my head. I already knew that. But I couldn't tell him the other thing that was occupying my mind, so I went for the cord story.

"Don't even say it," I said after I showed him the note. "I'm off the McMahon case. It's Les's baby, not mine. I just feel sorry for the kid. I don't know if finding her mother's murderer will make it better or worse for her. I predict years on the couch, probably wouldn't hurt for her to start now. You should've heard some of the things she told me about her mother. How the woman would pick fights with anyone who walked by, how they couldn't leave a restaurant or store without Fuzzy demanding someone be fired, accusing everyone of sleeping with Ashlee's father, though that wasn't really so off the mark. When she got drunk enough, she'd even wake up the poor kid in the middle of the night and drag her to the barn, convinced that Bobby McMahon was down there poking the latest female boarder and she wanted to show her daughter just what a sleazeball her father was. Horrible things like that. I know, I know, Fuzzy didn't have it easy being married to a tomcat like Bobby McMahon, but she could've kept her daughter out of it."

Henry was now wearing his concerned daddy look, and it about broke my heart. I've never felt so pulled apart in my life.

"I have an idea," he said. "Come to Morrison's with me and the boys tonight and call Ashlee to see if she can join us."

Dinner with Chet and Hank was always entertaining, if for nothing else than to see how much food Chet could get on his clothes and how particular Hank could be about removing every last piece of skin from his fried chicken.

"I'd love to," I said. "But I already made plans with her. I'm taking her bowling. We'll be at Queen City Lanes if you want to join us."

This was my morning for phone calls. Once again it started ringing, and once again I went through the spiel.

"Can it, Gold, who are ya kidding?" Les's sneery voice was coming through loud and annoying. "So it looks like your girl's off the hook, for the time being."

I mouthed to Henry I'd catch him later. "You mean because of those weird circle marks all over Fuzzy? Just because the shovel wasn't the murder weapon doesn't mean Sarah Jane had nothing to do with it. Much as I don't want it to be her, I'm still not counting her out, completely. She claims she's being set up to look like it was her, but she's been claiming a lot of things since I've known her. You'll never believe what I did yesterday morning. She's a horse communicator, right? So I took her to talk to the only known witness to the crime, Ashlee's pony, Blue By You."

Les could barely contain his laughter before I even got to the part about Blue refusing to talk any more. When I got to that point, he erupted into a big snort of a howl, and I thought he was going to upchuck he was laughing so hard.

"Give me an f'n break, Gold. I can't believe you did that. What'd you expect her to say, 'The pony says it was me who killed Fuzzy'?"

"No, but I did think it might be interesting to see whom she'd try to frame, assuming she were guilty and assuming horses really can't talk."

That was too much for Les. He couldn't even catch his breath between guffaws.

"Les, Mr. Butthole, you still there?" I screamed into the phone. "I've got a serious question for you."

"Yeah, what? Like is there a little green man on my shoulder?"

"No really, about those weird circle marks. Ever seen what a blacksmith uses to clinch down the nails? That would leave a circle indentation."

"Still got a hard-on to nail the blacksmith husband, huh?" Les said. "Boy, he must've done you dirty. Forget it, kid. I asked your cop friend about blacksmith tools and he said the husband or wife is always the prime suspect so that was the first thing they checked. Nothing a farrier uses makes that kind of mark. Whatever did it not only left a circle, but a pretty deep hole at the top. There must've been a pointed end on top of the circle. Weird. Well, let me know if you hear anything, I'm still working the story, though there's not much to work."

"Count me out," I said. "I'm off the case, back to how long you should be wearing your skirts when you dress in drag. I'd say an A-line suits your figure type."

He harrumphed and hung up, and bingo, I had myself a fashion column idea. Two of them, in fact. If I worked anywhere else I'd have gone for idea number one: drag queen fashion—my personal role models in how to dress. Maybe I'd even have done a phoner with drag queen extraordinaire Anita Man or her sister act, Anita Drink. But this was *The Charlotte Commercial Appeal,* all the news that happens from the neck up, so I settled for fashion idea number two: apples and pears, our figure types and how to dress them. I didn't say it was the most exciting fashion column idea.

CHAPTER 48

Bowling. Another thing in life I don't get. Right up there with eating Spam and playing golf. But who was I to talk? I spend all my recreational hours and dollars searching for the elusive, perfect takeoff spot before the jump I've been trying to find atop my horse for the past twenty years.

I hadn't hefted one of those big, black balls since the time my friend and I stole my mother's Luckys and made ourselves sick smoking in the bowling alley bathroom. I gutter-balled them then and I gutter-balled them now.

Ashlee thought it was a riot. She, being the natural athlete she is, got the concept right away. After her fifth strike, I finally hit a few pins. Three.

"It's because I don't see depth," I started to explain to her. She was giving me a get-real expression. "No really. See how my left eye floats out in space? My witch friend says it's the mark of the coven, that I'm really a witch. Whatever, my eyes don't work together, so things look flat."

"God," she said, "how can you jump fences, then?"

That one was easy: "I have a great horse."

"Gee, I bet you're really upset about Brenda. I know when Blue hurt himself last year, I could hardly eat. That's when Mom started buying those junior horses. She said it'd be the perfect time to move from ponies to horses. All I ever wanted to do was ride Blue, though."

"So you will this weekend," I said. Between her strikes and my gutter balls, we made plans. Because it was her spring break, she wanted to leave Wednesday, which would mean I'd have to take three comp days. No problem there. *The Appeal* had long ago stopped paying overtime. Between all the late night parties and weekend fashion shows I'd been assigned to cover, I'd accumulated almost two weeks of comp time. I told her I'd be happy to drive my car and she could ride along. It was March, so air-conditioning was not an issue, which was good because I didn't have any.

Just as we were about to leave, Henry and his boys walked in. The five us played a game together. Hank mostly wanted to throw his balls at Chet, and Chet mostly wanted to act cool around Ashlee, which resulted in him throwing the balls so hard they landed in the next lane. At least it looked as if I wouldn't come in last.

When Ashlee got up to throw her final ball—another strike—Henry leaned over and quietly asked what I'd heard from Gail.

"You could've asked me in front of Ashlee," I said. "She knows pretty much everything. Anyhow, nothing's new. I called Gail all day at the barn and her house. I just got answering machine after answering machine. Monday's her day off, and knowing her and Torkesquist, they were going for full-body grass stains someplace."

Henry laughed, flashing those perfect pearly whites. "Those two are certainly a perfect match," he said. "You should consider the matchmaking business."

Yeah, right, I thought. Matchmaker, heal thyself.

I smiled wanly and said, "I might have to. Richards e-mailed me, telling me he wants to meet with me tomorrow afternoon. You can bet it has something to do with what I said to Quarrels. But I'm not going to think about the fact that I might already be an unemployed journalist with an ailing horse and vet bills up the wazoo. Not now, at least. It might affect my bowling."

Everyone laughed at that.

Ashlee beat the pants off all of us and it was nice to see the kid smile. I'd been hearing for years what a terror she can be, but I'd yet to see that side of her. Then I remembered what a terror I'd been at that age, and that too was a side never seen by the one person who took the time to dig through the bunker of anger I'd buried myself in: Ellie, the kindly camp counselor with the wavy brown hair and worn buffalo sandals.

Henry and I never really had a chance to be alone. That was probably for the best because I didn't know what I was feeling for whom. He was pretty cute, though, trying to referee his scrapping boys with reason. That was about as effective as a rubber snaffle bit on a runaway horse. Chet and Hank took every opportunity to call each other any number of names, all of which involved body parts below the waist. When they weren't sparring verbally, they were going at it physically.

Their antics were nothing compared to what went on between my brother Larry and me. We're pretty good friends now, but growing up with only sixteen months between us, we almost set the record for sibling warfare. I say *almost* because the other week when I was doing a story on sibling fighting and what to do about it, I learned that the animal kingdom has honed sibling torture to a fine art. Get kittiwake baby gulls mad enough and they'll give their annoying sibling the old heave-ho out of the nest and over the cliff. This is before they learn to fly. That's kid stuff compared to sharks, who truly define the word precocious. Even as embryos they've got their role in the universe down pat: they sustain themselves by feasting on their squiggly fellow wombmates.

I couldn't let the evening pass without offering that nature lesson to Hank and Chet, which actually awed them into a few moments of silence. Henry took that as an opportunity to slip his arm around me and kiss me good-bye. Hank thought that was hilarious and singsonged, "Daddy's kissing Nattie."

Chet, who was skyrocketing into prepuberty and trying his

261

hardest to demonstrate his maturity to the Teen Goddess Ashlee of Long Legs and Perky Breasts, rolled his eyes.

"Grow up, Hank," Chet said. "They're probably doing a lot more than kissing."

That got Hank good. He started whooping and jumping up and down, singsonging a new chant: "Daddy and Nattie are having an affair."

That got all three kids laughing, and me and Henry too. We were quite a sight, five laughing hyenas in the Queen City Lanes parking lot.

We said our adieus and left. I took Ashlee back to her grandmother's house in Eastover. Bootsie Feldman was there to greet us.

She was a tiny bullet of a woman, at least two inches shorter than me and twenty pounds lighter. Chronologically, she must've been in her sixties, but you'd have never known it. She, unlike Carter Evans, was a poster girl for the wonders of cosmetic surgery. She didn't have a line on her polished face, and da Vinci could not have done a better job sculpting her nose. Some might wonder how I knew she'd been rhinoplastied to perfection. Bala Cynwyd Junior High School is my answer. Along with reading, writing, and arithmetic, spotting shaved noses was a major part of the curriculum, because God knows there were plenty of them to spot.

Bootsie opened her mouth and started drawling. As a northern Jew, it was still strange to hear a fellow tribal member sound like she was the reincarnation of Scarlett O'Hara. In the thickest of Southern accents Bootsie Feldman oozed the following: "Nattie, thank you so much for taking Ashlee bowling. This poor girl has been needing a night like this. Ashlee, honey, why don't you run in and tell Pop-Pop you're here? Hurry on up now."

Like I said, a bullet of a woman. It was no request that Ashlee "hurry on up and run inside now," it was an order, and Bootsie Feldman was clearly used to being obeyed. I was starting to see firsthand why Fuzzy married the sleaze. What better way to say screw-you to Mama than bring home someone like Bobby McMahon?

My car was still running, sort of, and I was about to pull away when Mrs. Feldman locked her little fingers around my wrist.

"Nattie, if you don't mind, I'd like to talk to you. Just for a few minutes."

Not that I had much choice. Her fingers were stronger than a pit bull's teeth.

"Sure," I said and cut off my engine, praying it'd start again. "What can I do for you?"

Her lips turned up at the corners, but her eyes stayed the same: focused and searing into me. She and my editor Candace had that same below-the-eyes smile.

"Nattie honey, I know it's a newspaper's job to report the news, but really now, don't you think all this digging into my poor daughter's life is going just too far? I mean she *was* the victim of a horrible crime, and I just don't see what good can come from all these intrusive questions."

I got it. Les's snooping around, grilling Feldman family friends and employees, was making her squirm. His Sunday story had alluded to some problems in Feldman Family Valueland and hinted not many folks had many kind words to share about the late Fuzzy McMahon.

Her fingers were getting firmer and firmer. I smiled sweetly, obediently.

"Anyhow," she said, "Ashlee tells me you're doing some asking of your own to your horse show friends. You know Fuzzy was having a hard time with that baboon she was married to, she wasn't really herself these last few years. She was—"

"Mrs. Feldman," I said, "I know all about Bobby McMahon. What is it exactly you want from me?"

"You're sure a direct young lady, aren't you? All right, I'll get to the point. Will five thousand dollars get you to stop asking questions and make it so you won't tell that unkempt reporter what you've heard about Fuzzy from your horse show friends?"

If I'd been wearing dentures, they would've dropped out. I'd never been offered a bribe before, especially for something I'd already done. This was a true moral dilemma, as opposed to last night's episode with Tony which, pre-AIDS, would've been considered standard operating procedure by members of my free-love generation.

Five grand to a Feldman was mad money. To me it was the fortune I'd be spending on vet bills these next six months.

Oh my aching, tortured soul. Do I take the dough and go?

CHAPTER 49

I am the niece of the Fireman, a man who burnt down three businesses and collected more than a million dollars in insurance money.

So much for genetic predisposition.

"Mrs. Feldman," I said as I unpeeled her chicken fingers from my arm, "for Ashlee's sake, I'll pretend you're out here asking me who my all-time favorite Hornet is. It's Muggsy Bogues. Now good night."

I cranked up my car and for once it offered no back talk. I don't know which I couldn't believe more: that I'd just turned down the largest lump of money my bank account would ever see in one fell swoop, or that the woman was trying to pay me to stop reporting. You'd think she'd want as many people as she could get asking questions, trying to find out who murdered her daughter. Was saving face really that important?

I got home to a full house. Lou was in the living room, splayed shirtless under his $650 Chinese heat lamp that allegedly zooms healing minerals into your body.

"Lou," I said, "are you having chest pains again? You know that thing can't fix blocked arteries."

Between the whir of the machine and his hearing-aid-less ears, he didn't hear a word I said. Or he was ignoring me. I was about to unplug the thing and scream in his ear when Sarah Jane answered for him.

"No chest pains, Nattie," Sarah Jane said. "He was just cold."

I hadn't seen either of them since I'd dropped them off yesterday morning after Sarah Jane's talk with Blue. Despite McMahon's strange look her way yesterday, I still didn't want to believe Sarah Jane had any part in Fuzzy's murder, thereby a part in Brenda's death threat, but I'd be stupid not to, given her aversion to veracity.

Between that and my current state of agitation, I wanted too wring her neck just on the off chance it was her idea to scare me that way. She knew exactly how attached to Brenda I am. However, so did anyone after talking to me for more than two minutes.

My brother Larry could always withhold, which got him a lot more attention growing up. I've always been a verbal bleeder, spurting over everyone, with no capacity to tourniquet myself. I should've gone the Larry route, just shut my mouth and gone to bed surly. In another lifetime.

"Dammit, Sarah Jane," I said, "if you had anything to do with Fuzzy and everything else I swear I'll kill you myself. I'll find whatever it was that left that weird imprint on her and start swinging it at you."

Well, that took her aback—literally. She took three steps away from me. Maybe it was the crazed look of turning down five thousand dollars on my face.

Lou, of course, hadn't heard a word of my tirade. He just looked up at us and waved.

Sarah Jane was wearing that don't-hurt-me look that dogs who've been slammed around get when you raise your hand to pet them.

"Nattie, are you okay?" Sarah Jane said. "Did something happen to Brenda?"

I snapped. "How the hell did you know that? Huh? You and Bobby think it'd be funny for me to find that cord by her stall?"

I invaded her space, pressing my face to hers.

"Well?" I said. "Was that your handiwork? I know Bobby's not smart enough to spell all the words right."

Being five-two and not one who likes confrontation—usually—

I'd never truly terrified anyone in my life. Until now, and I'd be lying if I said a small, sick part of me didn't get a kick out of it. I inched closer and she inched back, until she hit the living room wall.

I guess that's when Lou noticed we weren't talking about the weather. He turned off his Dr. Feel-Good machine and bounded over to us.

"Nattie, are you nuts?" he screamed, because he has no idea how loud he talks without his hearing aid.

I'd lost it, plain and simple. Between Tony, Henry, Brenda, Fuzzy, Quarrels, Richards, and Bootsie Feldman, my brain was Chernobyling. There was no holding back anything.

"No, I believe that's your department," I hissed. "I think it's perfectly sane to be a little irritable when you're living with a possible murderess who thinks it's amusing to threaten to make a french fry out of your horse."

"What?" Lou screamed.

I repeated myself even louder, broke my vow to God about curse words and told Lou to find his you-know-what-ing hearing aid. That's when the banging from below started. It was my crotchety neighbor's way of telling us to shut up. He'd been working that broom handle pretty good since Lou moved in.

My hands were clenched in fists and I saw Lou glance down at them. He probably thought I was going to punch Sarah Jane. A reasonable assumption.

He dragged me to my bedroom and closed the door. "I don't like to say anything bad about anyone," he said, "but you've got your grandmother's temper." He wasn't referring to his mother. "Now just calm down. Take ten cleansing breaths and then tell me what's wrong."

I don't know why I listened to him but I did. The deep breathing worked. I wasn't Mary Mellow at the end, but I no longer wanted to use the heat lamp to fry Sarah Jane, who, now that I'd oxygenated my brain, was still innocent until proven guilty.

Lou put in his hearing aid and I told him everything that was eating at me. I even told him about Tony. That was the good thing about having a father who wasn't the prototypical father. He'd never cared what I did with my body, be it drugs or men. His words were always the same: "Just don't hurt yourself or anyone else."

"Look," he said, "you know I like Henry. I like Tony too. But that's for you to decide. You're not married to either one of them, so stop feeling bad. Just make a decision because judging by the way you're acting, it's too hard for you to like them both."

I plopped down on my bed and let out a deep sigh. "Easier said than done," I said. "My mind's mush. I wish to God someone would decide for me, and then after that fix things at work. If I don't have a job, I'm in deep trouble."

This is where the normal father would've come in handy. He would've there-thered me a little, assured me nothing was unfixable and then told me how to fix it. Here's what Lou said: "You do have a big mouth, Nattie. But don't worry, the universe will take care of you."

"Thanks, Ozzie Nelson," I said. "By the way, why's Sarah Jane still here? I thought she only stayed Saturday night because we came in so late. Why was she here last night? And why is she here now?"

A sheepish grin spread over Lou's face.

"Oh no, Lou, say it ain't so."

He started giggling, and I knew I had myself another long-term house guest.

"Her landlord changed the lock," Lou said. "She was a few months behind on the rent."

I gave him a see-I-told-you look. "What?" Lou said. "You've never been late paying your bills? Didn't I take a call from a collection agency last week? Besides, she didn't murder Fuzzy and she had nothing to do with threatening Brenda."

"Then how come she asked if something happened to Brenda?

Maybe she was worried McMahon got a little carried away with their plan."

"Why don't you ask her?"

"Okay, I will," I said, and walked to the door. "Oh Sarah Jane," I said in a fake nice voice, "could you step in here for a second? I want to ask you something."

She didn't exactly rush my way. It took Lou's going out and saying something to her that got her within ten feet of me. When she was close enough to hear me without me yelling, I said not very kindly: "How come you asked me if anything was wrong with Brenda?"

"Because that's the only thing that would get you so upset," she said. "Remember in Asheville when you found out she'd hurt herself? I thought you were going to snap off the steering wheel."

"What about the cord?" I said.

"What cord?" Sarah Jane said. Now she was getting annoyed. "*What* are you talking about. I don't know anything about any cord."

So I told her.

"God, Nattie, you think I'd do something like that to *you*?"

"Possibly," I said. "I think I don't know what to think you'd do."

She shook her head. "I don't blame you. It's my own fault. I've told so many lies, sometimes I don't even know what's true anymore. But I'll tell you one thing that's true, I'd never do anything to hurt a horse or you or your father. That's the truth."

She actually took a step toward me and put her hand on my shoulder. Give that girl an A for bravery. Then she said, "You know there was no love lost between me and Fuzzy, so I didn't really care who killed her. I thought whoever it was had their own karma to work out with her. But now that someone's threatening Brenda, that's another story. This person needs to be stopped. You shouldn't bring animals into your karma battles. It's not right. I wish there was something I could do."

She paused and you could practically see the Eureka! word bubble appear over her head. "I know," she said, "I'll ask Brenda who left the cord."

Oh boy, here we go again. Sarah Jane closed her eyes, white-lighted herself into the spirit safe zone and supposedly contacted my girl.

"She's feeling a little jealous of that new filly Rob is having you ride," Sarah Jane said.

I hadn't told Sarah Jane about Grace, but I'd told Lou about her when I was decompressing a few minutes ago, so it is possible she'd overheard. Or maybe she really was talking to Brenda. Who knew? After these last few days, I barely knew my name, let alone my current thinking on talking horses.

"She says it was a woman who left that note on her door, someone she's seen before at horse shows, but doesn't know who."

Okay, I'd bite. "Send her my love and ask her what the woman looked like."

Sarah Jane laughed. "She says she was a bay, other than that she doesn't know. She says all humans, except for you, look alike."

Great, she had brown hair. Big clue. The only suspect not on the list with brown hair was Sarah Jane. How convenient.

"Oh, and one other thing. Brenda says the woman smelled like summer."

I had a poet for a horse. It figured. So the woman smelled like summer, what was that supposed to mean? This should have been easy, just find the brown-haired lady who smelled like a season. I needed to go to bed.

"Give her a kiss good night for me," I said, and walked my tired self into the bathroom. As I did I muttered an apology to Sarah Jane for my previous behavior.

I didn't know who, what, where, or when to believe. Maybe Lou was right, maybe the universe would take care of me. It'd better, because I sure as anything wasn't doing such a good job of it.

CHAPTER 50

Tuesday was a blur. But a good blur. Just when I was expecting the worst—unemployment—came the best.

Hard to believe, but it arrived that way in the form of Candace. She was smiling and, surprise of surprises, it was an eyes-and-all smile.

"Nattie, could you step into my office?"

Could she really be so cruel that my demise would make her truly smile for the first time in the three and a half years I'd known her? I dragged myself in with the enthusiasm of meeting my guillotineer. Rather than give her the satisfaction of starting, I did.

"I know I was out of line with Quarrels, it's just that when people start using Jesus Christ as a reason for their intolerance, it makes me crazy because—"

She was still smiling. Whew man, she was sicker than I thought.

"Nattie, stop. Stop talking for once and listen. First sit down."

I did.

Candace was at full-puffed mast, and had she stuck her arms out, she could've sailed us to Gastonia.

"This is the first time in *The Charlotte Commercial Appeal*'s feature department history anything like this has happened," she began, and I had no idea where she was heading, which was making me even sicker. "Remember that story I assigned you, the one that turned into the series you did with Henry? 'Murder on the A-Circuit'? We just heard, it's a Pulitzer finalist for local reporting."

271

I screamed and the whole How We Live Team turned their eyes to Candace's glass walls. They probably thought I was being sacrificed. I know it sounded that way. In my delirium, I even jumped up and hugged Candace, which was like dancing with an iron rod.

"Congratulations, Nattie," Candace said as she extracted herself from me.

Time to say "Thanks, Candace" and not quibble with her revisionist history as in "the story I assigned you." Never mind that I had to call in a major favor from my buddy Gary, the managing editor, to get her to let me work on it. Never mind anything.

I was a Pulitzer Prize finalist!!!!!!!

"Thanks, Candace," I said.

For once my tongue listened to my brain.

Chapter 51

Henry could not have been any sweeter when he heard the news. For a button-down kind of guy, he really cut loose. He took me in his arms and waltzed me around the city desk. Because he was the one with the childhood dance lessons at the New Haven Lawn Club, I was the one whose feet remained unmolested. I wish I could say the same for poor Henry. You don't learn to waltz at Grossinger's, the one place I'd ever had anything resembling a dance lesson. And it was the cha-cha.

We made plans to celebrate—when I got back from Culpeper. He couldn't do it that night and neither could I. I had a zillion things to do to get ready, and Ashlee's trainers wanted me to ride Fritz before I got to the show.

In all the Pulitzer hysteria, I'd forgotten about Gail and what she'd found out about the bogus credit card incident. She'd called me a few times during the day, but I was so excited I could barely sit at my desk for more than five minutes at a stretch so I missed every one of her calls. Every time I sat down to call her, my phone rang with some newspaper buddy on the other end who'd just heard the great news.

Other than wrapping up my fruit salad of a fashion column, I didn't get much done that day. And Candace didn't say a word about it. She was too busy making the rounds, accepting congratulations from the other Team Captains about "her story" being chosen as a Pulitzer finalist.

Even Ron Riley didn't squawk about my lack of productivity. This *was* a day to be remembered.

Riding the wave of their magnanimity, I cut out fifteen minutes early. That was it, the end of my work week. And not a bad way to wrap it up at that. Lou had wanted me to stop at home and celebrate with him and Sarah Jane, but I was antsy to get my legs around a horse. So we postponed the apple cider bubbly until I got back from Anyday and they came home from their Sai Baba Be Happy meeting.

I wasn't so antsy that I couldn't stop at my barn to check on Brenda. She was fine and there were no new gifts for me. I gave her more hay, kissed her good-bye, and snuck down to Grace's stall. Maybe horses did feel jealousy. I wasn't taking any chances.

I rubbed the filly's neck and gave her some hay too. "Don't tell Brenda," I whispered to her. I was joking—I think.

When I got to Anyday, Fritz was groomed and dressed in his best party clothes: an exquisite custom-made Bennetts bridle and a Butet saddle. I'd sat in one of those three-thousand-dollar babies before, and it was like riding on a down-filled leather couch.

"I'll be right there," I said to Ashlee's trainer, Eli, who was holding Fritz. "Let me just make a quick pit stop."

I walked into the lounge, and who should be there? Everyone. Carter and Ralston Evans, Jeannie Sukon, Ashlee, even the Bullet, Bootsie Feldman, who was giving me the evil eye.

I said my hellos quickly and dashed into the john. It wasn't until I was seated that it hit me: the smell in the lounge. Honeysuckle. But it was March, a good three months shy of the first bud. I was sure I'd smelled something sweet and even more sure it was honeysuckle. I'd never confuse that smell with anything else, it's my favorite smell of summer.

Smell of summer, well, hit me upside the head with a jackhammer—because that's practically what it took for me to figure out what Brenda was talking about, assuming she *was* talking and

Sarah Jane wasn't even more clever than I'd figured her for and made the whole thing up, knowing one of her fellow suspects wore honeysuckle perfume.

But which woman was it? Short of doing a sniff test on each human bay mare in the lounge, I had no way of knowing.

"Ladies," I said to the bunch, "if you'll excuse me, I have a date with a very handsome stranger."

Was he ever, in his own way. Fritz was the Nicolas Cage of horses; his individual features were a little off, but all together he was one yummy piece of equine flesh. And that was before I sat on him.

Beauty is as beauty does. In Fritz's case, his allure was far more than a pretty, though unusual, face. He was exactly the machine I'd heard he was. And Eli was exactly the unbelievably nice guy I'd heard he was too.

"That's right, Nattie," Eli said. "Just take a light feel of his mouth. Exactly the way you're doing it. He won't need anything more. You ride him well and you look terrific on him."

A horse trainer was directing the word "terrific" my way *and* telling me I ride well. First the Pulitzer finalist news and now this, it was almost too much to take in one day. If I didn't watch out, I'd swoon right off Fritz and into the ground-up Nikes piled ankle high in Anyday's indoor arena.

Fritz and I flatted, as they say in the horse world, for about fifteen minutes. Flatted, as in working on the flat—walk, trot, canter—before jumping fences. He was as adjustable and flexible as a rubber band. He moved off the slightest touch of my leg and stopped when I just wriggled the reins. This was one well-trained animal, as well he should be with a staff of two personal trainers and a multitude of grooms to tune on him.

"Nattie, canter up the line," Eli said. "It's a normal four."

That meant four strides between fences one and two. I pressed my outside leg on his side and he arced into his perfectly cadenced rocking-horse canter. He didn't slow down, he didn't speed up. His pace stayed exactly the same. You could've set a metronome to him.

And that is the key to finding the right takeoff spot before a fence. As much as I adore, love, and cherish Brenda, sometimes she sucks back before a fence. Then I have to push her on with my legs, and sometimes I push her on too much. In hunter parlance, I push her beyond the distance, so she ends up either taking off from the too-far leaping spot or jamming in an extra stride, called chipping the fence.

There was none of that with Fritz. It was very Zen. All I had to do was sit still. Believe me, that's easier said than done. Just ask any rider.

I forced my body to be quiet and did the old horse shower's trick of repeating 1-2-3 over and over with the beat of his canter. Because his pace never varied, we nailed the first fence perfectly and he marched down to the second in four equally perfect strides. Riding Fritz and riding other horses was like the difference between skiing in the East and skiing in the West—almost a different sport.

"Amazing" was all I could say as I stroked his neck.

"Yeah, he's a good guy," Eli said. "Ready for a course?"

I'm not normally the bravest rider over fences, but Fritz made it so easy. "You bet," I said.

Eli gave me a course of eight fences to jump, including an ugly oxer, a double-railed obstacle I've always had an unreasonable aversion to even before I broke my leg over one.

"Sure you know where to go?" Eli said. "Fritz is as uncomplicated as a horse comes. But if you have any questions or concerns, I'd be happy to talk about them first."

My eyes must've widened to silver dollar size.

"You okay, Nattie?" Eli said.

"Yeah, I mean, I'm just not used to talking during a lesson. That's all. No, it's great, everything's great. I've got the course and I don't have any questions really. But thanks for asking."

Eli looked at me a bit oddly.

"I train with Rob at February Farm," I said.

"Oh, that's right, I remember now, Ashlee did tell me that," Eli said. "Okay, got it."

I smiled knowingly, he smiled knowingly. Had we known each other better, I'm sure I would've heard his famous wit at work.

"Okay then," Eli said, clapping his hands together and smiling wide, "let's do it."

We did. And what a do it was. God, this was heaven. If I'd died right there on the spot, I'd have expired with a big, fat grin on my face.

"Nattie, that was terrific. You ride him like you've been riding him every day." It was Ashlee. She'd come into the indoor on Blue and was trotting him around. That pony could float his feet. I could see why he was unbeatable.

"I really had very little to do with it," I said. "You could probably strap a monkey on this horse and he'd canter around just the same."

"Been there, done that," Eli said. "His name was Brian. Now that was a child who should've taken up croquet."

"Brian Masters?" I said. "Isn't that the kid who won the equitation finals a few years ago?"

Eli nodded. "One and the same. He was the only rider whose horse did all the strides right, and that's because Fritz ignored every one of Brian's gyrations and figured out how to get around the course himself."

"Here's hoping he does the same for me at Culpeper," I said.

"No need for that," Eli said. "Ride like you did tonight and I see a tricolor in your future."

"Just being able to ride him is good enough for me," I said.

"Oh pah-LEEZE," Eli said, smiling. "The last time I heard someone say they didn't care about the ribbons, it was a pony mom who was also trying to find someone to put her kid's competition out of commission. We *all* care about winning, that's why we go to horse shows. Otherwise we'd just stay home."

277

He did have a point. It would be nice to carry home the streaming tricolor of division champion, but even if I didn't I knew it was going to be a show to remember. Now if I could just get past my queasiness about where it was: Culpeper, formally known as Commonwealth Park, but better known as the place where Christopher Reeve's life was turned upside down.

I fed the reins to Fritz and let him walk around the ring as I watched Ashlee school Blue. She was wearing an ear-to-ear smile. The same could not be said for Carter Evans or Bootsie Feldman, both of whom were standing by the observation window in the lounge looking as if they were doing facial isometric exercises.

Why Carter was angry was easy to figure. With Ashlee back in the pony division, that knocked Ralston out of the blue ribbons. But what burr was under Bootsie's saddle?

The Bobby burr.

I hadn't seen him until I turned the corner. There he was, leaning his back on the wall, holding a Bud in his hand.

"Hey, Nattie, I hear you're going to Culpeper with my little girl," McMahon said as I walked by. "She sure's taken a liking to you, and there ain't many I can say that about."

"I like her too," I said. "She's a good kid."

For the first time I saw the slickness fall from McMahon's eyes. They no longer looked like two hunks of turquoise he'd plugged into the nearest wall socket. The mention of Ashlee was like disconnecting the electric fence around his soul. He looked a little sad and a lot vulnerable. I almost felt sorry for him.

"I can't say I've heard many people say that neither," he said. "With all that money her granddaddy's got, you'd think she'd have had herself an easy, good life. That just ain't the case. Poor kid's had a lot to deal with."

If he hadn't looked so pitiful, I might have mentioned something about his contribution to what she'd had to deal with. But he was down for the count and there was no reason to land one in his gut.

"Human beings are amazingly resilient," I said. "She'll be okay. See?"

Ashlee cantered by us, still wearing that ear-to-ear grin.

"I hope you're right, Nattie," McMahon said. "I hope to God you're right. I'll see you tomorrow."

That slapped me back to reality. "Tomorrow?" I said. "What do you mean you'll see me tomorrow?"

That brought the old Bobby back. Zap went the electric connection, watting his blue eyes up full mesmer strength. "Didn't Ashlee tell you?" he said. "I'm driving y'all to Culpeper. You didn't think I'd let my little girl ride up in that foreign tin can of yours that sounds worse than I do in the morning, did you?"

Now it was my face doing the isometric exercises.

CHAPTER 52

Thanks to the uninvited guest who smashed up my plastic horse collection last year, coming home to a dark apartment now gives me a small case of the shakes. Tonight they were a little bigger than small because I didn't know if Fuzzy's murderer/ Brenda's threatener had gotten the message I'd gone back to hemlines. Maybe he or she thought it was time to move to Plan B: murder me.

"Hello, anyone there?" I called out, as if a crazed killer would answer back. "Just me and my Magnum."

Quickly I flicked on the light switch and saw everything was as I'd left it, except for a big silver lump on the kitchen table. My heart started beating hard; another sick present to scare me off? I refused to even contemplate the possibilities—I'd seen *Fatal Attraction* and *The Godfather*, so I knew how horrible they could be. I dashed over to the table and lifted the foil. Darned if I didn't start to cry.

But these were happy tears, the best kind.

It was a healthy-looking cake with big turquoise letters that said, *Yay Nattie!!!* Underneath that was a hand-drawn Pulitzer Prize medal in yellow and black tofu-cream frosting.

In my rush to make sure the silver lump wasn't some kind of roadkill or worse, I hadn't seen the note next to it. It was Sarah Jane's flowery handwriting:

Nattie, do NOT lift aluminum foil until we get home. We should be back around nine. Yours in the light, sj.

Talk about guilt. I'd almost punched her in the nose last night, and she spent the day making me a cake.

The only down side was that I'd have to eat it. Sarah Jane's a fine cook, but it would've taken a magician to make something edible with no sugar, eggs, wheat products, or dairy—all of which are verboten to ovalacto vegetarian macrobiotics like her and Lou.

I could force myself to eat one small piece; the trick was to figure out a polite way to decline seconds. As I thought about that, I noticed the red light on my answering machine flashing me a come-here look. "You have three messages," the monotoned man inside said, sounding exactly like the robot from *Lost in Space.*

The first was from Denise. "I heard!! Congratulations!!! If anyone deserves it you do, if nothing else for putting up with my sister. She called me this afternoon to tell me she'd made the Pulitzer finals. It took me five minutes to get it out of her that you were the one who'd written the story. Just ignore her and bask in the glory."

Then Tony. I'd left a message for him at the sheriff's department. I'd sounded so excited, even the lady who answers the phone who always knows it's me knew something was up. "Darlene says you sounded like some'd filled you full enough to pop. What happened, they stop making you write about neckties? That doesn't mean you're back to murders, does it? I'll be talking to you, or better yet, seeing you. Soon, I hope."

Not that soon—I hadn't had a chance to tell him my travel plans with Miss McMahon.

The last message was from Gail. "Nattie, are you still alive? Did you do something else to piss off whoever you've already pissed off? Where *are* you? I called you all day at work and you weren't answering and you're not answering here. Call me as soon as you get in. It's important."

She picked up on the first ring. "Nattie?"

"One and the same," I said. "You happen to be talking to the only living or dead feature writer for *The Charlotte Commercial Appeal* to be a Pulitzer Prize finalist."

I heard a scream come from the other end of the wire similar to the one I'd offered in the newsroom earlier that day.

"Oh God, Nattie, that's incredible. That's great. I don't even know what to say. Way to go, girl!!"

"Thanks, sweetie," I said. "It's been an amazing day. You'll never guess where I'm going tomorrow."

I gave her the details, ending with Eli. "You should've seen me, Gail. I couldn't make my mouth work when he asked me if I had any questions or concerns before I jumped a course."

She laughed. "Not exactly our Rob's style, is it? Enjoy it while you can. Listen, I hate to ruin your day, but you know what I was doing all yesterday?"

"Exploring the Kamasutra with Torkesquist."

"I wish, besides, we did that last week. No, I was driving everywhere looking for Allie. The gate to his pasture was open when I woke up yesterday, and I know I closed it the night before. You know how I am about things like that."

I knew exactly how Gail was—obsessive. She always checked, double-checked, and triple-checked stall doors, gates, and water buckets.

"What're you saying, Gail? Someone let your horse out on purpose?"

"You got it. And it isn't too far a leap to think that was the same person who sent me on the credit card run and the same person who left the cord by your stall and probably the same person who killed Fuzzy. I thought you said you were going to stop asking questions."

"I did. Both say it and do it. I don't care about it anymore. I really don't. I swear. I just wish that person would get the message."

"So does that mean you don't want to know what I found out from the girl at the convenience store?"

"You know me too well, Gail," I said. "Just this one last time. After that not another mention of Fuzzy McMahon. I promise. So what'd you find out?"

"It was an old guy who brought in the envelope," Gail said. "The only other thing the girl could remember about him was his teeth. They were dark."

An old man whose pearly whites had lost their youthful sheen. It was a good thing I wasn't working the story any longer. More vague clues like that and I'd be banging my head against the wall. Let this one lie; I had more important things to think about, like having the time of my life at Culpeper.

CHAPTER 53

Seven hours, three people, one truck bench. At least Ashlee sat in the middle.

But truth be told, the ride was fun. I'd been focusing so much on McMahon's negatives, I'd forgotten his positives. He's a heck of a storyteller, and that does come in handy on a long haul. Before I knew it, he was turning his truck into the show grounds of Commonwealth Park.

So this was it, the famous Culpeper I'd been reading about for years in the *Chronicle of the Horse.* There were sprawling expanses of flat green ground, rows of sturdy stalls, four show rings, a cross-country course, and cute little buildings in the center of it all for concessionaires to sell their wares in.

We were met at the guardhouse and given our stall location by a kindly woman who couldn't wish us enough luck. She must have said it five times before we pulled out.

"Y'all have a great show," she called after us, "and good luck."

Did she know something I didn't?

The horses were already unloaded, bedded, and groomed when we pulled up to the stalls. Eli and Jackson were there to greet us. With smiles, instead of orders. I could get used to this.

"Why don't you ladies get on and hack those boys around a little," Eli said. "We'll be down in a few minutes to school you. Nattie, I've entered you in a low hunter class, just to get the feel of Fritz in a show ring."

"Low hunter?" I said. "Are you kidding? I'll be the only non-professional in it. I might as well just light a match to the twenty dollars it takes to enter."

Eli laughed. "Wait a second, aren't you the person who doesn't care about ribbons?"

"You got me," I said. "I lied. I was just trying to show you what an evolved soul I am."

"I think that may be a few lifetimes from now," Eli said. "Now why don't you take your unevolved self and change into your show clothes. We'll get the horses tacked."

Next thing I knew, I wouldn't have to spend three hours after the show, cleaning tack, feeding and watering horses, and cleaning their stalls. I *was* getting used to this, along with the real bathrooms.

Another plus for Commonwealth Park. Most horse shows have Porta Potties that never seem balanced. So I usually end up changing clothes in my horse's stall, rather than risk an unspeakable bath. This one not only had flushable toilets, but big mirrors so I could see what I was doing.

Getting dressed in full show attire is torture for someone who's not a detail person—i.e., me. Not only does everything have to be shiny clean, but it has to be put on just so. The worst of it is the hunt cap. If you've got long hair, there's a specific architecture to the structure of how to confine your flowing tresses underneath the black velvet. It involves many hairnets, many bobby pins, and many attempts to get it right. The hair has to swoop down, cover the ears, and swoop back up, all with not a stray wisp to be seen. I used to just pile the whole mess on top of my head, let my ears poke out under the harness and be done with it. But a trainer I know, Richard Slocum, pulled me aside at one show and said: "Nattie dear, your ears are showing. Just remember, over $125,000, ears covered; below five thousand dollars, ears showing." He was referring to horse price, meaning if I wanted to look like I had an expensive horse, do my hair right.

For someone who resents authority and willfully flouts fashion trends, it still surprises me how hard I try at horse shows to make myself look like everyone else. Not that it worked. I still had a set of expanded thighs to deal with.

I was on my fourth attempt to wrestle my hair into control when Ashlee took over. "Let me do that for you."

"Hey, Ashlee, how are you?" My back was to the door, so I didn't see who had come into the women's room. It was a young girl's voice, probably someone Ashlee's age.

"Hey, Jenny," Ashlee said, sounding an awful lot like Marlon Brando since she had a jawful of bobby pins in her mouth. "You here with Cedarhill?"

"Sure am," the girl said. "Sorry to hear about your mom."

"Thanks," Ashlee said. "I hope things are better with you and your mom."

The girl mumbled something. She didn't have anything in her mouth but her tongue, so I took it her mumble meant the answer to Ashlee's question wasn't affirmative.

"Finished, Nattie," Ashlee said to me. "What do you think?"

I think I finally looked like the rest of them—from the waist up. "Wow, we should start calling you Miss Ashlee and get you a job at Roland's House of Beauty."

As I'd turned around to look in the mirror, the girl Ashlee had been talking to walked into one of the stalls. Because my walleye, which I now think of more poetically as my witch's eye, floats so far afield, I almost have the peripheral vision of a horse on the left side. So I caught a pretty good but fleeting look at the kid.

I spun my head around to get another look at her. But she'd closed the door. I knew her and my brain was sending some kind of alert, this is important message. I just couldn't remember why she was important.

As we walked back to the barn I was about to ask Ashlee who the kid was. Unfortunately, we ran into an old friend who walked us back to the Anyday stalls, which were now more decorated than the Charlotte Symphony's annual designer house.

Fritz was once again dressed in his best party clothes. This time, though, he was in the equine equivalent of top hat and tails: the previously mentioned exquisite bridle and cushy saddle, topped off by a perfectly braided mane, French-braided tail, and freshly polished hooves. He took my breath away.

"Hellll-LO gaw-JUS," I said to him.

"Loved that movie." It was Eli; he was in the stall next door.

Of course he did. Show me a gay guy who doesn't love Barbra Streisand and I'll show you a closet heterosexual.

"See you in the ring," I said. Before I had a chance to lead Fritz to the mounting block, there was a groom by my side giving me a leg up and rubbing my boots with a clean, white towel.

I *was* getting used to this.

Fritz and I flatted. He was even more perfect than he'd been last night, if that was possible. I was sure Eli or Jackson had already been on his back, getting him malleable for the amateur—me. I popped him over a few jumps and into the ring we went.

"Have fun," Eli said.

How could I not? Once again Fritz arced into his perfect canter, never varying his pace. And once again we nailed every fence as if it were written in stone that Nattie Gold and the horse called Fritz could find nothing but perfect takeoff spots.

"Give that girl a blue ribbon," Eli said as I came out of the ring. "Hop off and catch your breath."

I swung my right leg in back of the saddle and onto the ground. Before I landed there was a groom holding his reins, ready to take off his saddle, wipe down his back, and get him ready for the soundess trot in front of the judge, should we be in the ribbons. All of which I'd always done for myself.

"Eli," I said, "I don't think we need to hang around here for a ribbon. He's a great horse, but look whom I'm competing against, every professional horse person between Washington, D.C., and Charlotte."

Not to mention their mounts: all the top horses were in this class. The pros used the low hunter division as an opportunity to school for the important divisions such as green or working hunter.

"Stay," Eli said. "You're getting a ribbon. I'll bet my Butet on that."

Well, I didn't win his saddle, but I did get the second call—a red ribbon in the show's biggest class against some of the fanciest horses in the country. Practically the only one missing from this ASHA hall of fame was Rox-Dene and that was because she'd been retired to become a mommy.

I would've walked Fritz back to the barn, but big surprise, the groom got there first.

"Come on, let's go get a soda to celebrate," Ashlee said.

As we were walking to the indoor eating place—another anomaly for a horse show, indoor eating—the girl from the bathroom passed by walking a big, gray mare. Now that I'd finished riding, it started bothering me. Who was she and why was my brain telling me to pay attention?

"Ashlee," I said, "that girl walking the gray, the one you spoke to in the bathroom, who is she?"

"You mean Jenny?" Ashlee said. "Jenny Fulton? She goes to my school. We sorta used to be good friends. She used to come out to my barn. She'd help Cathy with the stalls or feeding or grooming, and Cathy'd let her ride some of the horses. We kinda got in a big fight, that's when she started going to Cedarhill instead. We just started talking to each other again."

"What'd you fight about?"

"Stupid stuff. She called me a spoiled brat and I called her 'Carrie' 'cause her mother's one of those religious nuts."

Bingo, that made the connection. Her mother was the one

who'd escorted me to interview the Total Female, the one who'd asked me about riding equipment because her daughter had just started taking riding lessons, the one who claimed her son had been molested by Quarrels. Now I knew why the kid looked familiar to me. I'd seen her at horse shows walking around with her mother.

"I know I shouldn't have said that," Ashlee said. "But it makes me so mad when people think I'm a brat. It's not my fault I'm rich."

"Ashlee, what'd you mean in the bathroom when you asked Jenny if things were any better with her mother?"

"Well, that's why I shouldn't have said that about her mother being nuts and all. Right before we had our big fight, we went to a show in Camden and sat up all night talking. It was just me and her in the hotel room. Our moms weren't there. Mine was home drunk and hers was in the hospital. You know, the crazy part of it."

"You mean the lockup floor for the mentally ill?"

"Uh-huh," Ashlee said, and nodded. "I mean like her mother's really nuts. A schizoid."

Ashlee's hand flew to her mouth. "Oh God, I'm sorry, Nattie. I forgot about your father and all."

"It's okay," I said. "He's fine now." I skipped my standard mental-illness-is-nothing-to-be-ashamed-of spiel. As I recall, she'd heard it before, and I wanted to hear more about Jenny's mother. This was something Henry needed to know about, pronto.

Ashlee told me about their slumber party confessional. She said Jenny was torn up something horrible because her parents were in the middle of a divorce and that was flipping her mother out even more.

"Her mother was trying to get Jenny to lie and tell her teacher her father'd been doing bad things to her down there," Ashlee said. "She told me her mother said she'd never let her ride again if she didn't. And I thought *my* mom was bad. She said I was the only one she'd ever told, except her minister. I wished I'd have had someone like him I could've talked to. He sounded way cool. Then that next week at school, she was her old self again. I asked her what happened, and she said her minister fixed everything. See what I mean? Way cool."

The Reverend Rowe Quarrels way cool? He'd certainly come to the rescue of that poor kid, and I had to admit it, maybe he was doing God's work after all, in between torturing my life.

"Ashlee, I've got to make a phone call, I'll meet you at the barn." I dashed to the closest pay phone and punched in *The Appeal*'s 800 number. I got Henry's voice mail. It took three calls to spill the whole story.

". . . don't you see, this must be that woman's twisted way of getting even," I said fast, hoping to squeeze in my finale without having to call back a fourth time. "Get her child to accuse whomever she's mad at of being a molester. I feel sorry for those kids, but according to Ashlee, their minister—you've got it, none other than the Reverend Quarrels—has been the proverbial savior to that girl, and I'm guessing the boy as well. Sorry to ruin your shot at another Pulitzer, my dear, but don't you think two is enough anyway? I know, I know, I'm counting my Pulitzers before they're awarded. Even if we don't win, it's an honor just to be a finalist."

A big laugh escaped from my mouth. Who was I kidding? An honor just to be a finalist? Like Eli said, not in this lifetime.

CHAPTER 54

Seeing as it was still March, the sun was well on its way to a dip over the horizon by the time I'd gotten back from calling Henry. And it wasn't even seven-thirty yet. Ashlee was sitting on her tack trunk talking to Eli and Jackson.

"Ready to go?" she said.

I looked around. Nothing was put up for the night. Not the tack or the horses. Bridles were hanging on hooks ready to be cleaned, the saddles were out, and the blankets were draped over the stall doors.

"Leave? With all this stuff still to be done?" I said. "I think I should stay and help."

As much as I liked the kid, it was easy to see why Jenny Fulton, who had to shovel poop just to ride, called Ashlee what she did.

"No, come on with me. They'll get it," Ashlee said, motioning to the six or eight or ten—I'd lost count—grooms milling around. "Daddy's taking us to dinner with Eli and Jackson."

Oh boy, breaking bread again with Bobby McMahon. This should be a night to remember.

Ashlee went with Daddy, and I went in Eli and Jackson's dually—a he-man, muscle head of a truck with dual rear wheels. We followed McMahon to a small strip mall shopping center, where tucked in the corner was what Jackson promised us was the best restaurant in Culpeper, John's.

Inside we were greeted by a gregarious waitress with a big head of platinum country-western hair. She hugged Eli and Jackson as if they were her long-lost sons.

As it turned out, McMahon wasn't the only gifted storyteller. Eli and Jackson cut loose. They had a pair of tongues that could slice warm bread, except this night what was being served up wasn't food. It was the horse show crowd. When you get a collection of really, really, really rich people with too little to do and too much money to spend on that too little to do, it's a perfect breeding ground for odd, and oftentimes unattractive, behavior. Given the peculiarities of the bunch, it was like shooting lame ducks.

I heard about one woman who liked to play Russian roulette after horse shows. So far nothing but a radio had met its maker. That was because everyone was so drunk, they kept dropping the gun.

Then there was the feminine care products heiress who carried her spoon collection from show to show. Jackson said her assistant swore the woman took them all out at night, lined them up in an X formation, and danced on them to the background music of Sammy Davis, Jr., singing "The Party's Over."

"You know it's not as if we're the only crazy bunch of people," Jackson said. "At least Ms. SummerMorn-PantyLiner isn't hurting anyone with her spoons, not that her assistant knows of. But look at all that Jon Benet little girl beauty pageant stuff. If you don't think they're all not a few petals shy of Daisy Fresh, you're crazy. And did you read about that dentist in Texas? He sharpened the buckle on his son's football helmet so the kid could score more touchdowns. The kid shredded half the opposing team on his way."

By the time I finished my spaghetti, I'd heard so much about so many horse people, I could've written a book that would've gotten everyone guessing who they were. Though right then, with the Pulitzer finals stirring up the ink in my blood, I couldn't imagine doing anything else that could make me as happy as cranking out newspaper stories. Even the fashion columns. But you never know where life will take you.

I did know where McMahon was taking us. To the Holiday Inn. He dropped us under the car port in front while he parked and I looked around. I was a long way from the Motel 6, and I wasn't talking miles. Fifteen of Mr. Patel's lobbies could fit in this one.

Ashlee checked in and got our room keys. We walked past the pool and up the stairs to our room. I could also get used to this: towels with enough fluff to actually absorb water, beds firmer than an aerobic instructor's tush, and a ventilation system that didn't sound like it was, as they say down here, kin to my car. It produced a steady, soothing stream of white noise that I knew would drift me gently down to the river of sleep.

Ashlee and I talked for a while. What about? Easy. What does one horse-crazy woman who never grew out of being a horse-crazy girl say to another horse-crazy girl?

"Did you see that big, steel-gray gelding Peter Foley was schooling by the colonels' ring? Was he gorgeous or what?"

"Yeah, and did you see Devon Shields's new horse? He's gonna clean up in the jumpers with him."

We went back and forth, reviewing all the horses we'd seen that day. We were like two thirteen-year-olds talking about all the cute boys in ninth grade. We probably could've gone on all night, and the lack of sleep surely wouldn't have fazed Ashlee the next day. I, on the other hand, had long outgrown my capacity to pull an all-nighter and still be able to walk and talk, let alone ride, the next day.

"Kiddo, I gotta get me some sleep so I don't crash your wonder horse through an oxer," I said.

I slept so deeply, if I had any weird dreams, I didn't remember them. I woke in a bit of a panic because the clock said seven and usually at horse shows I've been up for at least two hours by now. Then I remembered whom I was with and that her swarm of worker bees were buzzing their little hearts out, doing all the jobs and then some that I was used to doing at horse shows.

Ashlee was in the next bed doing the teen thing—sleeping in.

No need to wake her just yet. I stepped into the shower and, to my delight, there was enough water pressure to spray away the soap from my body. Another first in my horse showing travels.

I wrapped myself in a fluffy towel and tried to be as quiet as possible as I rooted through my cosmetic bag for my skin goops. The older I got, the more the bottles mated, leaving me with so many offspring I could barely remember which cream went where and when. Even though a dermatologist I'd once interviewed for a story assured me you could just as easily slather Crisco all over your face and get the same results as the sixty-dollar-a-jar bio-engineered eye cream made from blowfish intestines, I still was a sucker for wonder goops. Especially now that my face was approaching that dried riverbed stage.

"Hey, Nattie." Ashlee had arisen. She was standing by the window, eating something. "This is good, but like, what is it?"

She was holding a piece of silver foil, and in that, a slice of the celebration cake Sarah Jane had made me. Ashlee was right, it was good; far better than I'd expected. I'd been worried about how I was going to decline seconds when I should've been worried about fitting into size 28 riding pants after scarfing down four slices of it.

I'd brought along some to give to Ashlee. She'd asked about the weird things my father eats, so I wanted to let her taste something made with whipped tofu and barley malt. But I was sure I'd stowed the cake in my backpack, along with a few books and some documents Henry had asked me to read about child abuse.

Though I am at the opposite end of the obsession spectrum from my buddy Gail, I was pretty sure I'd zipped up the backpack when I left yesterday. And I was certain I hadn't gone in it since I'd arrived.

"Cake," I said. "Health-food cake. Hold on to your stomach, my dear, because you've just ingested soybeans, barley, seaweed, and, if I'm not mistaken, kudzu, or was that kuzu? I can never keep those two straight. Not bad, huh?"

"Yuck!!" Ashlee said. "Seaweed? You're kidding. That's what your father eats? And I thought my dad was weird for eating pig feet."

It was my time to yuck. "Pig's feet?" I said. "Ashlee, that's truly gross."

We both started laughing when there came a knock on the door. Though Holiday Inn towels do cover all private body parts and more, which can't be said for my usual motel's linen offerings, I was still naked as a jaybird underneath.

I slipped into the bathroom and Ashlee got the door.

"It's Daddy," she called in to me. "He says we need to leave in five minutes."

No problem. I've always been a sprinter. As it turns out, so was Ashlee.

We beat Daddy to his truck.

CHAPTER 55

What could I possibly say about the next couple of days? Had I died and gone to heaven, had I finally paid back all my bad karma, had the gods who've been playing my hand upstairs gotten a royal flush? Or was I really Pam Ewing and this was all a dream?

The long blue, red, and yellow streamers of the tricolor ribbon were doing their job, blowing poetically in the breeze as I walked back with it to Anyday's stalls. That's right. Fritz took me to the top. Division champion. We beat them all, even the ones who go from horse show to horse show fifty-nine weeks of the year. What made it even sweeter was the judge who'd judged us best: Rodney Jenkins, the redheaded phenomenon I'd grown up idolizing.

He pinned us over everyone. Including Mrs. Gordon Wheeler, on her two heavily chromed chestnut machines; Ruth Douglas, on her up until now unbeatable bays; Wrapped in Red, a roan quarter horse who was the second-year green hunter champion of the country last year; we even beat the reigning queen of the adult division, who's been wearing the tiara for the past twenty years, Leslie Jones, on her big copper gelding who was half brother to Brenda.

Speaking of. I missed her something awful. I loved riding Fritz, but somehow it didn't seem right being at a horse show without Brenda. I cleared my mind of all the chatter, the way Sarah Jane taught me, asked the heavenly policemen for spiritual protection from floating Ted Bundys and did my best to ring up a connection.

I don't know if she answered, but I talked. Thank goodness Ashlee was on Blue and I was alone.

"I wish it was you here," I said.

I'm sure it was hopeful thinking of a bird flying overhead, but I could've sworn I heard some one or thing say, "Me too."

Ashlee had an equally good show. No surprise there. Ponies don't come any fancier than Blue By You. He was grand pony champion, winning every class he stepped a hoof in. Even her Olympic mare, Kiss-Me, performed well. Or at least better. She wasn't champion, but she didn't slam on the brakes once with Ashlee. And the kid stayed on board in all her jumper classes.

Everyone at Anyday was happy. Me, Ashlee, Jackson, and Eli. Even the surly braiders were smiling. And that's saying a lot.

I take that back. Not about the braiders. They were smiling, even though they had no reason to be. Their fingers always hurt; they get up before the sun has a chance to think about rising, and practically as soon as they're finished braiding the horse, they have to turn around and rip the darn things out so they can start fresh for the next day. An easy life it's not.

What I meant was not everyone at Anyday was grinning. Carter Evans was hot enough to double as a portable water heater had she stuck her head in a bucket. I was the only one at the barn when she and Ralston came back from the ring, dragging along Wishbone, heretofore large pony champion everywhere since Fuzzy had retired Blue.

They didn't see me because I was in the grooming stall cleaning tack. I know Ashlee told me not to, but old habits die hard.

"I finally get that witch out of my hair and her daughter switches back to ponies," she said, and yanked the pony's reins. "I can't believe my luck."

"Ma-AHM," Ralston whined, "*your* luck? I'm the one who's riding, not you. Besides, if it bothers you so much, how come you and Daddy didn't buy Blue when Ashlee stopped riding him? Ashlee told me they were only asking a hundred and twenty for him because his X rays weren't clean. You could've had him then, but no, you always have to do things your way."

There's something wrong when a thirteen-year-old girl puts the word "only" before 120 as in $120,000 and is referring to a pony's price tag.

"Don't you open a mouth to me, young lady," Carter snapped. "And for your information, we did try to buy Blue. Fuzzy wouldn't sell him to me. She laughed in my face when I asked if he was for sale. You'll have to make do with Wishbone, until we can find you something to beat that gray pony of hers."

I suppose this put Carter Evans right back in the prime suspect seat. But the truth was, I really didn't care anymore. One newspaper series about the nasty side of horse showing was enough for me, especially now that it was a Pulitzer finalist.

Not to sound too much like Sarah Jane, but all that negative energy's not good for the soul. I'd just finished what would have been a perfect week—except for Brenda not being there—and I wanted to hang on to these warm, fuzzy feelings. I would've too, had Ashlee not dropped her little bomb. We'd just finished showing and her father had driven us back to the Holiday Inn to pack our bags.

"Nattie, I hope you won't be mad," she said, "but I'm not driving back with you and Daddy."

"What?" I said, trying to make myself sound calm. Up until now I'd done a pretty good job not letting Ashlee know I thought her father was one small step above smegma.

"Sorry, Daddy just told me Grams and Pop-Pop are on their way up. They should be here pretty soon. He said they're taking me to Washington for the rest of my spring break. We're going to their apartment, it's in that famous fence or something place where that president—what's his name?—got caught doing something."

Didn't they have history classes at Charlotte Country Day School?

"You mean the Watergate?" I said.

"Yeah, that's the one. It has those funny-looking teeth on the balconies. Anyway, they're taking me there. I asked if you could come, but Daddy says Grams wants it to be a special vacation for me, 'cause of Mom and all. Sorry."

"I couldn't have come anyway. I'm a working stiff. But that's nice of you to offer. You know," I said, trying to sound nonchalant, "maybe I'll catch a ride back with Jackson and Eli. I wouldn't mind seven hours of horse show gossip."

"Yeah, that'd be fun. But you can't," she said.

Steady, calm, I told myself. I even tried the 1-2-3-4 trick to keep my voice from racing off in an out of control shrieking gallop. "Really, why not? . . . Two-three-four-one-two."

"Nattie, how come you're counting strides?" Ashlee said.

Ooops. "I don't know." My voice was quickening. "Why can't I ride with Eli and Jackson?"

"Their truck's full. One of the grooms' cars broke down. So they've got to take three of those guys with them. How come you sound so funny? Daddy doesn't bite, you know."

Oh really? I *did* know something she didn't.

Okay, seven hours alone with Bobby McMahon. Cosmic payback for having such a stellar week. I could handle it. I took three deep breaths and repeated my old TM mantra.

"You're not mad, are you Nattie?"

"Nah, don't sweat it, Ash-peeps. Your daddy and I'll get along just fine. How about giving me a hand getting these boots off?"

She grabbed the heel of my right boot and yanked hard.

"Ya-owza," I screamed. "Let go, quick."

I must've turned the color the Holiday Inn towels. "Nattie, what'd I do? Are you okay?"

I stomped my heel back down and caught my breath. "Ooooh, that's better. You didn't do anything. It's that stupid doctor who left the head of the bolt jutting out of my ankle. It catches on the inside of my boot. If I ease it off slowly it doesn't hurt as much. Do you have a bootjack?"

"Yeah, it's in Daddy's truck, behind the seat someplace."

"Be right back," I said, and limped out.

McMahon had parked his truck next to a gooey patch of mud, and I was wearing the custom-made Dehner boots I'd stopped eating a week for. I did my best Florence Joyner impression and tried to leap over it. I wouldn't have made the jump-off in that class; I landed with my feet gush down deep into the squish. They made a sucking noise as I pulled them out, leaving behind two perfect imprints of the kicking end of my body.

I climbed into the cab of McMahon's truck, trying not to paint it brown with my feet. It was difficult, because my boots were a muddy mess and I had to swivel myself around to reach behind the seat. I flailed my arm around back there making grabs for whatever my hand caught. It was like one of those hands-on exhibits at a science museum where you stick your arm through the top of a box and try to guess by feel what's inside.

I was getting pretty good at it: four beer bottles, no doubt Buds; one horseshoe rasp—ouch on the fingers; six spent shell casings, I didn't know enough about guns to know what kind; two two-inch squares of foil with a circular something inside—at least he was being careful; and a few packages of cheese crackers. But no bootjack. My right leg was starting to throb.

I leaned way over and reached under the back of the seat. My hand latched onto some kind of double-armed tool. My fingers played twenty questions with it, but I wasn't getting any answers. I pulled it up toward me and looked at it.

Even a new set of senses couldn't help me figure out what it was. It looked like an overgrown pliers or cinch or something that squeezed. I put it on the seat next to me and swung my arm back over, still in search of the bootjack. As I did I accidentally kicked the mystery tool out the door and into the mud.

Yuck, now I'd have to clean the thing. But first I'd have to get it without stepping in the mud again. I hung onto the steering wheel with one hand, lowered myself down to reaching distance, and made a grab for it. Got it on the first try. I started to hoist myself back up, but my brain froze the winch cranking me back in when I looked down into the mud.

There it was, a perfect impression of the tool in question. A flat circle with a deep hole at the end. The same weird mark they found all over Fuzzy.

CHAPTER 56

"Open the door. Right now, this second, before I kick it in. And if you don't think I will, just try me. Here I go . . ."

The door opened, with Bobby McMahon standing behind it.

"What's your problem, Nattie?" McMahon said. "I thought you and Ashlee were packing to get ready to go."

"Shut up, just shut up," I said as I pushed past him into his room. "This is my problem." I held up whatever kind of tool it was other than a murder weapon. "Or more accurately, your problem. I'll give this contraption to Tony and I'm sure his boys will be able to find something of Fuzzy on it. You killed her, didn't you, and then tried to scare me off? It makes perfect sense. No one could find you that day someone played target practice with my head in Asheville. You used to shoot the whiskers off groundhogs for sport, you could easily shoot the split ends off my hair, which you did."

I took three steps toward him. "I always thought it was you, but Tony told me you had an airtight alibi. I guess you had yourself an oxygen mask? Who was it? Who'd you do it with, sweet Sarah Jane of the white light? Carter Evans? Jeannie Sukon? Or another one of your little conquests? You better start talking quick or else I'm going pick up this phone and dial 911."

McMahon sank to the bed.

"Go ahead and call. It had to come out sooner or later. You were right, Nattie, but not right about everything. I killed her and I wished I'd have done it sooner. But it was just me. Not Sarah Jane or anyone else. Fuzzy and I had some unfinished business."

"And that's the way you decided to finish it? I knew you weren't bright, but I didn't think you were a coward. Only cowards hit women. I hope you rot in jail, McMahon. I'm calling the police."

"No don't. Stop, Nattie. Please."

I turned around. It was Ashlee with tears running down her face. I hadn't heard her come in.

"He didn't kill her—"

"Stop talking nonsense, Ashlee, and get out of here. Now, I said."

"No, Daddy. I'm not leaving. Not with Nattie thinking you killed Mom."

McMahon bolted up from the bed, grabbed Ashlee, and tried to push her out of the room. But she was a tangle of flailing arms and legs.

"I'm not leaving until she knows what really happened. I killed her, Nattie. It was me. Daddy's trying to protect me."

The mystery tool fell from my hand, and this time I sank to the bed. Ashlee? The kid I was trying to play Ellie to? The kid I thought just needed a big ear to hear her problems. No wonder Blue wouldn't talk. Ashlee, a cold-blooded killer?

Not exactly a cold-blooded killer, it turned out, but a killer just the same. I practically had to duct-tape McMahon's mouth to get the story from her.

Fuzzy had been in one of her drunken rages. She woke Ashlee that night, screaming at her to get dressed so they could go down to the barn.

"She kept yelling over and over that Daddy was down in the fields pretending to be checking his cows when he was really there cheating on her with a new boarder again. She grabbed me by the arm and dragged me into her car to take me down to where his truck was so I could see just what a 'whore monger, pussy eater your daddy is.' "

Ashlee was really crying now, and her father was still trying to get her to be quiet. But she kept talking.

"Daddy was there, but he wasn't with anyone like Mom said. He was helping an old cow have her baby. But that didn't matter. Mom was still crazy, screaming and yelling. Daddy tried to get away from her, but she kept after him. He got in his truck and she kept yelling for him to come out and fight like a real man."

Then Fuzzy started kicking his truck. That's when he got out with the heretofore mystery tool in his hand. Mystery solved, I now knew what its official function was—something that sends shivers down the spines of baby boy cows. Though his plans for it were not what I'd thought.

He held the thing up before his wife's rage-filled face and said, "See this, Fuzzy, this is what you are. A walking, talking, breathing, drinking emasculator."

Emasculator, that is the official name of the tool in question.

That's when Fuzzy started swinging. McMahon dropped the emasculator so he could cover his face with his hands.

"She was beating Daddy up, again."

"Again?" I said.

"She beat him up all the time and he never did anything. He just stood there and took it. He never even called the police on her."

That explained all those bruises and shiners I'd seen him with. I looked at McMahon sitting there, deflated; he'd been too macho a man to let anyone know his wife was beating the you-know-what out of him.

"I couldn't stand it anymore," Ashlee said. "She'd just given him a black eye, I couldn't let her hurt him again."

That's when Ashlee picked up the emasculator and started swinging. "I didn't mean to kill her, I just wanted her to stop hurting Daddy."

"Ashlee honey, run on down to the car." Another voice. This was turning out to be a party. I turned around to see the Feldmans by the door. Bootsie's face was crimson and Mo was standing there silent, chomping on a big cigar.

I took a deep breath to steady myself.

Then I smelled it. Summer in March. Honeysuckle perfume.

I walked toward Bootsie, and if she hadn't been old enough to be my mother, though she could've passed for my sister, I'd have landed a fist in that perfect nose of hers.

"You're the one who threatened to kill my horse," I said. "What is it, like daughter, like mother?"

This time it was my personal space that was being invaded. She took the final steps to me and pressed her face to mine. "You don't know what you're talking about," she hissed. Now hissing with a Southern accent is truly a wonder to the auditory world. "Fuzzy wasn't anything like that before she met *him*. It was *his* fault, everything is his fault. This whole, stinking mess we're in now wouldn't have happened if he had been any kind of husband."

Mo took the cigar out of his mouth and it looked as if he might finally say something. That's when I noticed his teeth. They were stained almost brown by all those stogies. *An old guy with dark teeth.*

I spun around to face him, and for the zillionth time in his life, a female cut him off before he could get a word out.

"And you're the one who sent Gail on that phony credit card run," I said. "Did you open the gate to her paddock too and let her horse run loose?"

"No," McMahon said. "That was me."

We all started screaming at one another until I looked over at the little girl on the bed. Ashlee was looking smaller and smaller. I thought she might disintegrate before our very eyes.

"Everyone be quiet," I screamed. That silenced them. "You guys have the rest of your lives to fight and throw blame. Right now let's figure out how we can help Ashlee."

CHAPTER 57

Here's how it went down: McMahon agreed to pay me back for my slashed tires and then ditched the emasculator in the Dumpster out back of the Holiday Inn. I agreed never to say anything to anyone on two conditions. First and of utmost importance, they get Ashlee to a shrink right away and then enroll the rest of themselves in some kind of intensive family therapy. Second, I didn't want to hear one word about how they halted or side-tracked the police investigation or Les's story for *The Appeal*. Not one syllable. I knew with Feldman's money they could do it; I just didn't want to know the who, what, where, or when of it. And I wished I didn't even know the why.

I did drive home with McMahon, and he wasn't telling too many stories. Neither of us were. It was a long seven hours.

Things did not improve when I left his truck. Tony was in my living room looking very glum. First I thought somehow he'd found out and was there to arrest me.

That might've been better. At least I would've seen him on occasion.

For once he got right to the point. No meandering Faulknerian sentences or strange country metaphors. "Sharon's pregnant," he said. "She doesn't want an abortion, can't say as I do either. It's fine for other people, just not for me. I'm sorry, Nattie, I thought you and I were going someplace special. We can't now. This baby deserves a mother and father—together. Sharon's agreed to go to a couples therapist. I don't see as I have any choice. I'm sorry."

I remembered what I'd said to Lou the other night after I'd gone ballistic with Sarah Jane. I was wanting him to play Big Daddy and tell me what to do about Henry and Tony, and he was telling me it was something I'd have to decide myself. I told him I couldn't decide, that I wished to God someone would do it for me.

Slow cut to my face. My tortured eyes, my long nose, my quivering mouth.

"Be careful what you ask the gods for," I said, looking past Tony, past the turquoise walls of my apartment, past the heat lamp, the rebounder, the magnet collections, past all the gadgets my father has crammed in my living room. I looked out of Charlotte, into my future. I paused; cinemagraphically, dramatically, profoundly. Then I said, "They just might be cruel enough to grant your wish."

EPILOGUE

I'm accomplice to a crime. Big deal. Taking a bribe is one thing, sending a kid to the meat grinder media is another, and that's exactly what would've happened if I'd turned Ashlee in. Thank God I've got enough of my father's antiauthority genes in me I can sleep at night. Though that's not to say I didn't wrassle with myself but good.

What would it have done besides move Kathie Lee Gifford off the cover of the *National Enquirer*? Ashlee needed help, not reporters shoving microphones down her throat. Both Bootsie and Bobby adhered to my conditions: they got her to a shrink, fast and often. She's now going to the Good Doctor Greene five times a week. His bad toupee gives us something to giggle about when we meet on Wednesday nights. That's right, we have a standing date, Wednesday night girls' night. Dinner at Gus's Sir Beef, then bowling at Queen City Lanes.

One time we even invited a special guest: her daddy, Bobby McMahon. Like he said to me many moons ago, "Nattie, people ain't always what they seem." That was true in McMahon's case. He did and probably still does have a big zipper problem, but he's a good father in his own way and he only wants the best for his child, which is something we both want and are both willing to bend the law to do. Being as we're now co-conspirators, there's a new intimacy between us. But we have something more in common than a crime: we both love Ashlee and want to make sure she's got a fair shot at life. That's moved us into a comfortable friendship with no eye locks.

I wish the rest of my personal life was as easy to figure out. I never told Henry about my night with Tony. And that does keep me up at night. While Tony and Sharon are preparing for "And Baby Makes Three," Henry and I continue upon our slow path to something.

Once again Lou has stopped taking the Zoloft, convinced the Saint-John's-wort has kicked in. He's a grown-up, of sorts, so all I can do is be there in case he falls down that dark hole again.

Sarah Jane finally got her car and apartment back. Mr. Patel's very handsome nephew had to come to Charlotte for something, so he fixed her Mercedes and drove it down. Or so he said. I have a small suspicion Mrs. Patel sent him here after seeing Sarah Jane. Mrs. Patel's the one who should go into the matchmaking business. Her nephew Raj has been a regular at our dinner table ever since.

And finally, my girl Brenda. I wish I could say she was up and ready to go, but this suspensory healing business can be tricky. One wrong turn can tear the thing again. And that's just what she did. Now Doc Loc says it could be as much as a year before she's sound.

But that's why God made memory. Even though riding Fritz was the equine experience of a lifetime, when I close my eyes at night, it's still a chestnut mare I'm sitting on.

Brenda Starr, you'll always be the horse of my dreams. You hear that, girl?

ABOUT THE AUTHOR

JODY JAFFE has long experience in both the worlds of journalism and horse shows. For the past twenty-four years she has been riding and showing hunters, and she spent ten years as a feature writer for *The Charlotte Observer.* Her first novel, *Horse of a Different Killer,* was nominated for an Agatha Award for Best First Mystery. She is also the author of *Chestnut Mare, Beware.*